Lady Odelia's Secret

THE SCOTT-DE QUINCY MYSTERIES

BOOK TWO

Published by Aspidistra Press

❀ Created with Vellum

BOOKS BY JANE STEEN

The House of Closed Doors Series

The House of Closed Doors

Eternal Deception

The Shadow Palace

The Jewel Cage

The Scott-De Quincy Mysteries

Lady Helena Investigates

Lady Odelia's Secret

Lady Odelia's Secret

THE SCOTT-DE QUINCY MYSTERIES

BOOK TWO

JANE STEEN

I never was attached to that great sect,
    Whose doctrine is, that each one should select
    Out of the crowd a mistress or a friend,
    And all the rest, though fair and wise, commend
    To cold oblivion ...

True love has this, different from gold and clay,
    That to divide is not to take away.

— PERCY BYSSCHE SHELLEY, EPIPSYCHIDION

1

LOYALTY AND ETERNITY

Sussex, September 1882

The Scott-De Quincys, Earls of Broadmere since the Norman Conquest, were indisputably the most important family in our remote corner of Sussex, and our significance to the small town of Littleberry never showed to better advantage than in church. The second Sunday service at St. Michael and All Angels saw us neatly arrayed in our gated section of pews, which were decorated with our coat of arms lest some impertinent stranger should entertain the idea that all seats in God's house were equal.

By long tradition, we shared our seats with the wealthy Whitcombe family, to which I had united the Scott-De Quincys by marrying the late Sir Justin Whitcombe, baronet. As his widow, I was the sole representative of the Whitcombes and thus entitled to a prominent position on the front pew next to my brother Michael, the current Earl of Broadmere.

"Here I am, Helena." Michael's harsh voice sounded above and to the left of me as I descended carefully from my carriage, guided by my footman's hand, my vision almost completely obscured by my widow's veil. Feeling the cobbles beneath my feet, I reached out toward the vague shape of the earl. I felt Michael—who hated to touch, or be touched by, other people—flinch as I rested my fingertips as lightly as possible on his arm and prepared to play my usual part in our regular Sunday duty to the town of Littleberry.

We were, as always, a large group, especially since my sisters Blanche and Odelia were staying with me at Whitcombe House. We arranged ourselves in order of precedence, with Blanche on the front row beside me, since she was the Marchioness of Hastings, and our eldest sister, Gerry, behind us with her husband, Sir Edward Freestone, mayor of Littleberry, and their children. Our unmarried sisters—Odelia and the twins, Alice and Annette—had to be content with a less prominent pew farther back. On the very last rows, a variety of governesses, nannies, and nursemaids strove to maintain discipline among such of the youngest generation as were deemed old enough to attend the church service.

The rustling noises behind us were dying down. Guided by Blanche's hissed, "Now," I raised my hated veil—I could not read my prayer book when I wore it—and did my best to view the rest of the congregation despite the obstruction represented by Blanche's somewhat stout figure. The center of the nave was taken up by the gentry, while the town's more prosperous merchants sat at the rear of the nave, and its humbler residents were consigned to the side aisles. Our pews were at right angles to the rest of the congregation so that we could both see and be seen.

It was to the merchants' section that my gaze was drawn, quickly identifying the dark heads of Gabrielle Dermody and her husband, Quinn. Seeing that Blanche had fixed her cold blue eyes on me, I looked to the front again, aware that I was blushing faintly, but I had seen enough. Mrs. Dermody's brother, Armand Fortier, had not yet returned from France.

I struggled for a moment with the gold clasp of my prayer book, which was emblazoned with the Whitcombe coat of arms of three scallop shells. I hesitated over the inscription in my late husband's handwriting—*J. Whitcombe, Bart., to his beloved wife, Helena, on the occasion of their wedding, this twenty-second day of June, eighteen hundred and seventy-eight*—before rapidly turning over the gilt-edged pages to ensure I had the correct lessons for the day.

It was the fourteenth Sunday after Trinity—September the third—seven more weeks before my first year and a day of mourning was over. Much as I had loved Justin, he would not wish me to emulate the Queen and mourn forever, so in seven weeks I would relinquish my veil and widow's cap, even though I fully intended to wear black for another twelvemonth.

The voices of the choir soared to the rafters of the ancient church and, as was my habit, my attention shifted to the ponderous swing of the great bronze pendulum high above the heads of the churchwardens. It was part of the movement of the church's venerable tower clock, and, along with the great banner of the Lion and Unicorn holding the royal arms, it had been my friend since I was a small child. In those days, I had seen nothing of the congregation, tucked as I was into the very last pew, next to a round stone column more massive than any tree I had ever known.

"I can never see anything, Papa," I had complained to my father on one of the rare Sundays when I managed to evade my nursemaid and attract his attention. "Everyone's so tall, and all I can ever see are the pendulum and the Lion and Unicorn. Why can't I sit with O?" Even then, my sister Odelia had been my favorite of all my siblings.

"Because Odelia is fifteen, a young lady almost ready to take her place in society, and you are five." The words were stern, but my tall, handsome father had softened them with a smile. "One day you'll be grown up too—but for now you have the privilege of looking at the most important things." He had pointed at the pendulum and the banner.

"*Why* are they important?" I had put my hand into Papa's large, warm one and marveled at the way a ray of sunlight from the clerestory made his thick silver hair glow. "When I was little, they made me frightened, but I'm braver now."

To my delight, he had swung me up into his arms and kissed my cheek. "You *are* brave, Baby—almost as brave as O. Now, do you see what's written on the banner? *Semper Eadem*. Do you know what it means?"

I had shaken my head, a little afraid that he would think me stupid. But he had called me Baby, and he only used my family nickname as an endearment, so I had resolved to be brave.

"Lydia says it's Latin, and she says girls don't learn Latin." Lydia, my niece, was almost a year and a half older than me, the great disparities between the ages of the Scott-De Quincy siblings blurring the lines of our family relationships to a puzzling degree.

"No more they don't." Papa had kissed me again and set me down on a pew, seating himself beside me. "Well, it means *Always the Same*. It declares that we're loyal to the Crown. Loyalty is one of the most important rules for the nobility, Baby, and as an earl's daughter you must remember that. And the pendulum shows us the other most important consideration for the nobility, which is Eternity. We must strive to endure. Loyalty and Eternity will govern your life, little Helena, and don't you forget it."

I had barely understood, but I had never forgotten. As I grew older, I had fancied that the tick of the pendulum whispered "Loyalty" and "Eternity" as it swung back and forth. In my imagination, the fierce, rolling eyes and sharp claws of the Lion and the Unicorn's snorting head with its lethal horn were guarding its power from harm. Now, older still and reeling from my recent discoveries about my parents' true history, I could not shake off the notions instilled in me by years of watching the great bronze disk count down the seconds of my life.

Loyalty had prevented my sisters telling me about my father's affairs and their effect on Mama. Loyalty now restrained me from telling anyone else the chilling truth that Mama had poisoned my father. Only two other people knew the words of her confession, hidden deep in one of her paintings: Michael, who had stored the information in the inscrutable caverns of his unique mind, and Fortier, whom I trusted to keep our secret. On this ordinary Sunday morning, participating prominently in our weekly display of power and influence, I could only pray that the sense of loyalty and eternity that was the foundation of my world would help me carry the burden of the secrets that underpinned it.

NOT THAT I EVER CONSCIOUSLY CARRIED THAT BURDEN INTO the suite of rooms at Whitcombe House where Mama now lived, lost in senility. What would be the point? I entered her sitting room with a cheerful smile, knowing I would find her with my good friend Julia, Michael's wife.

"Ah, you're back at last."

Julia's plain face lit up with pleasure as she looked up from her tiny son's sleeping form. She was the one family member who had not attended the service since she was nursing two-month-old Julius and considered her maternal duty incompatible with her role as countess. Having promised to stay for luncheon at my house, she was now sitting on the settee next to Mama, who was no longer capable of remembering how to hold the child but appeared to enjoy looking at him.

"The rector has promised to come to Hyrst before evensong to give you communion," I informed Julia as I bent to kiss Mama, who was crooning softly as she ran a frail finger over Julius's wisps of blond hair. "Isn't he beautiful, Mama?"

The infant in Julia's arms instantly captured me. He was so new-looking, so perfect with his velvet-soft skin, beneath which you could almost see the blood flowing. Would I ever experience such a miracle myself?

"Did Michael behave?" Julia's smile broadened as she put the infant into my arms, warm and heavy and wonderful.

"He fidgeted. He's always so much better when you're there." I moved a little closer to Mama so she could see the baby better.

"You say that every time," Julia teased.

"Because it's true. After the service, Blanche disappeared to talk to some friends of hers from Broadmere, and that set Michael off. You know how he hates having to wait. Will you be ready for luncheon in forty minutes?"

"Cabbage water." Mama seemed to tire of the baby suddenly and retreated farther into the settee, folding her arms and legs so that her frail body appeared much smaller. "All pretense." She screwed her eyes tight shut and set her mouth firmly.

I grimaced at Julia. "Mama hates it when we talk over her. I wonder if 'cabbage water' means she's thinking of food, though? She does like green vegetables."

"Talking of green—" Julia, who had risen to her feet to give me more room on the settee, positioned herself so she could speak softly into my ear. "Is O wearing that glorious green watered silk again? It looks dreadfully expensive. You're not dressing her as well as paying for Blanche's gowns, are you?"

I sighed ruefully. Julia was the only person to whom I had confided that Blanche invariably wormed the price of a dress or two out of me on every visit. "O never asks me for money," I assured my friend. "She must have sold a painting. I'm doubtful whether the allowance Michael gives her would stretch to that dress."

"I'm entirely sure it wouldn't." Julia's tone was dry. "I hope she's not getting herself into debt. Is she trying to catch a husband, do you think?"

"That would make Michael happy." I rose from the settee and settled Julius more snugly into the crook of my elbow, moving to the window so Julia and I could talk more comfortably. "I know Papa's debts are a burden to you and Michael, especially with there being no real prospect of the twins ever marrying. If it ever turns out that O has been foolish, I will make sure I pay her bills, I promise you. To save the family's honor as much as anything else." I dropped a kiss on little Julius's head as he stirred, laughing as he pulled a face in response to some internal process. "And for the sake of your children, whom I love as much as if they were my own."

"I know you do, bless you. I just pray you'll have your own one day. Ah, hello, Belming." Julia turned as Mama's attendant came quietly into the room. "We're going to have to leave, I'm afraid. I can't go down to luncheon in this dress, and Lord Broadmere will be getting impatient."

"Yes, my lady." Belming, who had been with our family since Mama's condition had become apparent, smiled sympathetically at the two of us as we headed to the door.

"I can tell Belming thinks she has the better part of it, not having to sit through a family luncheon." Julia wrinkled her nose at me as we left the room. "How was church?"

I grimaced. "The rector chose to speak on 'pride goeth before destruction, and a haughty spirit before a fall' instead of on the Good Samaritan, as you'd expect from the day's lesson. Blanche claimed he was looking straight at us all the time and spent half the drive home telling us how much *better* the church at Broadmere is. She takes offense far too easily."

"There's an old saying that fish and guests begin to smell after three days." Julia's deep chuckle accompanied her words. "I suppose it's my fault that you've had both Blanche *and* Odelia for two and a half weeks already. Aren't they showing any signs of leaving?"

"I'm really not blaming you for having a baby and then having him christened." I laughed. "Come and be my protector against my siblings during luncheon, and then I'll insist that O go out for a nice long walk with me once you and your family have gone back to Hyrst. We can leave Blanche to her afternoon rest. It's time I showed Justin's monument to Odelia; she hasn't seen it yet."

2

THE PAST AND THE FUTURE

I took my terrier, Scotty, out with us once Odelia and I were free to go for our walk. He had been snoozing in the conservatory during luncheon and was now far too full of energy. As soon as I had shut the cemetery gate behind us, I let him off the leash, watching as he raced madly between the graves in search of rabbits.

"I always worry the sexton will appear and scold me for showing so little respect to the dead," I admitted to Odelia as I watched my dog's wild dash. "He's such a crotchety old darling, and having known me since I was a tiny child, he thinks nothing of telling me off."

"He'll be asleep in front of his fire." Odelia looped her arm through mine, urging me toward the Anglican funerary chapel. "Besides, it's his fault there are so many rabbits. He should set snares."

The gravel path that circled around a young cedar of Lebanon crunched under our feet as we rounded the chapel. As usual, I experienced the strange shock that it was my husband—my Justin—buried under the tall new monument, set apart within its own patch of closely scythed grass.

9

"What do you think?" I asked my sister.

"No railing?" She raised her eyebrows.

"I didn't like the thought of Justin being put in a cage."

Odelia's only response was to kiss me briefly on the side of the head before inspecting the monument, which gleamed in the soft light of the fine September afternoon. A weeping angel presided over a large square pedestal engraved with Justin's name, title, dates, and the simple legend: *Beloved Husband.* The mason had carved the other three sides with a splendid design of tulips to symbolize our love. Against the base of the pedestal leaned a spray of three or four late rose blooms and astilbes, placed there by my head gardener, Taylor, who refreshed the floral tribute every morning.

"I like it," Odelia said after a minute's contemplation. "Not very original, but nicely executed, although I know a woman who could have done it better for you. The tulips are pretty."

"Yes, I liked the idea of the tulips." I reached out to touch the polished stone.

"You haven't left much room for your own name." Odelia tilted her head to look at me, curiosity written on her lean, handsome face.

"Plenty of room on the lower pedestal." I was aware I sounded defensive. "Should the need arise."

"Hmmm."

"I didn't want to leave a large blank space."

"Especially if you should marry again." Odelia's eyebrows rose. "Do I take it you don't intend to be the weeping widow forever?"

"You're putting words in my mouth." My voice sounded sulky in my ears. "My *intent* is to remain loyal to Justin forever. He is my husband."

A sudden wave of unexpected emotion passed over me. To declare loyalty seemed instantly to suggest the possibility of *dis*loyalty. But how could I be disloyal to Justin? I cleared my throat and tried to speak, but no words came. O filled the silence.

"You have an awful lot of life left before you, darling one. You're a mere twenty-six years of age. I'm not going to be like the others with their eternal introductions to suitable men, but nobody expects you to remain celibate forever. Justin certainly wouldn't."

I tipped my head up to frown at my tall sister. "I suppose it's no secret to any of you that I'd love a child of my own. Matrimony appears to be the best way of achieving that aim. If I can. Justin and I were just unlucky."

The fight went out of me suddenly, my shoulders slumping as if I were laying down a heavy burden. I twisted Scotty's red leash between my hands. "I'm torn, O. I want to be Justin's wife forever—but how can I be if I become someone else's? And yet, if I remain loyal to Justin, I'll be alone forever. And I don't want that."

"It wouldn't suit you, would it?" O gazed at me, her expression thoughtful. "If you ask me, you need a man in your life just as much as you need a child."

I could feel the braided leather of Scotty's leash digging into my palm through my glove. My right hand strayed toward Justin's monument again, seeking solace, but there was none to be found in the unyielding gloss of polished marble.

"Don't look so tragic, darling." Odelia's smile was warm. "It's far too soon to make a choice. All you have to do is wait till that choice becomes obvious."

It was time to change the subject before Odelia mentioned Fortier. "And what about you?" I asked. "Since you take such an extraordinary interest in my marital prospects, you could at least hint at yours." And put Julia's mind at rest, perhaps. Supporting three unmarried sisters was an expense Michael could ill afford.

Odelia chuckled. "I? At thirty-six?"

"Why not? You're handsome, intelligent, and an earl's daughter. Don't tell me nobody's interested." It felt almost pleasant to be the one doing the prying for a change.

"I *do* tell you so." Odelia pursed her lips. "Haven't I made it clear enough? I have no interest in marrying. And I find the idea of children repellent. Not children as people, you understand—I like them well enough if they're pretty little things and reasonably well behaved—but the notion of bearing my own, of being tied to them, revolts me. I am wedded to my art and wish for nothing more than absolute freedom to practice it." She looked around. "Where's that dog of yours?"

I narrowed my eyes. It was typical of Odelia to poke her nose into my private life and then deflect any inquiry into her own. But her answer had been quite definite. Julia would have to hope one or both of the twins might marry, as unlikely as that seemed, given their attachment to each other.

Odelia was already calling for Scotty. To my surprise, he appeared, panting loudly and with very dirty paws.

"Oh dear." I clipped the leash to Scotty's collar, ignoring his growl of protest. "He's been digging again. Scotty, you know the sexton will flick you with his whip if he catches you. Come along, you naughty dog." I turned up the hill toward the road with O following, but she put a hand on my arm so I had to stop.

"I didn't mean to upset you," she said. "It's a perfect torment, always being asked when one might marry. I've had to put up with it for years. It's just that—well, behind your back, your marriage seems to be Blanche's and Gerry's chief preoccupation. They're both quite worked up about your Frenchman."

"He's not mine, and he's gone to France, and—oh, Scotty, do behave." I tugged on my dog's leash, wishing I could curb my family as easily as I curbed him. "Honestly, anyone would think I was carrying on with a groom rather than forming a harmless friendship with an educated, well-bred physician."

"It's not the educated and well-bred part that worries them. It's not even the fact that he has a profession. After all, with the way landowners' incomes have dropped in the last few years, more than one landed gentleman has had to find a way to make a living. It's the fact that he's a physician. Doctors are simply beyond the pale. I don't know why they should be so very different from, say, a lawyer, but you know very well they are. Something to do with the original surgeons having been butchers, I think. And his sister married to a merchant too. People one does not invite to dine."

"No? I thought Scott-De Quincys did what they pleased?" My cheeks were hot. "Gerry's husband is a merchant."

"Of impeccable lineage and considerable wealth, and a Sussex man to boot. There was still an enormous scandal, I've heard. A Scott-De Quincy marrying into trade." Odelia frowned. "I've always wondered why Mama and Papa allowed it to happen, you know. I was just a little girl at the time and remember nothing of any trouble. It's tiresome, all of us being so far apart in age."

"There's no proof at all that Fortier's lineage isn't impeccable." I raised my voice to be heard above Scotty's barking as a large rook landed near us. "Furthermore, it's highly impertinent to assume he has no wealth or prospects."

"My, how you defend him." Odelia put a slender arm over my shoulders. "No, don't shrug me off. You know I'm only teasing. I just want to see you happy, darling girl. Gerry no doubt feels that as the eldest daughter she must stand in for Mama and protect the family name, and Blanche—well, Blanche is Blanche. A roaring snob from the day she was born."

"It's all so ridiculous. They'd be happy if I married a

nobleman, even if he was decrepit and had a string of mistresses. Because a nobleman is the highest prize in the marriage stakes."

"As long as he isn't a physician." Odelia laughed. "We've all heard the story of the cook who went to work for a baronet but gave notice when she discovered he was a medical man. Of course, servants are always more snobbish than we are."

"That idea that aristocrats shouldn't work for a living has ruined many a family," I said. "Bored men gamble and live too high, and if you're not working for your money, you can easily lose sight of the gap between your income and expenditure. Justin said he'd learned that lesson before he reached the age of wisdom and settled down in the country. The blessed sheep kept him too busy to gamble and drink."

"Being a gentleman farmer is an eminently acceptable occupation, especially if he is as successful at it as Justin was." Odelia grinned. "You could marry a poet, of course—or a painter or a writer, as long as he's enough of a gentleman to be free of any taint of money-grubbing. A talented man always has the chance of being knighted."

"And look at all those Americans marrying their daughters into the aristocracy," I interrupted, warming to my subject. "None of us despise money from trade if it's enough to rescue an estate from bankruptcy."

"You could even get away with a nice dull clergyman or scholar, as long as he's one of us." Odelia was laughing again. "The funny thing is, it's much easier for a man to get away with marrying someone who's beneath him socially. All you have to do is send the girl away for a year or two to learn to speak properly and use the right fork."

I kicked at the gravel of the path with the toe of my boot. "Really, O, you sound just like Mama."

"I can't help it." Odelia shrugged. "I learned my lessons at her knee, as you did ten years later. Aren't we all afraid, somewhere deep down, that we'll make the dreaded unsuitable marriage and be forced to go live on the Continent because nobody in our own country will receive us in their houses?"

"You're quite ridiculous." I picked Scotty up, heedless of the marks his paws made on my black dress.

"Perhaps. And maybe I should just leave you alone to decide your future for yourself."

"I'd appreciate that."

"Would you take one piece of sisterly advice, though? Not about matters of the heart. There's something I've been trying to discuss with you for days, only we've all been so busy with Julius's christening and Blanche insisting we visit every bore in the county. I hope you won't be cross. I like the little changes you've made around your house, but don't you think it looks a little shabby overall?"

"Shabby?" In my surprise, I put Scotty down again and straightened up. "Some of our things are a bit old, but Justin always said a gentleman's home should be comfortable." I frowned. "Since he died, I've bought one or two little pieces."

"*Little* pieces, that's the point. That beautiful house is yours now. You can do what you want with it. And, even if I do sound like Blanche, you have plenty of money. I imagine a year without a single house party has filled the coffers to overflowing. Why not spend some of it?"

"On what?" I was perplexed.

"On bringing back some of Whitcombe's glory. It must have been a simply marvelous house a hundred years ago, but it's showing its age. Oh, the bedrooms are comfortable enough; some of them are really quite nice. But the reception rooms—how can I put it? They're faded. I think that became truly apparent when you put together your pretty workroom, which somehow unbalances the entire house. Why not make something of the rest of the downstairs before you

have some man in your life telling you how he wants everything to look?"

I thought about that. "I suppose you have a point," I
conceded at length. "But where would I start?"

"I know exactly where." There was a look of almost
febrile enthusiasm on Odelia's face. "And I know exactly the
right people to help you. Regardless of whether you marry
again, Helena darling, I'd like to see you be the young woman
you are. You should do something adventurous. Won't you
let me give you some advice? I know something about decoration. I've never been able to do much at Scott House
because my allowance won't stretch to it and Michael can't
afford any more than he already pays for its upkeep, but I've
helped a few friends improve their homes. Do you remember
the Hayter-Savidges? We visited them the last time you were
in London. You admired their house tremendously."

"Oh yes." A memory stirred. "They praised you to the
skies for your help. All right, O, I'm willing to listen."

"Good." Odelia smiled brilliantly. "You won't regret it."

"But you'll let me say no if I want to, won't you?" I lifted
my chin. "Just as in the matter of marriage, I would like to
make the decisions about my house by myself. I've let this
family steer my life for long enough."

3

THE NIGHTINGALE

By the time we returned to Whitcombe House, we had worked up a good appetite for tea and I had listened to some of Odelia's ideas concerning decoration in general. Odelia, Blanche, and I gathered in the main drawing room, joined by our nephew Thomas.

Thomas had done us the great favor of keeping Blanche amused once she had finished her post-prandial nap. It was like him to do so. Kind and good-natured, he had become a great favorite with everyone since coming to live at Whitcombe. My servants, all of whom adored him, affectionately called him Mr. Thomas rather than Mr. Freestone. To me, he was almost like a brother, a less difficult version of Michael. Now he sat quietly, consuming a prodigious amount of sandwiches and cake, listening to Odelia as she repeated some of the notions she had introduced that afternoon. Scotty snoozed beside her, occasionally letting out a whimper as he dreamed of rabbits.

"I must say, Odelia, I think you have a point." Blanche was clearly in an exceptionally mellow mood after her nap since she almost never agreed with Odelia on principle. "After all, this house will be Helena's for life, won't it? Under the new law, it won't become the property of her next husband. And one day she'll want to entertain on a large scale again." A pleased look stole into her calculating eyes. She had many friends in Broadmere and took pleasure in inviting them to my house whenever she could. "This season of retirement from the world would be an ideal time to prepare for that happy day."

Thomas took a large gulp of tea, no doubt to wash down all the food. "I rather like Wh-Whitcombe the w-way it is."

"Yes, dear, but you're a man." Blanche's smile was condescending. "Men always love dust and shabbiness. It is the role of the gentler sex to create beauty wherever we can. In the end, the men are always happy with the result."

"If you s-say so, Auntie Blanche." Thomas looked around the room. "Now you point it out, I c-can see this room needs repainting, at the very least." With his good arm, he indicated one corner of the room near the great row of windows that looked out toward the sea. "There's still a w-water stain where you had to have that corner repaired during the b-bad weather, Auntie Helena."

"I fully intend to have the room repainted." I lifted my chin. "But your ideas go beyond redecorating, don't they, O? You keep talking about doing far more with this room, but I wish you'd explain exactly what you mean."

"Very well." Odelia rose to her feet, surveying her audience with the air of an actor about to embark on a grand Shakespearean prologue. "I think we can all agree this room has perfect proportions, and the view out to the sea is remarkable."

She gestured to where the ocean showed as a dark blue line on the horizon. The land beyond the house sloped to such a degree that the view was entirely unimpeded. We were some two and a half miles from the coast, and the valley that separated us from the English Channel was bounded by Littleberry on our left, a jumble of red bricks and tiled roofs surmounted by the distinctive silhouette of St. Michael's church, and Broadmere to our right, its church and houses almost hidden behind tall trees. Justin's father had insisted there be no doors to interrupt the long sweep of windows, in front of which there was an inviting low seat that gave family and guests a chance to face into the room or sit dreamily looking outward, according to one's mood.

"We agree that the room is a little faded," Odelia continued. "But the real problems are those dreary paintings of undistinguished landscapes and religious themes. They're trite—uninteresting. This room compares badly with the green drawing room, where the paintings are quite remarkable."

I nodded. "I can agree with that—but you're not proposing we move the portraits from the green drawing room in here, are you? They're perfect where they are." The green drawing room on the north side of the house was vibrant with color from the life-sized portraits of Justin's ancestors. I had given that drawing room to Thomas for his own use, it being too long and narrow for a large party of guests.

"Th-those portraits were m-made for the room, weren't they?" Thomas asked. "It's like stepping back into the last century to s-see them there. Sometimes I feel th-they could almost step out of their frames and talk to me."

Odelia nodded, a half smile on her lips, as if Thomas had said something clever. "You're right, they were painted for the room. *That's* why the green drawing room makes people gasp and smile when they enter it for the first time. It has a scheme and thus produces an effect. That's what *this* room, which is supposed to be the public heart of your house, is lacking."

"I could concede that point," I said.

"Very good." O smiled at me. "I propose the remedy of a suite of paintings that reflect the beauty of the sea and the loveliness of the countryside on a summer's day—I admit it can look lovely when the sun is shining—and yet provide life and color on those tedious days, by which I mean at least half of the year, when the sky is gray or all you can see is rain. The rest is decoration. Silk brocade on the upper part of the walls and that splendid ceiling freshly gilded and made more colorful. Fresh paint and re-gilding on the paneling and gilt-work below the paintings, and everything else made new. Keep this lovely old furniture but re-cover it, I think. Although I would defer to the artist's opinion on that."

"Which artist?" I asked. "You haven't mentioned a name. I was starting to think you were proposing to do it yourself."

Blanche's plump lips stretched into an unusually wide smile. "But you're not, are you?" she said to Odelia, sounding as if she'd just seen the answer to a riddle. "You're trying to get a commission for one of your impoverished artist friends."

Odelia folded her arms and regarded our sister coldly. "It may interest you to know, Blanche, that many of my friends are established artists who are not in the least impoverished. Quite the contrary. I am *trying*, if you would allow me, to introduce the idea that one of them—a painter of great repute—has a project in mind that needs a suitable room. I have persuaded him to consider this one, if Helena is willing. I thought of her as soon as he mentioned it because it's based on a story she loved as a child. One I used to read to you, Helena. *The Nightingale*."

Sudden enlightenment spread over Blanche's face, and she sat up a little straighter. "A fairy tale—do you mean that

Dorrian-Knowles man? The one who painted the picture with the little children, all ice and snow—what was it called?"

"*In the Halls of the Snow Queen.*" Odelia looked, and sounded, startled. "Great heavens, Blanche, I never knew you could describe a painting."

"Don't be ridiculous. I know who Dorrian-Knowles is." Blanche looked truly interested. "Francis and I saw the *Halls of the Snow Queen* picture when we were visiting the Stranges at their London house years ago. They took us to a private showing—very *advanced*. All the talk was about the fairy-tale picture, that's why I remember it. People think he's a rather wonderful painter, don't they?"

"Even in the d-depths of the Sussex c-c-countryside, we have heard of the painting of Kai and Gerda in the *Halls of the Snow Queen.*" Thomas smiled. "I even have an engraving of it somewhere. It reminds me s-strongly of a picture in a book of Hans Christian Andersen tales we used to read as children. I liked that b-b-book, b-but it disappeared years ago. M-M-Mama was annoyed because it was one you'd all read as children too, and she was fond of it."

"*In the Halls of the Snow Queen* was the first of the great Andersen cycle. It was the painting that made Sir Geraint Dorrian-Knowles's name." Standing before us, Odelia could have been a teacher lecturing a group of students.

"*Sir* Geraint, of course. I'd forgotten he'd been knighted." Blanche's expression was avid. "Is he a baronet or an ordinary knight?"

"A baronet," Odelia said shortly. "I wish you'd all stop interrupting. Sir Geraint wants to crown his career with a grand series of paintings on *The Nightingale*. But he needs the right setting, and I think this room is just perfect."

"Do you know him well?" Blanche asked.

"Well enough." O waved a dismissive hand. "A few of us were at his studio—I'm an admirer of his work, as so many are—and when he spoke of wanting to put the sea into two of the paintings to symbolize eternal truth, it came to me all at once that there could be no better setting. It would be magnificent—it would restore this lovely house to its proper place in the world. It would both celebrate the splendid legacy that Justin has left to Helena and give her a public space she could truly claim as her own, don't you see?" She turned toward me. "If you're serious about making Whitcombe your lifelong home no matter what, shouldn't you start right now to put your own stamp on it? I think that's what you've been trying to do, in a small way."

"It would be *dreadfully* expensive." Blanche's face bore an inward look, as if she were calculating the advantages and disadvantages—to herself—of a restored and splendid Whitcombe.

"I won't pretend it wouldn't cost a great deal." Odelia sat down, looking at me intently. "It would also take a long time —two to three years, perhaps more. So the cost would be spread over that time, and would include the hiring of the right artisans and decorators to ensure the setting was correctly executed. The entire room would be a work of art. Can you see that? Sir Geraint would supervise everything, so in some ways you'd get a better bargain than if you hired your own people. Your man of business would have to advise you and draw up a proper agreement setting out all the terms of the work. It's not something to be undertaken lightly on either side, but it's a venture that will have lasting value. You will see all kinds of sketches and so forth before you sign anything. Sir Geraint is absolutely thorough in his preparation."

I stared out at the distant sea for a few moments before I spoke, an odd feeling of excitement in the pit of my stomach. "I'd have to give the idea a great deal of thought," I said finally.

"You'd need to understand every detail." O nodded her head vigorously. "There must be no doubt in your mind. Why don't you come up to London next month once your first year of mourning is over? You could meet Sir Geraint and get a better idea of his work. I'll arrange it all. You won't have to decide a thing straightaway."

4

THE REAL LIFE OF A LADY

he next day, Odelia announced her imminent departure. Blanche, ever eager to criticize and especially so where O was concerned, favored me with her opinion that Odelia had stayed so long precisely so she could introduce the idea of a commission.

"But it's not such an outlandish notion as all that, Helena," she said once Odelia had returned to London. "There's no reason you shouldn't live with a certain style, even as a widow. It would be far less *eccentric* to be a patron of the arts than to mess around with herbs the way Mama did."

"I *enjoy* messing around with herbs," I replied.

"But it's surely not your—what's the word? *Vocation*, that's it. I mean, you're not going to fret and fuss if you can't run around the countryside healing farmers and workhouse inmates all day, are you? Particularly if you remarry. Papa used to get quite cross when Mama wanted to dash away to some cottage instead of entertaining his guests as a countess should. And then she'd shout at him over healing being her purpose in life; so *unpleasant*. Usefulness to the people below her enhances a lady's reputation, but she must strike a balance with her social obligations, don't you see? Those obligations are the true vocation of women like us, Helena. Mama just made herself miserable. You were perfectly happy, weren't you, when your life revolved around Justin? You looked after him so well. Your dinners and house parties were the best in the county, not a detail missed. Did you need anything else in your life then?"

"I suppose not," I conceded.

"Well, then." Blanche looked pleased. "By all means, follow in Mama's footsteps with a few simple remedies here and there—some of your little concoctions are really quite pleasant—but don't get *obsessed* about them like Mama did. That's my advice. I believe Odelia's scheme might really do something for you socially. Sir Geraint Dorrian-Knowles is a member of the Royal Academy, so it's not as if she's foisting one of her dreadful bohemians on you, is it? Perhaps this is your opportunity to meet some more *suitable* people."

More suitable than Fortier, she meant. I could tell that by the way she was looking at me.

"I've promised O I'll go to London next month to meet Sir Geraint," I informed Blanche. "In fact, I'm hoping to persuade Michael to stay at Scott House instead of at his club when he's up for the parliamentary session, so I'm going up early to get the house ready. There are a few improvements that could be made."

If I hadn't known it was Blanche, I could almost have said she beamed. "Now *that's* much more suitable than making potions, isn't it? My goodness, if you could make dear old Scott House habitable, I might even risk a visit to London myself. I have so many dear friends I haven't seen for years . . . Yes, a trip to Town is a very sensible idea, Helena. A fresh start. A return to your *real* life. No more gallivanting about poking your nose into death and illegitimate babies and goodness knows what. Perhaps you can keep yourself busy with improving Whitcombe, and the first year of your widowhood will begin to seem like some kind of extraordinary fantasy, an escape from the real world. You'll see."

Blanche set off to her home in Tunbridge Wells on the fourteenth of September, so I had the pleasing prospect of an entire month at Whitcombe with just Thomas, Mama, and the servants for company. Of course, I was busy making arrangements to ensure Michael's comfort at Scott House, and I toured Whitcombe with my housekeeper, Mrs. Eason, to make a list of areas that needed improvement. It was an alarmingly long list. I was seeing the house with unaccustomed eyes now that it was entirely mine. I became increasingly convinced that Odelia had a point.

Searching through Whitcombe's libraries for a copy of Hans Christian Andersen's fairy tales, I eventually found one in the small library. It was not the pretty illustrated copy I remembered from my childhood, but it refreshed my memory of the story. I soon found myself relating it to Guttridge.

My lady's maid, who seemed to thoroughly enjoy her other role as my workroom assistant, had suggested an early morning expedition. Accompanied by an under-gardener and Scotty, we had set off to collect marshmallow plants near Scott's Folly, the local name for the gaunt Jacobean ruin that had once been the home of the Scott-De Quincys.

A mile's walk in a bracing damp wind over land formed by centuries of storms at sea was excellent exercise. By the time Guttridge and I returned to our workroom, the plants had been well washed and kept in the cool stillroom so that their downy leaves were unwilted and their crooked white roots fresh, plump, and promising. We set to work with a will, and I entertained us with the story of *The Nightingale*.

"I never did hold with fairy tales." Guttridge, whose long, strong fingers were making short work of peeling the roots, sniffed as I began with the Chinese emperor whose palace built of porcelain was the most splendid in the world. "Horrible, most of them. I wouldn't let Auntie read me any because they gave me the shivers."

"This one's not like that," I assured her. "I always loved the idea of the emperor's garden stretching down to the sea, containing a nightingale so famous for its song that men wrote books about it. The garden was so vast that the emperor never heard of the nightingale until he read those books, and then, of course, he wanted to summon it to sing for him. But the only person who knew the whereabouts of the bird was a little kitchen maid."

"Well, I can believe that. The gentry don't know half of what the servants know." Guttridge watched as I chopped the peeled marshmallow root into small pieces suitable for drying. "You could be a kitchen maid yourself, my lady, doing work like that. Why don't you let me do it all? You'll ruin your hands."

"My mother always dug the plants herself—*she* wouldn't have taken a gardener with her—and prepared them too, from beginning to end," I said. "She didn't care about her hands." I gathered the chopped root in my fingers and dropped it into a bowl, then reached for another root. "Anyway, in the story the courtiers offered the kitchen maid many privileges to tell them where the nightingale was. Eventually, they persuaded the bird to sing for the emperor. The kitchen maid was allowed to listen behind the door because she had been promoted. The nightingale sang so sweetly the emperor cried, and they made the bird live at the palace."

"Put it in a cage, you mean."

"More or less." I watched Guttridge cut another root from its stem. "We'll hang the leaves to dry to make tea, won't we?"

"We'll put aside a few leaves to use for poultices—they told me at breakfast that the country people swear by them for bruises and rashes." The fine strips of peel fell onto the table's marble top, and Guttridge handed the peeled root to me. "Was the bird happy in the palace?"

"I imagine not. The Emperor of Japan sent the Emperor of China an artificial bird, all covered with jewels, and while everyone was admiring it, the real bird flew back to the green woods near the shore. So everyone decided the artificial bird was better."

"There's gratitude for you."

"Indeed. Well, of course, one day the artificial bird's clockwork broke. They repaired it, but it could only be wound once a year, which was sad enough—and then, five years later, the emperor fell ill to the point of death. He lay in bed with the cold moonlight shining on him and the useless bird. When he felt he couldn't breathe, he opened his eyes to find Death sitting on his chest, wearing the emperor's golden crown and carrying his sword and scepter."

"You said it wasn't gruesome." Guttridge put down her knife. "They're not going to make a painting of Death to hang in your lovely drawing room, are they?"

"I wouldn't agree to it." I chopped carefully and steadily, shaping the rest of the story in my mind. "The emperor's good and bad deeds came and whispered to him, and he pleaded with the toy bird to sing so he couldn't hear what they were saying. But it remained silent because there was nobody there to wind it up."

"Didn't he have anybody to watch over him as he lay dying?" Guttridge tutted as she began making bundles of the marshmallow leaves, tying them with coarse string. "They should be ashamed of themselves. Funny people, the Chinese."

"I don't suppose Andersen ever went to China, so it's all made up. Everything was still and silent, save for the terrible whispering in the emperor's ears, but suddenly the song of the real nightingale arose from outside the emperor's window. The bird had come to save him. As it sang, the ghosts disappeared, and the emperor grew stronger."

"And it got rid of Death too, I'll be bound." Guttridge was clearly interested now.

"Of course. It sang so sweetly that Death handed over the crown, sword, and scepter just to hear more of its song. Then the bird sang of Death's peaceful garden until Death floated away, like a mist, back to his home."

"All right, I suppose that's nice enough. Is that the end of it?"

"Only that the nightingale agreed to come and sing for the emperor as long as it remained free to come and go as it pleased. And the servants came in the morning to look at their dead emperor, and lo, there he stood, wearing his crown and holding his sword and scepter, and he said: 'Good morning!' I always liked that part best."

"I like the kitchen maid." Guttridge grinned. "Will she be in the painting?"

"I don't know."

"It'd look funny in a drawing room, a kitchen maid in a painting."

"But it's a fairy tale. I suppose you can have anything in a fairy tale—dragons, toys that talk, magicians, enchantments. It's pure imagination. Like Lady Odelia's medieval pictures but with even more license for the artist to do as he pleases."

"I like a painting with real people and a nice moral, never mind imagination." Guttridge finished tying the last bunch of mallow stems. She would leave the cleaning up to Tilda, the workroom maid.

"But you approve on principle of making the drawing room look more—well, more splendid?" I asked her. "I should have thought of it when Sir Justin was alive. What would he say to such an extravagance, I wonder?"

"I'm sure he'd have paid for anything you wanted, my lady." Guttridge's voice was unusually soft. "He doted on you. But you never asked for much."

"Younger daughters learn not to ask." I ran a hand over the soft leaves of the plants, smiling as Scotty yipped softly in his sleep. "Well, we've got plenty of leaves for drying and a nice lot of roots. We'll dry some of those root pieces for later and use the rest for fresh extracts and syrups. Excellent for coughs and stomach upsets."

"And they make a nice confection, my lady. I saved some roots for Mrs. Foster, so there'll be marshmallow sweets with your coffee after dinner."

I was thoughtful as we carried plants and chopped roots into the stillroom that adjoined my workroom. "You know, Guttridge, occasionally I feel it's impossible to live in the real world when one has 'Lady' in front of one's name. Lady Hastings said something about my real world not being my herbs, but my role as a hostess, wife, and, if I were fortunate enough, mother. Yet sometimes, when I've been outdoors or in the town or even in this workroom and I go into the rooms where I live, I feel as if I've walked out of the real world into a fairy tale. Does it ever strike you that way?"

"Oh, servants are forever moving between one world and another, especially the upper servants who spend time with the gentry." Guttridge's voice was brisk and cheerful. "We get used to seeing both sides of the picture. A place in a large house with the nobility might fill some with envy and resentment, but if you're sensible, you just enjoy it. I take pleasure in seeing your pretty dresses and your silver and fresh flowers and all, and then I can go back to my room and put my feet up comfortable. That's what I always wanted, and it's why I stayed in service even when my friends called me a slavey. I'd much rather be a lady's maid than marry and live in a poky cottage where I have to cook my own food and scrub my own floors."

"I'm glad you're happy," I murmured.

"You don't mind me being frank, do you, my lady?" Guttridge, who had been hanging up the bunches of plants, turned to look at me. "It's a pleasure serving a lady I don't have to be mealymouthed with, although I hope you'll tell me if I ever forget my place."

"I rather like your frankness." I smiled as I spread the pieces of root on a rack taken from the drying cupboard. "Anyway, I asked you for your opinion. Now, what do you think of inviting Mrs. Dermody to luncheon? I've been wanting to do so for some time. Lady Hastings would have had conniptions if I'd told her, so I didn't. Lady Geraldine will also disapprove, no doubt, but she married a merchant, so I don't believe she has a leg to stand on, as the vulgar phrase goes. I don't see why my social circle should be entirely confined to people of my own class, and Mrs. Dermody is perfectly ladylike. Why should I be bound by a rule that says I should never invite people in trade to dine?"

"Her husband's a little rough around the edges." Guttridge, who like most upper servants could weigh the niceties of caste with a grain of sand, screwed up her brow as she thought. "And he's quite opposed to the nobility, my lady. Always agitating and complaining, wanting to give the poor people feather beds and bathrooms. If you weren't who you were, I'd say to be very careful in case the company you keep reflects badly on you."

"That would be Lady Hastings's argument. Lady Odelia

would say I should keep the company I want to keep." I shrugged. "And my brother doesn't care one way or the other."

"I don't see any of the Whitcombe staff giving notice because you invite a merchant's wife to tea." Guttridge shook her head slightly. "No, I can't think of anyone who would. You're too good an employer."

"And that's just as well because losing good servants is far more of a disaster than being the butt of the gossips of Littleberry." I was thoroughly enjoying this conversation.

"Well, if they didn't leave last year over Susan Hatherall, I doubt they'd leave over Mrs. Dermody. There *were* one or two people who talked about leaving when Susan died that horrible way, but they know when they're well off."

"I won't embarrass you by asking who they are," I said. "Very well, Guttridge, I'll write a note to Mrs. Dermody asking if next Friday would be convenient. She's quite the most intelligent and interesting woman I've met in Littleberry outside the family, and I'd like to know her better."

"Of course, my lady."

5

A MEETING OF TWO WORLDS

The week passed quickly since I was engaged in Littleberry business, and I was happy to indulge in a lazy morning before dressing for my luncheon with Mrs. Dermody. I was no less delighted to see my brother-in-law Sir Edward Freestone in the Great Hall when I was on my way downstairs to take the air while waiting for Mrs. Dermody's carriage.

"Ned!" I held out my arms to the mayor of Littleberry, laughing at his enthusiastic, fatherly salute of big kisses on both cheeks. "What brings you here? Would you like to stay for luncheon? I've invited Mrs. Dermody."

"That fact has already done the rounds of the Littleberry gossips, and I wouldn't dream of spoiling your *tête-à-tête*. Thomas has asked for a few more minutes with his tutor, but as soon as he's free, I want to go out to Holhurst with him and get his thoughts on the mill there. Littleberry needs a better mill, in my opinion. I know a place we can get a bite to eat and it will be good to talk."

I smiled. Since Thomas had announced his intention to join the church instead of clerking for his father, Ned had begun treating his crippled son more like an equal and seeking his company more. I suspected he missed Thomas's presence in his wine business and was eager to cultivate his friendship now he didn't see my nephew every day. All to the good, of course.

"So what are the gossips saying?" I slid my hand under Ned's elbow as, by tacit consent, we turned toward the terrace. Scotty, who had clearly been somewhere on the grounds, appeared to sniff at Ned and then followed us, darting erratically around in search of enticing aromas. Autumn was late in appearing, and Taylor's bronze dahlias still made splashes of bright color in the flowerbeds, yet the trees in the valley below us were taking on their autumnal tints. The distant sea had the hazy green-gray look to it that usually signaled bad weather.

"Oh, I think your reputation will survive the experiment." Ned scratched at his thick beard with his free hand. "Some people are quite pleased. They see it as a *rapprochement* of town and county that's long overdue. Not that Gerry hasn't frequently dispensed tea and cakes to the ladies on her committees—and it's quite pathetic, really, to see how thrilled they are to come to our house—but a private luncheon invitation is quite another thing. They have, of course, jumped to the conclusion that this is all for the sake of Mrs. Dermody's brother."

I started and felt my cheeks flame. "It's not that at all," I said before reflecting that my denial was perhaps a little too vehement. "I took tea with Mrs. Dermody last summer—I was passing, and she invited me in—and found her to be most pleasant company. I don't have many friends who weren't more Justin's friends than mine."

"Of course, my dear." Ned's arm squeezed mine a little. "Don't think I have anything against Fortier anyway. A most able fellow. In fact, I'd like to involve him in a little project of mine if only he would settle down in Littleberry and stop disappearing for weeks on end. Well, not a little project; rather a large one, in fact." He grinned down at me. "I'll talk to you about it someday."

"I don't see how I could help you with your grand schemes for Littleberry." I shrugged, watching the rooks swooping and fluttering in the breeze almost at eye level. The land below the terrace swooped down steeply so that birds could often be seen in flight before one's eyes. The rooks were most entertaining, pausing at moments to glide on the breeze before changing direction with a playful squawk. I kept a firm hand on Scotty's collar, although in his four years my dog had not yet jumped off the terrace.

"You underestimate yourself, my dear." Ned's tone was light, but there was an underlying seriousness in his voice. "You have more potential for good than you realize. You'd make a fine mayor's wife. Like your sister, who, God bless her, has been my light and strength since I first laid eyes on her all those years ago."

"I could never match Gerry."

"You think not?" Ned's expression was serious again. "In some ways—and I hope you'll forgive me for saying so—you were wasted as Justin's wife, as a mere companion and ornament. You have a deep and sincere wish to do good, and you have considerable reserves of strength and nerve. If you must marry again, make sure it's to a man who brings out the best in you."

I didn't know what to say to that, so I said nothing. We stood in companionable silence, watching the life of the valley spread out before us, until Ned started and pulled his watch out of his pocket with a murmured oath.

"Two minutes to twelve," he announced. "I hope Mrs. Dermody isn't one of those ladies who arrives early. Come on!" And grasping my hand in his large calloused fingers, he towed me toward the house, both of us laughing and followed by a madly barking dog.

"I TOO MUST GO TO LONDON IN ABOUT A MONTH'S TIME," SAID Gabrielle Dermody as we passed through the glazed outer doors into the Great Hall. We had eaten a good luncheon of brill and shrimp sauce, roast hare, and lemon pudding and then refreshed ourselves with a walk around Whitcombe's gardens, laughing at Scotty's antics.

"Really?" I had been telling Gabrielle—we had decided to call each other by our first names—about my forthcoming trip to London and explained a little about the commission into which Odelia wanted me to enter. "To visit friends? Or to see your dressmaker?" I was sure my new friend had her clothes made in London since they were more fashionable than one usually saw in Littleberry.

Gabrielle's smile was sad. "To spend time with my father," she said. "He is very ill. Armand doesn't think he has many months left. It's very hard on my brother to be absent from England at this time."

"I didn't know." I was instantly mortified. "How unfeeling I must have sounded. Your brother didn't say anything to me."

Gabrielle was silent for a moment. "I wondered if he had," she said eventually. "Armand can be extremely reserved at times. Then he will suddenly take you into his confidence . . ." She paused again. "He told me he's in love with you."

The heat rose to my face. "Ah," was all I could think of saying.

"And that he told you as much, quite recently. I must admit, I wasn't all that surprised. There was something about the way he behaved that day in my garden . . . . I could sense something, a connection perhaps. Or a longing in him. He has a romantic soul, just like our father." She hesitated. "Do you mind?"

I, too, waited for a few moments before replying. "I can't deny I feel an attraction between us. But it's far too soon for me. I have lost two loves, and now I must be alone until I can be sure who I am and what I want. I feel as if I was born as a new person the day my husband died, and until I know who that person is, I can't know whether she wishes to bestow her hand on anyone in particular."

"Do you miss Armand now he's gone?" Gabrielle's eyes were serious, her expression poised between affection and concern.

"Yes." The answer came before I had time to reflect. "Leaving all other considerations aside, we have become friends. I wish we could continue in that friendship for the time being. That and nothing more."

"Armand said something similar to me." Warmth replaced the note of concern in Gabrielle's voice. "He's rather shocked to find himself in love. He never has been before."

Was it idiotic to feel pleased about that? And there was also relief in knowing that Fortier did not perhaps intend to woo me yet.

"It's not just my uncertainties—nor yet my family, whose opinions I don't feel I can ignore." I took a deep breath. "To be honest, your brother hinted at an impediment—a wife who is not a wife—and until I understand that situation fully, I couldn't possibly accept his advances. I don't understand why he couldn't tell me."

I saw the corners of Gabrielle's expressive lips turn down and knew she wasn't going to tell me either.

"It's not my secret, and I won't betray it." Her expression was momentarily bleak, but then her brow lightened. "I will encourage my brother to be more forthcoming when he sees you, at least if he feels it safe to do so. I understand the frustration you must feel."

"Safe?" I seized on the word that had leaped out at me.

"The happiness, and perhaps the lives, of other people are at stake. Armand will not tell you more than he absolutely must. I'm sorry." She hesitated again. "He has carried a heavy burden since he was a boy of seventeen—a burden that should never have been thrust upon him. I suspect you are torn between your desires and your loyalties; so is he. Please forgive him, Helena."

And with that I supposed I had to be content.

6

THE FINAL DAY OF PURDAH

*M*ichael hated having to vary his routine, and the thought of traveling always made him anxious. He considered he had made an enormous concession to my whims in agreeing to stay at Scott House instead of his club, so the closer we drew to the date of my own departure, the more exacting he became.

"I will require to be met at Charing Cross at five twenty precisely on the afternoon of October the twenty-third. Brandrick has purchased the tickets and written out a memorandum for you." The fingers of Michael's right hand curled inward to scratch his palm, a sure sign of anxiety. "I intend to be present at the debate about Egypt. Some chaps have asked for help."

"Do you ever speak in the House of Lords?" I asked, curious.

"On occasion." Michael pushed aside the teapot to make room for his plate. "Only when I must. I don't hold with making speeches just for the sake of getting my name in Hansard. I'm going there to look out for certain deliberate mistakes, if you must know."

"Really?" I raised my eyebrows. I knew my brother had an astonishing memory for facts and figures. I also knew that he sometimes had his steward, the odious Brandrick, write to the printers of the Hansard parliamentary reports on his behalf to correct errors. Those errors were not in their reporting of the debates, but in the words uttered by the hapless aristocrats who had aroused Michael's wrath with their lax grasp of the truth. I was never sure how his complaints were treated, but I was sure the peers in question made fewer mistakes thereafter.

"Briggs will attend me at Scott House at six fifteen and will stay for dinner. He has to read the newspapers to me and tell me what's been happening." Briggs was Michael's London agent. "It's tiresome that I can only arrive the day before the debates, but I won't miss Quentin's birthday."

"Don't forget Helena's missing our son's birthday for your sake, Michael." Julia looked up at her husband as she put little Julius into my willing arms.

"Hmph." Michael merely glared at the fireplace.

"I think you mean 'thank you.'" Julia was occasionally given to a little glaring of her own. Michael glanced at her face, and his shoulders slumped.

"Thank you, Helena."

"You're welcome." I held my brother's baby son close to my face so I could breathe in his warm scent. "I suppose it's fortunate the House of Lords only meets occasionally. Just think of the havoc you could wreak in a Commons session, Michael."

"He does the country a great service by keeping the worst idiocies from being perpetrated." Julia settled comfortably into her armchair.

"I do my duty. I don't enjoy it." Michael pushed back his chair, rucking up the rug, and crossed to the open French windows, stepping out for a moment to watch his older children playing on Hyrst's large lawn. Their lively voices mingled with the admonitions of the nursemaids and Scotty's high-pitched barking, the scene so charmingly domestic that, not for the first time, I regretted my promise to spend a few weeks in London with Odelia.

"When are you meeting with Sir Geraint Dorrian-Knowles?" Julia asked.

I sighed. "Apparently, Odelia believes an informal meeting would be the best way to introduce me to Sir Geraint's work, so she's dragging me to a 'gathering' on the twenty-first. A sort of party, I think."

Michael, who had turned back into the room, scowled. "What party? You're in mourning. You can't possibly go to a party outside the family circle."

"In case you've forgotten, the twenty-first marks my year and a day." I felt a twinge of sadness that Justin should have been gone so long. "The final day of purdah, so to speak. Guttridge is even now working on making some small adaptations to my dresses to signify a second year of mourning for a husband, and naturally I'll have some new clothes made while I'm in Town. I'll still look like a crow, but I'll be over the worst. I don't see why one day should make a difference."

"You'll do as you please, I suppose. You women always do in the end. Just don't expect to give a party at Scott House while I'm there." And with this edict, Michael disappeared outdoors again.

"I'm glad you'll mark that last day with an outing rather than sit at home remembering." Julia's expression was thoughtful. "And that you won't be at Whitcombe. I'm sure your memories crowd around you there."

"They do somewhat." I hugged Julius a little closer. "In the oddest ways: when I turn a corner or walk past a door or open a drawer. And yet—do you know, Julia, the sense of Justin's presence is growing thinner every day. I don't hear his voice answering my thoughts very often now, and at the beginning that happened all the time. Some days I have difficulty summoning up an image of his face."

"Oh dear. But you have a cabinet photograph, don't you? I seem to remember you had them made for each other."

"Yes, when we were on our honeymoon in Paris." I smiled at the memory. "It's a wonderful likeness too. I had it framed and keep it by my bedside. But it's the living, moving memories that are wearing out somehow. They're becoming static, two-dimensional, like the photograph. It's unnerving. You're right—it's best that I spend that day surrounded by strangers."

"Without a veil." Julia smiled.

"It would be inappropriate for a party, wouldn't it? Besides, I never weep over Justin now. I can't somehow. I come near to it at times, but I think I'm afraid to sink too far into sadness. When Daniel died, I let the sadness swallow me up, and I don't want that to happen again."

The baby in my arms was beginning to stir. I smiled as he opened his eyes, and to my delight his mouth stretched in a wide, answering smile as he kicked his legs, wriggling his torso vigorously. Love and longing suffused me to an almost unbearable degree, and it was not grief for the past that made my eyes prickle and constricted my throat. I swallowed hard and disguised my emotion in a laugh that was shared by Julia.

"I can hardly bear to leave this little man when he's changing so fast." I hugged Julius to my shoulder, undaunted by the dribble of spit that trickled down my neck or the fact that the little boy now definitely needed changing. "You must write to me often, Julia. You know I'll begin disliking London as soon as the novelty of being there has worn off."

"I'll let you know all the news of the children," my friend assured me. "And you'll tell me all about Sir Geraint, won't you? I'm quite envious of you, meeting such a great artist.

Whoever would have thought O knew him well enough to broker a commission? She never tells us about her life in London, and I've always been curious."

"And I never have. She went to live there when I was nine, and I suppose I've always just accepted that she lives in a different world than mine. I'm not sure if letting the two worlds meet is a good idea."

"You can judge that when you meet Sir Geraint." Julia sighed, a little wistfully. "I wonder what he's like?"

THE CELEBRATED ARTIST TURNED OUT TO BE A TALL, WELL-favored man in his fifties, with dark hair streaked with just enough gray to enhance it and a thick, pointed beard. His eyes, an interesting shade of gray, met mine in a direct, penetrating stare, and between his brows was a short but deep line that gave him a studious look. He had the air of a man who had spent his life studying the human race but who had still not yet come to a verdict on it.

Odelia had arranged for us to arrive at Sir Geraint's home at three, well ahead of the other guests, so that Sir Geraint could show us both the building and the paintings that adorned it. The house was a large brick-built edifice of fairly recent construction, surmounted, Odelia had informed me, by a huge studio that occupied the entire upper story. According to my sister, it was the fashion for successful artists to build such "studio houses" in Holland Park, and belonging to the Holland Park Circle was a sure sign of greatness.

"This was the first large painting I ever sold." Sir Geraint raised his hand toward the vast canvas that hung over the dining room fireplace, its gold frame standing out sharply against the dark red of the wall. "*The Young Hera Welcoming the Dawn.* I sold it, as I said, and then purchased it back a few years later for ten times as much as I'd originally received for it."

He laughed. His teeth were strong and even, and he laughed and smiled often, as if he knew the expression suited him. His mellifluous voice, softened by the faintest trace of a Welsh accent, was a well-tuned instrument; he talked fluently and easily, dominating the conversation, as most men did.

"My pictures didn't sell so well in my first few years," he admitted. "We were terribly in debt. I could barely afford models, so Millie—my wife—sat for most of my early studies. I upset her by selling the painting, which is why I bought it back once I could afford it."

"Is that she? It's a striking picture." I gazed up at the composition, which showed a tall, slender woman standing with her arms outstretched and her head thrown back, wavy red hair cascading to her hips, eyes closed as if in ecstasy. Her white gown was lit to a rose color by the rays of the dawn rising above undulating green hills. Here and there the light penetrated the gauzy fabric, making it glow with an inner radiance. Columns suggested she was standing in or near some Greek temple. A dish of pomegranates was by her feet, the fruit torn open and spilling its jewel-like seeds over the dish. A peacock pecked at the bright seeds while a cuckoo sat atop the one intact fruit, its beak full of bright green caterpillars, as if it were about to go feed its young. But the cuckoo, I remembered, left its offspring to be reared by others . . .

"Yes, that's Millie." Sir Geraint's voice broke into my wandering thoughts. "I was fond of classical subjects in those days." He made a dismissive gesture with one long, powerful hand.

"You saw yourself as Zeus, no doubt," Odelia murmured.

She had not said much as Sir Geraint and I talked, walking three paces behind us and paying little attention to our surroundings.

"Prometheus." Sir Geraint twisted round to grin at my sister, but she did not answer his smile. Their allusions meant little to me, yet I liked the painting. It was chaste, but not entirely innocent; there was something about the look on the young woman's face and the flush on her cheekbones that subtly suggested she had just risen from her nuptial bed. The draperies did not entirely hide the outline of her form, as if the artist could not bear to conceal it entirely. He had painted her with love, I thought, and that made her even more beautiful.

We passed from the dining room into a long library with low bookcases, only waist-high, leaving ample room for the paintings that lined its rich blue walls. The large windows opposite gave onto the garden.

The paintings were all magnificent, but there was one that dominated all. I knew it must be *In the Halls of the Snow Queen*. I had never even seen an engraving of the celebrated picture, but I didn't hesitate in putting a name to it. Oddly, now that I saw the painting, I felt I knew it. The composition seemed familiar to me, like the memory of a long-forgotten dream. I stared, mesmerized.

A vast cavern of ice receded into the background in a jumble of glittering walls, held up by frozen columns on which multicolored lights cast their reflections. The floor of the great hall comprised shimmering particles of frost upon a lake of clear ice. The frost formed patterns that looked quite deliberate until one's mind tried to make sense of them, at which point they skittered away into randomness.

In the center of the picture sat two children. The boy's face and hands were as white as the ice, tinged with a delicate shade of blue. His eyes were also blue, with a slight cast to them, as if he were blind—or dead. Strawberry-blond hair curled around his face and fell upon his collar. He knelt on the ice, one hand resting on his hip while the other splayed long fingers, pitifully thin, against his thigh. He was suspended between life and death, staring straight out of the canvas into the eyes of the observer, the blank stare of one lost to the world. I shivered to see those eyes; I wanted to look away.

The girl embracing him, by contrast, was the picture of life itself. Her hair was red, like Hera's, unbound and falling down her back, although now the image was one of untouched beauty, maidenly innocence. Her arms were around the boy's neck, her pink lips near his face, as if she were about to touch his cheek with a sisterly kiss. One hand clutched a rose that was withering in the cold; a tiny trickle of blood stood out where a thorn from the rose had pricked the young girl's hand.

"It's odd," I said after a few moments. "It's extraordinarily like a picture from that book we had as children."

"I daresay every household with children has such a book." Odelia sounded bored. Of course, she must have seen the painting many times.

"I'm sure you're right." I turned to the artist. "It's quite spectacular. Did you paint the children from life?"

"Very much so." Sir Geraint smiled. "That's Edmund, my second-born son. He's his mother's favorite. The girl is Cassiope, my eldest daughter. I love the way I've captured her motherliness. She is a mother herself now. Phil, my eldest son, was far too sensible and strong-looking to put into this painting. Edmund was always delicate. We nearly lost him when he was two years old. My wife stayed at his bedside for three weeks at a stretch, feeding him tiny mouthfuls of bread and milk, as if he were a little bird. She saved him, I'm sure of it."

His pleasure in his children made me warm to him. "So you have three children?" I asked.

"Five. Phil, Edmund, Cass, Galahad, and Jane." Warmth shone from Sir Geraint's eyes. "My greatest creations. I'd have had fifteen of them—or even fifty, if I could. All creation is sacred in my eyes. If I have one regret in life, it's that I don't have more children."

"Shouldn't we go to the studio before there's a crowd?" O said abruptly. "People are already starting to arrive."

Sure enough, we could hear carriages outside. Sir Geraint led us back through the spacious entrance hall, richly patterned with blue-and-white tiles and adorned with stuffed peacocks, to the staircase.

"Sir Geraint's most recent work is in his studio," Odelia explained as we made our way toward the voices. "We need to see it before it gets too crowded. There will be so many people once the quartet starts playing."

"Music? How nice." I glanced up at Sir Geraint, who had offered me his arm. "Not all for my benefit, I hope? I don't like to think you've put yourself to any extra trouble."

"We always have music." Sir Geraint's Welsh tones were more obvious when he spoke lightly. "Phil, Edmund, and Galahad play, and we've hired a violin. It used to be Cass, but she's married now. Here's my one child who doesn't play."

He waved a hand over a very young woman who was descending the stairs at rather a hoydenish pace. Her red hair —the same shade as the woman in the Hera painting—was caught back loosely, her dress an approximation of medieval costume. "This is Jane, my youngest. Say hello to Lady Helena Whitcombe, Janie."

"Hello." The girl flushed and ducked her head at me in greeting, then darted across the hallway and disappeared behind a door.

Voices raised in shouts and laughter outside the front

door revealed that more guests were arriving. Sir Geraint quickly led us upward, past a sort of gallery on the second floor, to the vast studio at the top of the house.

"This is recent work. Most of these are already sold, recently exhibited, or about to be exhibited." He indicated the canvases hanging on the walls or displayed on easels. "I wish I had more time to explain them to you—although, of course, they should not need explaining. Art should be beautiful above all, and the beholder will either find a thing beautiful or not. They cannot, and should not, be persuaded into seeing beauty."

"They're splendid." And they were. Perhaps they lacked a little of the fire and passion of the earlier paintings I'd seen downstairs, but to my untrained eye, they were simply marvelous. And extremely large. I was getting an idea of the scale of the work that was being proposed for Whitcombe.

"Are there no unfinished paintings?" I asked, suddenly struck by their absence.

Sir Geraint grinned like a boy. "I'm sensitive about too many people seeing my unfinished work. Besides, we'd never get all our guests in here if I were to clutter up the space with all my canvases. I can never abandon a piece once I've started it, but I will put it away for a few weeks or months or years until I can see my way clear to continuing. I rent my neighbor's stables for my messes and use this studio mostly for entertaining or for working with models. The poor dears complain so when they're made to sit in a cold barn. Fortunately, I am not a portraitist, so most of my work with models is in the way of preliminary sketches or studies."

We had been talking against the background of a quartet of musicians tuning their instruments on a dais at one end of the studio. Now they burst into the joyous strains of a Mozart quartet, and I turned to look at them.

"Are they your—?" I turned back to Sir Geraint, but he

had been captured by two gentlemen, one tall and cadaverous and the other rotund and bearded, who appeared to be arguing jovially with one another and wanted Sir Geraint to judge which one of them had the right of it. People were pouring into the large room, almost shouting at one another in their eagerness to communicate.

A massive samovar on a table at one side of the room was clearly the origin of the cups of tea a group of young women were handing out to the arriving visitors. One was thrust into my hand as a shiny-faced young maiden asked me how many pieces of sugar I would like, dispensing the required amount straight into the cup with a practiced hand. By the time I had recovered from this unexpected hospitality, Odelia had vanished into the crowd and I was left alone.

7

THE LADY OF THE HOUSE

efore long, the studio filled with chattering people, all of whom seemed to know each other. Nobody paid any attention to me.

I made my way as best I could toward the dais where the musicians sat. The sound of the instruments would be loud at such close quarters, but no louder than the noise the people were making. From there, I reasoned, I could get the best view of the huge paintings and try to imagine such work on the walls of my drawing room.

The musicians were playing very well. Once I was closer to them, I found I could hear the intricacies of the music better and thus enjoy it more. Had Sir Geraint not said that his three sons would play? Since one of the quartet was a woman—the better of the two violinists, in my opinion—the other musicians must be the sons. A tall, dark-haired man played the other violin, frowning at his music with an anxious air and plying his bow with earnest precision. The small line between his eyebrows was like his father's. His beard was considerably less full, his lips less finely drawn, but the resemblance was plain.

A very thin man with red-blond hair was so clearly the adult version of the child in the Snow Queen painting that I knew immediately he was Edmund. He played the viola with effortless grace, his long, thin fingers dancing and sliding on the strings, a small smile on his lips. The third man weighed as much as his two slender brothers put together; he had an intelligent, handsome face and the brightest red hair I had ever seen, a wild riot of small curls waving around his perspiring brow.

By now, it was sweltering in the large room, and all four players' faces shone with perspiration. It was a pity only a handful of people appeared to be paying them any attention, but they seemed quite accustomed to being ignored and were entirely absorbed in the intricacies of the music.

I lost myself in the beautiful sounds, thirstily drinking the tea replenished at regular intervals by the friendly young ladies and occasionally accepting a sandwich or tiny cake from the servants passing through the crowd. Nobody sat down to eat. The guests waved their food at each other as they spoke and only occasionally remembered to take a bite.

From my vantage point, I could see Odelia, surrounded by some younger women and several oddly dressed men. Apart from Odelia, all the women wore some version of artistic dress of the kind O often wore at home. On this occasion, Odelia was more fashionably dressed, in the rich, deep colors that suited her so well. She looked like a queen holding court.

I lost sight of my sister as the musicians, after forty minutes of hard playing, entered upon the final flourishes of the composition. I put my cup and saucer down so I could applaud. A few other guests clapped, but the rest paid the musicians no heed whatsoever.

"Did Sir Geraint desert you too?" Odelia had somehow found me in the crowd. She smiled at me in a friendly fashion, her slight moodiness of the earlier afternoon quite vanished. "I suppose he's being shouted at by Burne-Jones and Morris. Did you enjoy the music?"

"Yes, but isn't it hot?"

"Always is at these affairs. It'll be quieter downstairs, if you want to escape. Nobody will mind if you wander around down there."

"Listen, O—is Lady Dorrian-Knowles still living? I'm quite perplexed. I realized nobody ever introduced me to her. Is Sir Geraint a widower?"

"Heavens, no." Odelia took a long sip of her tea, her eyes sparkling over the rim of her cup. "Millie will be downstairs somewhere, supervising the help," she said when she had refreshed herself. "They always get extra servants in for these events, and those London agency servants need constant chivvying. That's Millie's job."

"Goodness. Doesn't anybody introduce her to her guests? She *is* the lady of the house after all."

"I suppose so, but what does she have to do with a crowd of artists? She knows half of them anyway, and I shouldn't think she cares about the other half. She certainly doesn't like most of Sir Geraint's models." O sniggered.

"It all seems rather rude and offhand to me." I frowned at the milling, shouting people.

"It's the way we are. Nobody makes introductions at a crush like this. I suppose you haven't met anyone because you're waiting to be introduced. I should have told you. You just talk to people, and if you start liking each other, you might stick out a hand and introduce yourself after a while. The exchange of ideas is far more important than the social niceties."

I refrained from pointing out that the social niceties were of importance to a guest who was on her own and who knew almost nobody. Perhaps artistic people were simply so lacking in reserve that they could just walk into a crowd and talk to strangers without shyness. I did not lack confidence myself—it had been bred into me—but I had gradually begun to feel a little strange in the large room, particularly as I was the only woman dressed in black.

"Well, I don't have a single idea to exchange," I said rather sulkily. "And besides—" I leaned forward to hiss into Odelia's ear. "I'd be grateful if you'd show me where the WC is. I think I've drunk enough tea."

QUITE A FEW LADIES HAD THE SAME IDEA AS I DID, SO IT WAS nearly half an hour before I was finally free to return to the "crush." Odelia had waited with me for about ten minutes, then vanished to talk to a lady whose piercing American accent had been echoing through the tiled entrance hall in a never-ending monologue.

I had no wish to return to the studio. The downstairs rooms were far less heavily occupied, the people in them gathered into small groups. Some were sitting on the broad windowsills of the library, which looked like my best chance of getting a seat. I would be well placed to contemplate either the garden, which was empty and serene in the fading light, or the paintings on the walls.

I took my perch, feeling rather self-conscious. The group of people near me was discussing the merits of pictorial invention versus the "truth of nature," a phrase that seemed to mean whatever they wanted it to.

A few minutes of listening to the impassioned arguments on both sides made up my mind. I would abandon the idea of rest and ease and seek to make the acquaintance of my hostess. It was quite unheard of, in my experience, to attend a gathering without even seeing, let alone being introduced to, the lady of the house. I'd said as much to Odelia when we were going downstairs, hinting that she should be the one to make the introduction, but "Millie doesn't like me" had been her only response.

I drifted through the various rooms, my eyes on the paintings as if I were interested primarily in them, trying to spot a woman who looked as if she inhabited the house. She would be red-haired, that I knew from the Hera painting. Or would she have gone gray? Was she, for example, the invalid lady in the bath chair who was berating a red-faced young man over his inability to remember the names of the Greek philosophers? Probably not.

My perambulations took me back to the hall, and I moved toward the front door. Could Lady Dorrian-Knowles be there perhaps, welcoming or bidding good-bye to the guests?

My hopes rose when I saw an interesting-looking woman holding forth to a small circle of female friends since her crowning glory was a mass of red hair held back by a hairnet of medieval aspect. She looked like an older and comelier version of young Jane Dorrian-Knowles and definitely resembled the woman in the Hera painting.

She was tall and somewhat stout, her heaviness not the fat of idleness or self-indulgence, but the figure of a healthy woman who had allowed nature, child-bearing, and the years to shape her body. She wore a loose gown of the artistic type, made startlingly beautiful by its embroidery of autumn-hued flowers on a background of deep ivory. Her face was strong, with high cheekbones and large, intelligent eyes. Her arms crossed over her considerable bosom, she was talking to her friends in a rapid stream of words.

". . . I'm late with the screen I promised Cass, of course. When do I ever find the time to do my own work? You'd think the children would be more help as they get older, but they seem to require more of my time every day. I spent all Wednesday on omnibuses and only had twenty minutes to look at silks. Sometimes I just want to scream out at the injustice of it all . . . Are you looking for someone?"

She had seen me hovering. The other ladies, who had their backs to me, turned to see who the newcomer was. Two moved aside to bring me into their circle, their expressions welcoming. I smiled my thanks at them and stepped forward.

"I'm looking for Lady Dorrian-Knowles. Are you she, or do you know her? I've been here since three o'clock, and I haven't met her. I wanted to thank her for her hospitality."

"Since three? Why?" The woman frowned. "*I'm* Millicent Dorrian-Knowles, and you're very welcome to such as I can give you, but I can't imagine why you were here so early. I've been down in the servants' hall."

She held out a large, well-formed hand. I shook it, relieved to have found my hostess at last.

"I'm Lady Helena Whitcombe. Sir Geraint invited me to come early. We're talking about a commission for my house in the country, and he wanted me to see his work in peace. I'm invited for dinner too, I'm afraid. I hope you were given some notice of *that*."

"Oh, dinner is always thirty or forty people once the Season's over, and I never know exactly who's coming. Once it gets too cold outside, I can put my foot down and insist on just a dozen people, but even in England we don't freeze to death in October." Her expressive mouth twitched into a smile. "I suppose Geraint will want you inside instead of in the loggia if he's trying to persuade you to give him a commission. Or are you trying to persuade *him*?"

I laughed. "I don't know how any of this works. I'm a complete novice in the world of art—never commissioned so much as a fire screen in my life."

"Then how did you—? Oh well, never mind. I won't interrogate you. Somehow you have met my husband, and somehow you have the idea in your head that he might paint something for you. For that reason alone, you are most welcome in my house."

She then introduced me to the other ladies, who all seemed friendly. From their dress, I assumed they were of an artistic inclination. Indeed, before entering this house I had never seen so many browns, dull greens, and ochre yellows, so many trims and furbelows of medieval style on the ladies, so many loosely tied silk bows gracing the necks of men. My black silk must have made me look like a very small jackdaw amid these colorful birds.

"Please accept my sincerest condolences for your loss." Lady Dorrian-Knowles had clearly noticed my mourning attire. "Not a child, I hope."

"My husband. We had no children." I hesitated, but something made me continue. "I entered second mourning today, in fact. Perhaps I'm a little hasty in returning to society, but I'm of an active disposition, and anyway, my first mourning was full of incident. I don't think I'm destined for seclusion."

"You don't have to apologize to *me*." Lady Dorrian-Knowles smiled wryly. "You may have noticed that many of the rules just don't seem to apply where artists are concerned. They live in a world of their own making, a dream of beauty and illusion. Fairy tales, in particular, are the purest and most visionary feats of the imagination, with no intrusive morality and no crudeness. Or so my husband says. Is it a fairy-tale picture you're seeking, Lady Helena? I thought Geraint had exhausted all the better ones, except—" She stopped suddenly.

"*The Nightingale*," I supplied, puzzled at the dawning look in my interlocutor's eyes. Was it a sudden spring of hope? Of desperation? Or a little of both?

"My heavens," said one of the other ladies quietly.

"That would be a considerable commission." Lady Dorrian-Knowles's voice had a slight tremor.

"So I'm given to understand. I haven't made up my mind about it yet, but my drawing room is beautifully situated with a view of the sea and in great need of refurbishment. It's an intriguing idea."

A slight wariness now stole over the lady's face. "Where is your house?"

"In Sussex. I live just outside Littleberry."

Nobody spoke, but I felt the atmosphere around me change. All the ladies were looking at Lady Dorrian-Knowles.

"Well," she said after a few moments' silence. "I suppose it's an ill wind that blows nobody any good. Are you a friend of Lady Odelia's?"

"She's my sister."

"Ah." She smiled suddenly, revealing white teeth. The odd impression I'd been getting from her dissipated, and I could see the younger woman of the Hera portrait, animated by happiness. "She might have told you we're not exactly the best of friends, but she's a great admirer of my husband's work. Chief among the 'Worshippers,' as we call them. Geraint has many admirers."

"As befits a great artistic talent," I said politely.

"Of course." She put her head on one side, regarding me. "You don't look a bit like her. Are you half sisters? You look rather younger. Although I'll say this for Odelia, she's kept her looks."

"We're full sisters. I'm the youngest daughter, ten years younger than Odelia. It was she who suggested the commission to me, of course."

"Of course. How thoughtful of her." She stretched out her hand in an inviting gesture. "I do hope you'll sit next to me at dinner, Lady Helena. And call me Millie, won't you? Everybody does. I can't bear the dreadful bucketful of syllables I've ended up with. I was plain Millie Knowles when we married. Geraint hyphenated his middle name to his surname for better effect, and it cost us two hundred pounds for the petition to the College of Arms. And I don't care much for the baronetcy, except for Phil's sake—that's my eldest son. Even Geraint might not have accepted the title if he didn't have a son to hand it down to."

"Every family has to start somewhere." I smiled, charmed by her frankness. "Your sons are fine musicians. I look forward to meeting them properly."

It was eleven at night by the time Odelia and I climbed into the carriage, and I was quite exhausted.

"How long have you known the Dorrian-Knowleses?" I asked.

"Oh, years." I felt my sister relax into the cushioned seat. I hadn't spoken to her at dinner since I was near the head of the table and Odelia was several places away. She had been animated—brilliant, even; I could see that by her expressions and movements and by the laughter and the quick flow of conversation around her.

I wished she'd been closer. I'd been subjected to Sir Geraint's considerable charm for much of the evening. Millie had let her husband do most of the talking, only intervening when she could see I was quite overwhelmed. The entire atmosphere of the dinner was overheated, intellectually speaking. The conversation was universally emphatic, the subjects very often over my head. Art, music, myths and legends, architecture, poetry, novels, the theater—I sometimes felt like a child among adults, tired and longing to be taken up to the nursery.

I had thought I knew something about novels at least, but these people were definitely what Blanche would call "advanced." The half-dozen people close enough to speak with me had thoroughly explored my ignorance. My brain had been shaken out, examined, found to be wanting, and all its pieces jumbled back into my head in a cascade of recommendations to improve my reading, travel more, or visit this or that gallery. The discovery that I could speak, read, and write French led to a lively discussion of the works of Monsieur Émile Zola and a detailed summary of his latest novel, which sounded so shocking I didn't think they would ever publish it in England.

"Your friends appear to know many important people," I told Odelia. "If I understood correctly, that man opposite me —the one they all called 'Rookie'—works for Mr. Ruskin *and* Mr. Morris *and* Mr. Burne-Jones and goodness knows who else. And sometimes for Sir Geraint, is that right? I didn't realize artists had assistants."

"The better ones do, the ones in so much demand that they can afford assistants and have enough work going at one time to keep them busy." Odelia yawned behind her gloved hand. "Were you terribly bored?"

"It was hard going at times," I confessed. "But whenever I began to think I was completely lost, Sir Geraint or Millie would rescue me. And Mr. Rooke told me all about his baby son."

"Ah, she has you call her Millie. She looked quite taken with you, despite whose sister you are."

"Why doesn't she like you?" I asked.

Odelia shrugged. "Because I'm a practitioner of the fine arts, I suppose. She's rather left out, artistically speaking. She's good at what she does—embroidery, weaving, and so on—but the applied arts just don't have the same cachet. Especially in Sir Geraint's inner circle, where 'art for art's sake' is the battle cry. And I'm younger than she is, and—well." Odelia patently refrained from pointing out that Millie had not kept her looks in the sense that people usually judge such things.

"I think she's rather splendid," I confessed. "She was trying to draw me out. I've been a hostess for long enough to know when someone's working hard to allow a guest to shine. She behaved as if I were a catch she'd made herself rather than a guest of her husband's about whom she'd known nothing before I introduced myself to her."

"I'm glad you like her." Odelia yawned again. "I imagine that's the last of the big dinners for the year. It'll just be a dozen guests inside from now on."

"I should think the neighbors will be grateful for less noise." Through the dining room's windows—just a little ajar, as the night air had been fairly cool—we had heard the diners under the loggia, far livelier than even the chattering guests inside. There had been shouting and singing, and at some point somebody had played an Irish jig on a fiddle. I had heard what sounded like chairs being knocked over.

"I think most of the neighbors were there. Sir Geraint likes to entertain expansively. He *is* a baronet after all, and he owes it to Phil and the other boys to live like a proper aristocrat. That's how they'll meet the right people and get on in life."

She curled her long fingers around mine. The motion of the carriage was jostling us together, a pleasantly intimate familiarity after a long day surrounded by strangers. "I hope you don't mind that I wasn't by your side much, Baby. I get terribly distracted when there are so many people I want to talk to."

"Don't call me Baby," I said lazily. The voices of the guests, which had been reverberating in my head, were softening a little in the darkness of the carriage. "I didn't mind all that much—and once I found Millie, I felt better taken care of. If only you hadn't put me off bringing Guttridge. I think she'd have enjoyed the guests, even if she only saw them from afar."

"Nobody brings a lady's maid to an evening like this. Most of those people don't *have* a lady's maid. Millie doesn't."

"There weren't many servants, were there?" I asked. "I never seemed to be able to find anybody."

"Not everyone wants a staff of thirty, Helena," Odelia said drily. "So," she hesitated for a moment, "what did you think of Sir Geraint? And his paintings?"

"He's charming, and his paintings are beautiful. I'm amazed he can come up with such fine compositions on such a large scale. And the light on the faces of the figures is unearthly. I did find myself wondering something, though. Where was the Snow Queen?"

"What?" O sat up a little straighter.

"The picture of Kai and Gerda was so beautiful. I just think there should have been a picture of the Snow Queen as well. They'd have looked good as a pair."

"What a funny little thing you are. And what an imagination for someone raised as a country lady with nothing to think of but the pheasant shoot and Justin's sheep. But there was a time when you always had your head in a picture book, telling yourself stories about the people in them. The whole point of the Snow Queen is that she's unseen." O shifted in her seat. "She's a hidden threat, larger in the imagination than she could be in any other way."

"Oh." I felt disappointed. "I'd have liked a Snow Queen."

"The point is, do you think you'd give Sir Geraint his commission? It really is most important to him. Artistically, I mean." Odelia's fingers tightened around mine.

"I couldn't possibly decide yet," I said defensively.

"You wouldn't regret it, Helena darling." O's voice was cool, almost ironic. "It's about time you brought a little enchantment into your prosaic life in the country."

"Enchantment." I smiled sleepily. "Do you know, I quite like the sound of that."

8

CHIAROSCURO

*B*efore retiring, I wrote a note to Sir Geraint, thanking him and Millie for their hospitality. Tired as I was, I had been taught that duty came before rest. I gave the letter to Guttridge, who would ensure that it went off by the early morning post.

I slept late and had my breakfast in bed. I didn't imagine Odelia would be up, although one never knew with her. She might be awake at dawn to catch the first light for painting or lazily dreaming the morning away, but she almost never ate breakfast with me.

"I may as well make the most of it," I told Guttridge when she came up to draw my bath and take away my breakfast tray. "I'd love some more coffee while the bath is filling, if you would. Oh, is that my post?"

"Yes, my lady." Guttridge handed me a silver salver bearing a small stack of around half-a-dozen envelopes. She, of course, looked as fresh and alert as if she hadn't sat up half the night waiting for me to arrive home. "I took the liberty of informing the dressmaker that you would be in London, and

I imagine the one on top is her reply. I could answer it if you wish."

"Mmm. I may wish." I shuffled the small envelopes between my fingers. One from Gerry, one from Blanche, one from Julia—I looked forward to seeing how the children were. One from old Lady Holland; how nice. She must have read in the society columns that I'd arrived in Town. And one addressed in an emphatically masculine hand. I opened that one first.

"It's from Sir Geraint." I read on. "Oh—he's going to call on me at two o'clock. Tomorrow." I frowned. "And with Lord Broadmere expecting to be met at the station at twenty minutes past five. Precisely." I sighed. "Oh well, it won't take long to get to Charing Cross, and I daresay Sir Geraint won't stay for long. Guttridge, cancel the coffee—let's get me bathed and dressed as quickly as possible, or I'll have no time to myself today."

"Did you really do these that night?" I gazed at the sketches Sir Geraint had laid out on a heavily carved oak sideboard. "Weren't you dreadfully tired? I didn't think your party had nearly finished when we left."

"It hadn't." Sir Geraint laughed. "I deserted my guests at one in the morning and locked myself in my study."

"Didn't they mind?"

"I don't imagine so. I felt I knew you so much better by the end of the evening, you see, and was in the grip of inspiration. They're just rough sketches to give you an idea of how the story will look. We start and end at the sea, of course, reading from left to right."

"I wish Odelia had stayed to see this," I murmured. "After

all, she made the introduction. I'd have thought she'd want to stay instead of visiting her frame-maker."

"She'll see them eventually." Sir Geraint smiled at me, and I felt my lips curve in response. Mama had told me once that she had a weakness for "handsome devils," and I suspected I'd inherited it.

The fusty hush of Scott House's front parlor, with its wealth of carvings and barley-twist furniture, its dark paneling, and lead-paned windows displaying the family crest of the Escottes, felt like an oddly intimate space when dominated by Sir Geraint's male presence. I reached out and straightened one of the large pieces of thick paper he had taken out of his portfolio, studying the sketches carefully. Scotty, who had barked furiously at the great artist upon his arrival, lifted his head in curiosity before sinking back into sleep.

"There will be side panels flanking each of the large pictures, you see, Lady Helena." Sir Geraint leaned in to point to the left-hand paper, and I caught his scent, spiced with cologne and tobacco. "We begin simply with the sea, a little storm-tossed—I'm not sure about that one as yet, but I know it has to be there. Then the first large painting—the emperor's garden, which ends in low bluffs overlooking the shore. It starts off wild, with majestic trees overhanging the cliff's edge and a tangle of briar roses, a little forbidding. In those trees sits the nightingale."

"And then the ornamental garden, with the flowers all tied with silver bells so they would make music in the slightest breeze." I smiled at the memory. "Odelia used to read me this story, and I always loved the idea of such flowers. I'd have tied bells onto ours if I could have found some small enough."

Sir Geraint smiled. "Lady Odelia told me you were an imaginative child." He swept a hand over the paper, not touching the charcoal markings. "And then, here in the *arrière-plan* is the little kitchen maid showing the courtiers where the nightingale is. I'll have to study the clothing of Chinese servants."

"Where would you find those?" I asked, my curiosity aroused.

"Limehouse, probably." He shrugged. "Down by the docks, certainly. The courtiers' dress will be easier. I have books about such things. And then a panel with the nightingale, his beak wide open in song, surrounded by briar roses. Their beaks are a wonderful yellow inside, just the color of the stamens on the flowers. Then the courtiers, probably. There is a door here, is there not?" He pointed to one particular spot. "Then, facing the sea, the emperor's throne room."

I hovered a finger over the middle composition, not wishing to smudge the charcoal. There was little detail in the sketches, which were mere suggestions to give an idea of the composition in Sir Geraint's mind, but I could see that the emperor's magnificent throne would dominate the scene.

"And here behind the door is the kitchen maid, now richly dressed." Sir Geraint smiled fondly at the vaguely executed figure, as if he already saw the girl in his mind and loved her. "The nightingale is here again, singing so sweetly that the emperor weeps—but can you see the great and magnificent cage that is prepared for it? It won't have its freedom for much longer."

"And are these the Chinese ladies taking water into their mouths and gurgling to imitate the bird?" I pointed to the next panel. "There was a picture of them in the book we had as children, and I always thought they were so graceful and languid."

"Exactly." The charming smile gleamed through Sir Geraint's thick beard again. It was even more vigorous than Ned's but trimmed far more neatly, coming to a sharp point some two inches below his chin. "In these court scenes, there will be a chance to show much beautiful and subtle color. And then the artificial nightingale in all its bejeweled splendor against some kind of dark background. I can never resist combining chiaroscuro with bright colors. I love both, you see, and cannot choose between them. Then the real nightingale escaping through the window. And then, on the side where the fireplace lies—"

"It's almost as if you'd seen the room already," I murmured, looking at the third sheet. "How remarkable."

"Lady Odelia described it to me. I have an excellent memory for such things. I'm thinking of incorporating the fireplace itself into this painting, as a kind of glow of coals underlying Death's garden. Here the warmth makes the flowers more exotic. They will suggest stillness and peace, with a mist hanging over them. I can't render that well in a sketch, of course."

"The mist is Death." I nodded.

"But there will be figures. I can't do without figures in such a large picture. Classical figures, not Chinese, because Death's country is not China. Fair maidens by a shore, I rather think. I could model one of them on you if you wish."

I blinked, taken aback. "I'm not at all sure about that."

Sir Geraint laughed. "In the background, if you're shy about it. There's a painting of James Archer's where a woman is speaking with a hooded sage on the shore, and I've always wanted to improve on that little detail. Perhaps you could be the woman. No? Well, I hope you can let me persuade you." The easy laugh again. "In the very last flanking panel, we see the kitchen maid again, now a prosperous and happy woman surrounded by her children, at play at the edge of the sea. The triumph of life over death."

"I'd like a picture of children playing."

"We'll have one or two little ones splashing at the edge of

the water. And there is your story, Lady Helena. I'll admit some parts of it have been a little vague in my mind, although I've always been absolutely clear on the weeping emperor and the kitchen maid behind the door. And your languid ladies with their pretty fans and tiny cups of water. Last night I saw the whole thing clearly and felt I had to show you. In the next few weeks, I hope to work up some more detailed sketches of the parts of the composition that are clearest in my mind."

I felt alarmed. "But I haven't agreed to the commission yet. Shouldn't you wait before wasting all that hard work in case I decide against it?"

"Not at all. I'll be doing it for my own pleasure as much as anything else." Handing me politely to one of the wing-backed armchairs, Sir Geraint took possession of the other, leaning back as if entirely at his ease. "I can't expect you to agree to such an important commission without a better idea of how the finished work will look. There'll be an esti-mate of the final cost for you and your man of business to look over, splitting it out over the time I think the whole thing will take. The frames will have to be specially built, but I have an excellent man for that, and my figures will be inclusive of the entire decoration and arrangement of the room." He leaned forward, his gaze sharpening. "I believe you are interested enough for me to proceed with my proposals."

"I am." Indeed, I felt a kind of giddy excitement at the idea of such a daringly extensive work of art in my house. Whit-combe House had its finer points—the green drawing room and the Great Hall were particularly nice, and both libraries were eminently suited to the standards of comfort and grandeur expected of a wealthy family—but I was beginning to grasp the idea of a splendid drawing room as Whitcombe's finest jewel. Perhaps one day I would have a child to whom the estate could be handed down, and it would be wonderful to give that child an improved and beautified house to live in.

Sir Geraint cleared his throat. "Did Lady Odelia mention I could reduce my fee a little in return for the right to exhibit the paintings—for one or two months—if suitable gallery space can be found in London, and in particular for the right to have engravings made from the paintings? The former would bring me some new commissions, and the latter would provide a small income. Such things are commonly done, and we artists particularly appreciate the income. We are accustomed to feast or famine." He laughed. "I'm not the only one to have several large pictures in the works that might take another five years or so before they produce any money."

"She hadn't mentioned it, no."

Sir Geraint adjusted his cufflinks, an action that drew attention to the fine shape of his hands and the length of his fingers. "I shall explain everything to you quite carefully. I'm afraid you'll have to put up with my presence while you're in London, as I have a great deal to tell you." He fished into his waistcoat pocket, pulling out a fine watch and pressing the button to open the cover. "But now I should leave you. Did you not say that Lord Broadmere is expected this after-noon?" He got to his feet and began gathering the papers to return them to his portfolio.

I hadn't thought I'd told him about Michael's arrival, but of course we had spoken at length in Holland Park, and I might have mentioned it. I rose and went to the fireplace, tugging carefully at the frayed silk bellpull. When I turned, I saw that Sir Geraint had opened the door to the hallway and smiled at him as he allowed Scotty to precede him into the outer space.

"You did well to work that out. It always latches too securely, and most of our guests can't guess the trick of it.

And we can't keep the blessed door open, no matter what we try. The servants say there's a phantom that closes it, but I believe the door's just too heavy."

Sir Geraint's dark eyebrows tilted upward. "I'm good with my hands. Will you allow me to importune you again soon?"

"As long as it's not when my brother's here. Any time from Friday onward should do." I held out my hand, and Sir Geraint kissed it briefly, then turned his grip into a more modern shake.

"I will look forward to the next time I see you."

Sir Geraint's winning manners were thrown into greater relief by Michael's lack of them. Not that he lacked manners; my brother knew how to behave when his mind was on the social occasion in question. It was simply that when he had a thought in his head, he had no room for the minor details that were important in society. Now he was putting my nerves on edge by fidgeting, spilling sherry on the furniture, and always talking too loudly. Still, after more than two decades of Michael, I had learned that the best way was to ignore his faults, try to soothe his tempers, and above all, be precise in my speech. Vagueness upset him.

"I should have come yesterday." Michael glared as if the date and time of his arrival were my fault. "Now I wish to speak to people, and I've barely got any time before the House sits tomorrow. I'll have to breakfast at six—can you arrange it? I don't suppose Odelia would give a thought to my comforts. And eat with me, won't you?" He gazed at the window, where the light outside was fading; the footman would soon come to draw the curtains. "I miss Julia. And Brandrick. One of them always eats breakfast with me."

"You could invite Briggs to breakfast," I suggested. Briggs

was an excellent agent with, as he put it himself, a finger on the pulse of political life. Papa had found him when he had first taken Michael up to Town, at seventeen, to get used to his future role.

It was entirely unnecessary for Michael to do anything more in the House of Lords than turn up and vote for the Tory interest, as he invariably did. His seat was his by birthright. And yet as much as he hated London, Michael was punctilious about attendance and seemed to have an excellent grasp of politics, even though he depended on Briggs to read documents and newspapers to him and write any letters that were needed.

"I don't eat breakfast with Briggs." Michael looked positively offended at the idea.

"Then of course I'll keep you company," I said soothingly. "If you make an early start, you could catch up with some of your business. Naturally, you had to stay at home for Quentin's fourth birthday. Did he like the rocking horse I had made for him?"

"Yes." It was unusual for Michael to elaborate on an answer, so it surprised me when he said: "Julia says he sits it like a born rider." I was treated to the rare sight of Michael's beautiful blue eyes looking directly at me. "It was kind of you."

"I knew he'd like his own horse." I smiled, thinking of the little boy's delight in any vigorous activity. "He was so envious of James starting riding lessons."

"I'd have had Quentin take lessons too—he's much better at sport than James—but Julia said James should have the distinction of going first." Something that was almost a smile flitted across Michael's countenance. "She was right, of course."

Michael had only mastered riding at sixteen himself, under Brandrick's patient tutelage. He had insisted that his eldest son, James, a sensitive little boy, not start until he was at least five. Our father had put us all on a pony at three and let us hang on as best we could. I had loved it and was already a proficient rider at four and a half, when it had been Michael's turn. Michael had screamed and made his mount panic; my pony had bucked, but I had hung on. From then on, Michael's screams of fear and rage had been a regular occurrence in the paddock until Papa had given up in disgust.

"James will make a splendid rider. You were right to have Brandrick teach him." I didn't like Michael's steward, but I had to admit, he was patient with my nephew. The memory of the terrified little boy my brother had been made me want to pat his arm, but I knew he would flinch away, so I merely sipped my sherry.

"What's this about Odelia persuading you to give one of her friends a job?" Michael asked so suddenly I almost jumped. "Who is the fellow? Some scruffy little man who smells like a goat and dresses like a farm laborer, no doubt." Michael looked glum. "You women and your constant changing of things. I *like* the drawing room at Whitcombe."

"Hasn't Julia told you? She and I were talking about the commission when I was last at Hyrst." I saw the conscious look on my brother's face and laughed. "Ah, you kept interrupting, and she never got the chance. It's Sir Geraint Dorrian-Knowles, who wouldn't look out of place at court."

"*Him?*" asked Michael ungrammatically. "Well, I suppose at least he's a proper painter and quite like a gentleman. Very clean."

"You've met him?" I asked, surprised.

"Run into him a couple of times, lounging around this house in shirtsleeves as if he owned the place."

That put a new light on things, and I opened my mouth to find out more. But Michael forestalled me.

"I say, isn't he going to be fearsomely expensive?"

"None of your business." I gave my little brother what I hoped was a severe look. Naturally, that sent him onto the attack.

"And where *is* Odelia?" He looked around the room as if he expected her to be hiding in a corner. "I want my dinner. Honestly, Helena, you could have made sure she's punctual."

As if I had a hope of controlling Odelia's behavior. "She'll be down as soon as she's bathed and dressed. She had a busy time of it at the frame-maker's." I kept my tone calm and even. "And there are still fifteen minutes to go before they ring the dinner bell. Now, about when you met Sir Geraint here—"

But Michael, hungry and irritable, was clearly working himself into one of the small tantrums with which he generally ended a long day of traveling. "And what do you *mean*, it's none of my business if you throw away your money? I'm the head of this family . . ."

He was still raging when Odelia arrived, and I had no chance of questioning him about what he had seen.

9

LOST AND FOUND

Unsurprisingly, my chief preoccupation over the next three days was Michael. Odelia drifted in and out of our lives occasionally, but I barely exchanged two words with her alone, as Michael's presence made conversation difficult. On Thursday morning, she was not down for breakfast.

"Typical of Odelia to not even bother to say good-bye." Michael fussed with his watch chain. "I expect she's lying in bed doing nothing. These women who won't marry are absolute parasites, Helena. And I have three of them on my hands."

"Oh really, Michael," I said briskly. "Is O's allowance such a burden? She seems to pay for quite a lot out of the money she makes from her paintings."

"And that's no occupation for a lady either."

"Many ladies paint. And as for Alice's and Annette's allowances, you can hardly claim they're anything but an asset to you. You're far better looked after than most men in your position." Our twin sisters, unlikely candidates for marriage, ran Hyrst with an efficiency that matched that of the best housekeeper. No money was ever wasted, no detail overlooked.

"Well, yes. I suppose." Michael pulled out his watch for the tenth time and opened the cover. "But Odelia—"

"We have plenty of time to get to the train, so stop looking at your watch every two minutes." I sighed. I was glad I didn't have to deal with Odelia as well as Michael. Her patience always gave out before mine did, and Michael never liked it if people were sarcastic to him, so I would have to expend time and energy on peacemaking.

"I've ordered the carriage for half-past ten, and it will be outside at exactly half-past ten," I continued. "It will get us to the station a full forty-five minutes ahead of time." And then the real ordeal would begin. Michael would become anxious and fret about the train being late, and the more anxious he got, the more difficult he was.

"Hmph." Michael stowed his watch in his waistcoat pocket, from where it would doubtless soon make a reappearance. "All Odelia ever does is what she likes, and if a fellow is paying, he should at least have some say in his sister's life. I want her to find a husband and remove herself from my list of responsibilities." He pushed back the skirts of his frock coat and rested his hand on his hip, glowering at nothing in particular.

"She's probably hiding in her room precisely because she knows how much you'll be fussing. Do you have your ticket handy?"

"I'm not a child, Helena." Michael patted his chest in the region of his breast pocket.

"Good. I've checked they loaded all your bags on the cart and sent it off to the station. I will be back downstairs in precisely ten minutes with my hat and coat on, and we'll be outside the door, waiting for the carriage, with ten minutes to spare."

I glanced out of the window. It was not raining. If it were —or even if it were blowing a hurricane or freezing cold— Michael would not budge from Scott House's simple but elegant flight of steps during the time allotted for waiting.

I inwardly agreed with Michael that it was too bad of Odelia not to come down. But O was a law unto herself, and there was no point in my trying to change things. Nobody in my family ever listened to me.

I RETURNED LATER THAT MORNING IN A BETTER FRAME OF mind.

"Well, that's one problem less," I said cheerfully to Guttridge as I crossed the threshold. "Perhaps we could concentrate on my new dresses today." I turned so Guttridge could remove my coat. "Do you think Lady Odelia would like to accompany us to the dressmaker? She does have rather good taste. She—"

But the flow of my words stilled as I looked up into Guttridge's face. There was something portentous about her silence and the look in her dark eyes. "There's nothing wrong, is there? Is Lady Odelia all right?"

I had experienced the sudden demise of a loved one three times, so it was perhaps not surprising that I suddenly felt a little breathless. Guttridge, always observant, put out a steadying hand.

"I didn't mean to alarm you, my lady. Come and sit down —you've gone as white as a sheet. I'm sure her ladyship is quite well."

I frowned. "What do you mean, you're *sure*? For heaven's sake, is she still abed? She won't shout at you if you wake her. She might pay more attention to *you* than she does to anyone else," I remarked hopefully.

"She's not there, my lady."

"Has she gone out?" I frowned.

Guttridge took a deep breath. "Her ladyship didn't sleep in her bed last night." After a moment's hesitation, she continued in a low, confidential voice. "I gather it's not the first time she's been out all night without an explanation to the staff. There's gossip downstairs."

"We'll have to put a stop to *that*. Servants shouldn't gossip about their employers. Although it *is* inconsiderate not to inform your household when you won't be there." I thought for a moment. "There's probably a perfectly innocent reason. A friend in distress, for example. I imagine she'll be home soon."

BUT THE DAY PASSED WITHOUT A SIGN OF ODELIA. AFTER A sleepless night, the morning found me in a state of considerable anxiety. And also, not unnaturally, irritation.

"This is unconscionable." I put down the morning's letters, among which I had hoped to find a note from Odelia. "If I weren't so worried, Guttridge, I'd be furious. How can she frighten me like this? What am I supposed to do? Summon the constabulary? She could be dead in the river for all we know."

I realized what I'd said and felt the blood drain from my face, seeing my emotions mirrored by the shock and sadness in Guttridge's eyes. Then the blood rushed back to my cheeks like an angry tide.

"If I don't hear from her by this afternoon, I *will* go to the police station, even if it gets into the society columns. I'm quite ready to have a row with Lady Odelia if she accuses me of interfering. In fact, I'll write to Lord Broadmere and have him come back up here. He insists he's head of the family;

very well, *he* can have the job of—well, of doing whatever one can do when one's sister disappears for days on end."

The footman, a gauche young man with large ears, stepped into the room carrying a salver, and Guttridge immediately turned to take it. A very small tussle ensued between them, which Guttridge won. The salver, which she held out to me, bore a neatly ironed and carefully folded copy of *The Times*.

"I thought you might like to look at the newspaper, my lady." Guttridge indicated, by a sniff and a look, that the footman had better absent himself immediately. She waited until he had left the room before continuing. "It occurred to me that perhaps her ladyship's been seen somewhere. You know how they sometimes list the guests at a dinner or a party. She might not have thought of writing you a line. After all, she's used to being here by herself, coming and going as she pleases." She waggled the salver very slightly. "We should exhaust all the lines of inquiry open to us before going to the police station."

"You're right." I took the paper and unfolded it, looking for the society columns.

"I could send out for more papers, if you like." Guttridge's expression, which had been grave, lightened slightly.

"Yes, anything you think might answer." I deposited Scotty on the floor to make more room for the broadsheet. "And you could help me read them. Two heads are better than one, aren't they?"

THE ANCIENT CLOCK IN THE HALLWAY HAD STRUCK ELEVEN some time ago. Guttridge and I were now sitting side by side amid a welter of newsprint that, at my insistence, they had not taken the time to iron. Our hands were inked;

Guttridge's nose bore a black smudge, and I didn't like to inquire too closely into my own appearance. The world smelled of ink. My eyes were sore, and my head ached. Guttridge, always thorough, had procured yesterday's papers as well as today's, and there was an awful lot to look at.

"My lady . . ." Guttridge sat up straight.

"You've found something?" I was tempted to snatch the journal out of her hands, but instead I too straightened my back, feeling the protest of stiff muscles between my shoulder blades.

"Yesterday's *Pall Mall Gazette*." Guttridge handed me the paper, pointing at a brief article.

"Celebrated artist taken ill in Holland Park . . . Oh! Sir Geraint . . . Social engagements canceled . . . Severe and unexpected indisposition," I read. I looked at Guttridge. "Sir Geraint was in excellent health when I saw him on Monday."

Guttridge nodded slowly. "So it's what *I'd* call a suspicious circumstance."

"Which may or may not have anything to do with Lady Odelia."

"It may *not*," said Guttridge in tones of deep significance. "But on the other hand, it *may*." And then, in a more normal tone of voice: "In any case, my lady, what's there to lose? Do you know any other of her ladyship's artist friends?"

"Not in terms of knowing their full names and where they live," I admitted.

"Well, then." Guttridge went to fold her arms, saw the state of her fingers, and abandoned the gesture. "We probably should have made inquiries there first. Perhaps Lady Dorrian-Knowles sent an urgent message for help to her ladyship?"

Millie doesn't like me, said Odelia's voice in my head. But Guttridge was right. I had no idea where else to look.

"Should I send a note?" I asked, perplexed.

"Saying what? Sorry to hear Sir Geraint's unwell, and by the way, have you seen Lady Odelia?" Guttridge's tone was dry. "No, we'll have to go round there. Of course, since he's ill, they're not likely to be at home to anyone." She rubbed her nose, widening the area of black on its tip. "Bring a gift for the patient."

"That still wouldn't get us into the house if they're not receiving visitors."

"Not at the *front* door." I could see the dawn of an idea on Guttridge's face. "I know what. You leave a card and inquire after Sir Geraint's health. A very welcome attention from an earl's daughter. I'll go out first, take a hansom to Fortnum & Mason, and have them deliver an invalid's hamper straight-away—beef tea, calves' foot jelly, and such. Straight to the cook, you see, with me on the delivery cart, as per your instructions. *Such* a delicate attention. And you'll want me in attendance on your way home, won't you? So you'll have to linger. And while you're lingering, you can ask if your sister's been by, as she might be expected to if she's heard of Sir Geraint's illness. No harm in that, and you won't look as if you've come over on purpose to ask."

"That's rather devious."

Guttridge shrugged. "It'll work, though. Cook will probably grumble about us thinking she can't prepare her own beef tea for her master, but I've never yet seen a servant who isn't interested in tasting the contents of a Fortnum's hamper. Even if it's just to find fault."

GUTTRIDGE WAS RIGHT. THE HOUSEKEEPER ANSWERED THE door and recognized me immediately from my recent visit. Once I had performed the ceremony of handing over my card and expressing my wishes for Sir Geraint's speedy recovery, I naturally asked if my lady's maid had by now arrived with a hamper from Fortnum & Mason. Even more naturally, the housekeeper showed me into the library while she made inquiries rather than leaving me waiting on the doorstep.

"Has my sister also come to ask after Sir Geraint's health?" I asked casually, turning around at the last moment as if the thought had just crossed my mind. "Lady Odelia, you know. I would think she might, if she's heard. I haven't seen her today." That was certainly true.

I watched the housekeeper's face, my heartbeat increasing. I could see warring emotions—the need for discretion, the instinctive desire to answer my question truthfully, and perhaps something like relief. It would be worth pushing just a little harder.

"I'm sorry to miss her, in fact." I smiled. "She could come home in my carriage. Silly that we couldn't have agreed to come here together."

Now I saw a faint hardening of the housekeeper's expression. I knew at that moment that *she* knew I was telling, or at least suggesting, an untruth. I looked her directly in the face, willing her mask to slip, praying that her loyalties would not come down on the side of asking me to leave the house. That was unlikely anyway. One advantage of having a title before one's name was that servants rarely believed it was possible to eject one from the premises.

"I think you know her ladyship's still here, my lady."

Relief washed into every extremity of my body, tingling the ends of my fingers and making me feel light-headed. I ventured a guess.

"*Still* here? When did she arrive?" I tried to interpret the look on the woman's face, and enlightenment dawned. "Is she refusing to leave?"

After all, Odelia appeared to be a devoted follower of Sir

Geraint's. Perhaps she'd lost her head over his illness and was making a nuisance of herself. One heard such stories about spinster ladies.

The housekeeper's discretion had definitely begun to crumble. "She's upsetting the mistress, my lady." She swallowed. "I *wish* she'd go."

"Is your master very ill?" I inquired in my gentlest tone of voice. "Is there anything I could do other than take Lady Odelia home with me? I could send along Sir Arthur Southam if Sir Geraint's condition is serious." Sir Arthur was a physician who would only deign to attend your bedside if your family had been in Debrett's for at least three generations.

"It won't be necessary, my lady." The housekeeper shook her head. "The master's hurts have been attended to."

"His hurts? I thought he'd be suffering from a fever or some kind of collapse. Has he injured himself?"

"Yes. He—he has injured—himself."

I suddenly realized what she meant.

"He has done himself some harm." This was an entirely new state of affairs. "Is there permanent damage?"

"No, my lady, I don't think so." Now the woman was fighting back tears. "The cuts are not deep, and the surgeon who attended him said they'll heal quickly. But we must watch him." She hesitated. "In case he tries it again."

"Oh, heavens." I looked her in the eyes. "I won't tell anyone, you know. My only concern is to find Lady Odelia, to tell the truth. Perhaps you could let her know I'm here?"

"Yes, my lady."

She left the room, pulling a large red handkerchief from her pocket to wipe at her eyes as she passed through the doorway. I was left to sit and stare at the huge painting of *The Halls of the Snow Queen* and wonder. Had this been a serious attempt at suicide or a feint designed to draw attention to a deep internal disturbance?

Sir Geraint had seemed like the most rational of men when I'd met him, but his paintings hinted at a depth of feeling that was almost startling. They were not sentimental like so many modern paintings, but they were certainly full of emotion as well as being exceptionally beautiful in themselves.

I was lost in contemplation of the Snow Queen picture, trying to discern the artistic temperament it betrayed, by the time the housekeeper returned.

"Lady Dorrian-Knowles asks that you would do her the favor of joining her upstairs in the family wing, my lady."

"Did you speak to Lady Odelia?" I turned away from the glittering halls of ice and picked up my reticule.

"I did, my lady. She told me to go away."

"Ah." This was clearly going to be awkward. "And what about Guttridge? Do you know where she is?"

"She's taking tea in the servants' hall, my lady. I'll send her up."

"Good." Clearly, Michael wasn't the only one of my siblings who might need managing from time to time. Guttridge could be a valuable ally in my quest to extract Odelia from a house in which she evidently wasn't welcome.

10

AN EMBARRASSING SITUATION

I was dressed for the carriage, not having intended to stay. I began to regret the amount of wool about my person once we left the part of the second floor I had already seen and entered the private wing, since the air was warm—but not silent; several voices were all talking at once, which hardly seemed the right atmosphere for an invalid.

"Mrs. B.!" A young man darted out from the room to the right. It was the red-haired Galahad, looking flushed and agitated. "And Lady Helena, isn't it? I beg your pardon—our mother asked me to intercept you. Mrs. B., would you just tidy up a bit in Father's bedroom before showing Lady Helena in?"

The housekeeper nodded and proceeded farther down the corridor while Galahad held the door open for me. I entered a large sitting room of a comfortable aspect, far less grand than the reception rooms downstairs but beautifully decorated with sumptuous tapestries and embroideries.

Voices stilled, and several faces turned toward me. I immediately recognized the other two Dorrian-Knowles brothers and Jane, their sister. The latter was in tears and darted toward the window to conceal her face. She could not hide her sobs, which punctuated the next few minutes at regular intervals.

The men I knew to be Philip and Edmund rose to their feet as I entered. Behind them, a rather cross-looking man of around forty took his hands out of his pockets and made a brief bow. The woman who had been standing with him moved forward to greet me. She was dressed in the height of fashion, her red hair beautifully arranged and surmounted by a hat of the latest Paris style.

"Lady Helena? I'm Cassiope Jowett." She held out an elegant hand. "I don't believe you've made the acquaintance of my brothers—Philip, Edmund, and Galahad. This is my husband, Morrison." She winced slightly as a loud hiccupping sob sounded from the window. "I believe you've met Jane."

"I'm so sorry to intrude at such a moment," I said.

"It can't be helped." Galahad's face flushed to the roots of his flaming hair. "It's a bit embarrassing for all of us."

"Nicely put, Sir Galahad of the Trite Remark." Edmund, seeing his older brother motion me to a chair, sat down again and put his hands in his pockets. "The best way to make a guest feel at ease is to point out that she's an embarrassment."

"That's not what I meant, and you know it." The crimson hue of Galahad's face was a most unfortunate match for his hair. "Somebody has to say *something*."

"It's quite all right, Mr. Dorrian-Knowles," I assured him.

"I say, you'd better call us all by our Christian names." Edmund's long upper lip stretched into what was almost an expression of mirth. "Or we're going to get into a terrible muddle."

"You're not helping, Ed." Philip, who had not sat down,

crossed to the window to put an arm around Jane's shoulders. "Come now, Janie, don't take on so. He'll be all right."

Jane's response to these soothing words was to howl louder and bury her face in her brother's waistcoat.

"Now look what you've done," said Cassiope to the room at large, rolling her eyes. "Edmund darling, be nice. Think of the occasion . . . and our guest." She dropped a kiss on Edmund's fair hair before joining Philip at the window, stroking Jane's back and murmuring consolingly.

"I do beg your pardon, Lady Helena." Edmund turned to me. "We're all at sixes and sevens, as you'd imagine."

"And rather cooped up here, if you don't mind me saying so." I raised my eyebrows. "Perhaps one of you could take your sister out to the garden? A little fresh air is effective in cases of hysterics." I longed for a little fresh air myself but didn't think I could leave without Odelia.

"Are you knowledgeable about the care of young ladies?" Edmund asked politely, but I thought I detected a hint of scorn behind the words.

"I'm knowledgeable about how it feels to receive a severe shock," I said quietly. "I've had the experience several times."

"Dolt." Galahad shoved his brother in the arm and turned toward the window. "She's right, though, Cass, we can't just let her go on screeching. She'll have a fit or something."

"Tea, then." Cassiope, who was now hugging Jane, spoke over her sister's head, addressing her husband. "Morrison, would you be a dear and see if either of the maids is actually *doing* anything? And make sure they understand they're not to admit any journalists. In fact, not *anybody*. Mrs. B.'s the only servant with any sense, and she *has* to stay up here. Make sure they bring up a cup for her too. The poor woman's been on her feet for hours."

"Haven't we all?" Mr. Jowett skirted the assembled members of the Dorrian-Knowles family and headed to the door. "*I* could do with a whiskey." He shook his head at me in passing. "Terrible business. Unheard of. Not becoming."

"I imagine we won't see *him* again." Philip frowned at the closing door. "He'll hang around the garden smoking cigars. Still, he might frighten off the newspapermen."

"Have there been many?" I asked.

"A few." Philip shrugged and dropped into a chair. A sort of calm descended. Even Jane's sobs lessened amid a few loud sniffs and nose-blowings. I could hear nothing from any other room and wondered what was happening.

After about three minutes of awkward silence, I attempted to find some subject of conversation. Philip, who had clearly inherited a great deal of Sir Geraint's charm and ease, roused himself to assist me in the effort.

On the principle that it is always easiest to allow people to talk about themselves, I tried to find out what the young men's interests were. Philip readily spoke about his burgeoning career as a portraitist and his new studio, of which he seemed rather proud. Edmund explained that he had been down from Cambridge for nearly a year and was trying to make a name for himself as a writer. Galahad confessed that he had not yet chosen his path in life and intended to travel to Switzerland in the spring, looking, as he said, for inspiration. None of us alluded to the topic that was clearly on all of our minds.

After some twenty minutes, Cassiope moved toward her brothers, her arm still around Jane.

"We're going to see what happened to the tea," she announced. "This is perfectly ridiculous."

"Would you look for my lady's maid?" I asked. "Mrs.—what's your housekeeper's name?—said she'd send her up here."

"Mrs. B.'s probably still in Father's bedroom." There was faint laughter in Edmund's voice, as if he'd said something indelicate and wanted us to appreciate the joke, but he spoke softly enough that Jane couldn't hear him.

"Her name is Mrs. Bretherton, and she's a faithful, respectable old soul." Galahad frowned at his brother as he answered my question. "She'll be doing everything she can to make the room nice and ease Mother's mind a little."

And Odelia? I took advantage of a halt in the conversation to rise to my feet—indicating to the men that there was no need for them to do the same—and crossed to the window that Cassiope had opened. Partially hidden by the gorgeously embroidered curtains, I looked out at the garden, sending up a prayer of thanks for the blessed stream of cool air that washed over my perspiring face. I could not have been in that room for much over thirty minutes, but no interval of time had ever felt longer. I wanted to see Odelia—I longed to see Guttridge—and there was a part of me that wanted to see Sir Geraint, to see if I could help him. We all seemed frozen in place, like Kai on his boulder of ice, victims of some endless enchantment, waiting for a savior.

It was a relief when the door opened. "He's asleep again," said Millie's voice. "Oh, for heaven's sake, hasn't anybody brought any tea? Where's Lady Helena?"

I pushed the curtain aside. Millie's eyes were red and her hair somewhat disordered, but mostly she just looked tired.

"Is there anything I can do?" I hastened toward her. "How is your husband?"

"Where's Jane?" Millie asked. I wasn't sure if she'd heard my questions.

"Cass took her downstairs." Edmund rose to his feet and stepped to his mother's side. "Don't worry about her, Mimi." He smoothed down the wisps of wavy hair on his mother's forehead and kissed it. "It's better to keep her away from Father at the moment, don't you think?"

"You're right. Thank God for Cass." Millie smiled at her

son, whose arm was resting protectively around her shoulder.

"Our sentiments precisely," said Galahad. "Cass is seeing to getting some tea sent up, I think. She sent Morrison to do it earlier, but I expect he escaped. He's probably in Knightsbridge by now."

"Poor Lady Helena's stuck here like a passenger in a railway terminal where the train never comes." Philip smiled at me.

"Yes. Sorry." Millie seemed to see me properly for the first time. "He was a little feverish and agitated, and I thought I'd better change his dressings." A look of triumph stole over her face. "That got her out—she's not so devoted as to want to touch his dirty bandages or deal with his chamber pot. She took herself off to the WC—and then there was a bit of a scene between us when she came back, I'm afraid. My fault, but can you blame me?"

"So has she gone?" Edmund asked, an expression of deep concern and affection on his face.

"Geraint told me to let her back in. Damn the woman —*damn* her. And damn *him* for doing this to us. What am I supposed to do? How am I ever going to let him out of my sight again?"

"Sit down, Mother." Edmund led Millie to a chair, into which she dropped heavily. He remained standing, holding her hand. "Ah, here's Cass."

Cassiope entered, followed by a maid with a large, and presumably very heavy, tea tray. Galahad, true to his name, immediately jumped up and relieved the perspiring girl of her burden, setting it on a table near the window. He pushed the window open with an impatient gesture, letting in more of the damp, cool air. It was getting late, the darkness gathering outside. Cassiope ran to her mother, putting her arms around her, much as she had done with Jane.

"Poor, dear Mother." She kissed Millie's cheek while Edmund stepped back, smiling fondly at the two of them. "I'll share the burden with you. I can send to my house for clothes and things. Morrison and the children can manage without me for a day or two."

"May I see if I can take Odelia home?" I asked Millie.

"Oh, would you?" Millie's tone was heartfelt, desperate. "Please, for the love of God, get your sister out of here. It's been two days—*two days*—and *I'm* his wife, not her. How would *you* like having your husband's mistress around your neck at a time like this?"

UNDERSTANDABLY, MY MOUTH FELL OPEN. I ALMOST FELL over; I must have tottered slightly, as the next sensation I was aware of was Philip's large, firm hands on my shoulders.

"I say, steady on," he said. "You look as if you're going to faint."

"Whoops." Galahad leaned forward. "I think Lady Helena may have just received a piece of startling news. Cass, do you have any *sal volatile*?"

"I don't need smelling salts." I shook off Philip's hands. "This can't be true. My sister—Lady Odelia Scott-De Quincy —it's impossible."

I watched Edmund's face, hitherto grave with concern for his mother, contort into an irresistible grin. In a moment, all three Dorrian-Knowles brothers were laughing— Edmund with genuine merriment, Philip with a worldly chuckle, and Galahad with a sort of embarrassed snigger. Even Cassiope's face bore the trace of a pitying smile, quickly suppressed.

Millie's face darkened with rage. "That's right." Her voice shook as she addressed her children. "Laugh at the situation.

At me. The idiot who accepted this—this arrangement. This living hell. Men—I hate the lot of you."

"I believe they're laughing at me for being a naïve fool," I said, but Millie had pushed herself out of the chair and was out of the room in an instant. I stood, frozen, not knowing whether I should run after her.

"I'd better go." Cassiope looked around at her brothers. "Give Lady Helena some tea, you utter—" She bit off the last word as she left the room.

I was hot and thirsty and didn't think any of the young men would get around to serving the tea before it was quite spoiled, so I crossed to the table, relieved to have something to do. I began setting out cups and pouring the refreshing liquid. My actions prompted a flurry of offers to help from Philip and Galahad, which I refused, and in a few moments we were all seated. I took a sip or two of the tea and felt the warm liquid moisten the inside of my mouth.

"That's better." I looked at each of the men in turn. "Obviously, I didn't know, and perhaps that makes me a fool. But my sister left home when I was just a child, and I usually see her in the country. How long has this been going on?"

"More or less since Janie was a baby, I think." Philip sounded matter-of-fact. "I was twelve years old when I first knew, but by that time she was well established."

I closed my eyes, taking a very deep breath. Jane was a child still in many ways, but her figure was quite womanly. If I was any judge, she was fifteen or sixteen. Suddenly, much of Odelia's behavior made sense—her disinclination to marry, her erratic comings and goings, her marked preference for London over any other place. Fourteen years? Fifteen? More than half my life.

And then a thought struck me, and I felt a coldness that had nothing to do with the open window. Did my sisters know? Did Michael? Was I the only one *not* to know? Dear

God, if that were true, no wonder they called me Baby. I had accepted Odelia at face value for all these years, trusted her . . .

Another horrible notion arrived swiftly on the heels of the first. "Is this known in London society?" I asked faintly.

Galahad wrinkled his nose. "Depends on what you mean by society. In Father's set, the artists and the writers and such, I expect quite a few people know and just don't care. They've all got mistresses, haven't they? Or they're sleeping with each other's wives and husbands." He coughed. "Sorry, Lady Helena. Not really a subject suitable for polite conversation."

"But an unfortunate fact among the aristocracy as well." I sighed. "Inevitable, I suppose, in a class where one marries to increase the family's fortune or land rather than for love."

My voice was steady, but I could feel a tightness near my heart. My father had hurt my mother a great deal by his infidelities, and I couldn't help feeling immediate sympathy for Millie. How I felt about Odelia at that moment was not a question I wished to explore.

"Strange, isn't it, how people turn a blind eye to what is preached against constantly? We've often discussed such matters." Galahad nodded at his brothers. "In wider society, they refer to such things as 'goings-on among the bohemians,' and people regard them as some kind of strange and exotic creature that doesn't have to play by the rules."

"Except that Philip, if he's to make his way as a society portraitist, will have to distance himself from 'bohemian' life." Edmund looked amused. "Can't have patrons imagining he's interested in the wives he's painting." He grinned at his older brother, who merely folded his arms and ignored him. I had the impression that if these parents had indulged any of their children, it was Edmund.

"Cass has always attempted to set herself apart from any

taint of unconventionality," Galahad remarked. "She's a dear, though—an absolute brick in a crisis."

"Indeed, she's a saint." Edmund hesitated, then turned to me. "I think you should understand, Lady Helena, that your sister isn't our father's only mistress, although she is the *maîtresse en titre*. There are two more regulars, and a few others have come and gone. The most astonishing aspect of all this is that Father has not yet presented us with any little half brothers or sisters, but I live in hope."

"Don't be a facetious idiot." Galahad scowled. "Father doesn't believe in monogamy," he said to me. "He says that any man who claims to pledge himself to one woman for life is a hypocrite, and that it's better to take mistresses openly than to visit—well, you know."

"He asserts that love is necessary to his art and swears that a chaste marriage would result in his losing all his creative fire. That's what he calls it." Philip's youthful face was stern. "As we got older, he began justifying himself to us, you see. Naturally, we've all sworn to become entirely conventional men."

"To worship women from afar, to woo and marry chastely, and to practice fidelity till death do us part." Edmund nodded, his eyes sparkling with what might have been enthusiasm or ridicule. "You know, it's all a terrible bore when you've grown up with it. Not that he usually entertains his women in our house, you understand. Mother tolerates them coming to Father's crushes, but they'd better be gone before the party ends or he'll get it hot. *This* party doesn't seem to be ending, obviously." He smirked.

I realized my cup and saucer were still in my hand. What tea remained in the cup had gone entirely cold. I handed cup and saucer to Edmund, who took them with good grace, and stood up. All three men rose to their feet politely.

"Thank you for the elucidation," I said as steadily as I

could, looking up at the looming masculine forms. "I under-stand the situation clearly now and will take the obvious course of action."

Galahad's bright eyebrows rose to his even brighter hair. "Which is?"

"Find your mother, to reassure her that I'm on her side. Find my maid, to reassure *me*—Guttridge is also a brick in a crisis. Then Guttridge and I will do the best we can to persuade Lady Odelia to come home with us. I believe we're the best hope you've got."

11

THE INJURED PARTIES

Since my pleas to fetch Guttridge had hitherto fallen on deaf ears, I went in search of her before entering the very private domain of the family bedrooms. I decided to take five minutes to refresh myself. Once I had neatened my hair, cooled my hot face with a little water, and washed my hands—which felt sticky and unpleasant, as if I had been handling something noxious—I felt more in command of my emotions. The lavatory had a large mirror over the washbasin, and I studied my face as I used my reflection to guide myself in replacing my hatpin.

How shocked *was* I? I was no *ingénue*; the countryside was hardly exempt from extramarital affairs. Justin had had a finely tuned ear for gossip and loved to regale me with stories about the people we knew. But to think of Odelia in the role of mistress . . . It was strange, but I had always seen my family, especially my sisters, as somehow exempt from the venality that appeared to lurk in every corner if one looked too closely. Did I love Odelia any less for knowing? I hoped not.

"And I've been here for—what? An hour? More?—and I

still haven't seen her." I told my reflection. "The truth is, you're afraid of the scene that might ensue when you try to make O leave. You've never known her to behave with anything but complete nonchalance, and now you're worried that she won't."

My reflection stared back. My regular features gave nothing away, as usual, but my front hair had lost much of the curl Guttridge had put into it that morning, giving me a slightly dispirited air. I cursed the hot room upstairs, gave one last little prod at my hat to settle it into exactly the right position, and went to find Guttridge.

I found her sitting in the servants' hall in the company of the two maids. The latter got guiltily to their feet as I entered. I surmised that without proper supervision, they were indeed inclined to do very little. Guttridge's face was a picture of relief.

"I've been asking and asking to come and find you, but they keep saying to wait for Mrs. Bretherton," she said as she pushed back her chair and put down her teacup. "And no dinner getting done until Mrs. Jowett came in and spoke to Cook. Is Lady Odelia ready to leave?"

I motioned Guttridge out of the servants' hall before speaking to her in a low voice. "Believe it or not, I haven't even seen her." I looked around. "Let's come away from here, and I'll explain."

When we reached the generous hallway, gorgeously tiled in blue and white, I rapidly explained the entire situation to Guttridge in an undertone. I did not leave out one detail of what I had learned. Guttridge was entirely discreet, and besides, she would learn soon enough. The look of dawning alarm—mixed, perhaps, with a faint tinge of hilarity that she did her very best to hide—told me that Guttridge, at least, had not known.

"Coo-er." Occasionally, when taken by surprise, Guttridge

let a little of her inner Londoner through her correct pronunciation. "You *don't* say. 'Ow—*how* did her ladyship manage that for all these years with nobody in the family knowing?"

"So you think nobody knows?" I let out my breath. "You haven't heard any talk?"

"Not a sausage. We all just thought she was one of those eccentric maiden ladies the aristocracy breeds."

"I'm telling you this in confidence, Guttridge."

"Of course, my lady." The eager tone of curiosity had gone. The mask of the upper servant slid gently back over Guttridge's face, but her dark eyes were shining.

"The situation's going to need careful handling," I remarked, looking up at the stairs.

"Definitely, my lady." Guttridge smiled. "Don't worry, we'll manage."

I proceeded upward with Guttridge close behind me. The sitting-room door was shut, and I could hear the brothers conversing quietly. I passed it, heading down the corridor. As we reached the room at the end, Mrs. Bretherton emerged, carrying a tightly wrapped bundle of bed linen.

"Sir Geraint's awake." A tremulous smile flitted across her pale face. "He said—"

But the formless howl of rage—Millie's voice—that issued from within the chamber obliterated her message.

GUTTRIDGE MOVED FIRST, DARTING PAST THE HOUSEKEEPER and pushing the door open. As I entered the room in her wake, I was aware first of the bed and Sir Geraint, who was in a half-sitting position, clearly struggling to push himself upright. His wrists had been neatly bound, but I could see what looked like fresh blood seeping through one bandage.

He had probably re-opened one of his wounds by using his hands to sit up.

"Who are you?" he was asking Guttridge as I entered the room. My lady's maid was advancing toward him, putting out a restraining hand.

"I'm Lady Helena Whitcombe's lady's maid. Sir—sir—please don't sit up. You're making your wrists bleed. Let me help you."

Knowing that Sir Geraint was in expert hands, I looked farther into the large room. Odelia and Millie were standing by a window at the far end. Their combative stances, frozen as the door opened, looked incongruous next to the restful arrangement of a settee, small table, and portable writing desk.

Millie was even more flushed and disheveled than I'd last seen her. Odelia was pale and cold-looking. She still looked elegant, even after her two days' vigil, but the dullness and slight greasiness of her facial skin and the dry, almost withered look of the hand splayed over her trim bosom spoke volumes.

"Helena." Odelia's expression went blank as she dropped her hand to her side. "I thought you'd gone."

Millie moved so she was between me and Odelia. "I—want—this—*bitch*—out." Her voice rose to a crescendo of rage and frustration. "Or so help me, I will hit her."

"Just try," Odelia spoke over Millie's shoulder.

"Nobody's hitting anyone." I almost wanted to stamp my foot with irritation at the disgraceful scene, but I could see Guttridge struggling to hold Sir Geraint up—he was clearly under the influence of some drug—and pile up the pillows behind him. I darted to the bed to help her.

With a hand under each arm, we helped the invalid to shuffle back on his posterior until he was comfortably propped up by the pillows and bolster. I was relieved to see that his eyes were a little lacking in focus but otherwise clear and that his body held the normal warmth of an awakening sleeper rather than the heat of fever. At that moment, I fervently wished I had Fortier with me to examine the patient and, perhaps, help us with the two women. They were still talking in low, tense voices, circling each other like two cats getting ready for a fight.

"Sir Geraint needs tending to," I announced as loudly as I could toward the other end of the room. "I think he's opened up one of his wounds. Do you have clean dressings? And he must need some food and drink. And some peace." I looked directly at my sister. "O, this has to stop."

"All she has to do is leave." Millie pushed past Odelia again. "Then I and my children—*our* children—can look after *my* husband in peace and privacy."

"But he wants me here." Odelia raised her eyebrows, speaking in the cool tones with which she had always maddened Blanche. "He has said so repeatedly."

"I would like the two of you to show some spirit of cooperation and friendship." Sir Geraint's voice was a little weak at first but strengthened as he spoke. "I'm sorry—I apologize to both of you. I have brought down trouble on my house through a foolish loss of control, but I swear to you it has passed. The laudanum is wearing off, and I am feeling better."

He pushed and pulled impatiently at the blankets and bedspread, wincing as he moved his hands, and then began kicking the sheets aside, preparatory to getting out of bed. Guttridge's eyes widened.

"*Not* with her ladyship present, surely, sir."

"She's probably seen worse." There was a tiny hint of humor in the artist's voice. "Be quiet and hand me that robe."

Guttridge rolled her eyes at me, clearly exasperated at this male stubbornness, but did as Sir Geraint asked. He managed to get himself to the edge of the bed with only a minimal display of bare flesh, an effort involving much tugging and swearing at his nightshirt. He wrapped the robe around himself, rose to his feet—and promptly fell back onto the bed as his knees buckled.

Odelia and Millie both rushed toward the bed. Their paths collided, and O tried to push Millie out of the way. Millie countered with an almighty shove that sent Odelia into a bedpost. She followed up this violent action with a resounding slap that only caught the edge of Odelia's cheek, and the momentum put her hand on a collision course with the carved wood. There was a nasty hollow sound, and Millie yelped.

Guttridge, who had been leaning over Sir Geraint, looked up at me, and I felt a momentary surge of fellow-feeling. I grabbed at Odelia. I was several inches shorter than her but quite strong, particularly in the hands, so when I got a tight hold of her, I was able to pull her away from the bed, no doubt aided by shock from the blow she'd received. Her cheek was bleeding, either from a ring or one of Millie's fingernails.

Guttridge, in the meantime, ran around the bed and grabbed Millie by the shoulders. Fortunately, they were much of a size, although Millie was the heavier party. Not that she appeared about to attack Odelia again. She was clutching her right hand in her left, her face white with pain.

Anguished whispering outside the door was quickly followed by the entrance of all the Dorrian-Knowles siblings except, thank heaven, Jane. Philip and Galahad darted to their father's side while Edmund and Cassiope surrounded their mother, their voices raised in shock at the injury.

"Lady Dorrian-Knowles tried to slap Odelia but hit the bedpost instead," I summarized rapidly. I didn't want them thinking that Odelia had injured Millie. "Both your parents need medical assistance."

"I'm all right," Sir Geraint gasped. "But I'll concede I'm weaker than I realized." He had managed to struggle into a sitting position again, and both bandages were now bright with patches of crimson.

"I'll run for Dr. Menzies." Galahad took another look at his father and disappeared through the open doorway.

"Odelia," I said firmly, giving my sister a little shake, "before the doctor comes, we will be out of this house. I won't take no for an answer. You can see he's going to live. This simply cannot go on."

"I'm fine, O." Sir Geraint inspected his bandages. "But I *am* bleeding a little. Stupid of me. It's the damned laudanum that made me dizzy."

"Menzies poured the laudanum down your throat because you were shouting about jumping out of the window, you fool." Millie's words came out in gasps; she was hugging her hand under her chin. "We had to wrestle you out of the bath—blood everywhere—and then you wouldn't calm down. Haven't I told you before about drinking that evil stuff of Shelbourne's? And then you got worse—your breathing— and you made everything unbearable by insisting that—that *woman* hold your hand." She stopped, clearly forcing back tears.

"Which is exactly what I did," Odelia snapped. "It's hardly my fault that Geraint wanted *me* by him. Baby, do get *off* me—"

"Don't call me Baby." I tightened my grip on my sister. "I daresay that between us Guttridge and I could carry or drag you downstairs—but you really don't want an undignified row, do you? You've helped to get Sir Geraint over the worst of this crisis. Now it's time to come home and rest. Look, you're hurt."

O gazed at the smear of blood on the clean handkerchief I'd just used to wipe her cheek and then seemed to see the way Millie was holding her hand for the first time. Acknowledgment of the disgraceful fight was in her eyes. Her gaze met mine, and she gave me a brief, shamefaced nod. I relaxed my hold fractionally.

"That's better." I stood on tiptoe to blot the oozing cut on Odelia's cheek. "Let's clean it properly when we get home. I have a salve I made that will help it heal and some arnica to stop you from getting a bruise."

O was watching Sir Geraint, who now had one tall son on either side of him, while Cassiope embraced her mother. Tears of pain were running down Millie's face, and she was biting her lip.

"Perhaps you should go now, Odelia, my dear." Sir Geraint sounded resigned. "You can see I'm quite myself again. Thank you for staying with me."

I believe I was the only person present to see the hurt in O's eyes. The next moment, the fire returned to them and her spine stiffened. She walked round to the side of the bed where her lover sat; at her approach, his sons drew back, doubt in their eyes. My momentary fear that she would cling to him dissipated when she simply bent over, graceful as always, and pressed her lips to his in a long, lingering kiss.

"I'll see you soon." Without looking back, Odelia walked steadily through the door, her spine perfectly straight.

12

THE SNOW QUEEN

By the time the three of us arrived at Scott House, Odelia's head had fallen onto Guttridge's shoulder in a doze of pure exhaustion. We took her straight upstairs to her bedchamber.

"I don't recall having been in this room since I was a girl," I admitted as we sat my yawning sister on the bed. "Do you think you could find Lady Odelia a nightgown, Guttridge?"

"I have one right here, my lady." Guttridge, who had used the single candle she'd brought up to light the elegant bronze-based lamp on Odelia's dressing table, had gone straight to a drawer and extracted a neatly folded confection of fine lawn and lace. Of course, I realized, she would have more reason than I ever did to penetrate into Odelia's inner sanctum. O had no lady's maid, and Guttridge was always willing to assist her in matters of hair and dress once she had finished with me.

"Perhaps her ladyship would prefer a bath or a wash before retiring?" Guttridge suggested as I looked for the fastenings on Odelia's gown.

"She would not," O spoke groggily. "I'll just pig it tonight, Guttridge. Tell Maisie to bring up hot water at ten."

"Yes, my lady. But you'll let me fetch those salves, won't you? We can't have you going around with a marked face."

Odelia merely grunted assent, and Guttridge left the room, pushing Scotty in front of her. My dog had been underfoot, which was not helpful. I helped O out of her dress, wrinkling my nose at the various stale odors resulting from her long vigil at Sir Geraint's bedside. Once she was stripped down to her combinations, I turned my back while she took them off and donned her nightgown, taking the chance to study the room.

I remembered the plain, dark paneling, the chimneypiece with its marble fireplace surround and carved fruits and flowers, the stately bed. But when I was a girl, the room had never had such beautiful silk curtains nor such fine hangings on the bed, nor had it displayed such bright jewels of art.

Most of the paintings were Odelia's, exclusively medieval subjects. Women in gorgeously rich gowns with trailing sleeves, unbound hair flowing down their backs, gazed adoringly at knights in armor or handsome lute players. Pages attended them, their hair cut straight over their noble young brows. The light from the lamp picked out the flowers and leaves curling around the edges of the paintings, and I recognized many plants from the fields and hedgerows of Sussex. At least O had incorporated some measure of the real world into these dreams of beauty and chivalry.

There were other paintings by hands I did not recognize. Friends of Odelia's, perhaps. But it was the painting mounted on the chimneypiece that really caught my eye. The Snow Queen at last. My sister.

The painting depicted Odelia wearing a mantle of deep blue trimmed with white fur, which flowed in luxurious folds over a glorious throne of ice in the middle of a frozen lake. The ice on its surface had shattered into a thousand pieces, reflecting the northern lights that shimmered in the great cavern's ceiling. At her feet lay a tiny, huddled child wrapped in a fur pelt, asleep with its cheek resting on one small hand, its face almost obscured by the fur surrounding it. Whose child? I wondered. Around the throne danced strange creatures that might have been huge snowflakes except that they also resembled animals or birds. It was an odd painting, hard to interpret, almost disturbing in its dreamlike nature. I found it hard to believe that anybody could have painted it without sampling the purported delights of the opium pipe.

"Was that painted at the same time as the one in Holland Park?" I turned back to Odelia as I pointed to the Snow Queen. She was climbing into bed, carelessly pushing her discarded clothing onto the floor.

"He painted it first." Odelia yawned and rubbed her hand across her face. "I'm not sure Geraint would have given it to me if he'd known how well his fairy-tale work would sell." She sniffed the air. "Dear God, I stink. I wish I had the energy for a bath. But I'd probably fall asleep and slip under the water."

"Don't say things like that." My imagination supplied an image of Sir Geraint lying in a bath full of water tinged red by his blood. "Here's Guttridge with the salves. May I put some on your face? The cut's stopped bleeding."

O smiled, her eyes closed. "Have at me with your potions, dear sister."

I used the fourth finger of my hand to smear a little salve made of calendula and marshmallow on the cut. Then, avoiding the immediate area of the slight wound, I carefully rubbed arnica cream into the whole cheek and the ridges of the eye socket.

"That's nice. You're very gentle." O yawned again, not

bothering to cover her mouth this time. "I've never wanted to make an enemy of Millie, you know."

"Probably not, but you drove her to the edge of desperation today." I screwed the lid onto the jar of arnica cream. "We have to talk about this, O. Do you promise me you'll do so tomorrow? And that you won't try to go back to the house in Holland Park?"

"I suppose I owe you that much." Odelia turned onto her uninjured cheek, stretching out under the covers. "Goodnight, Baby, dear."

"Don't call me Baby," I whispered under my breath. But O's eyes were shut tight, her breathing's rhythm already deepening. I waited until Guttridge had finished gathering up Odelia's clothing and preceded me out of the room, turned the lamp's regulator until its flame died, then picked up the candle.

The Snow Queen stared at me with the face of Odelia's younger self, her regular features and dark blue eyes unmarred by the small marks of age that had begun to appear without yet diminishing O's beauty. They were cool and ironic as always, those eyes; they were also triumphant. With one last glance at the sleeping form in the bed, I left the room to seek my rest at long last.

I AWOKE EARLY AFTER A DIFFICULT NIGHT. TO MY SURPRISE, when I summoned Guttridge, she informed me that Lady Odelia had been up for some time and had already sent for hot water for her bath.

I went through my own ablutions with a haste that had everything to do with the fear that Odelia might, after all, return to Holland Park. Yet I found her in the dining room, most unusual at such an early hour. She was sipping coffee and reading the new *Illustrated London News* with the air of someone who had few cares on her mind.

"It's nice to see you dressed in something less funereal," was her opening remark. "Gray suits you far better than black."

I looked down at my morning robe, which was bordered with ivy leaves embroidered in black. "I must admit, it makes me feel as if I'm coming back to life. How are you?"

I went to kiss Odelia before investigating the sideboard, noting that the cut on her cheek was healing nicely. She returned the greeting with a quick hug and a smile, which was highly reassuring in the circumstances. I filled my plate well—I'd had nothing since the cup of tea at the Dorrian-Knowles house—and seated myself, smiling uncertainly at O as she filled my coffee cup and added a generous portion of cream.

"Mmm, heavenly." I sipped the coffee, to which I'd added three lumps of sugar, and set to work enthusiastically on the kedgeree, bacon, and mushrooms on my plate. "Have you eaten?"

I looked up from my plate to encounter a cool blue stare, one eyebrow tilted upward in a familiar mannerism that meant Odelia was about to say something sarcastic, and put down my knife to hold up a defensive hand. "There's nothing wrong with small talk, O. I'd just like to eat in peace for five minutes before we get to the interesting part of our conversation."

To my relief, Odelia actually laughed. "*Brava,* Baby—I'm sorry, I mean Helena. It's refreshing to see you putting your own needs before everyone else's for a change. As you'll have surmised, *my* needs are incompatible with the promise I made to you last night, but I have *some* sense of honor. I will let you eat that mountain of food undisturbed and continue to entertain myself with this brave spectacle of our troops parading through London." She held up the front page so I could see the engraving of the military parade. "Behold the heroes of Egypt. See all those manly chins and mustaches. Perhaps I should marry a soldier."

I sighed loudly in exasperation, but I was ravenous, so I applied myself to my plate without further comment. A few minutes later, I put down knife and fork and nodded my thanks at the footman who had brought fresh coffee. I stirred sugar into my replenished cup slowly, listening to the tinkle of the small silver spoon on the delicate china, until I was quite sure the footman had walked away toward the back of the house.

"Does anyone else in the family know?" I finally asked the question that had been on my mind half the night, interspersed with visions of dancing snowflake-beasts and Sir Geraint in a bath filled with gore.

Odelia leaned back as far as was compatible with the straight, high back of a Jacobean chair. "Michael knows I have . . . someone. It's possible he knows it's Geraint, given that he's seen him here. He said something to me one day about my having no more morals than a cat. But he *understands*, in some peculiar way, I think. He's such an odd duck. I don't think he'd tell anybody, would he? Even Julia."

"No, I don't think he would." I frowned. "I'm beginning to wonder what other secrets are locked in that brain of his. Michael wouldn't betray a confidence unless he had a perfectly logical reason." I looked across at O, who had put down her journal and was regarding me gravely, her long forefinger with its bright ring making circles on the tablecloth. "As far as I can see, our brother discards everything from his mind that he doesn't require. But I don't think he ever forgets anything. I think it's all there somewhere, neatly shelved and labeled."

"Hmph." The red cabochon stone in O's ring caught a ray

of morning sunlight as her finger moved. "None of our sisters know, of that I'm certain. Alice and Annette are hardly a danger. Blanche never has the money to come to London, and besides, the circles she moves in are so stuffy that they take no notice of the world of art and literature. Gerry's entirely wrapped up in queening it over the society of Littleberry and Broadmere, which is quite the most *provincial* collection of people I've ever seen. When she married Ned, she turned her back on the real world. Of course, she'd say that *my* world is fantasy and hers is real."

"I might say something similar," I remarked. "So were you plotting to just *happen* to visit Whitcombe while Sir Geraint was there? Do you take me for an utter fool?"

"*No.*" Odelia sat up straighter. "I swear to you, Helena, I told Geraint I wouldn't—well, you know—at Whitcombe. Separate quarters and all that. No nighttime prowling." She looked straight into my eyes, curiosity in her expression. "I must say, you're taking this rather better than I thought you would. You always looked quite disapproving when Justin talked about the infidelities in your set."

"I just don't see the point of marrying if you can't be faithful." I pouted a little. "It was one point on which I agreed with Mama."

"Did you suspect?" O's eyes were watchful.

"Not in the least. I almost fainted when Millie told me you were her husband's mistress. I feel like a complete idiot."

O seemed to relax a little. "Well, you were a little girl when it all began. By the time you grew up, skirting around the subject of what I did with my time had become second nature. Blanche used to ask questions about how much my dresses cost, but she hasn't done that for years."

"She thinks I buy them for you." I straightened my empty coffee cup in its saucer. "As I do for her. Does Sir Geraint pay your dressmaker's bills?"

"He likes to see me well dressed." One corner of Odelia's mouth twitched up. "Although I do *actually* sell paintings, Helena. Not all of my finery is paid for by the sins of the flesh."

"Don't joke about it." I hated to hear Odelia talk in that way. Looking at her, I remembered Millie's face twisted in despair.

O held out her hand toward me in a cajoling gesture, smiling as I let her long fingers envelop mine. "I've always told you I live for my art, Helena, dear, and that's never been a lie. I don't want children or a home of my own. My art is my home, don't you see? I want *freedom*, and Geraint gives me that."

"But he's not free." I withdrew my hand from O's grasp.

"He's never gone behind Millie's back. He lives his life according to principles that he decided upon before I came along and that he made clear before he married her."

"Yes, his sons told me about his 'principles.'"

"And you don't approve."

"I think it all sounds very nice and convenient—if only it hurt nobody. But there are other people involved."

"He *is* very fond of Millie, you know. You saw how he deferred to her in the end." A small frown appeared between Odelia's straight eyebrows. "And *she* sees him every day. Geraint and I spend most of our lives apart—but that's what makes every moment a delight when we're together, whether that's in public or alone." A smile lightened her face as if in response to a sweet memory. "He has always been the most generous of men, and we have lived without jealousy or possessiveness or rancor for fifteen years." She shrugged. "I'm not his only lover, you know."

"They told me."

"Well, then. If it weren't me, it would be somebody else. Do you begrudge me my happiness? I'm a fortunate woman."

"You didn't seem happy yesterday," I said.

"I made a fool of myself yesterday." O's hand curled into a fist, her rings glinting blue and green and red. "I'm angry with myself for discovering I couldn't walk away when he told me he needed me. It's the first time I've seen him weak, you see—those damned drugs of Shelbourne's. Believe me, Helena, *I* would never touch them. I woke up well before dawn worrying that Geraint will be disappointed in me."

"Has he harmed himself before?"

"Never." The word came out fast and vehement. "But he's been low in spirits lately. The *Nightingale* idea's been positively haunting him, to the point where he has trouble concentrating on his other work, and it's been making him miserable. Or perhaps it's his money troubles—but he's always had those. He lives generously. Money slips through his fingers no matter how much he earns. Having three grown sons is expensive too, and they expect to live like gentlemen. Geraint *is* a baronet after all. I think it all got too much for him suddenly. I've seen that mood—fey and dangerous. Usually, he can channel it into his work." She bowed her head, pushing her fingers into her thick dark blond hair. "I keep thinking, has he injured his hands? I couldn't stand it."

"I think the cuts were superficial, or they'd have bled more. And he was using his hands fairly normally." I chewed the inside of my lip, thinking. "What he really needs is a private asylum. If his nerves have become overwrought, he requires a complete rest. Millie should have the assurance that he won't try to hurt himself again."

"Do you think Millie injured herself badly?" O looked anxious. "She's a tremendously skilled artist in her own right. Just the applied arts, of course, but very good."

"Does she help Sir Geraint in his profession?"

"Of course not." O looked almost shocked. "Morris and

Burne-Jones are always extolling the virtues of the decorative arts, but Geraint believes fine art does not stoop to ally itself with decoration." Her face brightened. "Except, I suppose, for *The Nightingale*, but the idea there is that the entire room becomes the frame in quite an exciting way."

"You people always seem to bend your principles to fit what you want to do." I stood, too restless to remain seated any longer. "O, I don't want to judge, but how can you stand it? To sit around waiting for a man till he calls for you, like a parcel? And supposing—" My hand flew to my mouth at the thought that had just entered my head. "No, I shouldn't ask. I'm sorry."

Odelia was silent for a good two minutes as I paced the floor, my heels sounding on the polished wood and well-worn rugs. *I won't pry*, I swore to myself. *I won't ask.*

I didn't have to.

"I might have known you'd get round to thinking of *that*." O paused as the various clocks in the house struck the half hour at reasonably close intervals. "No, you don't have any nephews or nieces that you don't know about." She was silent for a few more moments before suddenly saying: "You have Mama's herb books. Are you aware exactly how skilled she was?"

I froze. O's words had the inevitability of a whispered utterance in a nightmare. Yes, I knew how skilled Mama was. I had seen her hidden confession that she had killed our father . . . *Ab irato, lex talionis*. Revenge out of anger. But I didn't think Odelia knew that. I weighed my words, knowing all the while where our conversation was leading.

"I realize her journals stopped at a fairly early stage," I said. "At the time of the row over Mrs. Batch-Crocker."

"You know about that?" Odelia raised her eyebrows. "My goodness."

"The twins told me. They said Papa threatened to take

Michael and me away if she made a fuss. After that, she wrote nothing down." She had incorporated her confession into one of her superb botanical paintings, and Michael had found it.

"They also told me," I continued, "that you used the events of that year to persuade our parents to let you live at Scott House. I used to pray for you to return." I felt the sting of remembered pain. "But you never came to see me—you barely even wrote—except for that time when I was twelve and you came to Hyrst because you were ill." A memory from that incident crowded into my mind. Another time when I had been slighted, and which until then I had forgotten. "Mama wouldn't let me see you, and I was hurt because I'd been helping her in the herb room and saw myself as a healer."

I was creeping closer and closer to a secret that I could have guessed at if I'd been less naïve. As in a nightmare, I had no choice but to press on, to open the door I didn't want to see behind. I stared at O, feeling prickles of horror on the nape of my neck. Why had she come to Hyrst just then? And then she spoke, and I was certain.

"I didn't tell Geraint." There was something like shame in my sister's eyes. "He would have insisted I have the child since he always wanted more children. Mama seemed like my only hope." She raised her chin defiantly. "I chose my art over my womanhood, Helena. I never regretted it. And Mama agreed with me. She said she would use poison to cure poison."

"She saw a baby—her own grandchild—as *poison*?" I felt numb, sick.

"Not the child itself." Odelia shook her head slowly, almost sadly. "It was the hold people would have over me because of it. Mama certainly hadn't recovered from Papa threatening to take you and Michael away. She was the old

Mama on the surface, but something had changed in her. Something deep. 'Hold on to your liberty,' I remember her saying. 'I will help you sacrifice to the one cause worth upholding.' Whatever she gave me made me very ill. I've often wondered if she was trying to teach me a lesson."

"I tried to see you several times." My voice shook. "I thought you might die and I'd never see you again."

Mama stood before me in my memory, tall and slender, her bright blue eyes stern. *I don't want to see you here again, Helena.* But I had defied her, creeping in one night to watch Odelia sleep. *That* was the core of the nightmare, the memory of darting, terrified, under the bed when I heard footsteps. Sick at my want of obedience yet defiant because I loved Odelia so very much.

"I thought I might die too, at one point." O shrugged. "But here I am. Mama gave me some sort of tisane to drink afterward to prevent any more accidents. I drank it until she became vague and forgot to send it. But by then the cure was complete, and I've never been troubled by motherhood again."

13

POISONOUS WORDS

Unsurprisingly, Odelia's revelations lowered my mood. I spent the rest of that day alternately staring out of the window and trying to catch up with my correspondence, somewhat neglected because of Michael's visit and O's flight to Holland Park.

It was a long time ago, I told myself repeatedly. What was the point of moping over past events I hadn't even known had happened? But it felt to me as if another tentacle from my family's past had stretched into the present to slither around my shoulders, cold and clinging. Another event at which I had been physically present but entirely oblivious to the truth.

Odelia had climbed the stairs to her studio at the top of the house after breakfast, and I didn't know whether she was working or dozing in a chair. She didn't appear at luncheon. I spent the morning and the start of the afternoon in solitude, afraid to leave the house in case Odelia returned to Holland Park despite her assurances that she would not do so.

By the late afternoon, I had finally battled my way

through my correspondence and settled down in one of the drawing room's more comfortable chairs to read. The day was darkening, but it had been a splendid late October afternoon, and I had refreshed myself by spending time in the garden watching the yellowed leaves fall from the trees and the birds flitting from branch to branch, bush to bush, surveying my activities with their shiny black eyes. Now, in the late hush of the afternoon, with the candelabras and lamps reflected in ancient mirrors and polished paneling and a busy fire crackling in the grate, I at last felt safe and content. Scotty slept next to me, a solid and comforting presence.

When the latch clicked and Odelia walked in, I greeted her with a wide smile. Scotty barked excitedly, like me happy to have company at last. O came straight to me, putting a warm arm around my shoulders and bending to kiss me.

"Are we friends?" she asked.

"You don't have to ask." I put an arm around her neck. "I won't let this come between us, O."

"Even if I ask you about the commission? Because I'll be honest with you, Helena. That's what's been on my mind nearly all day." She was disengaging herself from me as she spoke, seating herself in her usual spot on the settee. "I thought now might be a chance to ask without the servants around." She hesitated. "I'm hoping very much that you'll tell me you won't let personal matters interfere with your decision."

I gave myself time to think, carefully putting a ribbon into the book I was reading and placing the volume on the small table beside me. "At the risk of sounding like Michael," I said eventually, "isn't it rather illogical to even discuss the commission right now? It entirely depends on Sir Geraint's health. His *continued* health. I hadn't really thought before how dependent such a scheme is on one man, and now he's . . . ill. For how long, none of us can tell. I'm not talking about his hands, although whether his actions have injured his ability to work is an entirely unknown factor. It's clear to me he also needs rest, mentally and spiritually. We must give him time. I wrote to them, by the way."

"You did?" There was a conscious look on Odelia's face, and then she clearly decided to be honest with me. "I wrote to Geraint too. To apologize for irritating Millie and thus upsetting him."

"It's Millie to whom you should apologize."

"Not as far as I'm concerned. But I don't want to argue the merits of the case. What did you say to Geraint?"

"I wrote to both of them, expressing my best wishes for Sir Geraint's health and making the conventional offer to call on me for any help they think I could give. I inquired after Millie's hand and sent various creams and salves over with instructions on how they should be used. Guttridge and I have had enough experience with burns, bruises, scrapes, and cuts among the servants by now to gauge their efficacy." I smiled. "Perhaps that's all I'll ever be good for as an herbalist."

"And perhaps that's enough." Odelia rested her head on one hand, gazing at me. "I'm not at all sure I want you to become a second Mama."

"I just wish I could do something for Sir Geraint's state of mind." I frowned. "I must do some research into herbs for disorders of the mental state. Clearly, it's not an area that can be approached willy-nilly." As I so often did, I felt the prick of longing to discuss the question with Fortier. It was frustrating that the one person I'd found who had the experience and knowledge to be a real mentor was now almost entirely absent from my life.

"We should wait until Sir Geraint has spent a month or

two at a private asylum," I insisted. "You know it would do him good. Can't you suggest that to him?"

"Asylums cost a lot of money." Odelia's expressive mouth tightened into a straight line. "As I said, Geraint's short on funds. You have to understand that an artist's life is a matter of feast or famine. Geraint spent a lot of money on having that house built when he was doing really well, but now fashions are changing, and clients can be so dreadfully fickle. He still sells more than most people—he's always going to be one of the great painters of his generation—but he's getting fewer of the really large commissions, the sort of money he can invest. And those boys of his have been horribly expensive of late."

"So you said." I felt impatient that Odelia was so concerned with Sir Geraint's income. "But—"

"There've been some letters from tradesmen in Oxford recently, the sort one can't ignore, about Edmund's bills." O continued talking, heedless of my interruption. "That boy's got no conscience whatsoever. And Geraint gave Phil a lot of money to set himself up in a studio in a fashionable part of Kensington. I agree you can't expect people of caliber to slum it when they go to have their portrait painted, and going to their houses is tedious, but I think Phil gets far better treatment than he should because of his expectations. Living up to his baronetcy is half of Geraint's problem, if you ask me. And then Galahad wants to travel, and Geraint won't give him shorter shrift than his brothers just because he's younger. It's a mercy the other two are daughters—only Cassiope's dowry was stupendous, and now I suppose he'll feel he has to do the same for Jane."

After knowing too little about Odelia's life for years, I was apparently now going to know too much. I held up a hand as she drew breath. "I have no intention of interfering," I said as gently as I could. "But," my voice strengthened, "I couldn't possibly make any kind of decision while Sir Geraint is ill. If I made any decision at all, it should be to have nothing to do with him in the future, so I'm being more than fair in waiting until he's better." I reached out a hand toward my sister. "I love you, O, and I want you to be happy, but I don't want to get dragged into this mess."

WE DID NOT DISCUSS SIR GERAINT AGAIN OVER THE NEXT FEW days. Neither, to my surprise, did Odelia make any attempt to go to Holland Park. I was sure she was writing to Sir Geraint, but whether she received any replies was beyond my ken. I was content to let the matter drop and quietly planned my return to Littleberry in good time to arrange some sort of Christmas celebration for the family.

The fine weather of late October gave way to a sobbing, blustering November. Odelia and I were more often indoors, our accustomed walks around the parks and shops curtailed by the rain and wind. One particularly bad afternoon, we had donned our most comfortable tea gowns and were sitting companionably by the drawing room fire when the after- noon post arrived.

"Julia confirms Michael won't return to Town till February," I told Odelia, who had tossed her own letters aside while she worked on a sketch of me. "I'd like to tell her I'll be back in Littleberry by the last week of the month, if you don't mind. Or would you prefer I stay a little longer?"

"You must do as you please." O's voice sounded detached, her mind on her drawing, but after a few moments her pencil stilled and she looked up, grinning. "That sounded wrong. I mean, I'm delighted to have you here, but I won't detain you. I know you miss the rest of the family."

"I do, rather." I read a little more of Julia's letter. "Julia swears she can see Julius's first tooth, and Annabelle Alice drew a picture of a dog for me. Look." I held up the sheet of paper so that Odelia could see the drawing.

"That's a dog?"

"She's only two and a half, O." I opened another letter and read some of it before looking up again. "Thomas writes that Mama is in good health and seems to like the rain on her windows." Feeling stiff, I yawned and stretched.

"No, go back to the way you were." Odelia frowned in mock annoyance. "I was trying to capture that dreamy look in your eyes. Go back to reading your letters."

"Am I going to end up as one of your medieval ladies?" I asked.

"I was thinking of doing a proper portrait of you."

"Slumped in a chair? How modern."

"Well, I might arrange a better pose." O smiled, her eyes on the paper as she added a few more strokes. "See?" She held up the sheet so I could see it.

"You've made me look too pretty."

"You *are* pretty. It's nice to work with a model." Odelia carefully put the sketch into the portfolio she had brought downstairs with her and reached for her letters. "Ah, here's one from Blanche. Did she write to you?"

"I had one from her last week. I hope she's not telling you about the Scottish laird she wants to introduce to me."

"He doesn't sound too bad." Odelia sniggered. "Only forty-three. And a sizable estate with a grouse moor, just fancy. Think of all the house parties."

"Scotland's cold, and I'd never see anyone from the family. Besides, I'm not leaving Whitcombe House."

"That shows a little sense." Odelia slid her letter opener under the seal on the next envelope. "This one's a bill from my dressmaker. I can safely ignore it for another month."

"Poor woman. Oh, look!" I waved the letter I had just opened at her. "An invitation from Gabrielle Dermody."

"Who? Oh, the Frenchman's sister. Why is *she* writing to you?"

"We're friends, I told you. She's in Town. She invites me—in fact, she invites the two of us, since she knows I'm staying with you—to her father's house in Kensington Square on Thursday. Will you come?"

"Kensington Square? The Burne-Joneses were living there when I first came to London." A reminiscent smile flitted over Odelia's face. "I was so excited to meet Edward Burne-Jones. It was at their house that I first saw Geraint." A shadow replaced the smile for a brief moment. "I suppose I could bear to sit and sip tea with Monsieur Fortier senior, if only for the fun of imagining what Blanche would say. What do you think he is? A banker?"

"What an absurd notion."

"A merchant, then. No doubt retired. His son and daughter appear to have had an excellent education, so let's say a well-to-do retired merchant." Her face brightened. "I could speak French with him, perhaps. My French is getting rusty and requires exercise." She picked up the next envelope. "What's this now? Not another bill, I hope."

"I'll write to Gabrielle straightaway, accepting her invitation for both of us." I stood up, stretching. "I've ordered a dozen new pens, by the way. The nibs on yours all seem to have spread."

I had put aside the best pen the day before and was trying to remember where I'd hidden it when I heard Odelia say my name. Her voice was so strange I left off searching.

"What is it?"

"I suppose you'd better read this. Be prepared, though. Some of the language is very vulgar." She rose, holding out a single sheet of paper. "I didn't know people really sent letters like this. I thought they only existed in novels."

I took the paper from her. "'How long will you get away with it, you—'" I stopped reading. "Good heavens, I've never actually seen that word written down."

"Good old Anglo-Saxon, as Papa would say." Odelia's voice wasn't quite steady. "Read on."

"'A dirty . . . like you deserves to' . . . *Ugh.*" My lips moved silently as I read the rest of the brief message, which was quite specific as to the fate Odelia deserved.

"What horrible filth." I stared at the paper. It was itself quite clean, but I felt soiled by my contact with it. "Have you ever received any of these before?"

"Of course not." Odelia's voice was high and strained. "It's from Millie, I'm sure of it. She's finally gone insane."

"You can't just accuse Millie without proof. Besides, she's hurt her hand." I turned the piece of paper over but it was blank on the other side, so I turned it back. The disgusting message was written in capital letters with a heavy pencil. All the lines were straight, giving letters that would normally be rounded an angular appearance, and the writer had gone over the lines several times.

"Let me see the envelope, O." I held out my hand. "Yes, the letters are formed in the same way. The address is written correctly, and there are no spelling mistakes—so the writer and the sender are one and the same, and they've had an education. I would say they were trying to disguise their handwriting as much as possible."

"In other words, someone who knows me sent it. Such as Millie. Writing it with her left hand, perhaps. After all, she's quite skilled with her hands, and one can practice."

"Would a woman describe the mutilations this vile person has dreamed up? They specifically involve the removal of your, well, female attributes." I shuddered. "Perhaps we should go to the police."

"But that bit about my creeping into men's beds . . . The police are bound to ask me questions I don't want to answer." Odelia shook her head. "No, Helena, not the police. I'll put it in the fire."

"Don't." I tightened my grip on the paper. "Let me keep it for the time being, in case you get more. And perhaps I should stay a bit longer—or should you come back to Littleberry with me? I don't like to think of leaving you alone here now I've seen that."

Odelia smiled, the tension in her voice quite gone. "If the walls and gates of Scott House can't protect me, then I don't think you'll be able to. Keep the dirty thing if you wish, as long as you hide it from the servants." She bent to kiss me. "Bless you for wanting to keep me safe—but don't forget, I've been on my own for seventeen years. The imaginings of a deranged mind hold no terrors for me."

14

KENSINGTON SQUARE

I did my best to put the nasty letter out of my mind. I hid it well, so not even Guttridge would see it. Odelia seemed to have forgotten it altogether. When we visited the Fortier house in Kensington Square on Thursday, she was in excellent form.

"I'm so glad you included me in the invitation." Odelia leaned back against the striped silk of an Empire sofa, looking superbly at ease. "I can finally say I've met somebody from Littleberry—outside my family, naturally—whom I actually like. It always astonishes me that our town can offer so little in the way of culture."

"You're quite wrong, Lady Odelia." Gabrielle, looking beautiful in a gown of ivory silk with lilac trimmings, laughed as she pulled out a book. "There's plenty of culture and sense to be had in Littleberry. You just have to know where to find it."

"If you say so." Odelia rose to see what Gabrielle had selected. "And do call me O. I can't be bothered with titles when I'm in the company of cultivated people."

We had drunk our coffee in the library amid the pleasant

smell of old book leather and spicy potpourri. A fire blazed against the November chill, lighting up the gilding behind the bookcases' glass fronts. Heavy silk drapes shut out the beating of the rain against the window and the genteel traffic sounds of Kensington Square. I had liked the elegant yet unostentatious house immediately; it had a timeless and comfortable feel to it, with books and paintings very much in evidence.

"There." Gabrielle laid down the enormous book, one of a large collection of tomes about Egypt that took up almost an entire bookcase, and opened it to a bookmarked page. "On this column we see lotus, on this papyrus, and on this palm leaves. Sir Frederic Leighton says . . ."

I quickly lost the thread of my companions' conversation about the rhythm of decorative elements, an artistic technicality that eluded me. That did not bother me since I wanted time to think. The voices of the other women soothed me, like gentle music flowing over the jagged edges of my tangled thoughts.

By this time, we had been in the house for an hour. Gabrielle's greeting had been as warm as I had expected. She and Odelia had taken to each other from the start, and even the news that Monsieur Fortier senior was too ill to see visitors that day had not disturbed my equilibrium beyond my natural feeling of concern for the invalid. No, it was the words "Armand is with him" that had apparently overthrown my common sense.

Odelia had been behind me at that moment, and I had almost felt the heat of her gaze on the back of my neck. "Oh, is your brother here?" she had immediately asked. "I thought he was in France. Do give him my regards."

I had pulled myself together. "Yes, and mine too," I had said. "When did he return?"

"Only yesterday afternoon. He asked me to apologize for

not being here to greet you, but he won't leave Papa's side until he can make him quite comfortable. It dismayed Armand to find him in such pain. He only snatched three or four hours' sleep last night, and I practically had to push him out of Papa's room this morning to wash and have breakfast."

"What's wrong with your father?" It was like Odelia to ask such a question outright where I hesitated to pry.

"He has a growth—a cancer—in the middle of his back," Gabrielle had answered with no less frankness. "It causes him much pain. Armand fears it is partly in the spine, and although he would operate if Papa asked him to do so, he doesn't believe it would do much good and could make matters worse. In any case, Papa does not want an operation. He doesn't have much time left."

We had spoken words of sympathy and comfort, and Gabrielle had soon rallied. She had ordered coffee, and our conversation had been lively and absorbing, but now, left to my own devices, I was scolding myself inwardly.

Of course I was going to see Fortier eventually. What kind of schoolgirl behavior was it to blush every time the library door opened to admit a servant? Perhaps the problem was that I had simply not expected to see him in London. On my own ground in Littleberry, I might have been more prepared to greet him the way I wanted to, as a friend and nothing more.

Gabrielle had informed me that Fortier was shocked to find himself in love with me, so perhaps he would also find our meeting awkward. The reflections to which I had been prey over the last few weeks, whenever I was unoccupied or couldn't sleep, had led to the conclusion that there was no insult intended by his misgivings. He was taking a rational approach to what could, after all, be just a passing infatuation.

I, on the other hand, was being highly inconsistent. I

wanted Fortier to leave me alone while I got on with the business of being a widow. Hadn't I insisted I needed time to think? And yet I craved his presence with the silly, sick longing of a heroine in a novel. It was fortunate I did not possess a handkerchief of his or a nosegay he had given me that I could preserve by pressing inside a heavy book. I might easily have made a fool of myself by sighing in secret over some idiotic memento. Wearing a scrap of ribbon next to my heart because he had once touched it, for example. It was a short step from such jejune behavior to falling helplessly into a man's arms behind some garden arbor on a warm June night.

Seen objectively, the trouble was that, as Gerry had so perceptively remarked, I liked men. It was a source of great annoyance to me, in the still watches of several dozen sleepless nights, to realize how much I missed certain aspects of marriage. It meant I couldn't entirely trust my own reactions to Fortier. Was it that he was the first—the only—attractive man I'd spent time with since Justin?

I sighed, gazing around the room. There were the possible—or likely—objections on my family's part to contend with, of course. Gerry had married a merchant, but Ned's relations were not outsiders in the county the way the Fortiers were.

And yet this house spoke of a family history of wealth and refinement. I was too well trained by Mama not to miss the signs that the Fortiers were perhaps not the upstart merchants of Odelia's imagination. Nothing in these surroundings was too perfect or too new. Everything I could see reflected taste and discrimination that would not look out of place in any English manor. Not that this room was English in appearance, but in these days of antimacassars and violently patterned wallpaper, a lack of Englishness could present an advantage.

I had just reached this evaluation of the room's appearance when the door opened and Fortier stepped in. I started like a visitor caught looking at the backs of the paintings for auction labels. It was only Mama's expert schooling in lady-like behavior that prevented me from leaping up and putting my hands behind my back in an attitude of culpability. My palms positively perspired from the effort of remaining still.

Fortier's gaze went immediately to me, and I glimpsed delight in their green-gold depths. But then the thick lashes swept down over the remarkable irises, extinguishing their light as he adjusted the setting of a cuff before speaking.

"The coffee is finished, I suppose? I'm disappointed to have missed it. But it's pleasant to walk in on such a comfortable scene. Lady Helena, I'm glad to see you in good health."

He had bowed over my hand in his slightly Continental fashion and moved on to Odelia before I had time to say anything. He then bestowed a brotherly kiss on Gabrielle's cheek. She, naturally, rang the bell for more coffee.

Once the business of ordering was over, Fortier, having watched us sit down, seated himself in the largest armchair with the air of a squire making himself at home in his own parlor. In a dark morning coat and striped trousers, he looked both out of character and perfectly in tune with our surroundings.

"I hope you're enjoying London," Fortier said to me.

Had I waited four months for this mundane conversational gambit? Two could play at that game.

"The weather has been atrocious." Out of the corner of my eye, I saw Odelia bite her lip to suppress a grin. "But of course, Town is always interesting. We were thinking of going to Madame Tussaud's waxworks to see the figure of the Khedive of Egypt."

"Is your father feeling a little better?" O gave me a

quelling look as she spoke, and I remembered where Fortier had been.

"Is he in a great deal of pain?" I asked, feeling a pang of remorse.

My question seemed to deflate Fortier a little. I noticed he was a mite thinner and that there were faint shadows under his eyes, but he spoke cheerfully enough.

"I've finally succeeded with the morphine." He looked directly at me as he spoke, and not for the first time I thrilled at his tone, the ease of a medical man discussing a case with a colleague. "The problem is to get the exact dosage and manner of injection right, and there have been changes since I last saw him." Turning, he smiled reassuringly at Gabrielle. "He's reading, Gaby, so he can't be feeling that bad now. He's delighted with the books I brought back from France. Where are the children?"

"Gertrude took them to the zoological gardens to see the elephant." Her brow creased. "Do you think I should send them home to Littleberry, Armand? Or should they—should they stay?"

Her voice was unsteady. Odelia and I looked at one another, knowing that politeness dictated we should leave.

"It has been quite delightful, but we must be going." O's smile was warm. "You are very good to invite us here at such a time, Mrs. Dermody."

I held out my hands to Gabrielle, and she took them as we both stood up. Behind her, Fortier was looking directly at me, and it was an effort not to return his gaze. I concentrated on Gabrielle, drawing her closer to me.

"If there's anything I can do for your father . . . or you," I said quietly. "I wish I had realized he was so ill."

Odelia had begun to talk with Fortier, and Gabrielle drew me away from the two of them. "You must come back soon and meet him when Armand has made him more comfortable," she said. "I'm so relieved my brother is back. To see Papa struggle with the pain brings back too many memories of our mother's deathbed."

"I will come back as often as you ask me," I promised her, and we embraced warmly. She went to summon a servant to go in search of my carriage, and I watched Fortier and Odelia discuss a painting of a young man in armor until it was time for us to leave.

"That was a refreshing change," said Odelia as we settled into our respective corners of the carriage bench. "Did you realize what that portrait was?"

"I missed that part of the conversation. Was it something exciting?"

"No less than a Rubens. Not a major work, but my goodness—I'm glad to have seen it. Your handsome Frenchman is now even more of a mystery to me."

"As he is to me. And he's not mine."

"He would be if you let him. But I admire your determination to make him wait."

"Could we change the subject, please?"

"If we must." Odelia stretched her long arms and rolled her shoulders, then threw herself back into the seat with a pleased expression. "I enjoyed that. I needed cheering up after all that's happened. What do you say to actually *going* to Madame Tussaud's tomorrow? I will bring my sketching materials."

15

PAINT, SOOT, AND LONDON MUD

I awoke the next morning looking forward to our outing. Odelia seemed determined to put the episode in Holland Park behind her, and I was glad of it. She had talked with animation at dinner of the book Gabrielle had shown her and we had parted for an early night with an affectionate kiss.

Even the weather had improved, with gleams of sunshine occasionally breaking through the massed, turbulent clouds. From my bedroom window, Scott House's walled garden looked cheerfully autumnal, the red-and-orange leaves of its neatly trimmed shrubs shivering in the breeze.

"I thought you'd like breakfast straightaway," was Guttridge's greeting as she entered with my tray. "Lady Odelia was up very early, painting, and has had her tray sent up to the studio. She left word that she promises to be ready by eleven."

"Then I have plenty of time to linger over breakfast." Pleased, I reached for my copy of *The Portrait of a Lady.* "Don't rush to prepare my bath."

I lingered lovingly over my food and was deep in my

novel, nibbling on toast and marmalade and drinking my coffee, when Guttridge returned.

"I'm not quite finished," I told her. She had, contrary to my instructions, "rushed back," and it was hard enough to concentrate on James's famed style without interruptions. I would definitely lose the thread of the story if I put the book down now, and I wanted to understand why the heroine had accepted a proposal of marriage *after* she had inherited an independent fortune. I was sure her friends had steered her into the marriage, and the idea made me uncomfortable.

I realized after another few moments had passed that, contrary to what I would have expected, Guttridge was not busying herself with soap and towels, linen and brushes. I looked up, frowning.

"You're hovering, Guttridge. Is there something wrong?"

"Yes, my lady. Oh, nobody's hurt or—or disappeared." She picked up the book I had dropped on the floor. "But somebody has to be informed, and we thought it might be you. Lady Odelia's inclined to shout at the servants when they interrupt her painting. And besides, you have a more practical turn of mind."

Which meant, evidently, that *I* had to sacrifice my interests to Odelia's. I sighed as the thread of Henry James's plot slipped away. I was always bad at following plots and would probably have to read the last ten pages again.

"I'm listening." I drew my knees up into a more comfortable position as Guttridge removed my breakfast tray.

"Well, my lady, we only knew about it when the butcher's boy called for the week's order. Somebody has painted a word—a bad word—right across the gate. Starting and ending on the wall. I gave the lad a shilling not to gossip, but we'll have to get it taken off quickly."

"What's the word?"

"'Bitch,' my lady." Guttridge said the word without hesitation and with as little emotion as if she'd been talking about cabbages. "In letters six feet high and a good few inches thick."

"Oh dear." *Not entirely the same word as in the letter, but in the same spirit.*

"In red paint, my lady."

I put my hand to my brow, thinking hard. "That'll get into the newspapers. Lord Broadmere won't like it. Yes, I know he can't read the papers, but my sisters read the gossip columns and they'll make sure he knows about it . . . Bedsheets!"

"My lady?" It was satisfying to know that, for once, Guttridge wasn't thinking ahead of me.

"There are bound to be old bedsheets somewhere in this house. We can hang them so that they cover up as much as possible, can't we?" I pushed aside the bedclothes. "Get Mrs. Coles to put one of the maids to work—the footman too— and have the other maid bring up my hot water."

"Shouldn't we bring a constable to see it first?" Guttridge asked. "I'm that put out that the bobbies didn't catch the wicked scoundrels. What use is it for them to walk the beat if they can't see what's right under their noses? Right in the middle of St. James's too."

"I suppose we'll have to report it." I thought of the unreported letter, now safely hidden with my correspondence. "Very well, Guttridge, get my bath going and then look for a policeman. I'll be down to talk to him as soon as I'm washed and dressed. Don't disturb Lady Odelia."

THE WALL AROUND THE GROUNDS OF SCOTT HOUSE WAS OF very hard brick, mottled dull carnelian and brown and blackened unevenly by London's ubiquitous soot. Bristling iron spikes on wall and gate ensured the garden was more or less impenetrable to intruders.

The gate was a heavy sheet of iron, ornamented with complicated scrollwork and studded bands of more iron. Ancient, heavy, and ponderous, it bore the Scott crest worked intricately into the design. Generations of thick black paint covered it, blurring the scrollwork and presenting the outside world with a forbidding appearance.

By the time I got downstairs, Mrs. Coles had had the presence of mind to send the butcher's boy, who was quite willing to interrupt his morning's work for an extra coin, to Vauxhall for the gardener. The latter had arrived in a cart with the butcher's boy, two of his sons, and some large rolls of hessian. The men were busy using the coarse cloth to cover the paint, a far more elegant solution than the worn bedsheets I had suggested. Scotty, who had been running around them barking, suddenly caught the scent of something and darted back into the garden, no doubt to dig among the shrubbery while we were all busy.

With a brief greeting to the gardener, I went to inspect what I could still see of the damage. The red paint was still tacky. Unlike the black paint of the gate, it was shiny and unpleasantly vivid.

"We'll go to the oil shop of a feller I know d'rectly, m'lady." The gardener stood by me as I gingerly touched the red slick. "Take a while to get this lot orf, though." He hissed air through his remaining front teeth. "Nasty mess, this."

"Couldn't you paint over it?" I asked.

"It'll show, m'lady." He shook his head regretfully. "My boys'll repaint the 'ole fing after. Nate's a painter by trade." The gardener jerked a thumb toward his sons and then hooked the digit into his waistcoat.

"Very well." I turned my gaze to the wall, which bore quite a bit of the letters *B* and *H*, as well as several random splatters of paint. "I imagine it'll be difficult to erase every trace, but do the best you can."

"If they'd painted it hownly on the wall, it would've been a sight 'arder to deal with. They missed a hopportunity there, m'lady." The gardener puffed out his chest. "Don't you worry, we'll get most of it. 'Bout time this 'ere wall 'ad a cleaning. There's a mort of dirt on it. All of London tahn is covered in sut."

And having dismissed centuries of patina, he lifted his cap at me and called to his "boys," turning up his coat collar against the morning's chill.

"The constable's gone to fetch his sergeant." Guttridge hove into view, pulling her heavy cape tighter around her. "Shall we go inside, my lady? It's perishing out here."

"And it looked like such a nice morning earlier." I looked up at the clouds, which by now had darkened to an unpleasant gray that let no sunlight through. "You know, Guttridge, Lady Odelia always says Sussex is dreary in the winter, but I find London far worse. The gardener's right; all London Town is covered in soot." I looked down at my feet. "And mud—if this *is* mud I'm stepping in." I scraped at the dense, gritty substance under my feet with the toe of my boot. "I'm beginning to miss Sussex."

"Yes, the mud there has a much cleaner look to it." Guttridge grinned. "Come on in, my lady, there's a nice fire in the drawing room."

"THERE'S A GENTLEMAN WAITING TO SEE YOU, M'LADY, NOW you've finished with the police sergeant. Are you at home?"

The footman was holding a small silver salver with a card on it. I recognized it at once. I had intended to declare myself not at home to visitors—in the circumstances, I would rather not have to answer questions—but I changed my mind.

"I'm at home to Monsieur Fortier, George. Just give me five minutes and then show him into the drawing room."

"Mrs. Coles says to inform you that Lady Odelia sent down to ask for her luncheon on a tray now that you won't be going out after all." George, who was rather on the short side for a footman—thus only entitled to a lower rate of pay—spoke to a spot somewhere behind my left shoulder. I longed to be back home with my own servants, who were far better trained than those at Scott House. "Mrs. Coles says Lady Odelia sends her apologies, but—" he thought furiously for a moment, and then his brow cleared as he remembered the message. "Inspiration has struck, and she does not wish to be disturbed. Would you like your luncheon in here, m'lady? Mrs. Coles thought we could lay a place for you at the small table."

I imagined my solitary luncheon and Odelia painting upstairs. Then my own inspiration struck.

"No, lay the table for two in the dining room. I'm sure my visitor will join me."

"I'M SORRY TO DISTURB YOU AT SUCH AN AWKWARD TIME OF day." At his entrance, Fortier's attention was distracted by a wildly excited Scotty, and the interlude seemed to put both of us at our ease—or perhaps I was wrong in thinking Fortier felt as I did?—so that by the time my dog had calmed down we were ready to greet each other as friends. His opening remark, however, was not promising.

"I'm going to be very sorry if you keep making banal speeches." I made a wry face to soften the impact of my words and saw Fortier's lips curl up in response. How long was it since we had conversed alone? I missed the freedom of the countryside and the comfort of being on my home ground.

"I'm still thinking in French," Fortier confessed, his smile warming me. "It always happens when I've been over there for a while. I keep having to suppress the urge to add in a few flowery linguistic flourishes that would make me sound like a horrible pastiche of a French dandy speaking bad English, so I fall back on conventional English phrases. I'll be over it in a few days."

"We could speak French," I said in that language.

"Of course, you speak my language very well. But," he switched back to English, laughing, "you're not helping me. Kindly be the Englishwoman you are and help me remember which country I'm in. What's happening at your gate?"

"I'll tell you in a moment. The hour is very late, the morning has been trying, and I'm hungry, so if you want to talk to me, you'll also have to eat with me. Odelia isn't coming down since apparently inspiration has struck. Living with an artist can be very trying. Or was it O to whom you wanted to speak? I thought you were getting on rather well yesterday." I smiled to show him I was not so petty as to resent his attentions to my sister.

Fortier's easy laugh made him look far less careworn than on the previous day. "Do you really want me to have luncheon with you?"

"If I said so, I must have meant it." I felt rather pleased with myself. "The footman will be in attendance, so let's exchange as much news as we can beforehand. Is everything all right in France?"

"Everything is perfectly damnable in France." He waited for me to sit before seating himself, and again it struck me as odd to see him in city dress of pinstripe trousers and a dark gray morning coat.

"I'm glad to be home," he said. "At least I'd rather be back in Littleberry. Obviously, I can't leave because of my father, but finding you in Town definitely makes London feel more homelike. Although it's strange to see you here and not in the country. You look different."

"I was thinking the same of you," I admitted. "Did you return because of your father?"

Fortier nodded. "I wish I'd returned sooner. He's been dosing himself, entirely inappropriately, trying to hide the extent of his suffering from the servants. When I received Gaby's letter describing his condition, my choice was made for me, thank God, and I've arrived in time to be able to help him a great deal. I was just a small child, and powerless, when my mother died of consumption, but now I can be his ally in battle." His eyes darkened. "We will not win the fight, but I will make his end easier for him."

Dismay suffused me. "I'm so sorry to hear you say that. How terrible for you and Gabrielle."

"We've been through it before." His lips twitched, his gaze on me. "My earliest memory is of the terror of impending, inevitable loss. Who knows?" He shrugged. "Perhaps that was what turned me toward medicine, the desire to save another small boy from experiencing that terror. My skills are useful now."

"Yet it will still be a great trial, I'm sure." It was hard to find the right words. "Death has always been sudden for me. I can't imagine what it's like to know what's coming. Doesn't that knowledge make it worse?"

Fortier seemed to consider the question for a moment. "I've been present at more deathbeds than I can remember," he said slowly at last. "Worse? I suppose I've learned that death comes in all different forms, but we all have to face it at some time or the other. I'm no longer the little boy who would scream when they took me away from my mother—

and my father is a courageous man." He smiled suddenly. "So your gate? Or do you wish to relate the tale with the footman listening? It looked to me as if someone had thrown paint all over it."

"Someone painted a vile word on it." I tried to make my tone unconcerned. Fortier had enough to worry about after all.

"Have you made an enemy? Or has Lady Odelia?"

It instantly annoyed me somehow that he had guessed so near the truth. Although, of course, I had no reason to be certain that the word on the gate was connected with the poisonous letter Odelia had received.

"I imagine it's just some deranged person who doesn't like the fact we have a large house."

"*I* imagine you're not being quite truthful with me."

"Well, perhaps a few secrets are a good idea. You're not going to tell me about France, are you?"

"*Touché.*" Fortier's lips twisted in an ironic grimace, but then he smiled again. "So here we are, friends prevented by loyalty from telling each other our secrets. We *are* friends, aren't we? Or has that changed since I left? I thought we parted friends."

My truculence melted at the look in his eyes. Truth to tell, something else inside me melted as well, but this was no time to behave like the heroine of a silly romantic novel. I summoned up the brisk, no-nonsense tone that was my best defense against the attraction I unequivocally felt.

"Gabrielle told me you preferred to meet as friends, and I quite agree. I don't suppose our paths will cross all that often."

Fortier, his gaze still fixed on me, quoted softly:

"Ships that pass in the night, and speak each other in passing,
　　Only a signal shown and a distant voice in the darkness;

So on the ocean of life we pass and speak one another,
Only a look and a voice, then darkness again and a silence."

"How terribly lonely you make it sound, Helena. But I will have to be content with meeting you, when our paths cross, with pleasure. Only—let's agree not to be ships on the ocean forever, shall we? *'O lost hours and days in which we might have been happy,'* and all that. Eventually, every ship has to seek its harbor."

The arrival of the footman to announce—with a careless air that did not augur well for his career—that luncheon was served was a blessed relief. Or possibly a jarring interruption.

With servants present, our conversation ran along conventional lines. Fortier pronounced the soles *à la crême* and roast mutton—from Littleberry, of course—excellent.

I found it surprisingly easy to talk with him on ordinary subjects. Of course, we had Littleberry in common, and a small country town provides a wealth of opportunities for anecdotes of all kinds. I told Fortier about Michael's children, delighting when he responded with some tales of his own nephews and niece. It was tempting to tell him about Odelia's scheme for redecorating the drawing room at Whitcombe, but the events of the last two weeks made such a venture seem less likely, and besides, the topic would undoubtedly lead me into a tangled forest of admissions I would rather avoid. If Fortier was keeping some of his concerns private, I was at least as evasive as he.

And yet before we finished dessert, Fortier made a request or two that seemed designed to bring us closer together. After two or three spoonfuls of the refreshing concoction of orange slices and raisins soaked in brandy, he put down his spoon and addressed me with the formality necessitated by the presence of the servants.

"Lady Helena, could I beg the very great favor of introducing you to my father before you return to Littleberry?"

"Of course." It was not mere politeness that shaped the pleasure in my reply. "But I thought he was too unwell to receive visitors?"

"He's somewhat improved this morning. I think he may rally a little after a few days."

"Thanks to your care."

Fortier nodded. "I won't put on a display of false modesty about a matter so very dear to me," he said. "I am exerting all my skills to make him more comfortable." He hesitated. "I'm asking you as a friend, but I must also appeal to you as a colleague. Would you allow me to write to you, once you're back in Littleberry, with a few requests for extracts? Nothing you couldn't easily prepare in your herb room with what you have on hand or could harvest from the countryside. I have some preparations in mind for Father and would value your help."

I felt a thrill run through me at the word "colleague" that had little to do with Fortier's physical presence. He was talking to me as if I were a man, and a competent and knowledgeable man at that.

"I'd be delighted to help in any way I can," I said. "But surely there are herbalists in London? Men with far more expertise than I have."

"There are one or two I like to use. But it's not as easy as you'd think to get exactly what I want. They think they know better than I, and in general they do, but I like to use the preparations I learned about during the Siege of Paris. I know exactly what I'm doing with them, and I can trust you to follow my instructions exactly."

I nodded. "You can."

"Good." He looked round as the sound of the hallway clock striking two penetrated into the dining room. "Is it really so late? I'm sorry, Lady Helena, I must leave. Will you give my regards to Lady Odelia?"

I promised him I would and walked with him to the front door. The damp chill of London seemed less oppressive now, and I accompanied Fortier to the bottom of the steps.

"About your gate . . ." Fortier spoke in a low voice, glancing toward where the gardener's sons were industriously scrubbing the gate with turpentine, as evidenced by the sharp, piney smell that hung in the still air. "I hope I'm wrong and the paint is a mere act of vandalism. But if there is anything troubling you, Helena—you will come to me for help, won't you?" He bit his lip. "I don't even know why I'm saying this. Instinct, perhaps. But please don't let loyalty be your watchword to the exclusion of your friends. Don't put yourself in any kind of danger."

"Danger?" I shook my head vigorously. "There's nothing like that. Don't worry—"

"I know I shouldn't. But listen, my dear." He glanced back at the footman, who was standing by the open door with an expression of studied indifference. "I will try to give you a little of my own story, or at least let my father tell it as he likes to do. Some family background. In return, can you promise not to keep me in the dark about anything unpleasant or harmful?" He grasped my hand in his, a gesture not of farewell, but of protection. "Do we have a bargain?"

"I'm not sure what I'm bargaining for, but I trust you." I tried to smile. "As a friend."

"That's more than I hoped for." He turned his hold into a gentle shake of the hand, then let me go. "*Au revoir*, Lady Helena. I'll send a note when Father is well enough to meet you."

16

THE LADY IN THE TOWER

Odelia did not make an appearance until the paint had been vanquished by the combined efforts of the men and they had taken their leave in the failing November light, with a promise to repaint the gate the next day if there was no rain. She professed little alarm at the idea of the vandalism, dismissing it as "nonsense."

"It's almost certainly Millie making mischief. Who else would it be?" She grinned. "The question is, did she sneak up to our gate in the middle of the night herself, or did she have one of the boys do it?"

"It's not funny, O." I watched my sister help herself to more cold roast duck and winter salad. She was eating supper with the concentration of someone who had not eaten in a month. Her tendency to stare blankly at the wall behind me at intervals and frequently lose her train of thought informed me that artistic inspiration was still clutching her in its talons. In between these creative fugues, she was in her most maddening state of coolness. I quite understood how she could have driven Millie into a fury of frustration.

"It's all a storm in a teacup—it will blow over. Or maybe it really is just a random London madman with a spare pot of red paint." Odelia shrugged. "After all, Millie has put up with me for fifteen years."

"That's the part I don't understand." I knew I couldn't have borne it for fifteen days.

"That's because you know nothing about the artistic life." Odelia sighed. "What Geraint means to me is about far more than physical affection. Artists share on a higher plane, that of the intellect—and that's a country that has no borders, no possessiveness. For me, Geraint is the center of that world. You have no idea what an effort it's been to stop myself from going to his house these last two weeks. I began throwing myself into my work to prevent myself from thinking about him. I finished off some pieces I'd been doing, and then I went through my studio looking for something to pick up again, and *then*—well, perhaps there's something to be said for a change of routine."

"What are you working on?" I asked.

"Actually, it all started with Millie." Sated at last, Odelia leaned back in her chair and picked up her wineglass. "I found a very old sketch I'd done of her, seated at her loom— from back in the days when you could still call us friends, I suppose. I have always admired her work. Well, it made me think of the Lady of Shalott—you know, weaving her mazy web forever in her tower—and then I knew I had to capture the moment when the lady steps three paces away from her weaving to look at Lancelot with her own eyes instead of in the mirror. It was Lancelot I thought of when I saw the Rubens portrait at the Fortier house, the soldier with the ingenuous face and all that wild, curly hair. Of course, as soon as she stops weaving, the mirror cracks from side to side—"

"I thought that happened because she looked at Camelot, not because she stopped weaving."

"She had to stop weaving to look out of the window, didn't she?" Odelia made a face at me. "She's only three paces from the window, so it makes a nice composition. The point is, she awakens the curse, as one must never do in a fairy tale, and her beautiful woven creation flies loose from her loom. Real life destroys the dream—the mundanity of everyday love is the curse of art—and now she must leave her tower and go to her doom. The story nicely reflects all I've been feeling somehow, and the lady is taking shape so exactly, even without a model. I certainly haven't made her look like poor Millie. If anything, she resembles me a bit, but what does that matter if she's coming out just right? I believe this one will sell rather well."

"Do all your pictures start like that?" I was, for a moment, genuinely curious. "I can't imagine what it must be like to create something from nothing."

"The elements come together," Odelia said lazily, gazing at the reflections of the candlelight in her crystal glass. "I see something that makes me think of something else, and maybe I then see a possible setting, or I remember a poem or story, and somehow—" She gestured with her long fingers. "Suddenly, there's a picture in my head. Some parts are obvious and some vague, but it's as if it's speaking to me or—or showing itself to me, so that I just have to copy it. Geraint says it's like being in a dream but having the drawing materials with you in that dream."

Geraint again. All our conversations seemed to come back to the man, now that I knew about him. As if a sluice were cracking and buckling, ready to drown the land with the weight of the water behind it—only it was the weight of memories, of fifteen years spent together without a word to me.

But I dismissed that fleeting thought, focusing instead on the creative life of the sister I now realized I barely understood.

"To have all that happening in your head and none of it real," I mused. "It's beyond me. I love stories, but I can't imagine actually creating them, either in words or pictures. You're a little like the Lady of Shalott, O, living in your high tower and only seeing a reflection of the real world."

"That's rather clever of you." Odelia rewarded me with a brilliant smile. "I do live half in the real world and half in the world of my paintings, not to mention that I can become quite lost inside the art that others create. But how else would I live? My soul craves the company of like minds and the solace of beautiful things."

She took a sip of her wine and set the glass down, her gaze thoughtful. Then she seemed to emerge from a dream and smiled at me.

"You won't see much of me tomorrow, by the way. I must catch every shred of light. How I hate the November sky . . . I can leave that beastly gate to you, can't I? I know it's wrong of me to make you do everything, but if it were left to me, I'd probably just leave it as it is."

"No, you wouldn't because it's Michael's house, and you have to look after it for his and Julia's sake, and for James after him," I said severely.

"Hmph." Odelia dabbed delicately at her mouth with her napkin. "Sometimes I think I ought to move out of here and live in two rooms in Chelsea. Especially at times like these, when all I want to do is to be in the studio. I'll join you for meals, of course."

"Very kind of you," I said drily. "I'll be out tomorrow morning anyway. I thought I'd make some calls."

17

A FISHING EXPEDITION

"*D*oes Lady Dorrian-Knowles know we're coming?" Guttridge, whose principal job during our carriage ride was to safeguard the boxful of chrysanthemums—one of three boxes sent up from Littleberry on the milk train to decorate Scott House—looked at me curiously. It was unusual to be paying calls in the morning, especially on a Saturday, and I had sent no note, but the flowers had provided me with an excellent excuse for a visit.

"I thought we'd surprise the household." I breathed deep, relishing the sharp, almost medicinal scent of the flowers and longing to wander the greenhouses of Whitcombe House, where Taylor, my head gardener, would be busy bringing on orchids and putting the final touches to the neat rows of winter vegetables under glass.

Guttridge, who had opened the box of flowers to ensure they were still all right, left off stroking the cool petals with her fingertips. "You can tell me to mind my own business, of course, my lady, but does this have anything to do with the word painted on our gate? Mrs. Coles was speculating that whoever put it there might have something against Lady

Odelia. Of course, she doesn't know about the goings-on in this house we're going to." Guttridge nodded significantly. "But who else would have anything against her ladyship?"

"Who else indeed?" I hesitated, but Guttridge was extremely reliable when discretion was required, and I needed someone with whom to talk the matter over. "Supposing I told you this had not been the first message directed against Lady Odelia? She received a rather nasty letter a few days ago."

"From Lady Dorrian-Knowles?" Guttridge frowned.

"From a person or persons anonymous."

Guttridge sniffed. "Cowardly, that is. Although I suppose Lady Dorrian-Knowles has tried confrontation and it hasn't worked. She doesn't seem the sort to just sit still and put up with the nonsense Sir Geraint has inflicted upon her. Even if it's the sort of thing that happens all the time among those artistic people."

"It's Lady Dorrian-Knowles's state of mind that interests me." I steadied myself as the carriage jostled over an older patch of road. "We're on a fishing expedition, Guttridge. I will fish upstairs, and I hope you will keep your eyes and ears open in the servants' hall. If we get into the house, that is."

"You're not the sort of visitor that usually gets turned away, my lady. Will you see Sir Geraint too?"

"I'm hoping to see Lady Dorrian-Knowles most of all. She was understandably angry the other day, but with luck, she has recovered her equilibrium and can talk to me sensibly."

GUTTRIDGE'S FIRM PULL ON THE DOORBELL BROUGHT NO answer at first. We waited, and eventually the door was opened by Jane Dorrian-Knowles. The child's expression was wary but relaxed a little when she saw us.

"I thought you might be Edmund, forgetting his key again," she confessed with what seemed like a sigh of relief.

"You're not fond of your brother?"

A tide of red swept up her cheeks. "Of course I am—but he can be so sarcastic, and I was hoping for a quiet morning. I'm helping Mother with some work. I suppose it's Mother and Father you came to see, my lady—madam?"

"Lady Helena is what you should call me, Jane," I said gently. I was inwardly appalled—such matters were the kind of thing one learned in the nursery. Was the child's education so neglected? But I smiled at her. "You should ask your mother or sister to explain the rules to you. They're quite easy once you've learned them, and we all have to start somewhere." A thought struck me. "Is Mrs. Jowett still staying here?"

"Oh no, Cass went home three days ago." Jane held the door open awkwardly, standing in our way instead of stepping back as a servant would. "Morrison—Mr. Jowett, that is —didn't like her being away from home."

"I suppose not. Would you mind awfully if we came in?" I gave Jane an encouraging nod, and she finally stepped to the side, but not enough to prevent my dress dragging against hers as we passed.

I looked at her face properly for the first time since I'd had a glimpse of her at the party; since then, I'd only seen her in tears. She had that aura of gaucheness that was common in big girls who were old enough to feel the need for constraint but had not yet learned the poise of womanhood. Out of all her siblings, she resembled Galahad the most, but her face, its pale skin dusted with small reddish freckles, did not have his intelligence. She looked like the sort of young lady who needed, as Mama would have said, to be "taken in hand"—taught the rudimentary skills of social survival and given some instruction on how to carry herself with grace and distinction. After all, she was the daughter of a baronet, even if he *had* hyphenated his names. Weren't they planning to present her at court?

"I'd like to see your mother, if it's at all possible. I brought her some flowers." I turned to take the box from Guttridge, it being the rule that gifts should be offered in person if possible. "My head gardener sent them up very early this morning from my house in the country. I know it's the wrong time of day to call, but I wanted her to have them fresh."

"Mother's in the library." Jane bit her lip, and then more words burst forth. "It's nice not to have my brothers at home. I miss Cass, though. I don't see her very much."

"Is she very much older than you?" I asked.

"Eleven years—Lady Helena."

I couldn't help smiling. "Then we have something in common. All of my sisters are very much older than I. The eldest became a mother before I was born, so I have a niece who is older than I am."

A shy smile spread across Jane's face, improving her appearance considerably. "I'm glad my niece and nephew are younger than I am. It's nice to have children to play with." And then the shadow was back. "But Cass hasn't brought them here much lately because of—of what happened—"

She stumbled to a halt, biting her lip.

"It will all pass." I gave her a gentle pat on the shoulder. "Every family has its trials. Now, let's find your mother."

18

THEORY OF LIFE

illie was so absorbed in her task that she didn't look up as we entered the library. Sir Geraint's paintings dominated the walls, but my eyes were instantly drawn to the needlework frame on which was stretched a piece of work that rivaled the paintings in color and fire and strength.

The lower part of the design, already stitched, represented an intricate meadow in which wildflowers tossed their heads. Insects and birds wove between their intertwining stems, almost coming alive on their background of pale, heavy silk. Higher up, half-finished, a tree spread its branches to shelter more birds and creatures among its fresh spring leaves and vibrant blossoms. It was nature but brighter and more beautiful still, and I instantly coveted it with a quite unreasonable longing.

"That's marvelous." I spoke quietly, hating to disturb the steady, skillful movements, the words forced out of me by the glorious embroidery.

Millie lifted her head with no sign of alarm, her eyes unfocused at first, so like Odelia's when she was in the grip

151

of inspiration. When she recognized me, her expression changed slightly to a mixture of wariness and politeness.

"Thank you." She straightened up. "What can I do for you, Lady Helena?"

"I brought you these." I opened the box of chrysanthemums. "My gardener sent boxes of them from Sussex this morning, and I thought you might like some."

Millie inserted her needle into a holder that lay on the small table next to a sketch of the design, worked out on square-ruled paper. Now a little closer to the work, I could see the faint pencil marks that were all she apparently needed to guide her hand. I returned my attention to her as she stepped forward to touch the flowers.

"Such delicate incurved petals. Like a Japanese drawing." She nodded with satisfaction. "Thank you, Lady Helena."

"Would you like me to take these to the servants' hall, my lady?" Guttridge said to Millie. "I expect Mrs. Bretherton can find me some vases."

"Yes." Millie ran a finger over the best flower, which was a deep orange-red on the inside of the petal and buff yellow on the outside. "Would you mind asking Mrs. B. to bring up some coffee? Or tea?" She looked at me, and I smiled.

"I like coffee very much."

"We'll have it here—there are no fires in the other rooms." Millie led me away from the magnificent work on the frame. "Were you looking for Geraint? You've come at the right time. He'll have a model in the studio in an hour or so, and it's always difficult to interrupt once they're there." She raised her eyebrows. "I've spent half my life waiting for the real art to be finished so I can talk to my husband."

"What you're doing is real art. I came to see you, really."

I let Millie lead me toward the fireplace, which was ingeniously tucked in beneath a window so one could both enjoy the fire and look out at the garden.

"May I see your hand?" I asked.

Millie held out the injured appendage, which was heavily bruised. "Your remedies were effective for both of us." She let me hold her long, solid hand in both of mine, not wincing as I ran my fingers over the marked flesh. "In the circumstances, you were very kind to send them. It's all right. It hurts a good deal, that's all."

"I know our previous encounters have been difficult." I curled my fingers around hers for just a moment before letting go. "It didn't seem right to just leave things as they are, without seeing if we could talk a little. I realize the fact of who I am makes it hard for you to like me."

I let the words hang there, schooling myself to stillness as I settled into my seat. I directed my gaze to the mingled greens and autumnal hues of the garden, in the center of which, I now realized, was a sizable sculpture. A mermaid sat on a rock, her slender tail curled to one side; she was leaning forward, one hand stretched out and downward, as if she were calling to someone below the surface of the water. Long hair hung to her waist, covering her breasts and the curve of her back. Had I ever been assailed by so many beautiful images? I felt myself swallowed up by the world Odelia inhabited, drowning in beauty.

Millie, who had been silent, suddenly took a deep breath.

"Do you approve?" she asked. "Of this—arrangement I find myself in."

I tried to discern what was in her eyes. Was she angry? Afraid? Or simply unhappy? A little of all of those, I suspected.

"I neither approve nor disapprove," I said. "What qualifies me to set myself up as some kind of moral arbiter? There are too many people willing to do that." I frowned. "I also find I can't turn my back on my sister, whatever I may think."

"But do you think this is *right*?" The last word emerged in a rising pitch, driven by the force of passion—and I completely understood.

"No, it's not right." I could see Guttridge and Mrs. Bretherton in the garden, both carrying trugs. Cutting greenery, perhaps, to go with the flowers. I turned to Millie. "It's making you unhappy, and that's not right. And I had the impression, speaking with your sons, that they didn't like it either." I heard Philip's voice: *Naturally, we have sworn to each other to become entirely conventional men.* "A theory of life is all very well, but all parties to it have to agree for it to be an honest venture."

Millie snorted. "The children never got the chance to agree or disagree. He took your sister as his mistress when Janie was a tiny baby. Only she and Galahad were too young to understand what was going on. The others—well, it's surprising what children are aware of. Of course, if it hadn't been for the children, I wouldn't have minded half as much. When we were young, I too believed in Geraint's theories. The exultation of the body and the freedom of the soul. I saw the death of my faith in the puzzled looks on my older children's faces."

"I'm sorry." I didn't know what else to say.

"Not your fault. She wasn't the first anyway. Geraint had had affairs before, usually when I was carrying a child. He would always *tell* me, after a while. He'd claim it was better for my health and his if he satisfied himself elsewhere." Her generous mouth twisted. "I always knew anyway. He has a look about him after he's been with another woman. The same look as when he's finished a painting. The satisfaction of imparting his creative seed to the world."

A warning chink of china caused us to fall silent. We went through the ceremony of pouring and drinking the coffee the maid had brought. Millie sipped from her cup without speaking, her gaze on the two servants in the garden, while I looked at the huge painting of the Snow Queen's domain. Now it was at an angle to me so that I saw the layers of paint reflecting the light rather than the painting itself. However real the halls of the Snow Queen looked from one viewpoint, the scene was entirely two-dimensional until one was standing in the right place. Perhaps, I mused, I should strive to be less susceptible to the beauty around me, for did I wish to be part of a world that was all surface glitter and no substance?

"It's humiliating to be told, you know," Millie said after a few moments' silence. "But at the beginning, I reconciled myself to those episodes because they always ended. The women would cling too much or become boring, and he'd discard them. But then *she* started coming to the house. Young and beautiful, passionately interested in Geraint's art, and in enthusiastic agreement with his diatribes about freedom and generosity. A rare jewel, he said. And aristocratic, of course. That was before he became a baronet, and titles impressed him back then. Hers tripped so prettily off the tongue—*Lady Odelia Scott-De Quincy*. 'Just call me O,' she'd say. 'I don't care about titles when I'm among friends.' He lapped it up. The earl's daughter!" She barked a short, mirthless laugh.

My curiosity overcame me. "Did O make a play for your husband?" I asked.

"Who needs to seduce Geraint?" Millie's grin was almost genuine. "A man so easily seduced by beauty that I believe he's in a permanent state of arousal." Her mouth drooped. "I was the beautiful one once. His muse, his model—he couldn't stop touching me. When I gave birth to Phil, I was his Madonna. I regained my figure so quickly; he used to say that motherhood had only added to my beauty. But then there were Cass, Edmund, Galahad, and at last Janie . . . And Edmund was so ill I quite forgot, for a while, that I was a wife as well as a mother. With every child, the woman I'd been slipped away from me."

"Isn't that the natural course of events?" I asked.

Millie looked down at her body, which was swathed in a work apron embroidered with poppy buds. "I don't begrudge the loss of my beauty for the sake of the children. I wouldn't have missed any of them for the world."

"You're fortunate." I smoothed down my black skirts. "Sir Justin and I did not have children. His title and family line are now extinct, and I have nobody to remember him by."

"I don't deny my good fortune." Millie crossed her strong arms, which were bare to the elbows. "After we nearly lost Edmund, I cherished all my babies more than ever."

"And you *are* beautiful." I meant it.

"Geraint says that still, sometimes." Millie's expression softened a little. "I'm valuable to him as the mother of his children, the angel of his hearth." She pursed her lips. "I keep the house running, look after the children, and make shift to do my own work as best I can." She turned her head to look at the huge embroidery frame. "We hide all that away when we have guests, naturally. This house was built to display Geraint's work, not mine."

"Couldn't you use the studio as well?" I asked. "It's big enough, and your husband told me he often works elsewhere."

"I use it occasionally, but not when there's a model. Nasty, common girls mostly, parading around half-naked. No modesty. He flirts with them even when I'm in the room—thank you, but I've had enough humiliation. He says it's to put them at their ease, but they're all as brazen as brass. I'm sure they laugh at me behind my back, and I always wonder whether he's slept with them." She looked around the large room. "I like it here anyway. The light's excellent, and I can look at Edmund and Cass and remember happier times. The snake was already in the garden when this picture was painted, but I suspected nothing."

Not a snake, but a Snow Queen. There was nothing I could think of to say to comfort this unhappy woman, and I hoped, as far as I could, to at least clear her of the suspicion that she was persecuting my sister. So I asked the question that was on my mind.

"You told me there were other mistresses," I said. "Are they just—temporary?"

"Oh, I don't count the temporary ones." Millie waved her uninjured hand in a dismissive gesture. "Ultimately, I despise the models. No, these are the other two he fell in love with. He seems to need to do that every few years. Always young women who will make no demands on him. The bold kind, heedless of what anybody else thinks. Like your sister."

I tried not to wince. "Are they both artists, these other women?"

"Cynthia's a sculptress—she did *that*, which is the only time I've had anything really good out of the bargain." Millie pointed at the mermaid sculpture. "It's odd, but I'm fond of that statue. I don't mind Cynthia, really, because I truly believe she's only interested in Geraint in the physical sense. She has a way of keeping on everyone's right side."

"And the other?"

"An actress." Millie rolled her eyes. "Unoriginal—a sign of Geraint's advancing age, as I've told him more than once. A dainty darling with a mouth like a costermonger when she feels like it. I met her once, but I've told Geraint never to bring her near this house again."

"I'm sorry." I appeared to be repeating myself, as if perhaps I could make things right by apologizing—for Odelia, certainly, but perhaps for all the rest of Millie's trials.

"Yes, I think you really are." Millie stared at me. "You're not very like her, are you?"

"I'm not much like any of my siblings nor either of my parents," I confessed. "My father used to call me a wren among peacocks."

"That fits the bill." Millie grinned suddenly. "Your sister's definitely a peacock—I should say 'peahen,' but 'peacock' suits her better. Supremely self-confident. All the other birds have to get out of her way. Do you know, the only time I've ever seen that confidence shaken was when Geraint harmed himself. She actually *cared*."

I wanted to tell her how loving Odelia could be, but that would be a mistake. Besides, family loyalty dictated I shouldn't reveal anything to Millie about O. I sympathized with the poor woman, but if I absolutely had to take sides, I knew whose I'd be on.

"The one thing you have in common with her is that voice," Millie went on. "That damnably aristocratic voice, that accent that nobody can mistake and nobody can imitate unless they've been born with it. Nothing in England opens doors like that voice, does it? And that training—the way you hold yourself, the way you take off your gloves, the way you sit down. The very line of your back proclaims your breeding."

"You're very observant."

"I'm an artist—it's my job to observe. Everything about you reeks of privilege and wealth."

Millie looked down at her hands, and when she spoke again, she didn't look at me. "Are you going to walk away from the commission? From *The Nightingale*?"

There was something in her voice that told me that this, perhaps, was why she had spoken to me, why she hadn't just told me to leave, why she had accepted my peace offering. And there were lines of tension in her body that hadn't been there a moment ago. She was desperately anxious to hear my answer, but did she crave a no or a yes?

"Would you rather I did?" I asked. "Perhaps you'd prefer that your husband have nothing to do with me or my house, given who I am."

She flushed uncomfortably. "I can't say I'm happy about *her* bringing her family into this little *ménage à cinq*. I have wondered if it's all a ploy to prevent that foul little actress from getting too good a hold on him. O's not getting any younger any more than I am, and that little cuckoo is ambitious enough to try to push both of us out of the nest. But be that as it may, Geraint's been at a low point with commissions lately, and we've had some extra bills." Her generous mouth tucked in at the corners. "Worse, he's obsessed with *The Nightingale*. I can see all the signs. He may start on the series of paintings anyway, without a buyer, and that sort of project can take years. He doesn't like splitting up a series, so he'll hold out for someone who'll take the lot while his other work suffers. We've been through this before."

"Ah. Well, I wish I could give you a straightforward answer, but to be honest, I'm reluctant to say yes at this point, after what's happened. Sir Geraint should be resting, not painting—and I'm unwilling to get involved in the situation he and Odelia have created."

"And yet you came to see me."

"That's different. That's . . ." I hesitated, conscious that my motives for visiting were decidedly mixed.

"Kindness? Pity?" Millie gave me a half smile. "No, I take that last one back. You're being gracious, and I have no call to be rude to you. How did you grow up a Scott-De Quincy *and* turn out kind?"

"I have no idea."

"Leaving this whole wretched mess aside, how do you feel about *The Nightingale*?" Millie asked.

"That it would be the most wonderful venture I've ever embarked upon." My answer came before I could even think about it. "It's perfectly ridiculous that I should be even thinking of spending such sums on something I didn't know I wanted, but I want it beyond reason." I glanced sideways at the paintings on the wall behind us. "This house seems to reinforce that longing somehow."

"That's what it's designed to do." Millie swallowed hard. "Would you speak to him? To Geraint? He's in his study."

"Is he strong enough?" I frowned.

"As I said, he'll be working with a model this afternoon. He has decided he's strong enough to work, and there's little I can do about that."

19

A FOOLISH ACT

My fishing expedition was turning up some rather large fish, I reflected as I allowed Millie to lead me toward another part of the house. I smoothed my reticule against my skirts, feeling the crinkle of paper within. I had brought the foul letter to Holland Park just in case anything Millie said suggested that she'd sent it and I could confront her. But why, if she was eager for Sir Geraint to paint *The Nightingale* for me, would she attack my sister? She hadn't even shown the animosity against Odelia that I might have expected, just the weary, muted rage of a woman unable to free herself from an unbearable torment.

"I'll leave you to discuss the matter—*en famille*—and get back to my work," she said once she had opened the door at the sound of Sir Geraint's "Enter!" That *en famille*, with its clear implication of family intimacy, was the first hint of the strain my visit was causing her, and I was once again as repentant as if I were the guilty party.

But the man at the center of the whole sorry mess was rising to his feet, a delighted smile parting beard and mustache. As the door clicked closed behind Millie, he was bowing over my hand with the utmost politeness, thanking me for my kind letter and the remedies I had sent and asking after my health with solicitous charm.

"Please sit down." He hastily closed some books that were definitely ledgers, suggesting he had been evaluating his financial situation—or merely ensuring that the cook hadn't spent too much on chicken. "It's too good of you to come and see me."

"I came to see Lady Dorrian-Knowles." I wanted him to be quite clear on that point. "She asked if I would talk with you. I'm glad to see you looking so well."

Indeed, he did. His eyes were clear in the lamplight, and he had moved with the vigor of a man much younger than the fifty-seven years a little research in Debrett's had revealed to me. His wrists were bound with a very light dressing, and he could clearly move his hands without difficulty.

Like the library, this room was lined with low book-shelves, leaving plenty of space for the large windows, beyond which a November fog was invading the growing darkness. Miscellaneous images covered the walls—engravings of classical works, Punch cartoons, rough sketches, and a few carefully executed anatomical studies. It was the room of a man whose mind was unceasingly active, and I was sure he had read all of the books crowded into the shelves.

"I'm embarrassed," Sir Geraint said at length. "Before we embark on other topics, I'd like to assure you that there will be no repeat of my foolish act. I suffer from black moods sometimes, as many people do, and sometimes I resort to stimulants to drag myself out of them. That night I took too much and allowed myself to become overexcited. I gave in to despair and thought it would be noble of me to choose the moment of my ending. It's surprisingly difficult to do the deed, as I found, and once I'd made a feeble attempt, I wasn't at all sure I was brave enough to continue. I will henceforth suffer my trials as reasonable people do—with fortitude and consideration for others."

"I'm glad," I said. "I've had the misfortune to be present at the discovery of a successful suicide. One of my tenants. It was a distressing scene and had unfortunate consequences. I hope you can spare your family such disturbances in the future."

"You reprimand me like a sister—and you are clearly a woman of strength of character." He smoothed a finger over the bandage on one wrist. "How is O?"

"In good spirits. Except . . ." I hesitated, but if there was an opportunity to discuss the letter, it was now. "She received a communication that perturbed her very much. An anonymous letter—quite disgusting. And then someone left a message on our gate in red paint."

I saw Sir Geraint's expression change and knew I had struck the right scent. I waited for him to speak.

"What did the letter look like?" he eventually asked.

I opened my reticule and silently handed the letter over, watching his face grow paler.

"You recognize it," I said. "Can you tell me who sent it?" What if he told me his wife was a maniac who made a habit of writing salacious notes?

"Tell you who sent it?" He looked surprised. "Of course not. But I have received several. Half a dozen last spring and three since the summer. They haven't helped my state of mind. I try not to dwell on them, but some of the things they've said remain in my memory for too long. Whoever writes them knows my weaknesses. Millie thinks it's O."

"And Odelia thinks it's your wife."

"Millie?" His thick black eyebrows rose. "But they contained threats against our children." He shook his head. "I have always thrown them in the fire for fear of her seeing them. She knows I receive them, but I've told her they're just deranged rubbish. One gets strange things in the post once one is well known to the public."

"Have you not been to the police?"

He shuddered. "Would you? *Did* you go to them?"

"O's letter referred to her as, well, as a woman of loose morals. Naturally, she didn't want to go to the police in case they inquired into her activities," I said.

"And mine also contained some truths I wouldn't want to show to the police either." Sir Geraint's face was grave. "Not so much the remarks about my morality—more the allusions to the way I behaved over money when I was up at Oxford and rather short of cash. Or perhaps they were guesses. Doesn't every undergraduate do things they blush for in later life? In any case, they're not matters I want to discuss with the constabulary."

He closed his eyes and pinched the bridge of his nose, massaging the flesh where the small, deep line emphasized the intense look of his gray eyes. "I should ignore them, of course. Throw them into the fire unread. But I can't somehow. I find myself waiting for the next one, which can make it difficult to work. Everything seems to conspire against me these days. I was beginning to think I'd lost my creative fire altogether until *The Nightingale* was born in my mind." He looked straight at me now, as if he were trying to guess my thoughts. "*The Nightingale* is my salvation, Lady Helena. I pray you haven't come to deny me the honor of your patronage."

I was silent. Sir Geraint leaned forward, steepling his fingertips, his gaze more intent than ever.

"You *are* thinking of it, I perceive. Tell me, what has really changed? If you've decided you don't like my work, then I will concede defeat."

"I haven't decided that."

"Or you have set your mind on another artist? Perhaps one of the newcomers or a different style . . . please don't tell me you've conceived an enthusiasm for the Impressionists. Mere daubs—not art at all."

"I have no other artist in mind."

"Then it's a question of my stability, perhaps? Or my morals? I have already assured you that the . . . incident . . . was a temporary situation that will not re-occur. Most importantly, art has nothing to do with morality. The theories that resulted in pictures larded with moral lessons are outdated. It is beauty we should strive for, particularly on a large scale. You must have something that will last, not a reflection of the narrow morals of our time." He paused. "Not that there's anything immoral in the tale of the *Nightingale*. It is quite the purest story that exists, and it is absolutely timeless."

"Doesn't it have a moral, that the natural is better than the artificial?" I asked. "I entirely agree with that."

"That is a message—it's not the same as a moral." He smiled, stroking his luxuriant beard. "And it is itself an artifice—a fantasy. Perhaps you fear that O and I will disport ourselves in your house? We will not, of course, and would not do anything to arouse suspicion among the burghers of Littleberry. I will be in your house to work."

"But you and O said nothing about your affair until your actions brought it to light," I said. "I think my principal objection stems from the feeling that I've been manipulated. And now I'm aware of the situation, I would have to introduce you as Odelia's friend and colleague while knowing you're far more than that. You will make me complicit in your world of intrigue and deceit. I may be from the obscure country aristocracy, but in my own county my name—my late husband's name—stands for something."

"And yet you haven't upbraided O for immoral behavior

or demanded she leave me, have you? She says not, at least. If your concern were purely for your name, wouldn't you have walked out of Scott House the moment you discovered the truth about O and me? You're already complicit. Besides, the aristocracy are as bad as we bohemians when it comes to loose morals."

"Yes, but we play our games within strict rules, and when we lose, we know what to do. Go abroad or—" I stopped short, appalled at where my words were leading me.

"Or put a gun in one's mouth?" Sir Geraint's smile did not reach his eyes. "And yet you don't like to be faced with suicide."

"You're trying to talk me into running in mental circles." I felt exasperated, knowing I was losing ground to the man's quick wits. "I won't be herded. Wun't be druv, as we say in Sussex."

"So there's no hope for me?" Sir Geraint's demeanor softened, and I felt myself soften with it. If only I hadn't let Odelia persuade me to consider a commission. But I *had* been considering it, and to back out now because of immorality would surely mean I'd have to inquire into the morality of every artist and artisan I hired henceforth to work on Whitcombe. And to walk away from the *Nightingale* because I was worried about what people might think would make me . . . what? A coward or a hypocrite?

"I feel you haven't entirely decided." The charming smile was back on Sir Geraint's face as he stood up. "I have some sketches I was hoping to show you; will you look at them?"

At my mute nod, he fetched a portfolio from the other end of the room, returning to lay it before me. "I've been sketching ever since I felt myself well enough to do so. Partly, I was desperate to know whether my idiocy had done any lasting damage to my hands, but as soon as I held a pencil the *Nightingale* leapt to my fingers as if it had been waiting for me. These sketches have saved me from many an hour of harmful introspection and helped to speed my recovery. I've been collating my best efforts to show to you."

"They're exquisite." I stared with wonder at the drawings. The birds on the paper looked as if they were alive. Even the bejeweled clockwork bird seemed to shiver with life and movement. Another sketch showed part of the emperor's garden, full of flowers hung with small bells.

"If I decide against the commission, I will pay you for the hours you've spent working so far." I gazed, entranced.

"I wouldn't take the payment," Sir Geraint said. "Believe me, Lady Helena, I would have you come to me as a client eager for my services or not at all. Whatever it might cost me." He looked down at his bound wrists and flexed his long, strong fingers. "I don't expect you to give me an answer now, but as you can see, I'm willing and able to carry out the commission."

AFTER A BRIEF DELAY, I RETRIEVED GUTTRIDGE. ONCE WE were in the carriage, I gave my increasingly agog lady's maid an account of my conversations with both Millie and Sir Geraint.

"So Lady Dorrian-Knowles may not be the most likely suspect after all." Guttridge pulled at her long upper lip as she thought. "Unless she's devious enough to send letters to her own husband with threats against herself and her children."

"She could be, at that . . . what a suspicious mind you have, Guttridge. What about this? Lady Odelia's only had one letter, while Sir Geraint has been receiving them over a period of months. That must mean he's the letter writer's actual victim. But how would Lady Dorrian-Knowles benefit by hounding her own husband? What would be the point? Unless she wants him to take his own life—but look how upset she was."

"Perhaps that was remorse," remarked Guttridge severely before brightening. "Or she writes the letters while sleepwalking."

"Does she deliver them while sleepwalking, then? That seems highly unlikely."

"Hmmm." Guttridge narrowed her eyes. "We need to draw up a list of the likely suspects, it would seem."

"*I* suspect you read far too many accounts of murder in the illustrated papers, Guttridge."

"If I were a man," Guttridge crossed her arms, "I could be a detective in the Criminal Investigation Department." She wrinkled her nose. "'Cept that would mean coming to live in London again, and I'm used to the country now. I like a bit of green. I'm looking forward to getting back to Littleberry."

"So am I. Did you find out anything interesting from the servants?"

"Mrs. B's fairly tight-lipped, as is proper for a house-keeper. They *are* short of money, though; it's easy to spot when a household's being run on too little. I learned that the young men are costing their father a mort of money and that young Jane is unhappy. It's her age, and they think she misses having her sister there. She'd live with the Jowetts, only Mr. Jowett won't have it. Now *that's* one who's not well liked by the staff—I wonder if he could be making mischief? Or maybe one of the children. Maybe little Jane is miserable out of guilt. Like that Hatherall girl."

"Not *just* like Susan Hatherall, I hope," I remarked drily. "One case of incest is enough for a lifetime. I don't see how it would benefit the sons to persecute the father. It would be killing the goose that lays the golden eggs, surely? Without Sir Geraint's income, the house would have to be sold.

They'd have to work to support their mother and sister." I was silent for a few moments, thinking. "There are other possibilities, though. I'm afraid Sir Geraint has more than one mistress."

"No." Guttridge's eyes opened wide. "The dirty old—well, my lady, there are some queer goings-on in the world."

"Apparently, he has a theory of life that excludes monogamy." I shrugged. "You've been in service long enough, Guttridge. You know it happens in the aristocracy as well. People marry for the alliance and have affairs for, well, fun."

"Fun for men." Guttridge sniffed. "I could tell you some stories about the lower classes too, my lady. Old Farmer Crouch, now—they were twins . . ." She grinned reminiscently. "So how many more mistresses does the old—does Sir Geraint have?"

"Two. Lady Dorrian-Knowles told me enough about them that it should be possible to work out their identities, and then I can call on them."

"What for?" Guttridge looked shocked.

"I'm not sure. For the sake of interfering, perhaps." I frowned. "Lady Odelia is my sister, and she's being attacked. Whether or not she's the intended victim, I should find out all I can before I go back to Littleberry."

"I suppose it's a bit more interesting than twiddling your thumbs at Scott House while Lady Odelia paints." Guttridge pursed her lips. "What are the clues, then?"

"The what? Oh, the identity of the mistresses. One is the sculptress who created the mermaid statue in the garden."

"Miss Emery," said Guttridge without hesitation. "So *that's* what Mrs. B. was hinting at. Hoho, not so discreet after all. I admired the statue, and she said it was by Miss Cynthia Emery, who is a great friend of Sir Geraint. I thought at the time that there was something odd in the way she said it."

"Guttridge, you're making this far too easy. See if you can

guess the other one—she's an actress, and young, and rather free in her speech."

Guttridge looked taken aback. "There must be hundreds of young actresses in London, and most of them *not* very refined, I'll be bound. Haven't you got anything else to go on?"

"Well, she's probably small and dainty. Lady Dorrian-Knowles said she was a dainty darling."

Guttridge leaped to her feet, clapping her hands. Naturally, this action caused her head to come into violent contact with the carriage ceiling; the vehicle swayed suddenly, and she fell back, kicking my shin as she did so.

"Ow—sorry, my lady. I didn't tear your dress, did I?"

"Don't tell me you know the name of the other mistress as well." I brushed a mud mark off my skirt and rubbed my shin.

"I might, if her ladyship meant *the* Dainty Darling. That's Elisabetta Aldred. She performs at the Bulldog Palace of Varieties on the Haymarket, and she's the talk of the servants' hall at Scott House."

"Guttridge, you're a genius." I nestled myself more snugly into the carriage's velvet-covered seat. "Could you help me find out where they live?"

"I could try."

20

A WORLD OF DIFFERENCE

*T*hanks to Guttridge's intelligence, our task was much shortened. Thanks to her initiative in gathering up every directory in Scott House, not to mention acting as my guide through the maze of information, we soon located the first of our prey.

"Well, well." I had been running a finger down the list of sculptors in the London Post Office Directory. "Here she is: *Emery, Miss C.* All the other names are men, and tradesmen at that."

"That's because she makes monuments, see?" Guttridge pointed at the terse legend, "Children's monuments," after Miss Emery's name. "That's a trade. I thought somehow she might be gentry, but working for her living makes me think she isn't." She leaned over to peer at the list of names nestled between SCREWING TACKLE MANUFACTRS. and SCUM BOILERS. "But that mermaid statue makes me think she is. There's a world of difference between carving a monument, however beautiful, and making a proper statue. Did you look under ARTISTS, my lady?"

"It didn't occur to me." I went through the pages in

sections, searching. "ARTIFICIAL NOSE MAKER—good heavens. Ah, here they are: ARTISTS. Some women in this list . . . Yes, here she is again. Address in Chelsea, as before, and no mention of monuments this time."

"Because the more exalted readers of the directory would look at the artists first." Guttridge tossed her head. "Probably gentry, then. Living on family money, perhaps." She snorted softly. Scotty, who was dozing on the settee beside me, snorted in response.

I recommended running my finger down the list, hesitating for a fraction of a second over "Dorrian-Knowles, Sir G." and then moving swiftly down past Miss Emery's entry to the letter *S*. Odelia wasn't listed, which was just as well. Gerry and Blanche would have something to say about Lady Odelia Scott-De Quincy being listed in a tradesmen's directory. I breathed a silent sigh of relief.

"At least Chelsea's close enough." Guttridge tugged a piece of paper out from under the directory and noted the address. "Too far to walk. We'll have to take the carriage."

"We?" I grinned at my lady's maid.

"I suppose I'll have to stay in the carriage," she said grimly.

"Oh, I don't see any harm in arriving with my lady's maid in tow." I watched the brightening of Guttridge's eyes, my mood lifting. "Now, should I write to Miss Emery on my own notepaper or the Scott House paper?"

"Both have a nice, impressive coat of arms," said Guttridge with a practical air. "Your own, probably. That way she might not make the connection with Lady Odelia."

"But I *want* her to make the connection. I don't want her thinking I might be looking for a monument for a child." I stared at the closely printed pages on my lap. "You don't think we'll have the same luck with Miss Aldred, do you? Is there a listing of actors and actresses?"

"Easy enough to find. Look in the general index."

"There's an index?"

"You don't spend a lot of time searching for people, do you, my lady?" Guttridge took the heavy volume from my lap and settled it on her own.

"I know how to look people up in Debrett's," I mused, watching the quick movements of Guttridge's hands. "Fascinating what you find out."

"Very useful, I'm sure. No, my lady, there are no actors listed in this directory. I could see if I could find a stage directory of some sort. Or I could just go to the Bulldog and do some snooping." She peered at me hopefully.

"You have my ready permission to take the time off to go to the Bulldog. I'll contribute half a guinea for tickets and incidentals."

"I call that handsome." Guttridge beamed, as well she might. Half a guinea would ensure a very pleasant afternoon or evening indeed, with plenty left over.

"And I will write a note to Miss Emery. I'll ask if she would receive me at her home—or premises—or whatever sculptresses have. Don't you think we'd find out more that way?"

"I don't think we'll find out a great deal anyways, but it'll be interesting." Guttridge looked enthusiastic.

I turned as the door opened, feeling a little guilty in case it was Odelia. She would be bound to ask why we were surrounded by directories, and I didn't care to broach the subject of Sir Geraint's other mistresses just yet. I was quite relieved to see the footman with the three o'clock post on Scott House's largest salver.

"You can take Lady Odelia's post upstairs," I said after setting aside my own letters. Normally, I wouldn't concern myself with O's correspondence—she was entitled to her privacy—but since the anonymous letter and the vandalized gate, I had asked, where possible, for the post to be brought to me first in the hope I could spot any further attempts at unpleasantness. Odelia had received two letters—one from Blanche, one, I suspected, from Sir Geraint—and a solid, heavy-looking parcel that was doubtless yet more paint or other artistic necessity.

With a murmured "yes, m'lady" and a prolonged glance at the piles of directories, the footman departed. He would leave the post outside the door of Odelia's studio or, more likely, give it to a maid to take upstairs. No doubt the other servants would question Guttridge about what we were doing, but I knew I could rely on her to tell them to mind their own business.

I glanced at my own letters, noting that one of them bore Fortier's handwriting. I carefully placed my post on a small table next to the armchair I liked best before sitting down at the writing desk. Then, obeying the rule drummed into me by Mama and a variety of governesses—that I should complete all my tasks before allowing myself a little leisure— I began composing my note to Miss Emery.

I worked through two drafts with dogged application, aware of Guttridge bustling around behind me, taking away the various directories and ensuring the room was in good order. I nodded abstractedly as she announced that she would have my afternoon tea sent up and see to her own refreshment. By the time the tea arrived—a simple tray with the refreshing drink and some lemon biscuits since I was alone—I had signed and sealed the note to Miss Emery and was at liberty to sit in the armchair and read my letters.

I put Fortier's note at the bottom of the pile and began at the top. An inquiry from the dressmaker about trimmings— Guttridge could answer that. A letter from Julia—I read that through carefully, laughing over the incident involving Annabelle Alice and the ironmonger's donkey. A letter from

Blanche—mercifully, a short one, about her stay at Whit-combe at Christmas. An impertinent letter from a purveyor of oils and perfumes—could he send me some samples? No, he could not, and I was sure Guttridge would make that very clear in the reply I would ask her to draft.

And then, finally, Fortier's letter. Sealed, I was interested to note, with what looked like a hawthorn flower. His neat but slightly un-English writing gave a pleasantly curious little flourish to the *L*, *H*, and *W* of my name. I opened the seal.

I had to confess to myself that I was ever so slightly disappointed that the note was so short and to the point. Could I allow him to return the compliment I had paid him recently by joining him and his father for luncheon on the fifteenth? His sister would be visiting friends with the children that day but sent her affectionate regards.

I returned to the writing desk, selecting a piece of my notepaper and the best pen I could find. Matching Fortier's brevity, I wrote that I would be sorry to miss Gabrielle but would be delighted to accept his kind invitation. Then it was just a matter of ringing the bell and giving the footman this letter to add to the others going out by the evening's post.

I could, perhaps, answer Julia's and Blanche's letters as well, but I felt oddly restless. It was growing dark, so I took Scotty outside for a short turn in the garden. Watching him sniff under every bush and paw at the damp leaves that lay scattered on the grass awaiting the gardener's visit, I found myself longing for Whitcombe House, for my mare, Sandy, for the smell of clean earth, for damp that contained no soot. I even missed the sheep that by now would have been moved off the more exposed areas of the marsh into fields at the bottom of the valley, where they would be less buffeted by the winter winds. It would be so much more pleasant to wear boots, to take a brisk walk or ride past farms and fields instead of being hemmed up within these stone walls, aware of the cold dampness of brick and gravel beneath the thin soles of my delicate slippers. I wanted to wake up to the sight of the sea and know I could visit the shore whenever I felt like it.

Eventually, of course, I just wanted to be back inside. Scotty's tolerance for cold and damp was always greater than mine. I wiped his paws, ignoring his growls of protest, and headed upstairs.

I went to my room and rang the bell for Guttridge. Waiting, I fished my letters out of my pocket and stared at the note from Fortier, throwing the others onto my dressing table. He, at least, was a reminder of home. But how long would he have to stay in London? I felt a prickle of anxiety at the thought of meeting his father. Supposing I didn't like him? Supposing he didn't like *me*?

"Honestly, Helena," I reprimanded myself, preparing to toss the letter onto the dressing table with the rest. "You're twenty-seven, not fifteen." But instead of throwing the envelope on top of the others, my treacherous fingers strayed over the hard wax of the seal, finding the tiny ridges that represented the stamens of the hawthorn flower—and I put it into my trinket box instead.

21

THE SCULPTRESS

*M*onday morning's eleven-o'clock post brought a rather offhand reply from Miss Emery in large, looping writing.

"She says," I informed Guttridge, "that I should come round at four thirty if I like. As long as I don't mind 'the place' looking untidy, she'll try her best with the tea caddy."

"No servants, then."

"I believe there's a rumor going around that not everyone keeps a servant. Let's not think too badly of Miss Emery for having to make her own tea."

Guttridge grinned, unabashed. "I'll order the carriage."

Thus it was that at four twenty-five, Guttridge, who was clearly relishing our information-gathering sorties, was ringing the bell at the narrow red-brick house not far from the river. Miss Emery answered the door herself. I liked the look of her; she was tall and well-built, with thick, pale blond hair and shrewd, intelligent blue eyes.

"Lady Helena Whitcombe?" She put out her hand. "And," her eyes ranged over Guttridge, "lady's maid?" Her patrician accent and the fact that she had unhesitatingly guessed

177

Guttridge's station in life told me that although she may not have any servants now, she had certainly grown up with them.

"This is Guttridge," I said and felt rather than saw the tiny curtsey—a mere flexing of the knees since this was only a *Miss* Emery—that went with Guttridge's, "How do you do, Miss?"

"You'll have to excuse the mess." Miss Emery opened the door wider to admit us into a bare hallway, decorated only by an abandoned cleaning bucket and several pieces of raw marble. Another young woman appeared, pelting precipitously downstairs in answer to the bell. Seeing us, she stopped, said, "Criminy," and turned to rush upstairs again.

"My friend Miss Trelawney," said Miss Emery carelessly. "She writes."

She led the way into what was unmistakably a bedroom, where a screen had been hastily and ineffectively pulled around the unmade bed. I soon realized that one had to go through the bedroom to reach the sitting room, the two rooms being connected by a fair-sized archway that had once housed a double door. A huge, beautifully carved marble fireplace hinted at the sitting room's former splendor. Now, it mostly seemed to house books.

"This is it." Miss Emery smiled cheerfully. "All I need in life. Except for my studio." She opened a set of glass-paned doors to show us a cavernous room that had perhaps once been a conservatory. The bare, tiled floor was littered with stone chips and dust, and a damp chill pervaded the space.

"I could make tea while you ladies talk." Guttridge had remained in the doorway. "If you don't have anyone to make it for you, miss."

"How nice of you." Miss Emery's blond eyebrows rose high as she turned. "The kitchen's at the end of the corridor, turn right. There's cake. Lav's just outside the kitchen door, if needed. Be patient with the cold-water tap."

She turned back to me and motioned me through the glass door into the studio. "I expect you're curious. Most people are. That's my bread-and-butter work." She waved a hand over a finished piece in pure white marble depicting an infant asleep, its arms around a large cat, whose head lay on the little one's legs. It was carefully polished and spotlessly clean.

"Died of pneumonia, poor little mite. They'll collect it tomorrow. Fortunately, there's a nice big gate in the garden." Miss Emery shivered. "I should have lit the stove. Come on back into the warm."

We returned to the sitting room. Miss Emery moved a pile of newspapers from an armchair so that I could seat myself. "This is the *real* artistic Bohemia," she remarked as she settled in another chair. "Most of us can't afford to live like your sister does. I say, that was good of your maid to make the tea. Lady's maids don't usually like doing menial work."

"Guttridge is a rare jewel." I brushed a trace of stone dust off my black skirts. "You understand that it's Odelia I want to talk to you about?"

"What's O been up to now?" One corner of Miss Emery's expressive, slightly large mouth curled up. "Never been any family interference before." She looked hard at me. "You look a lot younger than her."

"I am." I stiffened my back. "This is about a rather delicate matter, I'm afraid."

"It has to be Geraint." Miss Emery didn't seem at all bothered. "He's what O and I have in common, apart from talent. Mine is greater than your sister's, by the way."

"I've seen the mermaid statue at Sir Geraint's, so I know

you're talented," I said. "I'm not artistic myself, sadly, so I'm no judge of comparative merit."

"Except for Geraint's. You must see how sublime his work is." Miss Emery's cool irony was replaced by enthusiasm. "It was a considerable coup for me to get my statue in his garden. Fortunately, Millie liked it." She smiled. "Odd, isn't it, that she doesn't mind me nearly as much as the others?"

"I find the whole thing very odd altogether." I tried not to sound too severe.

"O's a bit of a journeyman painter," Miss Emery continued, her mind clearly on art. "Lovely, polished work, but it lacks fire. She sells well among the bourgeoisie, though, and the money allows her even more scope to play the lady of the manor. Life is so much easier when you don't have to pay for the roof over your head, I imagine. I parted ways with my family ten years ago, so I can't compete with that." She stretched her arms over her head. "But I'm free in a way O could never understand. The other distinction between your sister and myself is that I won't let Geraint spend money on me. So I'll never appear with him in certain circles the way she does. And that's as it should be—O has such tremendous *style* that she's an enormous asset to Geraint. Rides to hounds like an absolute demon, they say, and always knows which fork to use and entirely the right thing to say and do."

"So do you, I suspect."

"Well, I do, but I have no patience with the upper echelons. I inevitably speak my mind at some point and insult people. Poor Millie just can't keep up at all, although she could if she were like O and didn't care what people think. Millie gets embarrassed and defensive over the smallest blunder, which is the wrong tack to take with these people. If you're brazen, they respect you."

I wondered fleetingly what social set she was talking about. I could think of one or two where O would be accepted as Sir Geraint's mistress quite openly, and both were quite close to the Crown . . . But as much as I wanted to explore this fascinating and unknown aspect of Odelia's life, I had my own line of inquiry to pursue.

"So you have no grudge against Odelia?" I asked.

Miss Emery laughed. "Of course not. Why, is there trouble?"

"You might say that. Not much—an anonymous letter and some damage to the gate at Scott House—but enough to worry *me*, even if it doesn't worry my sister."

"Ah, I see." Miss Emery's fair brow uncreased. "Well, if anyone would write a nasty letter, it would be Millie. She's a little unbalanced. Of course, if I had a husband who fell in love with a new woman every five years or so, I might be a little unbalanced too, if I cared for him. She *does* care, poor thing."

"So you deny any knowledge of any malicious acts?" I thought I might as well speak frankly with this outspoken woman.

Miss Emery spread her hands wide. "Do you imagine I would confess to anything if I *had* done it? You're not much good at investigating, if that's what you're doing. Of course I deny it. I'm not possessive about Geraint. I often don't see him for weeks. Most of the time, our paths cross somewhere, and he suggests we have dinner, that sort of thing. *You* know the sort of thing. After a pleasant interlude, we go our separate ways until the next time."

"How do you bear it?"

"Oh, it's delightful." Miss Emery positively glowed. "I wish life were like this for all women. I swear Geraint appears whenever I crave passion. He must sense my heat from afar, like a dog." She laughed. "And then I can return to the life I love. Why should a woman settle for cold, dry celibacy as an alternative to marriage? A man can go to a prostitute whenever he wants, but women are expected to just put up with—nothing. And yet we need *it* as much as men do."

I could not disagree. For a second, the thought flitted through my mind that I *could* become Fortier's mistress while I pondered the matter of my next husband. But he would never agree to that—and I wouldn't really like it either.

"We're very discreet, of course." Miss Emery smiled. "Everyone has the impression that I'm a maiden lady, perhaps one of those who don't like men. Marjorie—Miss Trelawney—helps me keep up that façade. I wouldn't get commissions if people knew about Geraint. I say, you won't blab, will you?"

"As long as you don't repeat anything I've told you."

"My lips are sealed. Heavens, your maid's taking her time with the tea."

Right on cue, Guttridge entered with the tea tray. Had she been hovering in the hallway? She carefully unloaded the china and cutlery onto the table Miss Emery was hastily clearing of papers and assorted debris and then announced she would return later to clear away. I blessed her silently for giving me so much time to talk with the sculptress.

"Well, blow me down." It was strange to hear this nautical expression pronounced in Miss Emery's aristocratic accent. "She's washed everything—scrubbed in all the cracks. May I borrow her?"

I grinned. "No." Miss Emery's answering smile was warm and genuine. I could see why Millie said she always managed to stay on people's right side.

"Could you tell me," I began once the tea was poured and I had taken two bites of the plain but delicious cake, "if there's anyone else who might harbor resentment against Odelia?"

"Well, she does rather queen it over people. Do you have

pencil and paper? You'll never remember all of them. Oh, listen, I'll write the names down." She stood, as if to look for writing materials.

"How many?" I sounded a little breathless. I *felt* a little breathless.

"Mostly women. Do you really want me to write them down?"

"Not if there are over twenty."

Miss Emery sat down again.

"I mean," I said, "anyone who might have a serious enough grudge against my sister to make real trouble for her."

Miss Emery shrugged. "Millie. Or perhaps that dreadful Aldred woman." She shuddered. "I met her once. What a horrible, vulgar shrew. Dainty Darling indeed. Awfully pretty, of course. That's what Geraint sees in her, I suppose. He's easily seduced by a certain type of pretty face."

"That's his other mistress?" I asked. "The actress?"

"You *are* well informed. I thought I was going to have to explain and shock you some more. Yes, the actress, if you can call her one. I believe she has aspirations to become a real actress rather than a music-hall act. Perform Shakespeare and all that. I assume that's why she collected Geraint."

"Collected him?"

"She's been seen with several other interesting people. Keeps us all busy speculating whether they're lovers or just friends. Mostly professional men, some gentlemen, one or two minor titles. A Member of Parliament or two." She waved an expressive hand in the air.

"And she knows about you and Odelia?"

"Of course." Miss Emery's lips curved in amusement.

"So what would she have against O?"

"I think she'd like to supplant O as *maîtresse en titre*. Be the one who appears with Geraint at all the best places. She's ambitious and clearly doesn't enjoy playing second fiddle. Of course, she thinks O is getting old." She raised her eyebrows mockingly. "She's quite young, this one—younger than Cassiope. Geraint doesn't like it if I tease him about *that*."

"I imagine not," I murmured drily.

"It's not that anything's changed, really," Miss Emery continued. "Geraint acquired both O and myself when we were freshly hatched into the world. It's just that *he's* older each time. Isn't it strange how everyone thinks men become more distinguished as they age, while women generally fade into hags? Or become unhappy creatures like Millie, married and yet overlooked, as soon as they have a brat or two and begin to lose their figures."

"I think Lady Dorrian-Knowles is rather splendid, if only she were to realize it."

"*Brava!* I agree." Miss Emery held out a hand to me. "I like you, Lady Helena Whitcombe."

"You're not so bad yourself." I shook the proffered hand. "I was surprised you even agreed to see me."

"Why not? I was curious. It's so odd to think of Odelia as attached to a family somewhere. She and I, and even Millie, sometimes feel like a little family in ourselves—Geraint's women. We're surprisingly polite to each other when we meet."

Most of the time. The memory of Millie's hand flying toward Odelia wasn't polite, nor were the remembered expressions on both their faces. Not for the first time, I wished Sir Geraint could remove himself and his appetites to the Antipodes.

A discreet cough at the bedroom door reminded me that Guttridge was still consigned to the hallway and kitchen, so I prepared to leave. Guttridge went to find our carriage while Miss Emery and I waited at the door.

"Do you really live entirely on your own resources?" I was

curious. I did not recall meeting another woman of my own class who did so.

"Entirely." Miss Emery smiled. "I'm proud of it. My family disowned me, you see. Or at least my father did. Mother would probably love to see me again, poor soul, and I her. But I have this unfortunate objection to doing what I'm told."

I listened for a moment to the shouting of voices from a nearby wharf. "If I can ever be of assistance in any way, do let me know," I said, without really knowing why I said it. "And please write to me if you can think of anyone who might have a particularly bad grudge against Odelia."

"I promise I will." To my surprise, Miss Emery kissed me on the cheek. "I'm glad she has someone to look after her."

FORTIER THE ELDER

My talk with Miss Emery had been interesting, but not terribly informative, and Guttridge—who had apparently combined a little sprucing up and tidying of the kitchen with some discreet snooping—reported that she had found nothing untoward among the various papers shoved into teapots and crammed into drawers. Since I didn't really need her to accompany me to the luncheon with Fortier and his father, we decided she would devote Wednesday to finding out more about Miss Aldred, the Dainty Darling.

I dressed with particular care on the morning of the fifteenth. After all, it was always pleasant to make a good first impression on a new acquaintance. It was because of this anxiety to look my best, no doubt, that my heart beat a little faster as I took my footman's hand to descend from the carriage.

Guttridge and I had devoted some of our stay in London to ordering new clothes from the dressmaker Odelia had recommended, and I was rather pleased with my new black silk. My hat was also new; although definitely suitable for mourning, it was so much nicer than my previous widow's weeds, and in point of fact had a certain allure about it. A lady always feels both pleased and apprehensive about a new hat, especially when she is not tall. I had spent some time in front of the mirror to reassure myself that I looked neither too frivolous nor too gloomy.

It did not help my oddly wavering confidence that Fortier was standing just inside the door as I entered. That strange impression that he was different in Town—that we were all different, like characters in a play—struck me again and made me stumble over my intended first words of greeting. He did not smile. He bowed over my hand, kissing my lace-gloved fingers lightly.

"That's a beautiful hat." He watched as the maid helped me with my winter cape. "Father apologizes for not coming to greet you. He's in the library. It's the warmest room in the house, and he suffers from these cold, damp English mornings. November is not a pleasant month for invalids."

"How is he?" I asked.

"He seems to have reached a certain plateau for the moment." Fortier dismissed the maid and led me slowly toward the library. "I've noticed in my profession that the road to death is a strange journey. There are mountains and valleys and detours, and sometimes there are moments when everything seems to stand still and the patient becomes pensive, reflective, almost docile in the face of the inevitable. This has been one of those weeks. We've been talking a great deal about the past. Living in it, almost. There have been moments when I could almost feel my mother's spirit in the room—if I believed in such things."

I wrinkled my brow, looking up at Fortier. "Forgive me— I know this is a painful experience for you—but there seems to be a certain luxury in having the time to reflect and talk."

Fortier's lips curved, his eyes lighting up. "There, I knew

you would understand. Luxury is the right word. Sometimes I ache to return to Littleberry and resume my interrupted life, but when I sit with my father, there are moments when the universe appears to have halted. As if I can endlessly stretch the moments we have left together because time no longer has meaning. Are you ready?"

It was as if he had sensed my apprehensive mood and deliberately slowed our progress until I felt more at ease. I nodded and smiled, and Fortier opened the library door.

I had expected to see an elderly invalid, so it was a shock to realize that here was a life about to be cut short. The man who pushed himself up from one of the room's elegant Empire armchairs to greet me was younger than Geraint Dorrian-Knowles. I judged him to be the contemporary of my brother-in-law Sir Edward Freestone, one of the most vigorous men I knew.

His dark hair was barely streaked with gray. He wore it longer than Fortier did and was shaved *à la Souvarov,* a neat handlebar mustache meeting curved sideburns. There was something of the dandy in his mode of dress, a Continental attention to detail that his son had not inherited. He was of a height with Fortier, but it was no doubt illness that stretched his skin tight over his cheekbones. I suspected he had once been a man of some considerable physical presence.

He switched a thick, silver-topped cane from his right hand to his left so he could take my fingers in greeting. *"Enchanté de faire votre connaissance"* were his first words, then in English: "My son tells me that yours is the pretty house on the hill, the house that one sees from so many spots around Littleberry. I've only been there twice and don't suppose I'll ever see it again. It's some of the loveliest country in England."

"It is a pretty house." I smiled, thinking of my home. "And I agree with you about the Sussex countryside. I think it's matchless. But then, of course, it's hard for me to be impartial. Have you never been tempted to live in the country?"

His lips split in a broad smile, giving me a glimpse of the handsome man he had been. "'You find no man, at all intellectual, who is willing to leave London,'" he quoted. "'When a man is tired of London, he is tired of life; for there is in London all that life can afford.' The great Samuel Johnson said that, and he was quite right. My greatest pleasures are in reading, writing, and discussing with other literary men and women, and I could not find that kind of life in the country."

I sat down because I could see that the knuckles grasping the cane were white. The two men were then free to sit.

"Of course, for the English aristocrat, life's greatest pleasures are to be found in the outdoors," Monsieur Fortier continued. "I'll admit it's a great enjoyment to see those young men when they're in town. So well muscled from riding, such fresh complexions." He gave his son a playful pat on the arm. "Armand is happiest with an active life, aren't you, *fiston*? Although he does not neglect his reading. And you, Lady Helena, do you like to read?"

"Only novels."

"And what are you reading now?"

"*The Portrait of a Lady.*" I smiled. "I find Henry James somewhat daunting."

"He's a splendid fellow. Speaks excellent French. Don't be ashamed of liking novels—all life is in them."

"I like stories," I confessed. "I enjoy reading about people who are real to me for a short time, knowing that if terrible things happen to them, I can comfort myself in knowing they have no existence but in the writer's head."

"And your soul is purged of its excessive passions."

I laughed. "I'm not sure if I have any of those. I'm far too English."

Both men laughed with me, and we spent a few minutes

discussing the plot of James's novel, which Fortier's father had clearly read. I noted his eyes were more like Gabrielle's than Fortier's. His accent was strong, to be sure, but his English was extremely fluent and idiomatic. Luncheon was announced while we were still deep in our discussion.

"I have a story to tell you." Monsieur Fortier leaned heavily on his son's arm as he got to his feet. "Armand has asked me to relate it to you. I'm afraid I will have to begin as soon as we are served, as I grow tired quickly. It's a little piece of family history."

23

A FAMILY TALE

We ate in an elegant dining room furnished entirely in the style of the First French Empire. Long windows gave an excellent view of the gardens at the heart of Kensington Square, their lawns showing green through the half-bare branches of the trees.

I barely noticed what I ate, although it was all delicious. I was engrossed in the tale Monsieur Fortier began, as he had promised, once the wine was poured, the soup served, and the servants dismissed.

"Have you read *A Tale of Two Cities*?" Fortier's father asked me.

"A long time ago." I had read the novel with Daniel, the two of us side by side by the fire in the library at Hyrst one snowy week in winter. Daniel had done much of the reading, his imagination fired by the story of spies and prisoners, adventures and betrayals. I, a fifteen-year-old girl just beginning to feel the stirrings of love for my quick-witted, mercurial cousin, had listened intently so I could answer the questions Daniel would fire rapidly at me at the end of every chapter, testing my memory and my grasp of the story.

"Then you know that our Revolution of 1789 was the best of times and the worst of times. It swept away an era of considerable evil and replaced it with even more evil before the great Napoleon took our benighted country in hand and made it something to be proud of. Do you remember the wicked marquis in the story?"

"St. Evrémonde." I nodded.

"Not all nobles were wicked. Naturally, they wished to keep their rights and privileges, but some did not abuse them. Like the aristocracy of which you are a member, they looked after the people who farmed their fields and worked in their houses, and they served their country as best they could. Many attended at court. Versailles was, after all, the place where one met interesting people. One such a man was Jean-Benoît Alexandre Chrétien Fortier de Maival."

I shot a glance at the younger Fortier, who sat across the table from me. He picked up his wineglass and took a hasty sip, causing him to splutter very briefly into his napkin. I didn't want to interrupt his father's tale, but I did need to clarify one point.

"Was this nobleman an ancestor of yours?" I asked the older man.

"My grandfather."

His reply told me that Fortier was without any doubt a gentleman and almost certainly one of noble lineage. The *de* in de Maival was not proof of nobility, of course, but combined with the claim that Fortier's great-grandfather was at the court of Versailles, it certainly suggested nobility of a high degree. How interesting.

"Jean-Benoît was something of a writer," Monsieur Fortier continued. "Witty epigrams, poems, a little philosophy, that sort of thing. He was perhaps a touch eccentric. He drank perhaps a glass too many. But he was not a bad man. At the time my story begins, he was thirty years old and unmarried. He liked women well enough, but he held an ideal in his head that no suitable noblewoman had lived up to. One of his poems, the best of them, in my opinion, tells us that."

He took a deep breath before continuing, and I saw concern in his son's eyes. He had drunk only a very little of the excellent soup, while Fortier and I had finished our portions.

"Jean-Benoît might have spent the rest of his life in untroubled luxury, visiting the court at intervals and writing his poems for his own amusement, but in 1789 the National Constituent Assembly abolished the nobility's privileges. In the next two years, it abolished titles, and aristocrats became ordinary citizens in the eyes of the law. Many emigrated, as I'm sure you know, to escape the rioting in Paris. The rumor grew that the king would also emigrate with his family. At that time, the Duc de Maival scorned those who emigrated as cowards, but he had his own moment of cowardice that would determine the course of his life."

I stared hard at Fortier. He responded with a tiny shrug, a barely noticeable movement as, having ensured that his father was finished with his soup, he rang a small silver bell to summon the servants. *Duc* de Maival, indeed. It seemed possible that Blanche's and Gerry's fears were going to be put to rest.

"In February 1791, on the day called the *Journée des Poignards* by history, Jean-Benoît fell in with a crowd of young noblemen bent on defending their king from possible harm. Fools, all of them; their Day of Daggers was not an act worthy of their rank. If they had carried their swords as noblemen should, they might not have been disarmed and humiliated. But they carried daggers, concealed out of fear— or perhaps, as they claimed, to mark them as members of a new chivalric society—and were easily outclassed by soldiers with bayonets and swords. Jean-Benoît was in the rearguard. Seeing the other men being shoved and disarmed, he simply turned and walked away, dropping the dagger he held."

"No doubt he was entirely sober by then." Fortier smiled at his father.

"You are stealing my words, *mon fils*." Monsieur Fortier gave his son a wry look before turning to me. "My apologies, Lady Helena. He has heard this story too often. Yes, Jean-Benoît was now sober, and shame at his cowardice overwhelmed him. He took the motto *Sans Peur et Sans Reproche* to urge himself to greater bravery in the future. Not original, of course—the Chevalier de Bayard was called 'the knight without fear and beyond reproach'—but a good sentiment, nevertheless."

"Did he remain a devoted monarchist?" I asked.

"To the death. He began writing satirical pamphlets against the revolutionaries under the name *Sans Peur*. At first, he made barely no secret of his activities. He went openly to the premises of a successful printer, René Durand, to commission and collect his pamphlets, and that is where he met young Thérèse Durand. A meeting that was to lead to his downfall."

He paused, lifting his wineglass and looking around at his audience of two as if expecting a reaction. I realized, seeing Fortier's expression, that he had asked his father to tell the story instead of relating it to me himself precisely because of the pleasure Monsieur Fortier took in the telling. I was quite willing to play along with the performance.

"I suspect a romance," I said.

"And you would be right." Monsieur Fortier bowed slightly in my direction, clearly pleased by my interest. "Thérèse was a sophisticated young woman of nearly twenty, who, unusually for the time, had received an excellent education. She had a lively mind and pretty face and differed greatly from the vapid, fashionable women of Jean-Benoît's social circle. The duke fell deeply in love—for the first time, apparently. It is a flaw in my family that we love once and forever."

I kept my eyes on the father but was all too aware of the son across the table from me.

"But Thérèse was also sensible and selfless," Monsieur Fortier continued. "He was a nobleman and she a commoner, and Paris was becoming dangerous. She persuaded her suitor to flee to England. With bourgeois cunning, she and her father urged him to move as much of his wealth as possible to London. Most of it was in land and property, but with the help of the Durands and some honest bankers, he could ensure that a fortune in gold and material goods landed safely on English shores. He left in December 1791, taking his mother's jewelry with him."

"Without Thérèse?" I asked. This was certainly better than a novel.

"She said farewell to him with tears but would not dishonor herself or her family by an elopement." Monsieur Fortier held up a finger. "But only four months later, Jean-Benoît returned to claim Thérèse as his bride. His love for her overcame every scruple. Her indulgent father eventually consented to a private marriage, hoping they could escape to England together."

"You've forgotten the confiscation, *mon père*," said Fortier.

"So I have." Monsieur Fortier wiped his mouth on his napkin; he had barely taken a bite of his fish. "Between Jean-Benoît's departure and return to France, the government declared the property of any émigré forfeit to the nation. The Duc de Maival returned to France to find himself stripped of his land and estates, no richer now than the prosperous Durands, who were themselves in the process of transferring their wealth to England."

"Nobody was truly safe in France at that time," Fortier commented.

"Nobody." His father's face was grave. "Everyone dreaded a denunciation, and before the Durands and the newlywed couple could escape, the moment of terror came. Armed men were at their door—a desperate attempt to escape was in vain—they were captured."

He let his hand fall heavily on the table like the blade of the guillotine, and I shuddered. The next course was being served, and we all sat in silence while my imagination conjured up the horrible moment of arrest, the brutality of the revolutionary guards.

Monsieur Fortier took up his tale once the servants had left. "The duke, his bride, and his parents-in-law were now the guests of the Revolution, in the prison known as the Abbaye. Worse, Jean-Benoît had lost no time in getting his young wife with child. He and his father-in-law spent the days of their imprisonment writing urgently to every friend or acquaintance who might help set them free."

"And those friends were few and far between, either because they had escaped themselves or because they were terrified to act." Fortier supplied the words with the ease of long practice.

"No help was forthcoming." His father thumped the table gently to emphasize the words. "The man who held the power of life and death over the prisoners of the Abbaye was one Stanislas-Marie Maillard, the captain of the national guard. He was known as the 'judge of the Abbaye' and could at times be generous enough to set prisoners free. Thérèse made a friend of him, of sorts. With her bright face and clever wits, her willingness to help others, she was a general favorite." He paused ominously. "The family was imprisoned in July. We have some idea of what they suffered in the ensuing month from the account written by

François Jourgniac de Saint-Méard, a survivor of the massacre."

I gasped at the last word. Monsieur Fortier favored me with a gratified nod.

"Yes, Lady Helena, a massacre. History has never learned the exact sequence of events. Captain Maillard, for reasons unknown, allowed many prisoners to be dragged to the courtyard and slaughtered in full view of their fellow sufferers. All we know is that by the fifth of September, Thérèse's parents, those honest bourgeois, were dead. Jean-Benoît had been taken to another prison. Thérèse, her belly swollen in pregnancy, was somehow free and walking out of Paris. A few days later, she arrived at the country home of some old friends, starving and with bloodied feet, her eyes those of a madwoman. So violent was the disturbance to her mind and soul that her friends thought she would die, but over time she recovered her wits. The only thing she would ever say about that episode was that she would atone for what she had done."

"She was your grandmother, of course?" I asked. I realized I was forgetting to eat and resumed my meal with a smile at Fortier, who was applying himself to his meat with a good appetite.

"She was indeed." Monsieur Fortier nodded. "She had not one but two children, both boys. They were born at seven months by her calculations and were thus very small and frail, but both lived. Thérèse gave rise to much speculation among her friends by insisting that the second-born be called Thomas Stanislas. Why did she give him the name of her jailer? The firstborn did not take his father's name either, as she gave him the name Louis, for the king, and René, for her dead father. Yet she wrote to her husband, who was still in prison, and received his full approval, underlined to emphasize that his wishes accorded with hers. 'Let them remember me,' he wrote. 'And let every generation of my seed remember me, even if history does not.' My father told me this story just as I tell it to you."

"Did the duke live?" I asked, but I knew the answer before Monsieur Fortier shook his head.

"The Duc de Maival went to the guillotine in January 1793, three days after his king. He died bravely, a royalist to his last breath. Thérèse stayed in the countryside, biding her time until the Revolution ran its course and then embarking on a campaign to recover the money transferred to England by her husband and father. By the time France was—briefly —a monarchy again and her sons were grown men, she had succeeded. She lived a long life, my beloved *grand-mère*, and held both of my children in her arms."

I let out my breath in a sigh, and Monsieur Fortier smiled at both me and his son. "Nothing mattered more to her than her family. 'I have seen more than enough history' was her invariable response to questions about the Revolution. She never returned to Paris."

Another pause ensued as the syllabub was served. I enjoyed the taste of sweet wine and cream, glad to see that Monsieur Fortier ate most of his.

"Louis Fortier de Maival was my father," he said at length. "Named after a king, I suppose it was ironic that he grew up with no great love for royalty. He was a man of moderate tastes and moderate opinions, a gentleman of letters who disdained politics and detested fashion. His twin, on the other hand, was a stalwart royalist. Although bound by love, the brothers spent little time together as adults. I rarely saw *Oncle* Thomas and my cousins."

He sat back in his chair and sighed, closing his eyes for a long moment. Fortier rose and went to stand near his father.

"Will you have your coffee served in your room, Father? You have tired yourself."

He was answered by a gleam of brown eyes and a flap of the hand.

"*Assieds-toi.* We will have coffee served at the table, if Lady Helena does not mind." He tipped his head toward me.

"I don't mind at all." I could see by the way he sat that he was in pain, but he was clearly determined to see out the meal. A brave and proud man, that much was clear.

"And then I will have to retire." He smiled at me. "I have told you our story at Armand's request, but I regret that there is little time for me to question you about yourself. I hope you will come back to see me again."

THE COFFEE WAS SOON DRUNK. THERE FOLLOWED A BRIEF ceremony of farewell, and then Fortier *père et fils* left the room, the father leaning heavily on the son's arm. Less than five minutes later, Armand Fortier returned.

"Don't worry," I said. I could see by his expression that he needed me to leave but didn't want to say so. "I've already rung for my carriage to be brought round. Your presence by your father's side is essential right now. Now that I've met him, I'm even more eager to help him, if my skills are sufficient."

"They will be." Fortier looked relieved.

"Under your guidance." Smiling up at Fortier, I was glad to see the tension around his eyes relax. "I will return to Littleberry very soon. I suppose you'll be here for Christmas."

"I'll write to you," Fortier said. We could both hear the front door being opened, no doubt because my carriage had arrived. "Not that much of what I'd really like to say can go into a letter." He frowned. "I mean, about my family and so on." His frown deepened. "Why does life have to be so complicated?"

I laughed. "You're asking *me* that?"

Fortier's response was to kiss my hand briefly and turn on his heel, exiting the room swiftly across the path of the servant who had come to tell me my carriage was ready. It was an unceremonious farewell, but I understood. He and his father were clearly on terms of great affection, and Fortier was worried about him.

It wasn't long before I was in my carriage. I stared with blind eyes at the wet streets and leafless, soot-blackened trees, seeing not London, but the blood-drenched Paris of the Revolution. Monsieur Fortier's story mingled in my mind with Dickens's novel so that I imagined the Abbaye prison to have an old man in it making shoes.

Fortier de Maival—Duc de Maival. If Fortier's father was the eldest son of a duke, to whom had the title passed? Was there still a title to be passed down? Fortier's father had introduced himself simply as Alexandre Fortier, so it was probable he had an older brother.

And what difference should it make anyway? I had thought no less of Fortier when I imagined him and his family as belonging to the middle classes. And yet . . . I had been born into a society that set great store by titles, even those no longer supported by land or wealth. The Earls of Broadmere were still earls, even if they had only two houses and a few hundred acres of marshland and hillside.

And why was it I suspected the tale of the Duc de Maival had something to do with this outlandish business of a wife in France who was not a wife? I felt I was being fed an explanation in small spoonfuls, and the puzzle frustrated and annoyed me.

I pulled my gloves off impatiently and worried with my thumb at a tiny chip in one fingernail. It was possible, of course, that Fortier simply wanted to pique my interest in him—and he'd succeeded, drat the man. In the meantime, I still had the entire business of Odelia and the Dorrian-Knowleses to contend with, not to mention needing to come to a decision about the drawing room. Why, as Fortier had asked, did life have to be so complicated?

24

A FAMILY QUARREL

By the time my carriage arrived at Scott House, I had shaken off my reverie and tried to focus my attention on mundane matters. The gate that guarded the entrance to our house was resplendent in fresh matte black, the Scott crest barely visible under the new layer of paint. The area of the wall that had been daubed had been scrubbed thoroughly, although I could still see traces of red that had resisted all the efforts with wire brushes. It looked oddly new, but I was sure the London soot would soon darken it again.

I pressed my nose against the carriage window, trying to see the repair work more clearly through the November drizzle as the footman jumped down to pull on the bell. A scarlet flash caught my eye, and I craned my head around to look. It was Odelia—I could not mistake that easy, gliding walk and the tall, slender outline, even though a large man's umbrella hid her head.

She had not simply returned from a walk or an errand, I knew that immediately. I recognized the dress—an evening gown, and it was not yet three thirty. She had covered it with an ordinary winter coat instead of an evening cape and had detached the train, which, no doubt, was inside the large carpet bag she carried. She hadn't seen my carriage, I thought, because of her umbrella.

"Wait." I spoke through the flap that communicated with the driver. "Don't go through the gate until I tell you."

It was less than a minute before Odelia tipped the umbrella back, having clearly seen the carriage's wheels. The surprise on her face quickly hardened into something like defiance. I tugged down the window.

"You may as well get in and save yourself a few steps." My voice had an acid edge to it.

"I'll walk, thank you, darling." Her tone was light, insouciant. "Did you enjoy your luncheon with the Fortiers?"

I stuck my head out of the window. "Don't imagine you're just going to disappear upstairs, O." I said it in French; among my sisters and I, that had always been our way of discussing matters we didn't wish the servants to understand.

One corner of Odelia's lips curved upward. "*Pas devant les domestiques?* How very serious you look." She yawned, covering her mouth with an elegant, slim hand. "I'll go in through the billiard room, if it's all right with you."

"And how do you know it's unlocked?" I hissed. And then, answering my own question, "Because you've arranged it, haven't you? Not for the first time."

Odelia switched back to English. "You're not going to be tiresome, are you, Baby?"

"Don't call me Baby." The nickname stoked my anger. "And yes, I rather think I am. I will come straight up to your room."

COACHMAN AND FOOTMAN HAD STOLID, INDIFFERENT expressions on their faces as I descended from the carriage. Servants' faces, hiding every trace of opinion or mood. Servants always knew all one's secrets, of course—but how could Odelia *do* this? The staff at Scott House were an unknown quantity to me, and it would only take one whisper in the right ear for O's reputation to be seriously damaged.

I shed my outer clothing with hands that trembled slightly, surprised at how angry I was. I had become so used to the role of the youngest sister who never criticized, whose opinion never counted, that it was rare for me to do other than accept my sisters' behavior. Yet now I felt as if I was the adult, while Odelia was the wayward child who needed to be chastised. No—not a child. No child would return home in broad daylight like this, brazenly advertising her absence.

Guttridge was out, and I took a little longer than usual to replace my buttoned boots with soft indoor pumps. Fifteen minutes after entering the house, I knocked sharply at Odelia's bedroom door. She opened it immediately.

"Help me get this off, would you, Helena?" she asked before I could say anything. "The skirt's a little tricky."

She had already unhooked the front of her low-cut bodice, and my attention was captured by her necklace. Fifteen or so garnets, perfectly matched and set in scroll-work, caught gleams from the winter sun that was now nearing the horizon, peeping from under the lifting bank of cloud. The choker she usually wore for the evening—six strings of pearls with a pretty intaglio at its center—lay on her bed as if discarded, and I instantly knew she had just been given the garnets. Mingled fragrances of cigars, rich foods, and wine hung around her, assaulting my senses as she moved.

"You've seen Sir Geraint, haven't you?" I took a firm grasp of her skirt, sliding my other hand down between her corset cover and the lawn lining of the heavy brocade to search for the hook and eye. The back of my hand registered the heat of her body, the slight dampness of perspiration.

She made no answer as I found the hook and worked it out from where it had caught. A faint animal smell came from her as the skirt came loose and fell down her hips—the smell of a man's bed. *No more morals than a cat*, Michael had said, and she *was* like a cat, elegant and indifferent. The weak golden glow of the fleeting sunlight made her dark blond hair look tawny. Her eyes narrowed to slits to avoid the sudden flash of light that reflected off a mirror.

"You're cross with me." She threw the bodice on the bed as she stepped out of the skirt, followed by the skirt itself. Petticoats, corset, and the rest followed until she was stripped down to her combinations. She rummaged in the closet set into the paneled wall and pulled out a wrapper, shrugging herself into the brightly colored fabric and pulling out hairpins as she wandered toward the bed. The sunlight was fading fast. I crossed to the fire to light a spill so I could set the lamp burning.

"You look drunk," I said as I passed in front of her. *Or drugged.* There was something about her eyes, something wild and restless, that made me think of Papa. Had I seen him return from just such a night?

"Is that why you're cross with me?" Odelia's long, slender arm intercepted me as I crossed her path, sliding across my shoulders. "Why? I was just celebrating a little. I haven't had a drop for hours. Just a little champagne with breakfast."

"Celebrating what?" I was too fond of my sister to break free from her grasp roughly, but I could feel the rigidity in my body. She was right. I could not hide my anger.

"I finished the Shalott picture, and it's rather good." Odelia smiled lazily. "We will have to have a *vernissage*, invite a few people. Don't sulk, Helena." Her fingers were under my chin, tipping my head up slightly. "You know how hard I've been working. Do you know, I've even told Maisie she can tidy up the studio a little. She might have finished. Won't you come up and look at my *Lady*?"

I refused to be thrown off the scent. "Don't you care about our family at all?" I asked. "You know how servants gossip."

"The trick is to treat them well." Odelia's gaze was directed at the setting sun. "Don't give them a reason to take revenge. Let them do as they like and they're yours for life."

"That's nonsense." My voice sounded high. "It's probably time someone looked at the household books. There's bound to be waste and probably stealing the way this house is run. It's Michael's money you're spending, and that's not fair. He doesn't have enough after the way Papa left things."

"Michael can't read the books. Why are we arguing about the servants, you disapproving little thing?" Odelia lifted her arm from my shoulder, stretching and yawning. "Goodness, I'll need an hour or two's sleep before dinner."

"We're *not* arguing about the servants." I wished I could shake her, but I'd never lain hands on anyone in anger. "We're discussing your behavior, which is appalling. Besides, I could always ask Brandrick to come up here with Michael and go through the household ledgers."

"But you *loathe* Brandrick, darling. Oh, don't be tiresome. And do stop talking about the running of the house. I've managed perfectly well for—goodness, how many years? Sixteen or seventeen. Living like a hermit in my little garret. I have very few debts, you know."

"Because *he* supports you. Did he give you that necklace?"

"Ah." Odelia squinted down at the garnets. "I'd forgotten this. Yes, Geraint wanted to make up for all the horridness."

"Everyone will know you couldn't have paid for that."

Odelia sighed. "I'll sell the Shalott painting easily—I know just who'll love it—and then I'll appear in public with my pretty new necklace and drop a hint here and there that I've done rather well out of the lady in the tower. People will naturally connect the one with the other. I'm not stupid, Helena."

She went to sit in the armchair near the fire, gazing up at the picture of herself as the Snow Queen. "You won't turn into Gerry, will you? Always talking about the rules and the family as if *she* hadn't broken a rule or two when she was young." She smirked. "As if the Scott-De Quincy family didn't do what it liked anyway. Papa always said our motto should be *Comme Il Me Plaît* rather than *Je Vive En Espoir*. You were never so prim when you first came out. And heaven knows Justin wasn't straitlaced. All this lady-of-the-manor business has changed you. Insisting on that silly rule of Mama's— twenty minutes alone with a man, no more, and the door always open. For heaven's sake, you're a widow, not a maiden who needs her honor protecting. Why don't you have some fun with that delectable Frenchman? I can see you want him."

My cheeks were instantly aflame. "We're not talking about me. Will you stop trying to distract me?" I folded my arms. "I'm glad I haven't given Sir Geraint an answer yet. You've made up my mind for me—he's not coming to my house. I can see I can't trust you. You may know how to avoid scandal in London, but you won't manage it in Littleberry."

Odelia's eyes widened in alarm. "But you must—not for me, for him. He's so brave, but he really needs to get away from Millie and the children for a while. He needs the money—"

"And yet he's given you a piece of jewelry that costs more than many people make in two years."

"He's a generous man." Odelia concealed a yawn behind her hand. "A generous, lovely man."

"A destructive, selfish man."

"All artists are selfish. We have to be. Destructive too, maybe. Geraint is simply mad about doing the *Nightingale* series. You can't imagine what it is to have the perfect painting inside you, the frustration of needing to work at that *one thing* and the way it stops you from working on anything else. He's asked me to describe your drawing room in detail a dozen times."

"Odelia!" I couldn't keep the irritation out of my voice. "That man has a *wife* and children and *grandchildren,* for heaven's sake. Your behavior—especially if you continue to behave this carelessly—will destroy them. The two of you may want to live in a little world of dreams and fairy tales, but *they* have to live in the real world, which is full of people who judge and condemn. I won't be the fool who lets you bring your lover down to Littleberry. I—"

But my words were cut short by the screams coming from the floor above us.

25

MAGGOTS AND NASTINESS

It wasn't just one scream either. The noise went on and on, shrieks that could probably be heard in St. James's Park.

The sound propelled me out of Odelia's bedroom and onto the stairs leading to the studio. As I followed the turn of the stairs, a flash of color in the corner of my eye resolved itself into Odelia just below me, clutching her bright wrapper in one hand as she climbed upward, noiseless in her black silk stockings.

"Maisie's having hysterics." Her brow creased. "Why? There's nothing shocking in my studio, not even my paintings."

I said nothing, saving my breath for the climb. The shrieking got closer. The studio door burst open, and the maid tumbled out, her cap askew and her face running with tears. She held her hands in the air, shaking them as if she were doing some eldritch dance.

I went to capture the jerking hands, but she held them even higher, stiffening so that I couldn't reach them.

"No, madam! I mean, my lady! Oh, I 'ave to wash them

straightaway . . . It's all over them. There's nothing on the rest of me, is there? Oh, oh, oh, those things ain't in my 'air, are they? I 'ave to wash them straightaway . . ."

"Why don't you use my washbasin, you silly girl?" Odelia grasped the maid's waist and began to turn her back toward the studio. "Did you get paint on your hands? Why are you making such a fuss?"

Maisie resisted Odelia's arms. "I don't want to go back in there. I 'ate maggots and nastiness." The girl's accent was pure Cockney, ugly sounds that contrasted with her pretty face.

"Did you find something nasty?" I kept my voice low and soothing, putting a hand on her shoulder. "You don't have to look at it, do you? You can just turn your face away from whatever it is, and I'll lead you to the washbasin." I had no idea where it was but supposed I could find it with Odelia's help. "You can wash your hands, and you'll feel much better." It was a little like dealing with Annabelle Alice when she was in a tantrum.

"I 'ave to wash them." The plangent sounds were subsiding into a whine.

"And you shall. Can you tell me where the nasty thing is?" I cast a puzzled glance at Odelia as I began to lead Maisie back into the room. A musty odor assailed my senses. Did O never open a window?

"It was on the table, but I dropped it on the floor. It 'ad maggots in it. They touched my 'ands." Maisie's voice rose to a howl. "I 'ate maggots."

"Are you talking about my parcel?" Odelia preceded us into the room, pulling her robe back up over her shoulders. "Faugh, it does smell in here." She crossed to the table, giving me a small push in the direction of the washstand, which was crowded with jars holding paintbrushes. I vaguely recognized the rugs on the floor from our childhood days.

They had been old even then and were now completely ruined.

"It can't be the parcel. That's just paint. I've probably left some food moldering somewhere." Odelia spoke behind my back. "I daresay I should let the servants clean more often—oh God!"

I turned just in time to see O darting toward the door, her hand over her mouth. A characteristic sound, accompanied by much splattering, told me poor Maisie was going to have even more unpleasant cleaning up to do. Honestly, couldn't Odelia have found a receptacle to be sick into?

I concentrated on pouring water into the basin, prompting Maisie to wash her hands well with the fresh bar of soap she'd brought up. The smell was stronger now, and I longed to open a window, but I held myself in patience while the girl washed her hands twice.

Looking around a little as she performed her ablutions, I could see that tidying the studio must be a daunting task at any time. Maisie had done about a quarter of the work, as evidenced by the difference between the ordered chaos of one end of the room and the absolute chaos of the rest. The smells of paint and turpentine mingled with the unpleasant odor, intensified by the sickening smell from the pile of crockery Maisie had gathered up into a pair of zinc pails, ready to take downstairs. I was going to have to have a word with Mrs. Coles about the state of this room. I would make sure I permanently countermanded any orders Odelia might give about not disturbing her domain.

"I rather fear Lady Odelia has been sick on the landing," I said to Maisie once she had splashed a little water on her face and dried herself on the clean towel that hung nearby.

"I don't suppose it can be worse than in 'ere. Blee—bloomin' nightmare it is at the best of times. We drew straws for it, and I got the short 'un. And wot a short 'un it was." She shook her fair hair, pursing her lips. I could tell she was recovering her native resilience.

"If you can bring yourself to finish the studio, I'll make sure there's an extra day's wages in it for you." I watched her face light up. "And I'll put in a little something extra for Iris if she cares to help you. I'm going to make sure these rooms are cleaned regularly from now on, no matter what Lady Odelia says. Now, are you able to cope with the mess on the landing? You can finish the studio tomorrow. I'll make sure the . . . the parcel is removed. Where are the candles? It's almost dark in here, and I need to see what I'm doing."

"It's gas, m'lady. 'Er ladyship keeps the matches on the mantelpiece."

"Of course." I dismissed Maisie to fetch what equipment and help she needed and gazed at the studio. Fetching the matches from the mantelpiece, I rather nervously lit the gas lamps, which I remembered from my young days. Once the yellow flares had transformed the sky outside the window from pale gray to deep black, I turned to face my next challenge.

Fortunately, I had a strong stomach. There were certainly maggots, and the smell, close up, was very strong indeed. A few splashes of liquid led from the table to where the parcel lay partially open. Mercifully, it had fallen onto a small rug—the cleanest one, of course.

I crossed to the fireplace, in which the embers of an earlier fire glowed gently behind a fireguard. I located the fire tongs and the poker and spotted a good-sized fire shovel leaning against a stack of canvases. Armed with these weapons, I confronted the parcel again.

It took me a few tries to get the thing a little more open without touching it. Eventually, I found that if I grasped the more intact part with the fire tongs and used the poker to work at the disintegrating bits, I made rapid headway. The string, which had been tied tightly and well knotted, was a real nuisance until I found a pair of scissors. The sender had used cardboard, possibly cut and folded to make a box, and had wrapped the whole in brown paper. Liquid had seeped through one side and, as Maisie had said, that side of the parcel had split open when she'd dropped it. The wriggling white maggots were mostly intent on their job of eating whatever it was and did not bother me. The few that had spilled out onto the rug were heading back toward their source of nourishment.

It was some kind of animal, as I had suspected, but I couldn't see exactly what. Black fur . . . a cat? A dog? And wait . . . there was something else. A few moments' work with the poker and fire tongs revealed . . . a knife? An ivory shaft and metal blade, possibly of medieval style. A letter opener, perhaps. And there was a piece of paper, discolored by the nasty-smelling, viscous liquid. I gingerly pulled at a corner that had remained dry.

Bitch. That word again—and it was the same writing as the anonymous letter. The handwriting on the outer wrapper was, as I had already noticed, painstakingly neat capital letters.

I could hear voices on the stairs. It was Mrs. Coles and almost certainly Maisie. I glanced around the room, spotting a small stack of newspapers. I spread several broadsheets on top of the split parcel and rolled it in the rug. That would at least do to get the mess out of the studio without getting anything on the floor.

Mrs. Coles walked into the studio without knocking. Behind her, I could see Maisie with a mop, pail, and bucket, muttering to herself as she set about cleaning up the mess Odelia had made. And where was Odelia? I wondered.

"Another unpleasant prank." I pulled the corners of the rug together more firmly. "No doubt one of those disturbed people who enjoy persecuting anyone with a title. I'd like you to have it taken to the toolshed, if you would. There is one at Scott House, isn't there? I want it kept in there overnight, and I would like it kept just as it is and not unwrapped."

"There's a toolshed, of course, m'lady, but . . . shouldn't it be burned straightaway? Maisie said there were maggots in it."

"We'll burn it tomorrow once I've had a proper look." I passed the unwieldy bundle to Mrs. Coles. "I'd rather as few people as possible saw it. Do you understand?" I waited for the housekeeper's nod. "And I'm afraid we will have to have words about the state of these rooms."

GUTTRIDGE RETURNED ABOUT TWO HOURS AFTER DINNER, BY which time I felt exhausted and peevish. My solitary dinner hadn't helped. It wasn't one of the cook's best efforts, coated in a sauce that reminded me rather too well of the glutinous mess that pooled under the sticky fur of the animal in the parcel.

Odelia had not joined me, pleading an upset stomach. I couldn't really blame her for that, but I was irked by the conviction that one of her reasons for not appearing was to avoid a repeat of the conversation interrupted by Maisie's screams.

All I'd really wanted to do after dinner was lie down, but I'd forced myself to go to the writing desk. After staring into space for a full twenty minutes, I'd thought of ringing for Guttridge to see if she could find the lavender and chamomile distillation we'd made to soothe just such a troubled brow as I now had. Finding that she was still out when I needed her was enough to plunge me into a state of headache and nervous irritation.

I could have looked for the lavender water myself, of course. Or rung for a cup of tea—or even a small brandy for its medicinal properties. But I had worked myself up into that mood where one refuses to seek relief for one's ills, a state of martyrdom aimed at justifying my bad temper while simultaneously stoking it. The result was that I stared with sore eyes at the blank paper, sighing out my griefs to an empty room—and it was not the events of the afternoon, but the luncheon with Fortier and his father that ran around the inside of my head like a rat in a trap.

Eventually, I realized the problem lay in the fact that I was seeing Fortier differently, and I didn't want to. His father's story had inevitably cast a somewhat romantic air over a man whose personality and, yes, drat him, physical attributes already had too much power to disturb my equilibrium.

And now I had to summon him to come to my aid. I couldn't think of anyone else I could ask for an opinion on the nasty mess now lying in the toolshed. Certainly not Odelia. I'd never imagined she'd have such a weak stomach. For heaven's sake, she was country-bred like me and therefore perfectly familiar with the grosser side of nature. When I was eight years old and she eighteen, she had come home from her first fox hunt with the blood from the animal's severed tail on her cheeks and a triumphant smile on her mud-splattered face—a savage princess, a true descendant of our warrior ancestors. Had living in Town really made her that fastidious?

I certainly couldn't ask any of the servants to help me. Perhaps if Guttridge had been there—but she was not and I was cross with her.

My note to Fortier no doubt sounded a little curt in consequence of my mood, but once done, I had signed and sealed it and rung for someone to take it immediately to the postbox without giving myself time to change my mind.

Then I had gone up to my bedroom, dragging my feet on the stairs in a way that would have earned me a good deal of correction from Mama, and sat stupidly on my bed until Guttridge finally entered.

"Where have you been?" I inquired without any other greeting.

"I'm sorry, my lady." Guttridge laid down the fresh linen and new bar of rose-and-geranium soap she'd brought up with her. "Would you like me to get a bath ready?" She was using her best lady's maid voice, cool and soothing, entirely impersonal.

"I'm too tired to bathe. Just the usual jug will be fine." I massaged my temples. "I'll make sure I scrub under my fingernails."

I watched Guttridge as she moved past me, wondering if I should demand a detailed account of her evening. After all, it had not been her free time. She had been on an errand for me, and she had stayed out unconscionably late. Undoubtedly, as her employer, I had a right to insist. Yet such a display of the power I wielded over her would probably end up being unpleasant for both of us.

I stared down at my black silk pumps, noting a small spot on the fabric that most likely originated from the contents of the parcel. If Guttridge had been there instead of Iris, she would have noticed it and supplied a fresh pair of slippers.

No doubt by the morning the spot would be gone in that slightly otherworldly way one's clothes had of healing themselves overnight. Even after I had gone to bed, Guttridge would still have to look over the day's clothing. Before seeking her own rest, she would send some items to the laundry, launder the most personal ones herself, and brush, clean, freshen, and carefully put away the rest. And she'd been out all day. No doubt she was tired too.

Guttridge had been moving around the room while I worked my way through to this somewhat humbling conclusion. When I finally looked up, a trace guiltily, she was holding out one of my handkerchiefs to me. It smelled pleasantly of lavender and chamomile.

My smile wavered as I took the square of lace-trimmed linen and applied it to my aching head. "Sit down, please, Guttridge. I apologize for being out of sorts. You don't have to tell me about your day if you're too tired."

Guttridge sat on a low chair near the fire. To my surprise, her carefully guarded expression transformed into one of obvious eagerness.

"But I'm *dying* to tell you, my lady."

"Oh! Are you?" I suddenly felt rather more awake.

"Did you enjoy your luncheon?"

"It feels like a lifetime ago—but yes."

Guttridge looked as if she would like to ask me more but then got a grip on her curiosity. "Well, my lady, as you know, I went to the matinee performance. I thought I'd leave plenty of time to get my work done after."

I felt crushed by the thought of her concern for me. "So what happened?"

"The Dainty Darling wasn't in the matinee. She was supposed to be, but they substituted another actress at the last moment." Guttridge folded her arms. "Well, my lady, I have to tell you that my blood was up. I decided then and there that I wasn't leaving till I got a sniff of my quarry. Perhaps I should have come back here—it's not that far after all—but I felt like if I didn't stay on the scent, she would elude me again." She smiled. "I knew you'd understand when I explained. So I made sure Miss Aldred would be in the evening's performance, bought another ticket, and got myself a bite to eat. I found a nice little establishment where I could eat and keep an eye on the stage door."

"You couldn't have tried to find her at home and save yourself the trouble of watching the performance twice?" I asked.

"Oh no, my lady. I know enough about theatrical people to understand you don't bother them before a performance. Besides, they wouldn't let me know where she lived, and I tried ever so hard. They thought I was one of those fanatics, those people who get obsessed with the performers and haunt their footsteps. Miss Aldred has quite a following—men, mostly, although there's no accounting."

"So did you see her?"

"She'll be here at eleven o'clock tomorrow, my lady. She didn't stay for her final curtain, and as soon as I realized, I nipped out of my seat and waylaid her, so to speak. I nearly got thrown out of the theater, but I'd taken the liberty of having one of your ladyship's cards with me, and when I said your name, I could almost see her ears prick up. It's funny how people behave when they get the sniff of a title. Anyway, I put on my best manner and requested the pleasure of her attendance in Saint James's. Worked a treat."

26

DISSECTING THE CLUES

When I awoke at seven, there was a note from Fortier promising to be round at nine thirty. He was true to his word.

"I hope this isn't too early." Fortier took my hand briefly and waited till I'd sat down before doing the same. "I'm mystified; is there something wrong again? More vandalism?"

I suppressed a tiny belch—I had hurried my breakfast—and wondered where to start. I would probably have to tell him everything. My silence must have unnerved Fortier since he leaned forward, an expression of alarm in his eyes.

"Forgive me, but I feel that something serious is happening. Is there anything really wrong? Nothing affecting Lady Odelia's health, for example? Or yours?"

"Heavens, no." I sat up straighter, hoping I looked healthy. "I'm in the pink, thank you. Odelia is also in good health, although she's had some upsets." I laced my fingers together. "Do you remember we, er . . . we had some red paint on our gate?"

"Of course I remember."

"The word was *bitch*, as it happens. There's now been another communication along similar lines, only this time it was in a parcel that seems mostly composed of a dead animal. And a knife—a paper knife, I think. And before any of that, Odelia received an anonymous letter that went much farther than just calling her a . . . you know."

I watched the emotions flit across his face and glimmer in the depths of his remarkable eyes. Curiosity, astonishment, and something deeper, something that struck an answering spark of warmth in my belly. We had sat like this before, hadn't we, discussing grave, out-of-the-ordinary matters? In the year after Justin's death, trying to make sense of a world that suddenly seemed a little more dangerous, feeling the thrill of that danger in a way that didn't need expressing in words. But Fortier's response was a simple question.

"Do you still have this parcel? And the letter?"

"Both." I smiled. "I asked you to come here to look at the parcel. You're the best person to inspect it with me before I have it burned. I know you won't be put off by how revolting it is. I started to pull it apart last night to have a closer look but thought better of it and had it put in the toolshed. The maggots won't be nearly such a nuisance in there."

Fortier's thick, black eyebrows rose at least an inch in an expression I found decidedly French. Then his face positively glowed with a smile that seemed to envelop me in warmth.

"What a woman you are, Helena. I can't imagine any other lady in your walk of life dealing with a situation like this with such aplomb. I'd think most of them would go off into a fit of the vapors and faint on the carpet."

"Then you don't know nearly enough aristocratic Englishwomen." I sniffed. "We're bred to rule, you know. Rulers don't have the vapors. Fainting is for the middle classes."

This time he laughed outright. "Did Lady Odelia also take

it all in her stride? Jump the fence head-on, as I hear she does on the hunting field?"

"She was sick all over the floor. On the landing, fortunately, and not right next to the evidence. It would have been an awful nuisance."

I joined him in laughter, ignoring my feeling of disloyalty to Odelia. After all, I had already decided to commit another act of perfidy.

"Before we look at it, I'm going to tell you something." My smile had faded. "It appears you're going to become acquainted with all my family's worst secrets. You know the very worst, about Mama—I suppose Odelia's isn't as bad. Although there is that saying about a fate worse than death."

"A ridiculous saying that any Frenchman worth his salt must disdain." Fortier spoke briskly. "We are practical people, and common sense tells us that there is, in fact, no fate worse than death. May I surmise, perhaps, that Lady Odelia's honor has been tainted?" He frowned. "Against her will?"

I snorted. "Very much *not* against her will. Did I tell you Sir Geraint Dorrian-Knowles wants me to commission paintings for my drawing room?"

"Gaby told me." Fortier's eyebrows rose again. "Does he have something to do with this?"

"Everything."

So I told him. A twitch of one corner of his mouth was his only reaction to the revelation that Odelia was Sir Geraint's mistress. A frown creased his brow as he listened to the tale of Sir Geraint's attempt at suicide and the subsequent altercation with Millie. When I told him about the letters received by Sir Geraint and recent events at Scott House, it was puzzlement that dominated his expression.

"Has Sir Geraint ever been the subject of such attacks as the paint and this parcel?"

"I have no idea," I confessed. "I suppose I could ask him."

"If not, we have an interesting development in the case. Lady Odelia has received only one letter. The perpetrator has moved swiftly to a simpler, very crude expression of hatred. And there is no blackmail, you say?"

"No demand for money." I shrugged. "And so far, no specific threats, although I certainly wouldn't describe this person's actions as unthreatening. As you say, it's an expression of hatred."

"He could be working himself up to something worse still."

I shivered as if someone had placed an icy hand on my neck. "Then you don't think I'm overreacting?"

"No, indeed."

"Good, because I've already spoken to one of Sir Geraint's other mistresses, and yet another is coming to see me at eleven."

The look on Fortier's face prompted yet another round of explanations. "Guttridge knows all of it," I finished after about fifteen minutes. "I can trust her discretion—and yours."

"I'm honored." Fortier drew a deep breath. "Now to the inspection of the parcel? I'm afraid I can't stay too long. I'm expecting a surgeon friend and don't want to keep him waiting. A second opinion on my father's case, you understand."

"Then shall we go to the toolshed?" I rose to my feet.

Fortier smiled. "How could I resist such an invitation? And I hope Miss Guttridge will join us, if she's willing. After the way she behaved at the deathbed of Susan Hatherall, I suspect she may enjoy the treat."

I HAD MY DOUBTS ABOUT INVOLVING GUTTRIDGE IN THE unpleasant task ahead of us, but in any event, going outside on a damp, chill November morning necessitated an extra layer of clothing. So I rang for her and put the question. The light in her eyes gave me my answer before she spoke.

Five minutes later, a strange little procession comprising a widow, a lady's maid, and a French physician in top hat and spats made its way toward the more utilitarian part of Scott House's garden.

I had taken the precaution of requesting the toolshed key from Mrs. Coles the day before since I didn't want any inquisitive servants interfering with what was bound to be the principal topic of conversation in the servants' hall. Accustomed to having doors opened for me, I found it some-what thrilling to insert the key in the lock and reveal the folded rug.

Guttridge watched eagerly as Fortier rummaged in a pocket, extracting a pair of thin cotton gloves to replace the fine doeskin ones he was wearing. He took a careful hold of the bundle—I was glad to see nothing was leaking out—and carried it onto the gravel path, where a spotted laurel shielded our proceedings from any watchers in the house.

"An excellent spot to conduct an investigation." Fortier surveyed the wall, glistening with damp, and the few spar-rows that darted hopefully among the branches of the surrounding shrubs. "Oh, thank you, Miss Guttridge." He took the physician's bag that Guttridge had carried from where he'd left it near the shed and removed from it a fear-some-looking instrument in the form of a hook with a wooden handle and something that resembled a cross between meat scissors and an instrument of torture.

"What are those?" Guttridge, who was carefully unfolding the carpet with her bare hands—she had not bothered to fetch her own outer clothing—gazed avidly at the strange implements.

"They are designed to assist in the swift and invariably

fatal extraction of a child when the surgeon has decided to save the mother's life at its expense." Fortier set the tools carefully on the edge of the rug. "I've never used them for their proper purpose. And this," he rummaged in the bag and pulled out a penknife, "is for sharpening my pencils." He smiled up at us. "But I keep it very sharp, and it may come in handy."

"I think you're showing off," I said rather tartly.

"Perhaps." Fortier put the penknife next to the other instruments. "It's a joy to have an appreciative audience." He began pulling the sheets of newspaper off from where I had thrown them over the parcel. "I'm glad we're outside," he remarked. "It's quite fragrant."

It was, and I realized I was standing downwind of it. My breakfast churned gently in my stomach, and I told myself severely that I would *not* be sick.

"Come and stand next to me, Lady Helena." Fortier had abandoned his contemplation of the parcel and was looking at me. "Breathe in through your mouth and out through your nose a few times."

"I'm fine." But I did as he said, and indeed the smell was less strong where he was standing. Guttridge seemed indifferent to the odor, watching carefully as Fortier used the instruments to take apart the nasty mess until the contents of the parcel were entirely exposed.

"That's a cat." Guttridge leaned over for a better look. "Crushed by the wheel of a carriage, if I'm any judge."

"I agree." Fortier, who was in a crouching position next to me, looked up from under the brim of his hat. "All right, Lady Helena?"

"I won't be sick." The first sight of the pathetic corpse had been bad enough—I hadn't realized a carriage wheel could do such dreadful damage—but I had seen worse things on country walks. Scotty was fond of the remains of deer . . . I could hear my dog barking from the servants' quarters.

"These might be the animal's inner organs." Fortier's voice tailed off as he used the hook to lever up one side of the defunct cat where there had been a particularly nasty mess. "Ah, no—do you know, I think this is ordinary butcher's offal."

"That's my guess." Guttridge nodded enthusiastically. "With the cat on top for maximum effect." She took possession of the hook and, at Fortier's nod, used it to tease out the knife and the piece of paper, whose one word was now almost obliterated by the liquid soaked into it. "That's just a cheap letter opener, the sort you could buy almost anywhere. Should I keep it safe, sir?"

"Mmm." Fortier was still crouching, gazing at the parcel. "I would feel happier reporting this to the police." He pulled off his gloves, inspected his fingers, and then looked across at me. "They might make more of the paper or the writing or the string . . ." He shook his head. "But you don't want to, do you? Or you'd have sent for the police rather than summoning me."

"They'll ask questions." I felt my shoulders slump. "It was bad enough with the gate, but at least we could allow them to believe it was an ordinary act of vandalism." I looked down at my feet, encased in galoshes but rapidly turning into blocks of ice in the November chill. "We didn't tell them about the letter."

"Because they would ask Lady Odelia if anyone had a grudge against her." Fortier's expression was sympathetic.

"And she'd have to lie—and so would I." I swallowed. "I'm inclined to follow Sir Geraint's example and burn the lot. I'm sorry. It was foolish to ask you to come here."

"I'll rinse these under the pump." Guttridge had been

gathering up the tools Fortier had used. "Don't forget you have a visitor in half an hour, my lady."

Fortier retrieved his doeskin gloves and dropped the cotton ones into his bag, watching Guttridge's retreating figure before reaching out to offer me his arm. I took it, and we turned away from the untidy scene, which seemed far worse somehow now that we had completed our entirely futile inspection.

"Don't ever regret calling on me for help." Fortier's voice was low. "Will you take Lady Odelia back to Littleberry with you? If she were my sister, I'd want to get her away from this person."

"She usually comes to Whitcombe at Christmas." I hung my head. "But we're not getting on entirely well—there's the matter of the commission, you see. Oh, Fortier, it's such a mess." I could hear Scotty's yelps growing more frantic, either to see Fortier or in longing for the enticing dead things I was handling. "I don't know what to do for the best, and I can't simply extricate myself from the situation no matter how much I'd like to."

Fortier released my arm as we neared the house, turning to me. "Sometimes, when we are in a corner, we have to let events play out until we can see our way clear to the correct course of action. That's the situation I'm in, and I'm sorry to see that you too are enmeshed in a web that's not of your own making. Just remember, my dear, that I am your friend —your ally—and don't hesitate to call on me again." One corner of his mouth lifted in the ghost of a smile. "Perhaps next time I can be of more assistance."

27

A PERFORMANCE

ortier left me at the door. Mindful that Guttridge was probably cleaning up the mess in the garden, I hastened to my room to neaten my appearance. My hands had thawed, and my feet, though still cold, were feeling a little more normal by the time I was sitting decorously in the drawing room, awaiting the imminent arrival of Miss Elisabetta Aldred with mingled curiosity and apprehension.

The undisguised awe in the footman's tone and the rush of blood to the tips of his large ears as Miss Aldred passed close to him to enter the room suggested he was one of her admirers. Scotty, who had just about forgiven me for going outside without him, greeted my visitor with one high-pitched bark before laying his head back down on his paws, eyeing me with the forlorn expression he reserved for when he felt he was hard done by. I rose to offer the actress my hand.

She *was* dainty, after a fashion. Perhaps an inch or two taller than me, she was possessed of a tiny waist, a rosebud mouth, and a magnificent head of hair the color of ripe wheat, curling around her face under a wide-brimmed hat trimmed with a huge feather dyed deep red. Her figure was a little heavy on top due to the overweening development of her chest, her cheeks and lips were touched with a hint of rouge, and her eyes were shrewd and mocking, but all in all she looked no more like an actress than many titled women of my acquaintance.

"It's very kind of you to come," I said conventionally as I offered her a chair and rang the bell for coffee. "I'm sure you're always very busy."

"It's my day off." Miss Aldred settled herself into her chair with an ease and confidence that bespoke a long acquaintance with being on show. "I don't even have a rehearsal today, for a mercy. Just an appointment with the costume-maker."

She spoke well. Was that the result of her background, I wondered, or many hours of elocution lessons? I had expected the overly refined voice often affected by those who had fought their way up from low beginnings. But then, how many actresses did I know? I thought of Gerry's or Blanche's reaction if they learned of this meeting and fought the desire to giggle.

"Your maid told me you wanted to talk to me about Geraint. And that you're O's sister." The Dainty Darling tilted her head on one side, regarding me intently. "How very curious was what I thought. I know O doesn't like me, but couldn't she speak to me herself? I've never known her to need an intermediary."

"Odelia's . . . busy." As far as I knew, Odelia was still in bed—in her *own* bed, in this house, I hoped. "Besides," I continued, "I had my reasons for wanting to talk with you myself."

"Yes, I don't suppose she'd have invited me here." The actress surveyed the room slowly, with evident curiosity. "To her ancestral home." She pursed her lips. "It's a little old-fashioned, isn't it?"

"It's handily located." I was not about to discuss my family's property with this young woman, whose age I judged to be around twenty.

Her gaze returned to my face, and her lips, just a shade pinker than might be natural, curved up into a smile that had an impish quality to it.

"Now you're making fun of me, Lady Helena. I *know* how select St. James's is—like a little village for the aristocracy. You'd never realize this house was here, would you? All hidden behind its walls, moldering away quietly for hundreds of years. I can just see O growing old here." She put a little too much emphasis on the word *old*. This was a woman who had learned to use her voice as a weapon.

There was something about Miss Aldred that reminded me of Odelia. Perhaps it was the same air of simply not caring what anyone else thought. Superficially, she and Miss Emery both had some slight physical resemblance to Odelia, which strengthened when it came to that ineffable quality people call style. Was Sir Geraint endlessly seeking a repetition of the first *grande passion* that had pulled him away from his wife's side? What an uncomfortable thought.

The coffee came, and I poured it into the tiny cups, decorated with the Scott crest by some Chinese pottery worker two hundred years ago. My spirits rose as I thought of all the permanence Scott House represented. I saw the sometimes inconvenient old house as a bastion against people like Miss Aldred, who was coolly eyeing the silver and china as if she were appraising its value. I got straight to the point.

"I've heard you'd like to take my sister's place in Sir Geraint's affections." I put my cup down. "Which means you'd like Odelia out of the way, I suppose. Have you been playing practical jokes to hasten her departure?"

Miss Aldred's shrewd blue-gray eyes narrowed to amused slits above her cup. She hastily swallowed her coffee before laughing out loud.

"You *are* a caution." She wiped a tear from one eye, a theatrical gesture rather than a natural one. "How old are you anyway? You should have some fun, not sit there in black, trying to find out if I've been a naughty girl. I suppose they married you off to some old man and now he's died."

I ignored her. "I'm trying to find out who's responsible for some nasty pranks that have been visited on my sister. Do you know anything about them?"

She spread her hands, which were slim, with narrow, tapering fingers. "I don't have an idea what you're talking about, I swear on my mother's head. If anyone's been playing pranks on O, it's probably Millie. She's half-mad, if you ask me." She raised her eyebrows mockingly. "I don't know why I get myself mixed up with these eccentric bohemians, I really don't." Her eyes brightened. "What kind of pranks?"

"I'd prefer not to relate any details." I felt as if I were getting stuffier every minute, ossifying into old age before this careless young beauty.

"Well, that's a shame." Miss Aldred finished her coffee, placing cup and saucer down with a gentle yet decided air. "If I'm not to know what's going on, how can I help you? Hardly worth your while calling me here. Certainly not worth *my* while, apart from the entertainment of seeing where the exalted Lady Odelia lives. And meeting your good self, of course. I'll enjoy dropping your name into conversations as the earl's daughter who invited me for coffee." She raised her eyebrows—which I was sure were plucked—at me again, the impish smile back on her pretty lips. "I hope you weren't expecting discretion, not from an actress."

"I don't have any expectations of you," I said steadily. "I thank you for coming here. If you wish to make social capital of having been invited here, you won't be the first." I narrowed my eyes. "After all, I—and Odelia—have the advantage of you, socially speaking."

Watching the scowl spreading across her young face, I had the same sense of triumph I'd felt as a child after Mama decreed archery lessons to improve my posture. I'd been an excellent shot in archery too—and right now, I knew I'd hit my target right in the gold. Sir Geraint's passion for Odelia might be waning, but I knew he valued the cachet of keeping company with an earl's daughter. I decided to press my advantage.

"Of course," I leaned back in my chair, "if you could be a little more forthcoming with me—perhaps search your memory a little harder as to whosoever might be an enemy of Lady Odelia's, or keep your eyes and ears open on my behalf—I could, for example, mention your name in certain circles as a remarkably good actress. You could leave the name 'Dainty Darling' behind—a little vulgar, isn't it?—and become 'the sublime Elisabetta.' Or 'the *divine* Elisabetta,' perhaps?"

A gleam of ambition lit her shrewd eyes. "What's the price? I won't give Geraint up, mind, till I'm good and ready. He's the most talented and interesting man I've met."

"I'm not asking that of you. This peculiar . . . arrangement . . . of Sir Geraint's private life shouldn't be any of my concern, except insofar as it gives some unknown person a reason to play unpleasant tricks on Odelia. If you can help me identify and get rid of the perpetrator, you will have my gratitude and my word in your favor wherever I think it may be useful."

"So you're not trying to make O give him up?"

"I would only make the attempt if I thought I could succeed."

There was silence for a few moments as Miss Aldred

appeared to reach some internal decision. She stood up, holding out her hand to shake mine.

"I can't promise anything."

"I know."

"It's a fair offer, though. By the way, my given name is Elsie. Elisabetta's my stage name." She hesitated. "Look, O's a rival, I won't pretend otherwise, but practical jokes aren't my style. You can consider me an ally."

ONCE MISS ALDRED HAD GONE, I TOOK SCOTTY FOR A LONG walk as an apology for excluding him from the exciting inspection of carrion, so it was not surprising that by the time I had eaten my solitary luncheon I was quite tired. My inquiry to Mrs. Coles elicited the information that Odelia had risen very late and had taken a little something on a tray in her room. She had eaten all of the little something, from which I deduced that her stomach must have recovered from the shock it had received the day before. Reassured that she was well and had not absconded again, I settled down to read after lunch and soon fell into a light doze.

I was awakened by the arrival of the footman at three o'clock to light the candles in an attempt to drive out the gathering November gloom. I changed into a more comfortable tea gown and let Guttridge arrange my hair anew while we discussed our preparations for returning to Littleberry.

I was downstairs again, busy writing a reply to Blanche's last letter, when Odelia finally appeared, looking well rested and quite beautiful. Like me, she wore a loose tea gown, and everything about her bespoke ease, elegance, and charm. On the surface, she was the familiar, warm presence of my childhood, but I found myself comparing her to the actress I had just met, reflecting that for years she had been playing a role for me and the rest of our family. I had believed, for well over a decade, in the version of reality she had presented to me. Did that make me a gullible fool?

O made no allusion to the events of the day before. After a few words of greeting, she launched straight into an amusing account of the new Law Courts—which she had somehow visited, even though the interior was not yet officially open—and on the latest fashions in hats. The two subjects were connected in her mind by their ornateness, and I could only nod in agreement as she provided detail after detail to bolster her thesis.

"And where will it all end?" was her conclusion. "As a nation, we appear to be in a fever of acquisition, forever adding new knickknacks to our drawing rooms and new swags and furbelows to our clothing. We will end up crushed under our own grandiosity, encrusted with unnecessary decorations, until we can no longer stand upright."

I espied the perfect opportunity to lead the conversation around to the subject that had been on my mind for days. "But isn't that exactly what you're asking me to do in my own home?" I folded my arms. "To decorate it to within an inch of its life? It may be a little faded as it is, but it has the dignity and quietness of the last century."

"It wouldn't be *unnecessarily* ornate." Odelia sounded almost offended. "There's a vast difference between the modern fad for overdecoration and the perfect harmony that a great artist like Geraint can achieve. And then there's the question of scale and appropriateness. What is excessive in a bourgeois parlor becomes sublimity in the right setting." Her face changed, as if she, too, had seen an opportunity. "Have you decided, then?" She sounded eager.

"Yes." I had to get it over with all at once. "I shan't do it, O."

I watched the warm color drain from my sister's face.

"Why on earth not? It can't be the expense. And you know that room desperately needs refurbishing." The color flooded back in an angry tide. "It's in retaliation for my friendship with Geraint, isn't it?"

"Retaliation?" My voice, like Odelia's, sounded high and strained. "Do you really think I would try to punish you for having a lover? You're putting me in an impossible position, O. If I agreed to this commission, I would have Sir Geraint at Whitcombe for weeks at a time—he would become part of my household—and you can't tell me you won't visit in all that time. We both know you will. You'll turn up unannounced as you always do, and with you and Sir Geraint in the same house, it'll be no time at all before somebody catches on."

"You don't trust me to behave myself?" Odelia's color was now decidedly high.

"Yesterday—*yesterday*—you came home tipsy and careless." I wanted to fling myself out of my chair and shake Odelia until her bones rattled, but obviously I would never do such a thing. "You've somehow avoided scandal in London, but that doesn't mean that everyone in your social set doesn't know about you and Sir Geraint. Perhaps it's just such old news that they don't care anymore, but it will be new gossip in Littleberry."

"And how that town does like to gossip," murmured Odelia.

"Precisely. And our sisters aren't as stupid as you think they are. Eventually, there'll be scenes and scandal, and all this will happen in *my* house, and heaven knows I don't deserve that." I took a breath and attempted to speak more calmly. "For once, Odelia, dear, I'm going to say no to you— for all our sakes. Even at the cost of a scheme I really rather like." I shrugged. "Perhaps you could suggest another artist. I agree that Sir Geraint is a fine painter, but he's not the only artist in the Royal Academy."

"But it *has* to be Geraint." To my dismay, I saw Odelia's cheeks and nose redden. Her face changed, losing its serene beauty as the hot tears sprang to her eyes and trickled down either side of her nose. "This is *his* vision—*his* masterwork. How can you reject something that's so artistically *right*?" Her voice was a high thread of sound, her face redder and shinier every second. This was a side of Odelia I didn't think I had ever seen, a raw vulnerability that brought a lump to my throat.

"He has to get away from London," she gasped out after several seconds. "He needs to be left alone. I need him to be left alone. And he needs a large commission. Don't you see that I'm the only one who can offer him this?"

"At my expense." But the words were uttered under my breath, and even I hardly heard them. Odelia was curling herself forward, digging her long fingers into her hair and pulling so hard I was afraid she would tear it out by the roots. The day before, she had been calm in the face of my anger, but now she presented a sight I had never seen before, and I quailed.

"He'll be all right." I had to stop this terrible distress. I rose from my seat and knelt in front of my sister, my hands on her shaking shoulders, trying to make myself heard above the noise of her lamentations. "He made it quite clear to me that he won't try to harm himself again. It's only a commission, O. Don't take on so."

"No." Odelia dragged her hands out of her hair, wisps of which came loose and waved Medusa-like around her swollen face and bloodshot eyes. Her irises were strangely bright, a far lighter blue than usual, in the flickering candlelight. She grabbed at my hands, removing them from her shoulders and bringing them between us. Her fingers wrapped around them and squeezed so tight I was tempted to cry out. I had never seen her like this. I had never even imagined her like this.

"Don't you see?" It had taken a few moments for her to speak, and now her voice was hoarse. "It's the solution to everything. If I can't be the one who saves him, I'll lose him. He's talking about selling up and returning to Wales, or worse. He says that maybe they should move abroad to save money." She gulped, and hot tears ran uncomfortably through her fingers onto my own. "A distinguished career finished—the end of everything. I'll do *anything* to stop that from happening."

I held tight to her hands, sensing that the worst of the storm was over. Indeed, after a few moments, her outburst appeared to be subsiding. She sniffed loudly.

"I mean it, Helena. I'll do anything. Even go away if you want." Her tears were rapidly calming. "To the Continent. To Rome." She took a long, shuddering breath. "I've never asked you for money, have I? Blanche does it all the time. But just a small favor, just this once, and I will go there and stay there. Send me to Rome, Helena, and there will be no danger of scandal."

"What will you do in Rome?" I asked, my voice faint.

"I'll paint. I'll study. My allowance will go farther on the Continent. I'll live like a nun. Geraint has often said I would benefit from studying more, from taking art more seriously." Her eyes brightened. "If I could take Cynthia as a companion—"

"Miss *Emery?*" I could not have been more astonished if Odelia had proposed taking Blanche as a fellow traveler.

"Two birds with one stone." Odelia nodded, her eyes red rimmed, feverish. "Cynthia's always dreamed of traveling, and she knows how to make the most of whatever money she gets. She's sensible and good with languages, and I know she'd jump at the opportunity. Geraint will take the summer off—he always does—and we'll come back during those months because Rome's not healthy in the summer, is it?" She seemed almost giddy with the idea.

"And if you lose him to Miss Aldred?" I asked.

Odelia wrinkled her nose. "She'll never come down to Sussex."

And if he wants to run up to Town for his comforts? I wanted to ask but refrained. "Will you come to Whitcombe for Christmas first?" I inquired instead. "I don't want to leave you in London at the mercy of someone who wishes you ill. Come home with me, and I'll consider the bargain sealed."

"And you'll agree to the commission?" O's face was pink again, but this time with relief. What mattered most to her, I wondered, the man or his art? Or perhaps Sir Geraint *was* his art as far as she was concerned. But—leaving aside the question of the commission, which I *did* want when I plumbed the depths of my desires—if it meant that Odelia would be away from England and safe from this person who might wish her harm . . .

"Very well, I'll consider it," I said at last and immediately wondered how I could be so weak as to consent to such an outlandish scheme. But at the same time, I felt a glow of excitement in my selfish heart at the thought of the *Nightingale* taking shape at Whitcombe, free of the fear of scandal, even more precious because I had been ready to give it up entirely.

"You won't regret it, Baby—*Helena*, dear."

"Perhaps." And perhaps, just perhaps, the separation would give Odelia other interests and tear her away from this man's side.

28

THE START OF AN ADVENTURE

In the end, I delayed my return to Littleberry by three weeks. This was because Odelia's note to Miss Emery asking if the latter would care to accompany her to Rome for an indefinite period produced what, to me, was quite an alarming reaction in favor of the project. The two of them—for all the world as if they were old school friends rather than rivals in love—decided they would not wait for the New Year, but would depart as soon as might be arranged, traveling down through France, Switzerland, and Italy in time to reach Rome for Christmas. They planned to see as many artworks as they could on their travels. Clearly, it seemed, art trumped affairs of the heart, at least temporarily.

"I'm heartily sick of *Bradshaw's Continental Guide*," I remarked late one evening to Guttridge as I sat before my dressing mirror, braiding my hair for the night. "Thank goodness Miss Emery has a good head on her shoulders for organization and that you can give them the benefit of your experience in traveling as a lady's maid. All I have to rely on are my memories of my honeymoon tour—and I suppose you made most of the arrangements for that." I smiled into the mirror, watching Guttridge as she gathered up my clothing. "We'd had hardly any time to get to know each other, do you remember? It was daunting to have a new husband and a new lady's maid, the first one of my very own, at the same time. I felt so shy of both of you."

"You knew how to behave." Guttridge picked up the silk pouch that held the day's underwear and put it on top of my dress, which was lying on the bed. "You did seem a little nervous of Sir Justin at first, but he soon put you at your ease."

"The two of you did everything for me." It had been the first time in my life I had felt as if I were truly the center of attention. "I suppose it'll be quite different for Lady Odelia and Miss Emery, but they seem happy about traveling with no English servants." Holding fast to the end of a braid, I watched Guttridge tie a ribbon around it. "I feel as if I'm not really being much help."

"You have quite enough to do arranging for this house to be shut up—for which Lord Broadmere should be grateful—and writing letters to your man in Hastings about Sir Geraint. What a blessed business *that* is. I never realized it would be so complicated to get some paintings done."

She left the room, her arms full of clothing, and I contemplated the truth of her words. I had discovered much in the last fortnight about the sheer work—and expense—involved in paintings of the scale Sir Geraint proposed. And it wasn't just the paintings. There were the artisans who would build ornate frames to house the enormous canvases and take care of the rest of the redecoration of the drawing room, including any repairs or restorations that might need to be made. All these people would have to be paid, and materials had to be bought.

I had spent far too much time checking provisional lists

of estimated expenses and had already advanced a sum of money to Sir Geraint that would have horrified me five years before. In the intervening years, of course, I had learned much about the rate at which a wealthy household spent money.

I brushed aside my front hair, which had completely lost its curls, and ran a hand down one of my shining braids. I remembered Mama doing the same the night before my wedding. "You will be somebody now," she had said. "You will be important."

By then, she had already been showing signs of the eccentricity that had worsened rapidly after my marriage, as if she could finally loosen the reins of her reason, but when it came to convincing me it was better to marry than to remain dependent upon Michael, her will had been as strong as ever. She had been right, of course, and I was about to put my mark upon the house I had learned to love far more than my childhood home.

"It *is* exciting," I confessed as Guttridge returned with a tray bearing warm water, curl papers, and the various implements necessary to complete my evening toilette. "It's giving me a strange feeling in the pit of my stomach, like galloping downhill."

"And Sir Geraint's the horse?" Guttridge dampened a strand of hair and wrapped the curl paper around it.

"You do have a dreadfully imaginative way with words sometimes, Guttridge." I closed my eyes as the familiar evening ritual continued, Guttridge's strong, deft fingers making short work of rolling up the curl papers. "I'm trying not to think too hard. What with Lady Odelia off to travel through Europe at Christmas and my drawing room about to be entirely torn to pieces, I need to keep my imagination from running riot."

"Lady Odelia will have a marvelous time, and we will

have a much smarter drawing room," Guttridge said firmly as she gave a curl paper that peculiar twist that ensured it would stay in place till morning. "And you'll still have time to say good-bye to the old one over Christmas." The corners of her mouth tucked in as she concentrated on her task. "It'll be good to see the old place again."

Parting from Odelia at Victoria Station under Miss Emery's ironic gaze was easier than I'd thought it would be. It was with a certain amount of relief, mingled with misgivings, that I returned to Whitcombe to prepare for Christmas.

The relief proceeded from rediscovering my ordinary life, with particular pleasure when Guttridge and I were able to start work on some tinctures for Fortier. The misgivings originated in my natural anxiety that I had made entirely the wrong decision about the paintings, mistaking my own selfish desires for sisterly affection. Add to this the qualms I had about inadvertently revealing Odelia's relationship with Sir Geraint, and it might be understood that the forthcoming transformation of my drawing room was not a subject I readily brought into conversations. It crept in anyway.

"Have you ever noticed, Michael, that the more money a lady spends, the less she says about it?" My brother-in-law's brown eyes twinkled under his heavy brows.

It was four days before Christmas. Ned and Gerry had asked me, Michael, and Julia to dine at Four Square. Outside, a storm was sweeping in from the sea, battering the solid brick walls of the Freestone residence with gusts of wind that drove icy sheets of rain against the windows.

Inside, all was comfortable, in the effortless way Gerry had of combining elegance with ease. Her well-trained servants moved noiselessly through the motions of clearing the meat course while Ned leaned back with a sigh of satisfaction, ignoring his wife's soft noise of protest as he gently patted his rotund belly to show his appreciation of the roast ribs of beef. I suppressed a smile. Gerry always made a point of disapproving of what she called her husband's vulgarities but spoiled him relentlessly, a trait that rather endeared my dignified eldest sister to me.

Across the table, Michael glared at Ned over his wineglass as he tried to work out whether or not Ned was making a joke. "Are you talking about Helena's drawing room?" he asked at last, his brow furrowing. "I'm not sure what I think about that. I suppose I have to be in favor of it because Whitcombe House is very large and very grand, and it is logical to spend a great deal of money on decorating the drawing room when one *has* a great deal of money."

Having reached that conclusion, he nodded emphatically. "It'll be well regarded in the county when the news gets out. And I—" he spent a moment in thought, his glass raised halfway to his lips, to the frustration of the footman who was trying to take his plate. "I agree a lady shouldn't boast."

"Hear, hear." Ned raised his own glass to me. "I admire your reticence, Helena. I can name a dozen owners of country houses who never stop talking about the improvements they make."

"And every single one of them men." Gerry shot an approving glance at the footman, who had somehow restored order to the cloth despite Michael's obliviousness, and watched as the servants readied the table for the cold and hot sweet dishes. "It's one thing to admire work after it's done. It's a dreadful bore to hear about it beforehand."

"To be honest, I'm quiet about it because I only have a vague idea what it's going to be like." That was true enough that I did not consider my words overly evasive. "Sir Geraint's going to provide me with some detailed sketches of how the room should eventually look after he's received all the measurements and photographs—he's only had O's description to rely on so far—and besides, if he comes here and decides it simply won't do after all, our agreement says he can cancel the whole thing. So telling the whole county about it would be premature."

"I'm rather impressed by O's powers of persuasion," Julia remarked. "Are she and Sir Geraint very good friends?"

"They've known each other for some years." This was exactly the kind of obfuscation I disliked, making me nervous at every mention of Sir Geraint. I avoided looking at Michael. "Sir Geraint appears to attract a good many artists to his side. He invited me to a sort of party in October, and as far as I understood it, there were many men of artistic and literary importance present. Some women too. It was awfully crowded."

"You must be happy to return to the peace of Littleberry." Ned smiled at me. "And Littleberry is glad to see you. We've all missed you, and not just the family. Don't forget I speak to a great many people in the course of my daily round, and even I didn't realize you did so much good in the town. As you leave your grief behind you, my dear, I'd like to urge you to do more—to join me in a cause that's very close to my heart." He leaned forward, his napkin crushed in one large hand. "The greatest problem for the poor of Littleberry is that problems are tackled piecemeal. There are many of us who support a more thorough approach."

"Ned, *no*." Gerry huffed out a sigh. "Not the hospital, not now. It's Christmas."

"And what better time to introduce the subject of caring for the poor and meek than at Christmas, when we celebrate the birth of the One who came into the world in a stable?" Ned's smile at his lady wife had a challenging glint to it. "Of course, if Helena doesn't want to be importuned this evening, I'm quite happy to request a private interview at Whitcombe, but now seems like a suitable moment to speak. It's my job to speak, you know." He turned to me. "It wasn't why I invited you to dinner, Helena, my dear. Don't imagine that. We haven't seen you for far too long."

I felt my lips curve upward. Ned was an inveterate raiser of funds for one cause or the other. His success in such endeavors was one reason he was so often elected mayor of our small town. Justin had often remarked that to drink a cup of coffee with my brother-in-law was to risk being included in a subscription, and to take anything stronger might well cost him a hundred pounds. Despite this, he and Ned had often spent time together.

I leaned back in my chair, prepared to be gently fleeced in a good cause. Around us the servants were busy offering dishes, including, for Ned's benefit, a dish of delicate partridge as an alternative to sweetmeats.

"I suspect this is one of those occasions where business and pleasure can mingle," I said. "Out with it, Ned. Were you planning to ask me for a great deal? And in front of Michael too."

"I already know about it." Michael's harsh voice was tinged with resignation. "Ned's been plotting all autumn while you've been away. He wants to build a new hospital." He took a sip of wine at last. "I'm on the list of subscribers."

"And so you should be." Ned's gravelly voice was tinged with amusement. "The earl must lead the way, eh? It's time we moved out of that ancient, insanitary building and cared for our sickest residents in a place where they can have light and air."

"And where would that be?" I asked, my suspicions suddenly aroused.

"Well, this is where you come in, my dear." Ned wiped his mustache with his crumpled napkin. "We can't have a hospital without land to build it on, and in my opinion we would do well to put our new building on the higher ground inland rather than try to find a space in Littleberry. I'm thinking of that field of yours between the new workhouse burial ground and Whitcombe Lane—or at least the part that's more or less flat before the land drops away. I'd have to have it surveyed, of course, to see if it's suitable for building, but there are many things I like about it. It's on the main road, for one thing, easily reached from the town, and it's a salubriously windy spot. Too windy for crops in summer and for sheep in winter, what's more. What do you think?"

Gerry pursed her lips. "Do bear in mind, Helena, that the new building is what people will see first when they visit you at Whitcombe. It's bad enough that the workhouse is at the top of the hill, but at least that's hidden from the road. The new hospital building might ruin the approach to the house."

Ned puffed out his cheeks in exasperation. "What approach? All that's there now is a low-quality field that sometimes has sheep in it, sometimes not. You'll never get a straight row of trees to grow in that windy spot, and Helena has a perfectly pleasant drive once you get closer to the house. A smart new hospital will look better than a field. We could call it the Whitcombe Hospital to boot, thus allowing your visitors to see you as a philanthropist as well as a patron of the arts." He chuckled. "I don't see how any reasonable person could object. You're not intending to lay out a park along the lane, are you, Helena?"

"She might be, now that she's going to have a grand drawing room." Julia smiled mischievously. "After all, the only thing Hyrst has that Whitcombe lacks is the allée of trees leading to the house. Helena could have *twice* as many trees as we do."

We all, except Michael, saw the joke at once, and there was a burst of general laughter. Michael regularly complained that Whitcombe had twice as many bedrooms as Hyrst, feeling—rightly, I supposed—that the house he had inherited did not measure up to the dignity required by an earl.

Michael, rather left out of the merriment, adopted an air of long-suffering patience. "Have you consulted Dr. Sharrock and Dr. Finch yet, Ned?" he asked once the laughter had died down.

"I've talked to them." Ned rapidly ate a few bites of partridge before continuing. "I'll consult them officially out of courtesy and then leave them out of it as much as possible." A movement in his beard suggested a wry twist of his mouth. "Gerry can soothe their wounded feelings while I bring in some younger men. It won't make much difference to their practices anyway, since the wealthier patients will prefer to be nursed at home where at all possible." He raised his glass in my direction. "I want Dr. Fortier to be in charge of the hospital, if he agrees. He's young and energetic, certainly doesn't lack ability, and his being Quinn Dermody's brother-in-law will find favor with the more radical merchants."

The story of the Duc de Maival flashed into my mind. Would Fortier be popular with Littleberry's merchant class if they knew *that*? But my overwhelming feeling was one of surprise, which must have shown on my face. "Have you told him?" I inquired.

"No, and I'd rather you allowed me to choose my moment." Ned smiled. "I need to get the agreement of the trustees first—need to officially announce the trustees, come to that—and it's a heavy responsibility. I don't want him hearing of it secondhand."

"He's in London, isn't he?" Julia asked before I could respond. "With Mrs. Dermody. Their father is ill, I hear." She would know, of course. Gabrielle would have told someone where she was going, and the Littleberry gossips were as efficient as any newspaper. "Did you see him at all, Helena?"

"I did." I faced the others squarely. "O and I paid Gabrielle Dermody a visit just after Dr. Fortier arrived, and later I met their father. But Dr. Fortier's not likely to return to Littleberry for some time. Perhaps you should write to him, Ned."

"It'll be weeks, perhaps months, before I can write to him officially." Ned tugged at his beard. "Maybe you should—"

But the entrance of Ned and Gerry's butler cut off my brother-in-law's words, and the ensuing events quite blotted the question of the new hospital from my mind until after Christmas. By the time I had consulted my man of business, talked over the matter more thoroughly with Ned, and finally agreed to deprive Justin's estate of a parcel of land I would little miss, I was expecting the arrival of Sir Geraint. My life in Littleberry was about to be invaded—influenced—intruded upon by the bohemian world that until then had been entirely separate from my own existence. Odelia was absent from my life, to be sure, but the events she had set in train were to dominate much of the ensuing year.

Except that Sir Geraint had other ideas. "May we take the air for a moment and view the façade of the house?" he asked as soon as the ceremony of greeting was over. "You and I, that is. Hay and Scoff should wait for the cart. There's a fair amount of equipment on it, and I don't want anyone else handling it. Don't make your staff wait outside in the cold, though."

I nodded at Dunnam and Mrs. Eason, who had heard Sir Geraint's request. "Anything that's not needed immediately can be stored in the game pantry until the drawing room's emptied," I explained to my guest as we turned away. "I've left the drawing room as it is for now, as you requested."

"We will take more photographs before we begin." His teeth showed white between beard and mustache. "You're going to find it all horribly inconvenient at first, you know, especially once the artisans arrive to prepare the room, but we'll all get used to each other. Besides, I hear you have another large drawing room to retreat to."

"I suppose you know all about the house from O." I felt the slight roughness of damp, crushed gravel under my thin-soled shoes as we embarked on the path that led to the terrace.

"Every detail. This house, Hyrst, Littleberry, your family have been part of the landscape of my imagination for years. It's almost strange to come here, like stepping into a story." He looked around. "It's quite tantalizing, the way you can't see the front of the house at all from anywhere close. Not a glimpse on the way from the station either. It's the same with Hyrst, I understand. Living in London, one forgets about the sheer exclusiveness of these country houses—in the sense that they exclude everyone from them who has no business there. One must admire them from afar if one can see them at all." His expression changed, his gaze sharpening as he looked down at me. "I don't think you have any notion of how much this commission means to me."

"No, I honestly don't think I have." His familiarity with my life and family had disturbed me, and my next words were probably an attempt to recover some of the distance to which he referred. "I hope Odelia has made my conditions —*all* of my conditions—clear to you. There are some aspects of this commission that can't be set out on paper."

Sir Geraint nodded. "The position is entirely clear." Now his expression was grave. "I give you my undertaking that while I'm at Whitcombe—while I'm in this part of Sussex—I will live like a monk. I'm not without self-control." He drew a deep breath. "To be honest, at this moment I'm happy to concentrate on my art, knowing that two of the women I love are experiencing the joys of France and Italy. It was a generous solution and one I'm grateful for. Things had become a bit . . . overheated." He laughed. "Or perhaps I'm just getting old."

There was absolutely nothing I could say to that. We had mounted the short flight of steps that led up to the main terrace, and I knew by Sir Geraint's fresh intake of breath that there was no need to pursue the conversation. This was the view that always struck a first-time visitor with delight, sometimes reducing them to speechlessness and sometimes provoking a babble of words.

To our left, Littleberry, red-bricked and red-tiled, rose on its low rock with the solid placidity of a town that had stood seemingly since time began and would stand to the world's end. At its apex was the tower of the church of St. Michael and All Angels, looking shorter than it really was because of the sheer size of the church, its squat silhouette a landmark that could be seen for miles. Far off on the right, Broadmere sat on its own promontory, hiding its secrets in its enshrouding trees. Between them was the great green sweep of the Ealy valley, the river where Justin had met his doom a gleaming thread among the lush green of the sheep-dotted pastures.

Beyond the fields, where the land rose again to form the low cliffs that looked out over the marsh, gleamed the English Channel. A lone ship rode the line where the sea, today a grayish green, met the overcast sky.

A gap had opened up in the clouds so that the sinking sun shone into our eyes. It was not late, but in just an hour or so it would get dark and the division between sea and sky would lose its sharpness, giving way to a misty vagueness. The cold, damp wind flattened my skirts against my legs, and I was grateful for my furs.

Sir Geraint said nothing, spending a few moments simply taking in the view. Then, like all visitors inevitably did, he drifted toward the balustrade of the terrace, which seemed to offer nothing more than empty air. I knew that as he looked down, he would see Whitcombe's formal garden stepping in splendid pomposity toward the lower terrace. Beyond that, there was only scrub growing in patches where the sheep had not been able to conquer it.

He then turned, as I knew he would, to take in the house's rear façade. I joined him, watching his eyes devour its regular patterns of red brick, pale stone, and white paint.

"The drawing-room windows are under that balcony." He gestured toward it with the confidence of long familiarity. "And there are no French windows in the drawing room because your late husband's father had it altered to put in a long sweep of window seats."

"He was fond of window seats," I said. "He restored the symmetry of the façade by having double doors put in either side. The balcony, of course, now serves no real purpose except to shade the drawing room from the worst of the midday sun. You may know that there used to be a ballroom above the drawing room, where the balcony is, but there's no door leading to the balcony now."

He nodded. "That floor was altered many years ago, and those bedrooms are not popular with guests. Some say it's because of the ghost of the drunken guest who toppled over the balcony during a ball in 1827 and dashed out his brains on the flagstones below—to the horror of the revelers in the drawing room."

"And others say it's because there's far too much sun in those rooms." I laughed. "If there's a ghost, I've never seen it. We've put you and your assistants fairly close together. There's a sitting room connecting to your bedroom for working in." How many hours, I wondered, had Odelia spent describing my house to him? Did he know Hyrst as intimately?

"About that." The line between Sir Geraint's brows deepened. "As much as we appreciate your hospitality—especially given the circumstances—I intend to make other arrangements for Hay and Scoff, and possibly for some of the artisans who'll be coming from London and Kent. They need their own space to be together, to talk and make noise and paint all over the walls if they can. We're like children, we artists, when we're together. You know the Bennett farm at Lower Broadmere, I suppose?"

"Yes, of course. It's almost as old as Whitcombe, I believe. I've been riding out to Lower Broadmere since I was a child. The family abandoned the farm ten years ago and moved to Pincham."

"Just so." Sir Geraint nodded. "Well, I'm going to take the earliest opportunity to inspect the house with a view to renting it."

"But it's half-derelict." I stared at him, puzzled. "My brother says the land has become impossible to farm, although he thinks it may improve now they've built the sea wall. It's a very pretty house, of course."

"And very large. O tells me it was a prosperous farm once upon a time, but the sea is always changing the land hereabouts, isn't it?" He smiled.

"Did Odelia suggest you rent it?" I had fully expected to host the three artists until the summer and was taken aback by the change in plans.

"Not in the least. I saw the sketches she made of it years ago and have always wanted to see it. I wrote to the owner recently and was delighted to find he'd be happy to make it over to me for a derisory rent if I were willing to renovate it. The boys will need something to do in their free time. As soon as they can make a room or two habitable and install a stove for heat, they could camp there. The owner assures me the pump in the courtyard still works and the well water's fresh. The village is only half a mile away, and they can walk to Whitcombe or buy a dogcart and pony."

"But you'll stay at Whitcombe?"

"Of course." He smiled. "And I'm sure Hay and Scoff will enjoy a few days of luxury. I understand you are quite the perfect hostess and keep an excellent table. Now, may we see the drawing room? I daresay the cart has arrived by now, and we are here to work after all."

WITH A HOUSE AS LARGE AS WHITCOMBE, IT WOULD HAVE BEEN petty of me to complain about a minor disturbance. Still, when I took refuge with Julia and the children at Hyrst a few days after Sir Geraint's arrival, it was with a feeling of relief that I entered the familiar quiet of my childhood home, whose former shabbiness was gradually being conquered by Julia as Michael's fortunes slowly improved.

"Guttridge went straight to the Pugs' Parlor with Scotty," I told my sister-in-law as I settled into one of the new, rather comfortable sofas she had bought. "She was absolutely bursting to tell your upper servants about the people who've been to Whitcombe House over the last few days. The photographer Sir Geraint told us about when you and Michael came to dinner turned out to be *very* grand—I got the impression that anyone below the rank of duchess was beneath him—so much better than the Littleberry man who took the photographs we sent Sir Geraint. His photographs are astonishingly good, so I suppose he was worth it. Apparently, he will photograph the finished paintings, and somebody will make engravings, and they'll all be sold in a dozen different ways. That's part of the agreement in return for a reduction in the fee."

"Your drawing room will be famous, then." Julia picked her baby son up from where he had toppled into the nest of cushions she had built for him. In the next room, I could hear my niece Annabelle Alice bossing her older brothers. The soft voices of the nursemaids were audible in the brief intervals when the little girl stopped talking.

"It might be, I suppose." I hesitated. "I feel an absolute fraud, Julia. Heaven knows I'm not fashionable or an arbiter of taste or knowledgeable about art. All I am is wealthy."

"That's the supreme qualification for becoming a patron of the arts, isn't it?" Julia smiled. "Look, Helena, dear, don't worry so much about it. If you don't think you know enough about art, ask Sir Geraint how you can learn. Or Odelia, when she comes back. There's nothing wrong with being an amateur with money. That's how all collectors start, isn't it?"

She leaned down to kiss her little boy and laughed as Julius, crowing with delight at seizing hold of his silver teething ring, stuffed it back into his mouth. "And you've balanced things out nicely by giving Ned land and money for his hospital. In my opinion, you're doing more good now than when you and Justin were constantly giving dinner parties and hosting the hunt and having shooting weekends. You don't seem eager to go back to that life."

"I have no enthusiasm for hunting or shooting. Not that anyone would expect a widow to give parties, except I suppose if she were an avid rider to hounds." I watched Julius bang his toy against the cushions, darkening them with spittle. "At least I enjoy giving dinner parties, but they can't be large or glittering ones, not with me still in black. I'm having to invite the people I feel should meet Sir Geraint in small groups."

"I've heard the news of these paintings is creating quite a stir in some circles." Seeing Julius yawn, his mother scooped him up and rose to hand him to me. "Here's Auntie Helena to rock you to sleep, little man. And here's a nice big piece of muslin so Auntie Helena's shoulder doesn't get wet." She sat down again, throwing the cushions to one side. "By the time they're finished, though, you'll be well out of mourning." She counted on her fingers. "Let's see. In three months' time, you can wear jet jewelry; how exciting. And by November, you'll be in lavenders and grays and mauves." Her smile was mischievous. "That dangerous stage when you're a threat to every debutante, and their mothers will refuse to invite you to their gatherings. There's nothing more attractive to men than a young, pretty, and wealthy widow in lavender. By June of next year—or the year after—you could hold a ball in your newly decorated masterpiece and dance in pink satin."

I made a face, my attention distracted for a moment from the baby. "Do you know, I can hardly remember what colors I wore before Justin died. You're right, though—I could do justice to the paintings by the time they're completed. I've already had letters from people who've never written to me in my life, hinting that they might like to come and see me once the drawing room is finished. People who are mere acquaintances, even if they *are* what Blanche would call important. An Irish graduate from Oxford who has dined with my fourth cousin once removed in County Mayo sent me a book of his poems—at pains to emphasize that it was a first edition of a very limited number—hoping he might call on me 'in a few months' to view the progress of the work."

Julia's chuckle brought a smile to my own face as I felt my little nephew, an easy baby, melt into sleep against my shoulder. A tuneless crooning announced Annabelle Alice, whose dancing steps slowed in response to a soft hiss and a finger on Julia's lips.

"Kiss Baby," Annabelle Alice decreed, and to her credit she did it very gently without waking her brother. "Kiss Auntie Helena," and a small sticky patch was imprinted onto my cheek before my niece sprang nimbly onto her mother's lap. She settled down with a sigh of satisfaction at finding that space, so recently usurped by the newborn, entirely hers.

I relaxed, feeling the warm, damp weight of the tiny boy in my arms and listening to James and Quentin, who, no longer importuned by their little sister, appeared to be setting up a game of some sort. I loved visiting Julia, all the more because she and Michael so often had the children around them, never banishing them to the nursery all day the way many parents of our class did. It had been settled between them that James, now five years old and the heir to the earldom, would begin his formal education with a retired clergyman when he turned six and that there would be no notion of sending him away to school unless and until he wished to go there.

"My drawing room's quite empty now," I said once Annabelle Alice's chatter subsided and the little girl's eyelids fluttered as she fought off sleep. "It looks smaller somehow. Six men came down from London. Mrs. Eason absolutely bristled, thinking they were going to tell her staff how to remove the furniture, but it soon became clear they were carpenters and other artisans who work only for artists. Almost every man who works at Whitcombe—except Dunnam, of course—was conscripted into clearing the room, and the chandeliers had to be taken down one bauble at a time and the whole wrapped in wool and put in tea chests. The men from London made strange marks on the walls and spent *hours* taking measurements, and Sir Geraint says he will soon receive plans and documents about the frames. It will take weeks to check everything, it seems, and only then will they build the canvases—and then it will take at least a month to prepare them."

"Gracious. Why so long?"

"Ah, I know something about that." I was pleased to impart some information Julia didn't know. "O has explained to me about size and ground, and has shown me how a canvas must be as tight as a drum before you begin. It's a part of the artist's work that can't be rushed, and from what I understand, when a canvas is as big as those Sir Geraint will be using, the task is even more painstaking. The carpenters will build the frames for the canvases and stretch them, and then Mr. Mountjoy and Mr. Scoffield will prepare the painting surfaces. They've decamped to Lower Broadmere, by the way—Mr. Mountjoy and Mr. Scoffield, I mean. They're living like gypsies in the Bennett Farm, spending the time before they're needed for the canvases in making the farmhouse habitable."

"Goodness." Julia's sensible face creased in consternation. "So much toing and froing. No wonder you're looking a little worn around the edges, darling. If it weren't for Sir Geraint staying with you, I'd tell you to move in here for a short while. And then having to entertain all the time . . . or do you and Sir Geraint dine *en famille* sometimes?" Dimples appeared on her cheeks at the thought. "He *is* a charming man."

"Thomas dines with us, of course." I dipped my head over the sleeping baby, afraid I might be blushing. If I countered Julia's lighthearted insinuation with the stern remark that Sir Geraint was married, I would feel a hypocrite, knowing what I did about Odelia, and having to avoid the subject embarrassed me. So I changed it.

"Don't think I'm never free to follow my own pursuits. Guttridge and I hide in our workroom whenever we can, and then there are all the usual things that one does. I don't have to spend my days with Sir Geraint, only my evenings."

"And what on earth does Sir Geraint do while all these preparations are going on?"

"He sketches and writes and has found quite a few books to interest him in Whitcombe's libraries. He walks a great deal too, apparently to understand the local scenery for the background of the paintings. I must say, Julia, I'm impressed by his capacity for work. Even after dinner, he sits in the green drawing room with us and works on something. He can talk and work at the same time. He's promised to show me a full set of drawings tomorrow."

30

THE EMPEROR

I had agreed to no particular time for the presentation of the drawings, Sir Geraint having suggested he simply come by the workroom in the midmorning to avoid an overly formal occasion. Guttridge and I were deep in the joint perusal of various books that recommended different treatments for asthma, sitting side by side at our twin desks with notepaper to hand, when a cough behind us made us both turn in our seats.

"I'm not disturbing you?" Sir Geraint smiled charmingly as he entered the room, a large portfolio under his arm. "I prefer not to make much of such moments. After all, they're only working documents, you might say. A necessary step, in my opinion, because the client is better served by being given some concrete idea of how the finished work will look, but you must understand that these drawings are as far removed from the ultimate creation as the seed is from the flower. I will change my ideas as the paintings develop, and if an element is wrong, out it goes. That's an excellent table for display." He moved to the huge marble-topped table in the middle of the workroom, pulling at the ribbons that held his portfolio closed.

"I become melancholy sometimes," he continued as he worked, "wondering at the fate of my pictures in the long years ahead. I always want as many people as possible to see them straightaway, and love them, I hope. They too are my children—but unlike children, who grow and grow and suddenly become strangers to the gentle little people they once were, they must endure unchanging while the world changes around them."

He paused for a moment and then smiled. "Don't listen to me—I'm in that nervous mood I always get into when I'm actually beginning a subject I've dreamed of for a long time. There's always that point of fracture between the ideal in my head and the scratches on the paper, and I have the client's expectations to deal with at the same time. No debutante could be more apprehensive than I am right now."

We stood in silence, watching as Sir Geraint laid out the large, sturdy sheets of paper. Even before he had completed his task, my heart had soared to somewhere near the heavens. I had already seen some sketches, of course, but they had been mere suggestions that had whetted my appetite for more. Now, here was the first hint of how the feast might look.

For a full minute after the last piece of paper was arranged and Sir Geraint had propped the portfolio against the wall, I couldn't utter a word. I could sense Guttridge beside me, completely immobile. Did she feel the same way, or did she see flaws where I saw perfection? I knew she was too well trained to proffer her opinion before I did. It was up to me to speak.

I breathed deep, seeking for the words. "I feel as if I've walked into my imagination. That of my childhood, I mean—

the time before my thoughts centered on real people. Are the figures drawn from life?"

"The emperor and the kitchen maid, yes." Sir Geraint touched the corner of the drawing that showed the emperor on his throne and the kitchen maid behind the door. "I had to haunt the Limehouse docks regularly until I found what I wanted."

"The emperor's so young." Guttridge peered at the handsome face, its beauty barely marred by the slant of the drawn-down brows, the brimming eyes, the fall of a single tear. "I hadn't expected that somehow. He's very handsome."

"The model is the half-Chinese son of a drunken porter." Sir Geraint's face turned grave. "The child who sat for me as the maid is a Kazakh, the daughter of a woman addicted to opium. Her grandmother became ferocious until I convinced her I just wanted to draw the girl, and I think she will keep the money I gave her away from the mother." He smiled reminiscently. "I drew the grandmother for good measure, for the sake of the lines on her face. One day I will paint her as Clotho, the spinner of fate. The girl resembles her, I think. In fifty years, she'll also be a crone, but for now there is the beauty of youth in that face, if no great beauty otherwise."

He turned toward me. "Or are their faces too exotic for you, Lady Helena? I can make them more ideal if you wish. Burne-Jonesify them, as it were. After all, you have to live with them. Ned Jones makes great claims for the artistic virtues of his expressionless lads and ladies, but the bald truth is that he does it that way because the buyers like them. Although his Merlin is rather fine."

"I think you should paint your figures as you wish them to be." I frowned. "If I don't trust you, wouldn't that ultimately spoil the painting? O would never allow me to criticize what she is doing."

"O doesn't have any dependents." It was the first time I

had heard that dry tone of voice when Sir Geraint spoke of my sister, and I wondered what it meant. But the moment passed as Guttridge, who had been studying the emperor intently, gave tongue to her thoughts.

"Do Chinamen really wear clothes like that, sir? He'd never be able to walk in those robes." She was right; they were impossibly long, flowing in silken folds down the steps that led up to his throne.

Sir Geraint puffed out a laugh. "That's the point, my dear Miss Guttridge. He's too powerful to need to walk anywhere, and the world comes to him. I'm fond of painting robes and drapery of all sorts, you know. And this is a fairy tale, so I don't have to be entirely accurate."

"So this is the painting that will face out to the sea." I smiled at the kitchen maid's expression of wonder and delight as she peeped from behind a door that seemed almost as richly ornamented as the emperor's robes. "Is that why the emperor is not looking at the nightingale? He seems to contemplate eternity. Is that why he's staring out to sea?"

"Your understanding is greater than you claim." Sir Geraint made me a little bow. "And that's not mere flattery of a patron, Lady Helena. Do you approve of my efforts?"

I studied the drawings again, but my thoughts were of Odelia's tear-streaked face as she promised to absent herself from England for the sake of this man and his art. I also thought of Justin and what he might say to my plan for such a drastic change to the heart of his house. But it was my house now ...

"These will certainly give your guests something to admire, my lady." Guttridge's voice broke into my reverie. "How do you get big paintings like that up on the walls?" she asked Sir Geraint.

"Very carefully." He grinned, merry as a boy, as he gathered up the large sheets of paper. "I always hate moving my work, but my carpenters are highly skilled and it is a matter of routine for us. The canvases will be exhibited first before finding their way to their ultimate home, you remember."

"You speak as if the paintings won't be done here." I frowned. "Will it be London after all? You haven't been very clear on that point, but I hope you understand you're welcome to stay here for as long as you need to. I have plenty of room."

"Not London." A conscious look had appeared on Sir Geraint's face. "And not here at Whitcombe House. That was the other thing I wanted to tell you, Lady Helena. I'm going to use the barn at the farm for the actual painting; its walls are sound and the floor superb. They tell me the area flooded before the sea wall was built, but there's no sign of it now. Even the rats have moved out for want of food, and we'll keep them away with a cat or two. My assistants have already arranged to have the barn roof rebuilt and windows put in." He sighed. "The Sussex light is superb, and down at Lower Broadmere it's a painter's dream. It must be the reflection from the sea, which, as you know, is silver like a mirror when it's calm. I'm quite besotted with the farmhouse, and the sea wall makes all the difference in sheltering it from the wind. There I can make my messes as I wish. I have my own way of working, which must look distressingly disorganized to most people."

"I shouldn't think I'd find anything messy after seeing O's studio," I said. "Of course, I haven't seen the one you told me about—the one in your neighbor's stable."

"I keep that well out of sight." He smiled. "I allow Mrs. B. in there once a year at most."

"Aren't your assistants freezing to death at the farm?" I asked. "I've been meaning to ask after them. Don't they want to come here for a little warmth?"

"They have one chimney working and are eating and

sleeping in the one room, with walls they've whitewashed and new curtains of plain linen. There's nothing wrong with the farmhouse except a few years of neglect. The boys have made friends with some lads in the village who'll do the heavy work, and they've ordered great quantities of lumber to be brought in via the river." His teeth showed again. "A few more weeks of work will make all the difference, and we're changing the name for good luck. We've decided to call it Edenholme."

31

EDENHOLME

Sir Geraint's absences from Whitcombe became more frequent as the weeks fled by. By the beginning of April, he had made plans to move out altogether.

In the first week of that month, he invited Thomas and me to see his future residence. It was the same day, he informed me, that his wife and two of his children were to visit him, and I looked forward to seeing Millie again.

The Bennett farm was a large farmhouse built in the last century, with that regularity of stone blocks and large sash windows that made Georgian buildings so pleasing to the eye. Seen with newly curious eyes, it was even larger than I remembered. Its view out to the sea was now ruined by the sea wall, and it was set too close to the new road, but it was an imposing property.

A crumbling low wall, pierced by an as yet intact iron gate thick with rust, fronted a small garden with two ancient apple trees. Those miraculous survivors were bent into weird shapes by the wind but still sported a mass of delicate blossoms. There was a drift of smoke from one of the tall chimney stacks and glass in some of the windows for the first time in many years.

Yet even the casual passerby could see this was no longer a mere farmhouse. A newly constructed arch over the gate winked subtle iridescence as Thomas and I descended from my carriage. It was covered with shells—the inside of oyster and mussel shells, glinting with mother-of-pearl, reflected the sunlight in pale gleams. They were fastened to a fantastical arch made of pieces of driftwood, so cleverly fitted together that at first they looked like a single carved piece. Some wood had been left bare and carved with fish and seabirds while strings of smaller shells shivered on copper wires, making an odd rattling sound in the ever-present wind. At the top of the arch, a twisted piece of wood, perhaps part of the sea-tossed root of an ancient, uprooted tree, had been smoothed and carved with the word EDENHOLME.

The path had been newly cleared of weeds and dressed with a fresh coating of crushed shells. As Thomas opened the gate for me, Sir Geraint stepped out of the front door, flanked by his family.

Millie's abundant red hair was caught back in a net of gold mesh, her magnificent matron's figure clothed in a deep green gown festooned with a riot of gold embroidery. Edmund wore the soberest of black clothing, and Jane sported a perfectly conventional travel ensemble of blue-gray wool, as if neither of them wished to be a part of the artistic world. Sir Geraint was in shirtsleeves and a long workman's apron, an informality that almost seemed to be deliberate, identifying himself with his work and his new premises rather than the world to which I belonged.

I hastened my steps to reach Millie, holding out my hands toward her, pleased to see a smile break over her face. "I'm glad to see you in good health," I said, shaking her hand cheerfully. "This is my nephew Thomas Freestone. What do you think of Lower Broadmere? Have you seen much of the village, such as it is?"

"Only what we saw on the way from the station." Millie shook Thomas's proffered left hand.

"Then you've r-really seen n-nothing." Thomas's stammer was a little worse than usual, as frequently happened when he met new people, but he was a man who took his fences bravely. "It's n-not so m-much a village as a loose association of houses, w-with quite a f-few eccentricities. S-such as boats used as d-dwellings."

Our visitors from London made the appropriate noises of amusement and astonishment at Thomas's words, and in the space of a few moments we effected introductions all round.

"I can see you're the man to talk to." Edmund, whose upper lip was now adorned by a wispy mustache to match the fine, silky sideburns that had sprouted on his cheeks, nodded approvingly at Thomas. "I intend to write an article about it all—the paintings, the house, the village, and so on. Plenty of local color. Father's going to supply a little sketch of the house—and perhaps one of Whitcombe?" He raised his fair eyebrows at Sir Geraint, who shrugged indulgently. "I'm sorry I won't have time to see your house, Lady Helena. But this little place is charming—or it will be once it's restored. Quite suitable."

"It's a fine house." I shielded my eyes against the sun to survey the façade. "The roof has lost a lot of slates, hasn't it? The attics must be in a dreadful state."

"Oh, they are—the floors are rotted through in places. But we can fix them." Mr. Mountjoy, the young assistant, had pushed up the lower sash of one of the front windows and was unabashedly listening to our conversation. "Our current preoccupation is cleaning up the kitchen. It's absolutely enormous, with one of those fireplaces you could roast a whole pig in and beams as thick as Scoffield's head. Janie, why don't you come and give us your opinion about the decoration of the kitchen walls? I'd quite like to do a mural. You could sit for me. I'll paint you as Hestia, the goddess of the Roman hearth, with a bowl of flame. Chastely domestic, of course." He rolled his eyes in a parody of prudishness at Mr. Scoffield, who had joined him at the window. "Won't she make a marvelous goddess?"

Jane, her cheeks pink, looked hesitatingly at her father before scurrying back into the house. She had lost some of her adolescent roundness and in her smart traveling clothes looked a little better than when I'd seen her in Holland Park, but she had none of her sister's poise and absolutely nothing of Millie's distinctive style. Millie tutted and turned to follow her, muttering, "Men," under her breath.

"Young puppies." Edmund, perhaps a year or two younger than his father's assistants, adopted a superior air, stroking his silky mustache. "Still, I'm glad they and the ladies are keeping themselves busy and out of our hair. I can't bear to hear little Scoff bleating on about brushwork. Father, you'll fill me in on all the technical details I need to put into the article, won't you? I can trust you to do so *briefly*, without boring me to death."

"You'll never succeed as a writer if you can't work up an interest in your subject." Sir Geraint ushered the three of us along the newly renovated path, which wound through a wilderness of desiccated stems and fresh green shoots, toward the large barn that stood at right angles to the house. It was on a slight rise; behind it, the land sloped downward to a large pond, whose shivering water hosted a number of birds.

"I'm interested enough in subjects, just not in Scoffields," Edmund replied laconically as we entered the courtyard through an arch in its enclosing wall. "In any case, the publication only wants enough technical detail to fascinate the more serious readers. It's primarily interested in an entertaining portrait of the great artist's new home. Lady Helena, may I take your hand? I wouldn't want you to trip over the door frame." He cast an eye at Thomas, who had steadied himself on the wall, the ground in front of the barn being a little uneven.

"Don't expect too much," Sir Geraint said to me as he slid open a heavy door set into the iron frame. "We've barely made a start—I warned you about how long the preparation work took—and paintings are built in layers, so what you see now will be mostly gone in a month's time. I hardly like to show you, but I thought you'd be reassured to see we're actually doing some work."

The cavernous barn was surprisingly well lit by large, carefully positioned windows, clearly new. I stared at the enormous canvas fixed on a massive easel of metal struts, at each end of which stood a towering wooden construction like a cross between a ladder and a hangman's scaffold.

Against a large area painted in shades of deep blue and darkest red, the head of the emperor stood out clearly. His handsome young face was pale with sad longing, a glistening tear on one cheek. In the background, a half-open door revealed the little kitchen maid, her half-ugly, half-beautiful face a mere sketch. Charcoal outlines showed the position of the nightingale and the litter of scientific instruments and books that lay on the floor around the throne.

"Haylock's putting on a background layer for Death's garden." Sir Geraint waved a hand at the far wall of the barn, where another vast canvas was partly covered in dark blue paint. "Scoffield's still finishing the preparation of the third canvas, which is a rotten job on such a big area. The preparation of the canvas is the most crucial stage, and every artist has his own recipe. Mine has stood the test of time, as my early work proves. If you get it wrong, the paint can crack."

"Paint cracks." Edmund made a note in a small book he produced from a pocket. "I remember you telling me that when I was a little boy."

"I h-hadn't realized they w-would be so large." Thomas's brow furrowed.

"The large canvases measure twelve by six feet." Sir Geraint waited for Edmund to note the proportions before continuing. "I like canvases that are half as high as they are broad. It's a pleasing ratio. The side panels will vary in width to suit the room." He motioned to me. "If you would care to step around the back of the easel, Lady Helena, you will see that two pieces of cloth have been stitched together and that we've incorporated keys and expandable joints into the stretcher in case the canvas should sag over time. They may not look like much," he indicated the work with a broad sweep of his hand, "but we've put in hundreds of hours of effort already."

"Goodness." I stared at the back of the canvas, where the vertical stitching was indeed apparent. "Are these the largest paintings you've ever done?"

"*The Emperor's New Clothes* was much larger." Sir Geraint smiled happily as he caressed the thick struts of wood. "The preparation of a large canvas is a marvelous operation. The frame must be exact down to one-sixteenth of an inch, the stitching done with great care, everything perfectly measured and calculated before we apply the first drop of size. The same goes for the subject. I work out each area of light and shadow, each expression, every line of each figure in a hundred studies before I begin work. Then we must transfer all of that—that *thinking*—to the canvas correctly so no detail looks out of proportion. The *arrière-plan*—background—is a vital consideration, and against it the figures must stand out sharply, as if lit by an otherworldly light, a little like the actors on a stage."

"I've never thought about th-that," said Thomas. "Are there to b-be no shadows on the faces?"

"Not in my world." Sir Geraint's rich voice held a note of amusement. "And it *is* my world, to fashion as I wish. That's the advantage of developing one's own style. In my earlier work, I didn't always get the effect I wanted because I rushed. Now I work fast—you'd be astonished how fast, especially once the earlier stages are past—but I never rush."

We moved out from behind the canvas into the brighter light of the studio, and I contemplated the emperor's face again. Realizing that Sir Geraint was looking at me with an air of expectation, I felt I had to speak.

"I'm not sure what to say. It's overwhelming."

"How w-will you move these paintings to Whitcombe?" To my relief, Thomas had thought of a more practical question than my untaught reasoning could achieve.

"The moving of paintings is an art in itself." Sir Geraint nodded gravely, as if Thomas had raised a most important point. "When they are taken to London for exhibition and then brought to their resting place in Whitcombe, it'll probably be a matter of detaching the canvases and rolling them, and then re-attaching them to the frame *in situ*. I will be on hand to make any necessary repairs." He rubbed his hands together. "To tell you the truth, I'm pleased with how much we've managed to get done since the New Year. To have a studio dedicated entirely to one commission is a luxury I have never had. That, and the isolation of this spot, make me more productive than I have been since I was a young man. I should miss the friends who would drop by at any hour in London, but I do not. The older I grow, the more I hear the rush of the stream of Time and imagine the day when it will close over my head and flow on without me, and that makes me want to work as much as I can."

"Besides, it's safer here." Edmund's cool voice sounded

from one corner of the studio, where he had found a seat to make note-taking easier.

"Safer?" My heart beat a little faster. Was he referring to the unpleasant letters?

"Far from charwomen, patrons, and other intruders." Edmund made a wry face. "Father's rather protective of his work."

"I'll admit to that." Sir Geraint shrugged. "Scoff and Hay seem like careless chaps on the surface, Lady Helena, but they've never caused me a moment's worry, and they're really the only ones I want near my unfinished work, except for Millie or my closest painter friends. I'll admit that the notion of any visitor to Whitcombe House wishing to admire my work in progress makes me shrink into myself like a snail in its shell."

"And you will have the privilege only on carefully considered occasions." Edmund spoke again, his eyes on his paper. "You will notice the omission of us 'children' from the list. He never liked us in his studio."

"There are many good reasons for excluding children." Sir Geraint spoke briskly. "Now, will you come and see the rest of the house? Millie has no doubt inspected it thoroughly and will be waiting to give me her opinion on everything. I quite depend on it."

"Does she give her opinion on every stage of a painting?" I asked, strangely fascinated.

"Oh, I'll consult her when it's time to put in birds, or flowers or any of the natural elements. She's never terribly interested in the figures." He shook his head, correcting himself. "No, she is—of course she is—but she's more critical about the figures than anything else, and then I sulk, so she decided long ago to leave me to do them the way I like them. Have you taken enough notes, Eddie?" he asked his son.

Edmund rose to his feet and kicked at a stray fragment of

wood with one well-shined boot. "I suppose it'll do for now. When are you going to move here?"

"That will depend on your mother's opinion." A faintly anxious look flitted across Sir Geraint's face. "I hope she likes the place."

32

HARMONY

Thomas and I stayed far longer at Edenholme than we'd intended since it transpired that Millie had brought a picnic lunch, and it would have been rude to refuse her hospitality. We ate in the one presentable room, the ladies seated in the three chairs and the gentlemen perched wherever they could find space. The pump in the courtyard had been repaired, and there was plenty of fresh water for tea, which Mr. Scoffield prepared in the desolate kitchen.

The habitable rooms were already a riot of bright colors that stood out against the starkness of freshly whitewashed walls, the decorations applied in places by the younger artists a far cry from the elegance of the Dorrian-Knowleses' London house. Yet the overall effect was one of harmony and simplicity, quite beautiful in its way.

There was time after lunch for some fresh air before the hour arrived for Millie and her children to catch the train. Millie and I decided in favor of a stroll along the wide path that topped the sea wall. The tide was out, a strip of sand showing along the water's edge, the regular thump and hiss of the waves muted by the distance.

"What is your true opinion of the farmhouse?" I asked after we had talked for a while about commonplace things. "It must have seemed a little odd to you after expecting Sir Geraint to live at Whitcombe. It was to me."

"But you're over the shock, I suppose." Millie stopped, turning to face seaward. She wore no hat; I regretted mine, at which the wind was tugging mercilessly. "I'm not really surprised. Geraint wouldn't be happy working in your house, however grand, and he's never satisfied with his studio space. He's in that stage of a project when all he wants to do is work, with the biggest challenges—whatever it is he's set himself—before him. When he's worked through all the difficulties and only has the finishing before him, he'll want more life around him again, but that's a long way off with this series of paintings. We're lucky he has a man in London who will handle his business correspondence for him. I've been sending everything on but the most personal letters."

"Is there a great deal?" I asked, and Millie laughed briefly.

"Of the personal things? If you're thinking he receives letters from Rome at the house, think again. He has an arrangement somewhere for getting letters he doesn't want me to see."

"I meant correspondence in general." I tried to smile. "But it's a relief to know you don't have to see any letters from Odelia."

We fell silent, watching the shifting clouds, behind which the sun disappeared at intervals, only to sidle out again and slide its light across the restless sea. It was a scene that lent itself to contemplation. Millie's still form, with the sun sparking light from her contained mass of red hair, reminded me suddenly of the painting of her as Hera, welcoming the dawn light. Before us were Edmund, who stood still, smoking a cigarette, and Jane, who was walking at the very edge of the water, sometimes skipping back as a wave threatened her boots. Sir Geraint had stayed at the farmhouse to work. He had asked Thomas, whom he seemed to like, to stay with him.

After a while, Millie sighed and turned to me. "This is what Geraint needs, I suppose. A complete absence from London."

"Do you mind?" I asked. "Not seeing him, I mean."

"There are advantages." Millie's voice held a trace of amusement. "The household bills have certainly gone down. And it's a quiet life for me: no models coming and going, no theater, no calls to pay, no parties—and no mistresses, of course. Just visits from my own friends and some old friends who remember us when we were young. The only nuisances are the young lady artists who write to ask if they can visit to learn from the great man. I have to answer those to prevent them turning up at my door. Sometimes they write back to ask where Geraint is. Don't they read the society columns? I suppose they'll all know he's in Sussex eventually, and then it will begin again, the pilgrimages, but at least for now I don't have to put up with them smirking and giggling at him." She looked me in the eyes. "Has he remained . . . quiet? No stimulants?"

"None that I've noticed."

She nodded. "There are some old habits he needed to shed. Will you keep an eye on him when he moves to this house?"

"I'll certainly invite him to Whitcombe regularly. Do you think he'll come?"

"He's too old not to pass up the chance of really good cooking when offered. He told me you keep an excellent table." Millie smiled. "He'll be tired of that aspect of the bohemian life soon enough. I've thought of sending Janie down to drudge for them, but I worry about Mountjoy's romantic intentions. I don't want her to marry an artist."

"I'd hate to see her drudging." I watched the young girl, who was now searching among the seaweed-strewn sand, presumably for shells.

"Oh, she's used to work. Far more than Cass ever was since we could afford more servants when she was this age. I'm hoping I can keep Jane close a little longer. I'm teaching her whatever I can on the handicraft side too. She needs a good deal of instruction, but once she's learned how to execute a piece of work, she does a decent, exact job of it. It's strange that neither of my daughters has my feeling for needlework. Cass loathes it. She was always going to be the sort of wife whose interests are limited to children, shopping, and complaining about her servants. Jane might make her own husband a bit happier when her day comes."

"And Edmund?" I nodded toward the young man, who was now flinging stones into the waves with a concentrated effort that might have been mistaken for anger. "Does he have matrimonial intentions?"

"He'll have to wait awhile if he does." Millie's face softened as she watched her son. "It was rather unfair of Geraint to help Phil out with the studio and reduce the other boys' prospects. Still, Phil, at least, has a definite talent and an inclination for following in his father's footsteps. Edmund has Phil's love of high society and good living, but not Phil's sense of vocation. Galahad's far more straightforward; he'll just find something to do when he's ready and go out and do it."

"I'm sure Edmund will find his path in time," I said, hoping to sound reassuring. But Millie's face darkened suddenly, spots of angry color appearing on her cheeks.

"It won't be any thanks to Geraint. Edmund was always a sensitive child, and he feels the whole situation at home keenly. That's what's at the root of his inability to settle down. I could murder the lot of them, those women—and Geraint too, at times."

"You don't mean that."

She sighed. "Most of the time I don't, I suppose. But I get so *angry*—sometimes I just can't be the good, meek, forgiving wife any longer. I say or do things I regret."

Unfortunately, I could not pursue this interesting admission since Edmund was striding up the shingle bank toward us, pocket watch in hand. He must have called or signaled to Jane, who was also approaching us with a cheerful smile on her face.

"I say, shouldn't we be getting back to the house?" Edmund's demeanor was unhurried, his young brow clear. "We don't want to miss the train. I can't wait to get back to London."

"Why?" Jane was panting slightly with the effort of ascending the shingle. "It's so nice here. Look what I found—isn't it pretty? I was determined not to bring a shell home unless it was a truly lovely one, and this one is. See, Lady Helena?"

I smiled as I took the shell from her. "These are my favorites. They call them jingles or mermaids' toenails, but I think they're a sort of oyster." I held it up; it was quite transparent, a golden yellow on the outside with a faint silvering of mother-of-pearl. "You're lucky. One rarely finds them with no chips or barnacles. I used to collect them when I was a little girl. I wonder where they went? Thrown out by some maid, probably."

"I hereby start my own collection." Jane's expression was more carefree than I'd yet seen. "I'll put it in a box labeled 'Do Not Throw Out' just in case." She passed it to her mother for inspection. "Isn't it beautiful here? The air is so pure, not like dirty old London."

"Beautiful?" Edmund rounded his eyes in mock astonishment, his voice an exaggerated varsity drawl. "It's the epitome of absence. No shops, no hansom cabs, no omnibuses, no theaters, no restaurants—and hardly any people. How Father can stand to live *here*, among the yokels and fishermen, is the greatest mystery of all." His gesture took in the beach farther along the bay, where a handful of men were busying themselves with keddle nets or digging for lugworms in the sand. "It's ludicrous."

"He said he'd come home for Christmas." Jane's young face had lost its serene look, and her voice was small and hesitant.

"Which is months away." A sneer lifted Edmund's lip, and Jane seemed to shrink even further into herself. "Still, I suppose at least he's working. Shall we go, Mother? We'll be so much more comfortable at home."

33

OBJECTIONS

Sir Geraint moved to Edenholme on the sixteenth of April. On the same day, I received a telegram from Odelia, informing me that she and Miss Emery would return to England on the twenty-sixth.

I suppose I could not be blamed for inferring that Odelia's principal purpose in coming back so early had something to do with Sir Geraint. I had no grounds for hoping that Odelia did not correspond with her lover, even though no letters from her had arrived for him at Whitcombe. As Millie had said, he would no doubt make arrangements, such as having her letters sent to a post office to await collection.

Ten days' notice would not give me time to write and inquire about Odelia's reasons for returning. Nor did the occasion seem to demand the dispatch of telegrams insisting that Odelia remain abroad. So, as usual, I submitted to my sister's whims and merely arranged for my driver to collect the ladies at Dover at the extraordinarily early hour ordained for their arrival.

But only Odelia stepped out of the carriage at Whitcombe. "Cynthia's gone straight up to London," was her first remark after embracing me. "She sends her thanks for your offer of a bed for the night, but she has a most important appointment. She's done terribly well in Italy and quite established a name for herself. This meeting may result in a significant commission. That's why we decided to come back now rather than waiting for the prospective client to visit Italy again. Strike while the iron's hot and all that."

I felt the warm weight of her arm about my shoulders as we ascended the steps into the carriage hall and put my own arm around her waist. I had missed her more than I'd realized. Our reunion had been almost effusive; we had hugged each other hard, laughed together at the small tear that had come to my eye, and O had kissed me with the full measure of sisterly affection.

"To be honest," Odelia continued, "it was only the thought of seeing you that prevented me from taking the train straight up to Town. I've sent all my trunks up already, apart from my small one, and I intend to be back in Scott House by tomorrow night. I've wired to Mrs. Coles to open the house."

My arm fell from my sister's waist, and I stepped back in astonishment. "But that means we'll only have a day together. Don't you even want to see the rest of the family? I was going to invite them to dinner tomorrow."

Odelia—who looked quite splendid, her skin gently kissed by the Italian sun—shrugged her slim shoulders and waved her hands in a decidedly Continental way. "The family will keep. After all, we've all been writing to one another, so I have all their news. It's not as if any of them have done something worth seeing. If Ned had shaved off his beard or Maryanne acquired some common sense, I might have been tempted to see the miracle for myself, but as it is, I just know I'm *doomed* to feel as if I'd never been away. I'll see Thomas this evening and will visit Mama tomorrow morning before I leave." She shuddered faintly at the prospect. "Ned will probably come to see me off—maybe Gerry will even accompany him—and that will be *quite* enough."

"But there's so much to talk about." I firmed my jaw, aware that my mouth had been open in amazement. "I never thought—well, don't you even want to see the *Nightingale* paintings?"

"At this stage?" Odelia, suppressing a yawn, began to undo the buttons of her winter paletot while Guttridge—who had naturally been in the welcoming party—hovered discreetly in the background. "It'll just be Geraint's assistants transferring the outlines from the cartoons, preparing the backgrounds, and so on. I know how Geraint works." She handed the coat to Guttridge with a smile. "It's nice to see you, Guttridge. In the pink?"

"In the best of health, my lady. You look very well yourself, if I may say so."

"You may. I feel very well. The Italian air agrees with me." Odelia unpinned her hat and patted her thick, dark blond hair. "Goodness, Guttridge, I'll need to put myself into your capable hands soon. This fine rain plays havoc with my hair. The contrast between the wet cliffs of Dover, as seen from a steamer, and my memories of the blue Mediterranean is positively distressing."

"I am at your ladyship's disposal." And Guttridge, with her most professional smile, melted into the background, no doubt heading for the laundry rooms, where she could ensure my sister's outer clothing was properly blocked for drying, after which she would remove any mud splashes and effect any necessary repairs. Any lady who passed through her hands left them improved and refreshed.

"It's a pity you arrived on such a nasty, squally day." I glanced at the window of the carriage hall, on which the rain was now dashing in gusty spurts, making a noise like the rattling of small pebbles. "Would you like to go to the drawing room to see the progress, or shall we warm ourselves up in the small library? I had them light the fire in there since it's nicer than the morning room on a day like this. Or would you just like to lie down on your bed? You have your usual room."

Odelia stared for a moment at the painting of Justin's ancestors over the fireplace before answering with a tiny shrug. "I suppose we could get the drawing room over with."

I followed, vaguely puzzled at her lack of enthusiasm, as my sister led the way to the drawing-room door. It was still early, and no artisans were yet there. My butler, Dunnam, who had, as always, followed our conversation while managing to obliterate the fact of his presence from our consciousness, mysteriously arrived at the drawing-room door at the same moment we did and produced the key from his waistcoat pocket.

"We keep it locked to discourage curiosity and prevent any overzealous maid from trying to clean things," I remarked as Dunnam swung the double doors open. "Naturally, it's a very long way from finished—barely started, really —but it's surprising how much our visitors like looking at it. Every time I give a dinner I have to put it on show. The main exhibit is Sir Geraint's drawings, of course."

"Of course." Neatly avoiding the tools of the trade left by the artisans—who always cleaned and tidied the room before they left for the day—Odelia made her way to where Sir Geraint had set up his framed drawings on a series of easels. She studied them in absolute silence, her face unreadable.

"It's strange to think of all of this going on while I was in Rome." Her tone was oddly flat.

I glanced around; Dunnam had left the room, shutting the doors behind him. "I thought you'd be more . . . well, interested, I suppose. You were so excited about this commission.

I thought you'd at least insist on dashing off to Lower Broad-mere to see the paintings." I took a deep breath. "To be honest, I'd been rehearsing speeches to keep you out of—well, to avoid—" I stopped, feeling a little flushed and flustered.

"You thought I'd run toward Geraint like a she-cat on heat." Odelia was still looking at the sketches, but her eyes had hardened. "You know, after all the promises I made, you could trust me a little more."

"I didn't mean—I wasn't—" I flung my arms around my sister. "Oh, for heaven's sake, O, I was mildly worried at the most. Something's changed, hasn't it? Have you and Sir Geraint quarreled?"

"We haven't written to each other in weeks." A small twitch at the corner of Odelia's expressive mouth made a tiny line appear as she very gently pushed me away from her. "At least, I haven't written to *him*. His letters to me are nearly always replies to mine. He doesn't like writing letters when he's in the early stages of a project." She cupped one side of my face with her long fingers. "I suppose you could say I've quarreled with *him*."

"Why?" I placed my hand over hers. "He's done nothing but work since he came here, I swear to you. I don't think this move to the Bennett farm—to Edenholme—has any motive other than art. And it was your idea anyway, wasn't it? He seemed to suggest you'd recommended the place to him."

"I did *not*." Now Odelia looked decidedly sulky, and I knew, suddenly, that I'd found the key to her odd mood. "I drew a sketch of it once—don't you remember? We went out on a long hack together, before Justin died, to see the seawall and the new road. I suppose I must have shown it to Geraint and said what a pretty place it was, but that was ages ago. It's also possible I recommended he stow his blessed assistants somewhere else before you lost patience with them—they're good artists but appallingly bohemian in their manners, and flirting with the maids wouldn't have been the half of it—but I thought *he'd* be staying with you. Nobody could have been more astonished than I when you casually mentioned the farm in your last letter, as if I knew all about it."

I frowned. "To be frank, O, I still don't understand. You wanted Sir Geraint to get away from London, and he's away. You wanted to keep him out of further trouble—of an amatory nature—and as far as I know, he's leading an entirely chaste life. I can't imagine Lower Broadmere has much to offer in the way of temptation."

That, at least, produced a smile. "No, romancing farmers' daughters or fishermen's wives isn't Geraint's style."

"And you know," I swallowed before continuing in this dangerous vein, "at least, you *must* have known that I would discourage any, er, intimate meeting between the two of you while you were at Whitcombe. Surely, you didn't get your hopes up about a—well, an assignation."

This time Odelia laughed, although there was little genuine mirth in the sound. "Yes, I did realize you'd take that stance, you funny, prudish little thing. It would have been quite amusing watching you trying to stop us. Surely, you didn't actually try to prevent the goings-on at your own house parties? Justin always thought it was staggeringly hilarious how much you disapproved."

I did my best to ignore that last remark. I *did* prefer spouses who were faithful to one another, which was probably why I was not terribly interested in inviting Justin's old friends to Whitcombe.

"So what is your objection to Edenholme? Eccentric as it is, I can't actually see anything wrong with Sir Geraint's decision."

Odelia flinched; just a tiny movement, but I was staring at

her and didn't miss it. "Edenholme. That horrid name. Like something you'd find on a middle-class seaside villa." She dragged her gaze from the series of drawings and fixed it on me. "I suppose, since you must plumb the depths of my every motive, that I don't like this arrangement because it has a nasty feeling of permanence about it. I didn't think for a moment he'd set up work in your drawing room. The light's entirely wrong, for a start. I thought he'd go back to London, where he could work comfortably in his own studio. All he'd have had to do would be to run down here twice a month to reassure himself about the progress of the decorative work. You'd have kept his room for him so he wouldn't even have to pack a suitcase, just leave a few things down here and come up and down by train as it suited him."

"And yet you made it sound as if the whole point of the exercise was that he'd be happier down here." I narrowed my eyes at my sister. "You haven't been entirely honest with me."

"I haven't been *dis*honest either." Odelia widened her dark blue eyes at me. "The last thing I imagined is that he'd actually be *living* in a freezing, damp farmhouse and painting his glorious pictures in a barn. And what's more, he'll be under the chilly gaze of little Scoff and horrid Hay, neither of whom like me." She rolled her eyes. "I couldn't so much as glance at Geraint without one of them saying something indelicate. So I have absolutely no intention of visiting *Edenholme*." She shuddered as she said the word. "I will go back to London, where I feel at home, and enjoy the Season, write Geraint a long letter, and see where that leads." She held up a slim hand. "In any case, I will keep my promise and return to Rome in September, with or without Cynthia. If Geraint wants to see me, he will have to return to his normal life. You won't know a thing about it. Your conscience will be clear."

"And yours?" I felt a spark of anger but quelled it. After all, we would have such a short time together. "I'm disappointed, O. I thought the change of scene might dislodge him from your mind."

"He doesn't live in my mind. He lives in my soul, in my heart." Odelia laid a hand on her chest rather theatrically. "I just wish he didn't live in Lower Broadmere."

34

A KILLING RAGE

"You've done sterling work this morning, Helena." Ned stepped onto Whitcombe's terrace, sighing in pleasure at the sunlight. "It was nice of you to get up and dressed so early for my sake."

It was a month after Odelia's arrival and immediate departure for London. The miserable wet weather of April had reluctantly given way to a glorious May. My brother-in-law tucked my arm comfortably under his as we set out together for a short stroll through my gardens, freshly tidied for the season.

"I did nothing but sign my name." I laughed. "And I'm not *such* an idle aristocrat that I can't get up early occasionally." But Ned's happiness was infecting me, and a smile tugged at the corners of my lips. My signature had made over a piece of my land to a trust set up for the purposes of creating a new hospital for Littleberry, and the very sound of the trustees' carriage rolling away down Whitcombe Lane carried promises with it for our small town. Now they could begin the task of raising funds. Now, construction of the hospital could begin as soon as the initial sums had been secured.

Ned and I had turned into the rose garden. We were marveling at the contrast between the stiff, barbed network of branches and the delicacy of new leaves and buds when my companion paused, lifting his bushy beard to the light breeze like a bloodhound scenting the air.

"Somebody's shouting for you." Ned, who topped my height by almost a foot, stood on tiptoe to look upward to Whitcombe House. "Good heavens, it looks like Dorrian-Knowles. An accident at the farm, perhaps?"

"He'd have gone to the village if somebody was hurt." I turned on my heel and began ascending the wide, shallow steps of granite and crushed gravel. "It would only take him a few minutes—he has a horse—Sir Geraint!" I raised my voice into as ladylike a shout as I could manage and waved, seeing the artist turn toward the sound and hurtle down the curving steps from the terrace.

Ned and I continued our ascent. Sir Geraint began talking when he was still some distance from us, frustrating my query as to what had happened.

"Is the drawing room all right?"

"I suppose so. The men haven't arrived yet." I frowned in puzzlement at the man in front of me, dusty from the road and sweating in his shirtsleeves, his shirt lacking a collar. "You could have just asked Dunnam to unlock the room for you."

"I wanted a witness in case of trouble. My studio was broken into last night."

My heart thumped, and a thousand questions crowded into my mind, but Ned spoke first. "Is anybody hurt?" It was typical of him to put people before property.

"Hurt? No."

Ned puffed out a sigh of relief. "Thank goodness. I'll stop

at the police station on my way to the Town Hall and ask them to send someone round." He had pulled out his watch as he spoke and was looking at the dial. "I'd better leave now. You'll have to excuse me, Sir Geraint; I'm supposed to be chairing a meeting at nine. Will you take Lady Helena up to the house for me?" He leaned forward to kiss my cheek. "Helena, my dear, I'll come by later to hear all about it. Of course, in the unlikely event that someone has gone on a spree and broken into your drawing room, you must send for me immediately."

Sir Geraint and I watched Ned's stalwart frame disappear around the corner of the house before I spoke. "He knows nothing of the events in London." I stared up into his intense eyes, a small knot of worry cramping my stomach. "What has happened? You wouldn't rush over here for nothing."

"I suppose I must look like an idiot to Sir Edward, making a fuss over a burglary." Sir Geraint grimaced. "But I didn't tell you the rest. Four months of work destroyed—you have to come and see for yourself. I can hardly bear to speak of it." He threw up his hands in a gesture of despair. "Please, first, the drawing room—just to reassure me."

We met Guttridge on the way back inside, and she immediately ran to fetch Dunnam. All four of us were soon assembled outside the drawing-room doors. Dunnam held the key, a look of brooding anxiety on his pale face that mirrored Sir Geraint's. A moment of suspense ensued as my butler turned the key in the lock, and then his expression changed to one of relief.

"I think you will find everything satisfactory, my lady." Dunnam sounded positively cheerful as he swung back the heavy paneled wood for us. As if to reassure ourselves, we all stepped into the large room, but everything was as orderly as one could wish. A good, clean smell of wood and glue hung on the still air.

"It's excellent, Dunnam. I'm sorry to have alarmed you." I turned toward Sir Geraint. "We'll take the brougham back to Lower Broadmere. A groom will bring your horse back to you once it's had a rest. And Guttridge will come with us— won't you?" I smiled at my lady's maid, who, although she stood silently in the background, positively quivered with investigative energy. "She's such a help at moments like these."

Sir Geraint had warned Guttridge and me that the damage was too great for any repair to be feasible, yet I was still unprepared for the sight of the emperor's riven face, contorted into a leer by the great gash running through it. The morning light filled the barn through the new windows and open door, oblique rays of sunlight picking out the worst of the damage as if nature were deliberately mocking man's attempts to imitate it.

Someone had attacked the *Nightingale* paintings with considerable energy. Their fabric, rendered stiff by the preparation rituals, bulged and swayed around long gashes and tears with frayed edges. Here and there the attacker had vented his fury on the edges of the canvases, creating great gouges in the wood of the frames and leaving large, raw-looking splinters on the barn's plank floor. Whoever it was had been thorough, climbing the tall ladder platforms that stood in front of the emperor painting to slash it at several heights and a variety of angles. The other two canvases, standing ready on low easels, had been slashed vertically at close intervals so that they looked like curtains of broad ribbons.

"It's an axe that's done the deed, you mark my words." Guttridge had been inspecting the damage with the air of a general reviewing her troops, her hands linked behind her back, her tread steady and martial. "Has anybody found the weapon?"

"There's an axe missing." Reid Scoffield had folded himself into a plain wooden chair and was sitting with hunched back and splayed legs, staring gloomily at the ruined work. "I noticed this morning when I went to the woodshed. I'll go round the place and see if I can find it."

"If you do find it, you must leave it be." Guttridge eyed the young man severely. "It might offer a clue."

Haylock Mountjoy had been leaning, with a dejected air, against the door frame. Now he interrupted a long stretch and gaping yawn to splutter with sudden laughter. "A clue? Do you think the fellow wrote his name on a ribbon and tied it in a bow around the handle?"

"Don't be rude to Miss Guttridge, Hay." Sir Geraint sounded exhausted. "She's trying to help."

"I beg your pardon." Mountjoy made a half bow toward my lady's maid, who nodded regally. "But my bet is that the murder weapon is in the pond anyway." He yawned again. "I suppose I should walk up to the post office and wire for more wood and canvas, and then I'll go to Whitcombe and recruit a couple of carpenters to help us start again. There's no point in crying over it. Scoff, why don't you go find the blacksmith and see about bolts and locks and bars? We'll make sure it can't happen again."

Scoffield rose to his feet, rubbing the back of his neck. "So much for the peace of the countryside. Let's hope it was just some passing maniac. I'd hate to think we'd made an enemy in the village."

"Didn't anyone hear the noise?" I asked.

"I slept like a baby." Sir Geraint shrugged. "There's something about the sound of the sea that soothes me, and I've been getting up at dawn to start work. I went to bed at nine and never heard a sound."

"And we made a night of it at the Red Lion." Mountjoy's careless drawl sounded from the doorway. "Scoff was sick on the road, and I can't remember how we got to bed." He rubbed his eyes. "My head's splitting. And this barn is built of brick and stone, as is the farmhouse—none of your tuppenny-ha'penny wood in any of these buildings, which is how they've stood so long. You can't hear much from the outside."

"Do you remember if you needed a lamp to light your way home?" I asked, suddenly inspired by the thought of the two young men staggering seaward from the village. "And do you remember what time it was?"

"Time? We barely knew what day it was." Mountjoy winced as he stepped out into the bright light. "But we didn't need a lamp, I know that. And," he held a finger in the air, "there was a bit of a moon. We howled at it."

"Did you indeed?" Guttridge gave the young man a look of contempt. "But you've given me an idea. What you need is dogs." She nodded emphatically. "Or one really big one. Nothing like a dog for putting the fear of God into mischief-makers." She thought for a moment. "My young man has a cousin who breeds hunting dogs. He can probably put you in the way of a nice big brute, the sort that barks at everything."

"Miss Guttridge solves the problem." A faint smile appeared on Sir Geraint's face as he turned to his assistants. "Off you go, then. Scoff, when you've seen the blacksmith, wire to Tom Rooke—ask him if he can spare a week to help us. Here's a shilling." He flipped a coin from the end of his thumb in a high arc. Scoffield caught it neatly, whistling as he pulled on his jacket and fished under the chair for his hat.

"We can still make progress, Lady Helena." Sir Geraint

turned to me as the young men walked out into the sunshine. "None of the smaller panels were damaged, so I can get on with those until my big canvases are rebuilt. We'll be faster the second time around because we have the feel of the composition. The days are long at the moment, and we will make use of every hour of light." He turned to look at the ruined emperor canvas, his fists resting on his hips. "We should probably drag all this out into the courtyard tonight and have a bonfire."

Guttridge and I emitted simultaneous yelps of objection. "And destroy the evidence? What about the police?" I asked. "This isn't minor damage." I waved an arm at the shredded canvases against the wall. "It's pure rage."

"A killing rage," Guttridge added dolefully. "With an axe. If one of you had heard a noise and happened upon the culprit while he was committing the deed, who knows what might have happened? A man who is capable of such an act of violence is capable of anything."

Her voice had strengthened and her vowels rounded as she delivered this rather fine speech, but she relapsed into her flat, London tones as she asked, "What kind of axe?"

"I beg your pardon?" Sir Geraint frowned.

"There are lots of different kinds of axes." Guttridge assumed the long-suffering expression she sometimes used with me when I professed ignorance about purely practical matters. "Was it a big, long, heavy one, the sort you need two hands for? Or the little sort of axe you use to split kindling?" She looked at the damaged canvases again. "It was good and sharp, I can see that."

"It was about this long, I suppose." Sir Geraint held his hands apart to indicate the length. "Not really short, but not really long, either. It belongs—belonged—to one of the craftsmen. He lent us an old one of his and a whetstone. He's been giving the boys lessons in working green wood—absolutely fascinating. Scoff's got some plan to build a bower in the courtyard."

"Probably a carpenter's axe, then." Guttridge walked up and down in front of the canvases against the wall, then stopped and stood on tiptoe, stretching an arm upward and miming a blow or two.

"Wait." I held up a hand before darting out of the door. I had seen the shed with the stacked logs, some of which were no more than thick branches. I selected a piece of about two inches in diameter, roughly the length Sir Geraint had indicated, and ran back to the barn, squinting in the bright light.

"Oh, well done, my lady." Guttridge sounded like a schoolmistress praising a normally slow pupil who had surprised her with the right answer. "May I try?"

"Be my guest." I blinked furiously to relieve my dazzled eyes. "In any case, we'd have to find me something to stand on before I could reach that far."

Guttridge's answering grin was that of a colleague. I watched as she walked up and down, making chopping motions with the piece of branch.

"A man, I'd say," I concluded after about half a minute. "Or a very tall woman, I suppose. Some five inches taller than you. Let's say six feet, maybe an inch or two more."

"Or taller still if he held the axe like a carpenter does, close to the head. See the control in these cuts?"

"You're right." A thought struck me, and I ran to one of the huge wooden ladders, climbing as swiftly as my skirts allowed until I was far enough up to see the slashes in the emperor painting up close. "Look, Guttridge. These cuts are wilder, as if he was swinging the axe around anyhow. Perhaps because it was awkward to attack from this height?"

"Or because it was a different person. There might have been two of them." I saw Guttridge's face tilted up toward mine. "See here—*these* cuts are lower down than the ones on the other pictures and not nearly as neat. Perhaps they were made by somebody who's not as strong."

"Or the same person who, by now, was simply exhausted." I wrinkled my nose, thinking.

"Or getting more and more upset?" Guttridge suggested. "That's dangerous, that is. My dad used to work wood—he told me many a tale of severed fingers and blades buried halfway into an arm where chaps he knew were careless." Her eyes gleamed with happy memories.

A guffaw from behind us made us both turn round, I somewhat awkwardly because I was still on the ladder.

"You ladies." The tension had quite gone from Sir Geraint's face. "I've never seen anything like it. You should be in the detective force."

"Is your astonishment due to the revelation that we have brains or that we use them?" I inquired mildly as I descended the steps, being very careful not to tread on my skirts.

"Oh, I always knew you had brains. Both of you. Millie said so." He held out a hand to help me off the last step. "Talking of Millie, I'd better write to her that the work's been delayed and I can't come home in June as I'd planned. She won't like it. But I could get the whole scheme of the side panels decided on while we're rebuilding." There was a spark of enthusiasm in his eyes. "I was going to start on them in earnest anyway. One can't work on the same painting for days in a row, you see, even the big ones, as the oils have to dry before I can do the next layer. I always have to have a good many pieces to choose from. The advantage of this studio is that I have no other work than your commission, so I won't get too distracted." He passed a hand over his brow. "I just pray we can secure the barn properly. Thank heaven whoever it was didn't touch the side panels."

"And why was that, I wonder?" Guttridge's brow creased. "If I wanted to destroy a place, I'd do a proper job." She looked around. "With all the oil and turpentine and what have you, a match would have made what you might call a final statement."

"The act of slashing just the large canvases might have been symbolic," I mused, trying to ignore the look of horror on Sir Geraint's face. "If, that is, it was somebody who had a grudge against you in some deep and personal way. Not just somebody who didn't like artists."

"But it's always possible some local person objects to your presence." Guttridge left off her contemplation of a stack of materials in one corner. "They're a queer lot in these villages —you can't rule it out. Broadmere proper is odd enough, if you ask me, but up there it's mostly the upper crust, and we're supposed to call it eccentricity. Down here, well . . ." She made an expansive gesture to suggest how strange she found the Sussex character.

"That would be a convenient explanation," I said. "Too convenient, perhaps. The alternative is that trouble has followed you from London, and that's far more serious."

35

A LITTLE DETECTION

We left Sir Geraint awaiting the arrival of the police, with one more reminder not to burn the canvases until we could derive no more information from them, and returned to Whitcombe.

"You don't think we should have waited for the constables, do you?" I asked Guttridge once we were back in our workroom and had greeted Scotty sufficiently that he'd calmed down. "Perhaps we could have been helpful."

"I do not." Guttridge snorted. "We'd have ended up having to explain ourselves, and that would have led to explanations about the nasty things that happened to her ladyship, and there'd have been no end to it. In any case," her eyes narrowed, "you and I, putting our heads together, are worth ten of any bobby. The *interesting* thing about this case could well be, as you so rightly pointed out, the personal angle. You don't think Sir Geraint suspects who might have done it, do you?"

She looked hopefully at me. I rolled my eyes. "For heavens' sake, if we're to develop a theory of the crime, let's hope Sir Geraint isn't in the middle of formulating his own. All he really seemed to care about was getting started again." I shrugged. "Which is reasonable—professional, even. No good crying over spilt milk and all that. I hope he and the young men *can* secure the barn. No," I bit my lip, "let's just think this through together and leave Sir Geraint to do the work for which I'm paying him. Get a pencil and paper and let's see if we can work out who it might have been."

We were soon settled side by side in our Morris chairs. Guttridge, who had the better handwriting, had taken one of my heavier herbals to use as a writing surface, and we were quite comfortable. She wrote "LIST OF SUSPECTS" at the top of the piece of paper, underlining it twice.

"One?" she asked, writing the numeral neatly. I hesitated, then plunged in.

"I hate to say it, but—"

"Lady Odelia Scott-De Quincy." Guttridge wrote my sister's name on the first line. "I can see it by your face, my lady. What makes you think such a thing?"

I shrugged. "A feeling, that's all. The look on her face when she inspected the drawing room—like jealousy." I fiddled with a length of ribbon, used as a bookmark, that had fallen out of the herbal. "Perhaps she was never possessive about Sir Geraint when she was younger, but she's definitely showing signs of it now, wouldn't you say?"

"Not half." Guttridge put a very decided period after Odelia's name. "If that business in Holland Park is anything to go by." She licked the point of her pencil reflectively. "And she came back early, didn't she?"

"Not, in itself, a suspicious circumstance since the return to England was prompted by Miss Emery." I quickly informed Guttridge of what Odelia had told me.

"But you haven't seen Miss Emery."

"No, she went straight up to London."

"Well, then." Guttridge emphasized that cryptic remark

by writing the number two on the next line. "Her ladyship's on a wild goose chase, if you ask me," was her next thought. "A man like that may play the field, but he'll never desert his wife."

"I sincerely hope not." I crushed the ribbon in my hand, feeling uncomfortably as if someone had just placed a cold hand on the back of my neck. "It would be an utter disaster if she and Sir Geraint ran off together. They'd have to live abroad. There'd be such a scandal, don't you think?"

"I *do* think, my lady," Guttridge spoke as she wrote. "Well, number two must be Lady Dorrian-Knowles. The injured wife has every reason to cause trouble, doesn't she?"

"But how would she get down to Lower Broadmere without anyone knowing? Come to that, how would Lady Odelia?"

"They could hire someone to do the work for them." Guttridge nodded. "Didn't you say that almost everyone who has an opinion about the letters has said Lady Dorrian-Knowles must have sent them?"

"I did, and it's a pity. I like her." I watched Guttridge put the final flourish on the *S*.

"We'd ten times rather it were her than one of *our* family," Guttridge pronounced stoutly, and I couldn't contradict her. "What do you think about the sons and daughters, my lady? I suppose if *my* dad had run off to the seaside, I might want to try something to get him back to London."

I wrinkled my nose. "It doesn't quite work like that with our sort of people. My own father was frequently absent. One expects a man to have his own interests. And the earlier letters to Sir Geraint—which he destroyed, of course, so we only have his word for it—made threats against the children." I sighed. "Put them down anyway."

"Two or more of them could be acting together," Guttridge suggested.

"Yes, but which of them?" I frowned. "That would really complicate matters. I might rule out Cassiope Jowett, though. A woman with a house and children might not have the time to run around making mischief."

"She could be the mastermind." Guttridge licked her pencil again. "They have those in the stories. A criminal mastermind doesn't do the work. He thinks up bad things with his devious intellect and communicates his plans to his subordinates." Her eyes shone.

"Colorful, but unlikely." I did my best to sound severe. "We might also have to rule out Jane Dorrian-Knowles because of her youth. Her mother must surely keep an eye on her whereabouts."

"The mother and daughter could be in *cahoots*. That's what Americans say when people are plotting evil deeds together."

"You're wasted as a lady's maid, Guttridge. You should be a writer of penny dreadfuls. Very well, note them down as number three. 'Philip, Edmund, Cassiope, Galahad, and Jane Dorrian-Knowles, either singly or in cahoots.'" My tongue lingered lovingly on the slang. "I wonder how I could introduce that word into a conversation? My vocabulary is so conventional." I turned my head to look at Guttridge, who was clearly trying to suppress a grin. "And if the words 'sheltered upbringing' are about to invade your mind, banish them immediately."

"Yes, my lady." Guttridge turned aside for a moment, ostensibly to cough, but I saw her shoulders shaking.

"Number four," I said loudly, "must be Miss Emery, and number five Miss Aldred. The latter definitely has the look of a woman who wouldn't take an insult lying down. So to speak."

This time the ruthless suppression of mirth was so clear on Guttridge's face that I almost laughed too until she spoke. "I don't see that actress getting her hands dirty, though. She might instruct a confederate. Lots of funny people hang around theaters, so she'd have plenty of choice."

"Agreed. So we have a list of nine possible suspects, some of whom may be acting together or with assistance. That's an awful lot."

"Eleven." Guttridge wrote on the paper. "We mustn't forget Mr. Scoffield and Mr. Mountjoy, although what their motive might be I couldn't imagine. But they are actually there, at the farm, and they're young and strong enough to use an axe. How do we know they were as drunk as they said?"

"And they were in London until recently." I nodded.

"And let's not forget 'person or persons unknown.' We could be completely wrong."

I flapped a hand at my lady's maid. "Don't write that. I forbid you to take such a defeatist attitude."

"Very well, my lady." Guttridge turned the paper over. "Now we have a list of suspects, let's make a list of actions."

I settled myself more comfortably into my chair, smiling. I could always rely on Guttridge and her lists. They were a familiar sight, whether we were discussing my wardrobe or the tasks to be done in the herb room. I watched as she wrote "ACTIONS" in neat capital letters.

"I could find out from Sir Geraint if he's received any anonymous letters or parcels while my sister was away," I mused. "If he had, wouldn't that exonerate her? And Miss Emery? It would be quite obvious if they came from abroad."

"Good." Guttridge made a note. "Unless Sir Geraint lies to you."

"What a mind you have." I thought further. "Here's one you could do. Could you go to the Red Lion and find out whether Hay and Scoff—I beg your pardon, Mr. Mountjoy and Mr. Scoffield—were really there getting drunk last night?"

"Nothing easier, if I have your permission to take the evening off." Guttridge looked pleased. "My young man won't mind a stroll to Lower Broadmere, especially if there's a public house at the end of it."

I was filled with curiosity and something like envy. "What are public houses like? I've been into coaching inns, but I can't imagine going into one of the small ones."

"They're crowded and noisy, and they reek of men and beer and worse things depending where the privy is," Guttridge said cheerfully. "On a nice evening, I'd rather sit outside, although Silas doesn't mind paying extra for the snug if he's got the money in his pocket."

"Is that your young man's name?" My curiosity increased.

"Silas Horniblow. You didn't know that?"

"I feel ashamed of myself for not asking before."

"Well, I never," Guttridge murmured as she wrote "Find out if H and S were really drunk," on the paper. "And what about the rest of the suspects?"

"We can't find out unless we go back to London." I groaned. "As unpleasant as the thought is, Guttridge, we had better plan on returning to Scott House."

36

TINCTURES AND SYRUPS

London had its compensations, the chief of which was seeing Fortier. We took with us several jars of hawthorn syrups and jams from berries we had harvested in the fall and, at Fortier's particular request, a quantity of dried blackthorn blossoms and a tincture of lavender he especially liked. Our luggage included gifts from Gabrielle, who had returned to Littleberry to spend a few summer weeks with her children.

We also took with us a basket of Taylor's hothouse strawberries that I carried up to London myself, making every conveyance we used smell like absolute heaven. They needed to be delivered to the Fortier house in Kensington Square as quickly as possible, so after I had greeted Odelia—and presented her with a similar basket of edible delights—I wrote a note to Fortier, asking if I could call that afternoon.

In the time we had taken to arrange our visit to London, May had replaced the brisk freshness of early spring with its warm, perfumed breezes. It was one of those afternoons when even London looked serene, bright, and cheerful, and I almost felt as if coming to London for the Season might one day be a possibility.

Our way to Kensington Square took us along the edge of the magnificent parks that made the city bearable. The sky was—for once—blue, and bright flowers, freshly planted, displayed their shining spring colors in neatly arranged rows. The late Prince Consort's statue shone in gilded splendor under its ornate canopy, and fashionable London tried to outshine both flowers and golden statue with its silks and well-brushed top hats. One might have thought there was never a richer, more prosperous place to live on the face of the earth.

Nor was that impression diminished when I entered the Fortier residence. Its quiet elegance enveloped me in the way only a really well-appointed home can. It had that indefinable essence that bespoke long-founded wealth and breeding, separating those who possessed such qualities from the ambitious parvenu.

It also had Fortier, smiling at me with unhidden pleasure as I stepped over the threshold.

"Guttridge has gone straight down to the servants' entrance with our footman, who is laden down with the remedies I promised," I informed him. "But I thought I'd show these off to you myself." I lifted the edge of the cloth that covered the strawberries. "A little of Whitcombe. I know you must miss the country."

Fortier's eyes brightened. "I hoped my nose wasn't deceiving me." He inhaled delicately. "I'm no gastronome, but I'm beginning to suspect the rumors about your head gardener's skill are well founded. Good heavens, my mouth is watering."

"I always feel a minor miracle has occurred when Taylor sends up the latest production of his glasshouses. Aren't I lucky?" I smiled, happy to be the bearer of such a gift. "Shall we send these down to the kitchen with instructions to prepare them for you? Guttridge has cream from the Pincham dairy—we were sure London could never supply cream as rich and yellow. There are all sorts of tinctures and syrups of hawthorn as well, all freshly made. You should see how well the trees on Whitcombe Hill are doing."

"It's very kind of you." Fortier smiled ruefully. "Father is frequently short of breath, and your remedies should help. He suffers from many troubles of the heart, lungs, and digestion. As he says, the business of dying is not an easy one."

"I'm sorry." The brightness of the day felt somehow diminished. "May I see him for a few minutes?"

"He's asked that you be brought to his room."

I COULD SEE THE CHANGE IN FORTIER'S FATHER IMMEDIATELY. His cheekbones were even more prominent, the hand that pressed mine thinner and more translucent, his eyes brighter with a look that seemed to see far beyond the veil of this life. Yet he uttered his greeting in a firm voice; it was not yet time.

"You find me dying by degrees," was his cheerful utterance. "No, don't tell me I look better or any of that nonsense. I strictly forbid it. It's only death after all, and I'm equal to it." There was still great charm in the smile that played on his lips. "I understand I owe the alleviation of my discomforts to your remedies. Armand swears they're better than any he can purchase in London."

"Plucked straight from the countryside and made with a careful hand." His son was arranging a chair for me. "Lady Helena has a gift for getting the proportions just right."

"I hope making them isn't an inconvenience for you?" the sick man asked.

"Of course not." I made myself comfortable in the chair. "Doubtless I'll never be the healer my mother was, but I enjoy making remedies. It's highly satisfying somehow. As my lady's maid would say, ladies must have their pursuits."

"Ah, the excellent Miss Guttridge." I could see a definite resemblance to Fortier as his father smiled. "Armand has whiled away many a long hour by telling me about Littleberry and its people. I can close my eyes and stand in your church in my imagination. I know where everyone sits. The vision of the Scott-De Quincys in their special pews, all those blond heads of hair catching the light of the chandelier, is clearly before me."

"And I the exception." I laughed. "When I was a child, they tucked me in next to the pillar, where I could see nothing and nobody could see me. Until I married, that is, and gained a status of my own—or at least my late husband's."

"You say that without rancor."

I laughed again. "As a sixth daughter, I didn't expect much in life. I simply accepted the circumstances into which I was born. One does."

"Not always." Monsieur Fortier sighed heavily, shifting a little against the pillows. "You'll have to forgive me, my dear. I am becoming sleepy. Armand gave me something a little while ago to dull the pain, but it delivers me into the arms of Morpheus. No—I don't want you to go." He put out a hand as I made to rise. "My dreams will be more pleasant if I drift off to sleep with your pretty face in front of me. Tell me, then, what made it so easy to accept 'not much in life'? You were born noble and comely. Did you not think you would marry well? A titled man, perhaps?"

"I used to think I would marry my cousin, who had no title. But he died."

"So a title is not important to you?"

I shrugged. "I've never really thought about it. I was born

with a courtesy title, and I suppose I'll bear it for the rest of my life. I've never been ambitious for more."

"And yet you are proud of your family name?"

"Of course." I smiled. "Our history is not always as noble as our name, but while I live, I will remain loyal to my immediate family." I frowned. "Although I suppose I would be loyal simply because they're my family and I love them."

"Well said." The sick man sighed again. "Love is the only real justification for loyalty. Human love, that is, and not just loyalty to a cause or an institution. Loving a person rarely leads us into error. Loyalty to an abstract idea has been the cause of many miseries."

"Except loyalty to the truth," Fortier spoke at last.

"But the truth is a constant, not an abstract idea." There was a challenge in the father's eyes as he looked at his son, but he returned his gaze quickly to me. "I remember my uncle haranguing my father about his 'great name' and shouting that he—my father—was not doing enough to ensure my loyalty to that name. It infuriated my uncle Thomas that my father, having inherited a title through the accident of being born first, refused to play a part in the life of the court. This was during the July Monarchy, the reign of France's last king, when we still used the name Fortier de Maival."

"Was that how you were christened, then?" I could feel Fortier's eyes on me, but I gave all my attention to his father, watching the gradual signs of relaxation and his struggle to keep his gaze focused.

"I was. After all the years my grandmother had spent recovering her husband's property, my father could hardly refuse to sign himself as a nobleman. I used the name myself for the first twenty-six years of my life, until my wife died and I moved myself and my children to England. Armand bears it, of course, but he is a better republican than I am and intends to renounce it formally."

He smiled hazily, reaching for my hand. "My own sympathies lie with the family of Bonaparte. I have a fondness for lost causes. And yet I still hear the whisper 'de Maival' whenever I say the name 'Fortier'—and so does my son."

"He'll sleep for the rest of the day, I expect. All night, if he's lucky." Fortier said as he came quietly into the library, to which I had retreated. I had left him and the manservant who had come in response to the bell to arrange his father more comfortably for sleep. After uttering the words "my son," the older man had stared at me steadily as if expecting me to say something significant. I had been puzzling out a reply when his eyelids closed, and I realized that what I had seen was an end to the struggle with sleep. His hand had been grasping mine with surprising strength. I had withdrawn my fingers as gently and slowly as I could, but he had not stirred.

"It's good to see you." Fortier lowered himself neatly into a chair, his eyes on my face. "Are you in London to see Lady Odelia? Or your dressmaker, perhaps?" He tilted his head to one side. "It seems a little strange to me that you should desert Littleberry just when London is becoming warm and crowded. I thought you disliked the Season." He smiled suddenly, and my heart jumped. "I don't suppose it would be on my account?"

"As a matter of fact," I said, trying to ignore the heat in my face, "I'm up here to make some inquiries. Did you know that Sir Geraint Dorrian-Knowles has moved to Lower Broadmere, to a place he calls Edenholme?"

"I read all about it in that rather long piece in the *Gazette*. Written by his son, wasn't it?"

"One of them."

"The writing wasn't to my taste. Rather too much purple prose. Weighty openings and grand declarations, that sort of thing. But it mentioned Littleberry and Whitcombe, and for a moment you appear on the page, 'sister of the Earl of Broadmere and of that ornament of society, the artist Lady Odelia Scott-De Quincy,' so I rejoiced and kept it." Now it was the turn of Fortier's face to grow slightly pink. "Pasted it into my commonplace book."

I coughed. "Well, I don't suppose you know that the barn in which Sir Geraint has set up his studio was broken into recently. The large canvases were attacked—cut to ribbons."

Fortier's attitude immediately altered from something perilously like flirtation to a keen alertness. "With a knife?"

"An axe—or at least we're pretty certain it was an axe. One that happened to be lying around in a nearby shed. The police came and all the rest of it. Ned used his influence to keep it out of the papers, of course."

"Of course." A shade of annoyance crept into Fortier's expression, but his frown was one of worry. "I don't like the increasing level of violence in this affair. I was thinking of the paper knife bundled in with the dead cat as a foreshadowing of an attack with a knife, but an axe is worse."

"No harm was done that can't be remedied. Anyway, I have come to London because Guttridge and I have made a list of suspects and intend to rule at least some of them out. All Sir Geraint seems to care about is getting back to his painting, but it's rather tiresome to have things *happening* around him and Odelia all the time. I am resolved to do something about it."

The worry on Fortier's face had shifted to a black scowl. "How?"

"By asking questions and confronting people. Odelia won't do anything either, so I'm hoping that if I do, eventually the person who's playing these silly tricks will become discouraged and stop."

"Or they'll attack you instead." Fortier glared at me in a manner worthy of Michael. "Didn't I ask you to call on me for help if you needed it? Honestly, Helena—"

"I *am* calling on you." I suddenly felt the lifting of a burden. "And of course I'll accept your help if you can be spared from your father's side. Guttridge has already partially eliminated two of the suspects: Sir Geraint's assistants. They said they were drunk that night, and according to the gossip at the Red Lion, they certainly were—royally. They might still have attacked the canvases in some sort of drunken rampage—and perhaps even forgotten about it by the next morning—but there was something controlled about the slashes in the canvas that suggests the perpetrator was sober. And a man, because they start from quite high up."

"Like the word painted on your gate." Fortier's brow had cleared, and now he simply looked interested.

"Yes. Guttridge is going to pursue the mistresses—trace the movements of Miss Aldred, Miss Emery, and, I'm afraid, Odelia because we can't entirely rule her out. I intend to go to Holland Park and try Millie again, in case it's her or one or more of the children."

"You could be doing this for months." Fortier's lips curved upward.

"Yes, and I *will* do it for months until they stop, whoever they are. So how would you like to help?" I gave Fortier what I hoped was a challenging look. "After all, you're quite busy with your father."

"I'm not needed at his side all day. The servants have detailed instructions on what to do, and I let them know where they can find me in case of need. Naturally, I don't wish to leave London—I absolutely have to be here in case he takes a sudden turn for the worse."

"And since most, if not all, of our suspects are in London, you don't have to." I felt quite cheerful. "So why don't you invite me to take tea—I hope it will include Taylor's strawberries—and I will tell you all about the discussion Guttridge and I had. Then we can decide what to do next."

37

THE WOMAN IN THE PICTURE

I returned to Scott House full of strawberries and cream and contentment. I was buoyed up by the comfortable feeling that Fortier would be a formidable ally in my quest to get to the bottom of the string of incidents that had beset my life ever since Odelia first mentioned the name of Sir Geraint Dorrian-Knowles.

In my cheerful mood, I decided I could easily eliminate Odelia from our list of suspects simply by talking to her. Why should I "investigate" my own sister? Better to unburden myself at once and be straight with her.

As I had expected, I found Odelia in her studio. The May afternoon was long and bright, the light still good. She was frowning at the half-finished picture of a woman. Once I had kissed her cheek, she leaned back and gestured at the painting.

"I'm not at all sure I like her." She sighed impatiently. "She's supposed to be 'a damsel of high lineage, and a brow May-blossom, and a cheek of apple-blossom, hawk eyes; and lightly was her slender nose tip-tilted like the petal of a flower.' I think she looks like a common milkmaid."

"Surely not." I squinted at the painting. "Is that Tennyson? It sounds like it."

"Yes, it's the *Idylls of the King*. That story of Gareth and Lynette and the Castle Perilous." Odelia sighed again. "She's supposed to be proud and scornful and petulant, but I think her expression is sly. I'll probably have to scrape her face back and start again. If anything, she reminds me of that horrid Hatherall girl." She shuddered. "That's the worst of painting from the imagination—one's inner light can be a wayward thing. If I paint Gareth, I might use a young Italian man as a model. They have that quality of eager beauty when they are very young, I find."

I said nothing. Once Odelia had mentioned it, I too saw something of Susan Hatherall in the painted girl's eyes. The business of where Susan and her child would be buried had occupied us for weeks, with Ned particularly vehement about them not being buried in the same grave as her father, who had also been her lover. The sexton had told me he often found rue and betony left on Susan's grave, flowers commonly used to ward off evil.

"Well, never mind." Odelia picked up her palette and took it to the washstand. "Nothing I do at the moment seems to come out quite right. Why are you here?"

"Why shouldn't I be here?" I asked. "I wanted to talk to you. Have you received any nasty letters since you've been back? Or anything else?"

"Letters?" A strong smell of turpentine arose as Odelia began to clean the tools of her trade.

"You know. The dead cat, the letter, the paint on the gate. That kind of thing."

"Good Lord, no. Haven't seen anything like that for months. You're not still fretting about it, are you?"

I stared at her. "Don't tell me Sir Geraint hasn't written to you about the destruction of his work."

"*Sir* Geraint." Odelia's voice had a far-off quality to it. "Always *Sir* Geraint, and always *Millie*. It's pathetically obvious where your sympathies lie."

"O." I crossed to where she stood, laying a hand on her arm. "O, darling, my sympathies lie with *you* at the moment." I gazed at her face, presented to me in profile as proud and scornful and—yes—petulant, as Lynette was supposed to be. "I think you're unhappy over something. You haven't been to Lower Broadmere, have you? Please tell me you've been at Scott House ever since you returned to London."

Odelia said nothing at first, merely turning her face toward me, and I quailed at the frozen, closed look of it. It reminded me strongly of an expression I had seen on Papa's face once—where and when? I groped in my memory for the thread of it, but it eluded me. I took a deep breath and stood my ground, fearing an explosion; but the words Odelia spoke next were like ice in my heart.

"You little beast." The words were a mere whisper at first, but then her voice strengthened. "Are you accusing *me*? I've done everything I said I would. I went away. And then when I came back, I exiled myself from society; haven't you noticed that? I am withering away here, body and soul, alone, so that no whiff of scandal should touch you and your ridiculous notions of morality. And you come to me with suspicion—"

Her tone had deepened, flowing over me like ice water, but she stopped as if what she said was choking her. I'd never felt afraid of my siblings before, but now I wanted to run. I wanted to get away from this house and this sister with eyes that burned like chips of deep ice, cold and blue in a white face. Yet I felt my fingers curl into the palms of my hands, seeking whatever strength I could find.

"I just need to know." My voice was unsteady. "I never wanted to become involved in any of this. If you hadn't disappeared without telling me where you were, I wouldn't have come searching for you. I might never have known about you and Sir Geraint, and I'd no doubt be better off for it." I swallowed the lump in my throat. "But I came looking for you because I love you. I'm here now because I love you. Loyalty and eternity, remember? I am bound to you forever —if everyone else deserted you, if there were a scandal great enough to engulf the whole of London, I would stand by you. I asked that question because I can't help you unless I know the truth. I want to be treated like the adult I am, not the child you all used to lie to because I was too young to know about grown-up things. Tell me . . . please."

I stopped because I didn't know what else to say, and because speech was failing me. I was shaking—I could feel the tremors in my arms and legs. I was balanced on the edge of a cliff, expecting to topple forward and fall.

Odelia moved, and I flinched. Her face changed—and suddenly I was enfolded in her long arms, the heat of her slender body against me, my face crushed against her shoulder. A great sob shook me and then another, and I was crying in my sister's arms like a small child, one that had been badly frightened and was desperate for comfort.

"Of course I was here." Odelia's voice, coming from over my head, was not entirely steady. "Didn't you ask the servants, you silly Baby?"

"Don't call me Baby." I groped in my skirts to find the pocket where I kept my handkerchief. "I didn't want to investigate you by questioning the servants. You're my sister, and I knew you would give me a truthful answer." Tears distorted my voice.

"Bless you for saying that." Odelia sniffed, dashing moisture from her eyes. "I was at a *vernissage* the night the damage was done—yes, I heard about it. I honestly don't have a clue why it happened. The next day I had luncheon with the dreadful old woman who wants the painting of Lynette—and Gareth too, if I can persuade her. She's tiresome and horribly snobbish, but she's wealthy and could make a good patroness." She crossed to the small desk that stood by the wall. "Look, here is her note to me the next day. I'm working, Helena. You must think the worst of me, but in fact, working is what I spend most of my time doing. 'I follow up the quest, despite of Day and Night and Death and Hell.' Can't you find your handkerchief? You're rather damp-looking under the nose."

In a moment, I felt the soft touch of a well-laundered linen handkerchief on my face as O dried my cheeks, just as she used to do when I was small. She then surrendered the cloth to me so that I could wipe my nose. I breathed deeply, trying to regain control of my emotions before speaking again.

"I thought you might be angry enough at Sir Geraint to destroy his work. I'm sorry. There's something so unhappy about you since you came back."

Odelia folded her arms, staring out of the window at the fresh green of St. James's new leaves. "I *am* angry with him," she said eventually. "For not writing to me much when I was away. For removing himself from our little world of London, where we've been happy. He's not even coming back to Town next month to visit me; did you know that?"

"Yes, I knew." Except that it was Millie whom he'd talked about not being able to visit.

"It was I who suggested Whitcombe House. I gave him the commission he's been looking for, the setting for the most important work of his life." Odelia's jaw tightened. "And now that he has it, I don't seem to matter anymore. The last thing I expected was that he would dig himself into the marsh and stay there. It means I can't see him. It would be too humiliating to chase him to Lower Broadmere. I shrink inside at the idea of walking into the Bennett farm, of all places, under the knowing eyes of Scoff and Hay. Why would I destroy his work? I would like it to go faster so he'll come home to London, where he belongs. He's everything I love about London—he always was, from the moment I escaped Hyrst—and now he's left me for the tides and the flat marshes and muddy, rainy Littleberry. So I'm angry with him and with myself for creating this situation. I thought that maybe if I came back, he would return to me."

"But he hasn't left you, has he?" I finished scrubbing at my face. "He's just absorbed by this new commission. I don't suppose his enthusiasm for the coast and the countryside will last through the winter." I made a noise somewhere between a laugh and a gulp. "Look at me, trying to reassure you when I should be rejoicing."

"Torn between loyalty to the family as a whole and loyalty to me personally?" Odelia's rather cynical smile was back on her face.

"Somebody told me today that love is the only justification for loyalty. And someone *else* suggested that loyalty to the truth is more important." I sighed. "It's important to me to find out who's behind these incidents, O. You should have seen the damage to the paintings—it was quite frightening. *A killing rage* was what Guttridge called it."

"Dear Guttridge." Odelia's smile widened. "It's Millie, you know, I'm sure it is. If anyone is truly angry at Geraint, it's she. Poor, foolish Millie, who should have walked out on him years ago and left him to stew in his own juice until he came to heel. I hate to admit it, but that would probably have worked."

"I suppose I'm willing to believe it's Millie." I thought of Guttridge's list. "But can we show that she was absent from home on the twenty-first? If it's not you, then it has to be someone close to Sir Geraint. Millie, or one or more of the children, or Miss Emery, or Miss Aldred."

"Well, it's not Cynthia." Odelia's fine eyebrows lifted. "I can vouch for her because she was at the *vernissage*. If necessary, I can ask other people to vouch for her so you can't say I'm protecting her because we're friends. And we *are* friends, you know—so unusual for me to have a woman friend. I like her independence."

"Thank you," I said. "That makes my life easier. I'm glad, you know, that it's not Miss Emery. I rather like her too."

"And you can easily find out whether the nasty little actress was at her so-called theater, can't you?"

"I suppose I can." I smiled. "Guttridge has already ascertained that Mr. Scoffield and Mr. Mountjoy were as drunk as they claimed to be that night. They impressed the patrons of the Red Lion by their capacity for ale."

"Stupid boys." Odelia rolled her eyes. "So how are you going to *investigate* Millie?" She sounded rather amused as she pronounced the verb. "Send in Guttridge of the Detective Force to question the servants?"

"I would like to do *some* of the work myself." I was suddenly very glad I had come to London. "Or at least in the company of Dr. Fortier. It turns out that he's fairly knowledgeable about art, so I am going to write a note to Millie begging the favor of bringing him to Sir Geraint's house in the persona of an enthusiast."

"Good heavens." Odelia shrugged. "Well, he won't look out of place. Half the fashionable young people in London worship there at some time or the other. Mostly female, which Geraint just adores. A charming young man will make a pleasant change for Millie."

38

A NEW LIFE

illie's answer to my note was that it was not convenient to receive me and my friend until Friday afternoon at two thirty. After sending word to Fortier that I would call for him at two o'clock on Friday, I settled down to a peaceful Wednesday with a clear conscience.

I was deep in the *Idylls of the King*, inspired to read it again by Odelia's painting of Lynette, and by three o'clock had reached the tale of Geraint and Enid. I had not long read the uncomfortable passage—

> *O purblind race of miserable men,*
>> *How many among us at this very hour*
>> *Do forge a life-long trouble for ourselves,*
>> *By taking true for false, or false for true;*
>> *Here, through the feeble twilight of this world*
>> *Groping, how many, until we pass and reach*
>> *That other, where we see as we are seen!*

—when George the footman astonished me by entering the room to inquire if I was at home to Miss Elisabetta

Aldred. I had not heard the doorbell nor any sound of a visitor being admitted, so absorbed was I in the story of marital misunderstandings. I foolishly leapt to my feet and stammered out that I was at home instead of giving myself a few minutes to achieve greater composure.

I regretted my haste as soon as I saw the smartness of Miss Aldred's dress—mine was definitely more suited to a quiet afternoon than to receiving calls—and the not altogether friendly expression in her eyes as she strolled into the room under the footman's admiring gaze. I motioned to him to remove Scotty, who had begun barking.

"Your lady's maid is asking questions again." Miss Aldred seated herself, her back perfectly straight and the large feather in her extremely fashionable hat barely disturbed by the movement.

"She is?" I had given Guttridge a few hours off, not feeling that I needed her. She had clearly decided to put them to good use.

"Flirting with the stagehands." Miss Aldred looked as if she would have liked to toss her head but had remembered her dignity. "I told Ted—he's the stage manager—to send her off with a flea in her ear. If you think I've done something, you could ask me yourself." She glared at me. "Well?"

"I didn't send Guttridge to spy on you. I apologize for her actions." I decided I might as well make a clean breast of it. "I imagine she was trying to find out, in a general sort of way, where you were two—or is it three?" I thought for a moment. "Two and a half weeks ago. I expect you know someone destroyed the paintings Sir Geraint is doing for me."

The expression of astonishment on the young woman's face was not feigned, if I was any judge. "You *what?*" she began, before correcting herself and reverting to her more polished actress's mode of speech. "I have no idea to what you're referring."

"Somebody broke into Sir Geraint's studio in Lower Broadmere—by the sea, hasn't he told you?—and cut three large canvases into ribbons," I explained patiently.

"And you think it was *me*?"

"We're just eliminating the possibilities. If you were at the theater that night, for example, and someone could vouch for you, we can remove you from the list and leave you in peace."

"You're telling me I'm on a list." Miss Aldred's tone was expressionless, but the look of mischief and amusement was stealing back into her cynical gray eyes. "Because you think I might have stuck a kitchen knife into one of Geraint's paintings." She bit her lip, possibly to fight back a laugh. "I've never heard anything more ridiculous. I've a good mind to go home without telling you what I came here to tell you."

"And what's that?"

"I remembered what you said, you see, about how you'd be grateful if I gave you information." She smiled suddenly. "Not that I need any help from *you* now, and I suppose I'll tell you why. I reckon you can keep a secret, and there aren't many people I can tell when it comes down to it, and you can't help being about as useful at finding out things as a monkey would be if you asked him to read Shakespeare. They bred you to be a useless aristocrat, and I feel sorry for you—really, I do. And your lady's maid is just your cat's-paw, so I suppose I won't harbor any hard feelings toward her either." Dimples appeared either side of her mouth.

"If you're quite finished being rude about me—and about Guttridge, which is worse—would you mind telling me where you were when Sir Geraint's paintings were attacked?"

"I haven't left London for months. Why would I want to go anywhere else? Except—" Her pink mouth softened. "Well, I wouldn't mind going to the country with the right person. You may as well know that I'm giving Geraint up. I was waiting till I saw him to tell him so. I haven't seen or heard from him for an age. What's he doing by the sea?"

"Working on a commission for me." I looked closely at Miss Aldred. "Last time I saw you, I had the distinct impression that you wanted to supplant my sister and get Sir Geraint to yourself. Do you no longer care for him?"

Miss Aldred directed her gaze to the windows, where the afternoon light was picking out the stained-glass escutcheons. "I'm fond of him, of course. I'd never want to hurt him. Or his paintings. They're beautiful." Her face transformed, an effect that was quite startling—*radiant* was the only word for it. "But—oh, Lady Helena, I'm in love. The kind of love that makes me want to forsake all others, including poor Geraint." A flush spread over her youthful cheeks. "I was wondering if you—if you might know *him*." The last word was said with reverence. "Can I whisper the name to you? Can I be sure that if I tell you, you won't tell anyone else?"

"I would never breach a confidence." I was bemused, almost touched by the young actress's faith in me and by the uncharacteristic hope and trust in her eyes.

"You treat me like a human being, you see. You're the only one of your sort—the only lady—who does. I know we can't be friends, but . . ." She shrugged.

"I will certainly never be your enemy. Whatever you tell me will never be used against you."

The only answer Miss Aldred gave was to half rise out of her seat so that her pretty pink lips were close to my ear. I was enveloped in the warmth emanating from her, caressed by the subtle perfume she wore, and then—I was staring at her, open-mouthed and wide-eyed, the name she had given me boring into my head with the shock of a blade.

"But he's . . . he's . . . practically royalty," I heard myself stammering. "I don't actually know him. My family doesn't move in such circles." I swallowed hard. "You don't believe he'll marry you, do you? Because I don't believe he can. The Queen would never allow it."

"I do know that." A slightly sulky curve of the lip accompanied the words. "He will marry for the good of his family. But I'll be the one who counts, you'll see. I've given notice to the Bulldog that I'll leave at the end of the week." The enthusiasm was back on her face. "I'm going to take private lessons in classical theater once I'm—that is, when I've moved to a more suitable house." She favored me with her puckish smile. "I'm staying at a hotel just off Piccadilly now, all very nice. Just think, we're almost neighbors."

"It's very sudden."

Miss Aldred's face underwent another transformation. "It's wonderful. As if I'm not the woman I was just a few days ago. Love can do that." She sighed. "I suppose I thought I loved Geraint too. He made me feel special. But this is far better—and he's young, isn't he? So very young and beautiful that I can't stop staring at him. I count the minutes until we can be together. But that wasn't really what I wanted to tell you."

"There's something else?"

"Something or nothing. It's just that one of Geraint's sons has been coming to the Bulldog."

"Which of the sons?" I felt a small surge of excitement. Perhaps a clue was emerging at last.

"I don't remember which is which." Miss Aldred pursed her lips a little scornfully. "Tall and thin with hair of that very light red."

"Edmund." I was grateful that the Dorrian-Knowles boys were so easily distinguishable in terms of looks. "Has he paid any especial attention to you?"

She shrugged. "He sits in the good seats like a gentleman and applauds when he's supposed to. Doesn't seem to be paying attention to anything other than the show. Arrives at the beginning, I think, and leaves at the end. Seems to enjoy himself. So that one's Edmund, is it?"

"The middle son."

"I only saw Geraint's family once, before we—well, you know." The mischievous smile again. "When Geraint was after me, he invited me to one of his artist parties. I think he wanted to show off what a big house he had. Men are like that when they're interested. They like to display themselves, like peacocks." She spread her slim hands, miming the opening of a peacock's tail. "Geraint showed me his paintings. Now *those* impressed me, far more than the house itself. Like walking into a storybook and all the characters coming alive around you."

"You're quite sure it was Edmund?"

"Oh yes. I don't forget a face. Geraint pointed out his children and said their names to me, only I forgot *those* straight-away." She dimpled prettily at me. "I remember thinking how sweet it was. Most men his age wouldn't want to draw atten-tion to having children out of the schoolroom. And then I saw his wife looking at me like she smelled a rat." She widened her eyes dramatically. "If *she* came to the Bulldog, I might be worried, I don't mind telling you. What a look on her face, like she was ready to drag me out by my hair. After that, I said to Geraint, no more invitations to his house. *Espe-cially* after I found out about the other women. It's against nature to carry on like that under the wife's nose, isn't it? Put hers right out of joint, I'll swear to that."

Poor Millie. I could just imagine her spotting her husband talking to the pretty young actress and *knowing*, and I inwardly thanked God that Justin had never shown such interest in another woman in my presence. But she had given me another clue—Millie's anger—although that, I supposed, I knew already.

"So you've never seen Lady Dorrian-Knowles at the theater?"

"No, and it won't make any difference after Sunday. Of course, the young gentleman may just be one of my admirers." She threaded her fingers together and looked at me winningly from above her clasped hands. "You'd be surprised how many gentlemen have a taste for stage performers. Well, I've told you all I can, and now I must get to my dress fitting. *Do* give my regards to Miss Guttridge." She smiled at me. "I'll have my own lady's maid soon."

"I FIND IT SIGNIFICANT THAT IT'S MR. EDMUND, DON'T YOU?" was Guttridge's conclusion after I had finished telling her about Miss Aldred's visit. "He's the only one of the sons who, to our knowledge, has visited the farmhouse so far."

"He is—and he's tall too." I picked up one of the hats Guttridge was sorting through, admiring the way the silk bow at the front caught the light. "But is his interest in Miss Aldred purely personal, or is he observing her on his mother's behalf?"

"I don't really think he'd have a personal interest, would he?" Guttridge spoke archly as she gently abstracted the hat from my grasp. "Knowing his father's been there before him, I mean."

"What an unpleasant thought."

"Much would depend on *why* Miss Aldred is leaving the Bulldog." Guttridge narrowed her eyes at me. Naturally, I had refused to give her the exact details about Miss Aldred's departure. Investigative partner or no, Miss Aldred had told me her news in confidence.

"I told you why. She has a better prospect." I was definitely not going to let Guttridge intimidate me into telling her more than I wanted to.

"Of course you did, my lady." Guttridge's tone had a slightly acid edge to it as she studied the hat. "I'm having second thoughts about this hat. This shape might go out of fashion."

I sat up straighter. "I *like* that hat, and it will do for the country, even if it's not acceptable for Town." I softened my voice a little, trying to sound conciliatory. "Be a good Guttridge; don't hide it away so I never see it again."

"As if I'd do such a thing, my lady." But the cadence of Guttridge's voice told me she would.

"I promise I will tell you everything she told me if it becomes clear that it's essential to do so. And you will come with me to the Dorrian-Knowleses' on Friday, won't you? That should be interesting, especially with Dr. Fortier there."

39

TOWN AND COUNTRY

Friday afternoon found me in the brougham, seated by a soothed and softened Guttridge, who had decided that, after all, the hat was eminently suitable for a London visit. She was greatly cheered by the prospect of an investigation. We were both rendered mellow by the glorious sunshine, which had already tempted some of London's fashionable people back for the start of the Season's high point.

My coachman had ordered the four matched bays to be brought up from Whitcombe and was driving the horses as a four-in-hand. The carriage had been repainted, the Whitcombe coat of arms of three scallop shells shining bright yellow and gilt against the polished black of the doors. Although I was still wearing black, I felt almost part of London society as we moved smartly along Knightsbridge and Kensington Gore.

I could hear a church bell tolling two o'clock as we entered Kensington Square. Fortier was waiting for us on the house steps. A laburnum tree in full, fresh flower hung over him as he opened the gate in the railings, its drooping racemes of pure yellow almost brushing the top of his tall hat. He tipped that hat to us before removing it to mount the low step into the brougham.

"Good afternoon, Lady Helena, Miss Guttridge. No, Miss Guttridge, I wouldn't think of depriving you of your seat. I will be quite happy to sit with my back to the driver."

Fortier smiled charmingly at Guttridge as he folded down one of the corner seats. Her expression, no doubt several degrees cooler than my own, gained a little warmth.

"Thank you, monsewer. I hope your father is as comfortable as can be."

"He is." Fortier suppressed a grin as we came to terms with the arrangement of knees inevitable when more than two people are in a brougham, but his face showed nothing but sincerity when he returned his attention to Guttridge. "I have you and Lady Helena to thank for the relief of many minor symptoms. The opiates I have to give him have some distressing effects, but your remedies are marvelous for his skin and stomach and far more to his taste than anything else."

Guttridge merely smiled gently, but I could feel her glowing with pride beside me. If Fortier was trying to win her over, praising our efforts with herbs was the right way to do it.

It was not far from Kensington Square to the Dorrian-Knowles house at the southern end of Holland Park, so we were soon past the bustle of Kensington High Street and back in the hushed streets lined with large new houses. I quickly related my meeting with the Dainty Darling—leaving out, once again, the details of her new *amour* and thus rendering my tale far less exciting than it could have been—and then we talked, as the English do, of the weather and the London life we saw around us while I tried not to stare at Fortier. I was conscious of looking at him too much, especially when his visage was animated with conversation, as it was now, and tried to glance out of the window whenever it was not impolite to do so. I watched for the ornate Jacobean outline of Holland House across the park, aware of Fortier's closeness in the carriage, his hands with their fine, straight fingers curled gently around his walking-stick.

"Are you wishing you were back in the country?" Fortier spoke softly, but his baritone was easily audible despite the noises of the carriage.

"I was thinking I should call on Lady Holland again. She's a contemporary of Mama's and was very kind to me when I was a debutante." I smiled at the Frenchman. "I suppose I don't really spend enough time in London during the Season. None at all after I married. Justin never liked it."

"I'd far rather be in Littleberry, riding Lucifer over the fields with the anticipation of sewing up wounds or lancing a quinsy. That is, when not in present company, of course. I long for fresh air and the simple flowers of the hedgerow, and for *work*, with almost a sickly passion. I can't tell Father that, of course." Something on the ceiling of the carriage seemed to attract his attention. "And then, when I begin feeling like this, I tell myself how fortunate I am that my father is still on this earth. I must remind myself to give him my full attention and not be preoccupied with my own concerns. Speaking of which, you seem a little preoccupied yourself—is there something wrong?"

I felt my face flame. "Nothing at all. I'm sorry if I gave that impression." How ridiculous that I should have put so much effort into not looking at Fortier that I'd made myself appear rude.

I was saved from further mortification by the sight of the large flat-roofed house, solid in mellow London brick. The brougham was slowing, and I could feel it rock as the footman stood, ready to jump down and open the gate giving access to the carriage drive.

In a moment, the brougham rocked again as the footman re-mounted, and we were almost instantly at the front door, the drive being short. Fortier—who, I suddenly realized, was also looking slightly embarrassed—immediately jumped out and lowered the step, holding his hand out to help first Guttridge and then me descend. The footman, hastening to prevent Fortier from doing any more of his work for him, marched smartly up the steps and rapped the heavy brass knocker three times. I glanced at Guttridge, who nodded and headed toward the servants' entrance while Fortier and I prepared to do our day's work.

"It's perfectly haunting." Fortier stood in front of *In the Halls of the Snow Queen*, drinking in the great painting with eager eyes. "I've read about it and seen the engraving, but I've never been in Town when it's been on show." He turned to me, genuine delight on his face. "These large canvases overwhelm the senses, don't they? They speak the language of childhood, the fairy tale, but they make it strange and wonderful again, as it was when we heard it for the first time."

I glanced behind me as I spoke in case Millie were on her way in. "It makes me feel like a traitor. Those children are Edmund and Cassiope, as you may already realize. Quite apart from my concerns about Edmund, this picture reminds me they are a family. That this is a home as much as a gallery of Sir Geraint's work."

"It's not treachery to expose the truth." Fortier had stopped looking at the painting and fixed his gaze on me. "I've told you before, Helena, I don't like this business. I feel it's heading toward danger of some kind."

We both turned as we heard footsteps. Within a few

moments, I was introducing Millie and Fortier to each other. Fortier bent over Millie's hand and kissed it—I heard the faint sound of lips on skin—then followed his salutation with words of delight and appreciation that could have come from any courtier at St. James's Palace. I reflected I had never seen him so *French*.

Millie smiled as if she were entirely used to such effusiveness, being accustomed, I supposed, to visits from admirers of Sir Geraint's work. Fortier having been introduced to her as a friend from Littleberry, she asked politely about his connection with the town.

"My sister lives there. Her husband owns Littleberry's main pottery." Fortier's gaze was now fixed on Millie, as he had the pleasant habit of really paying attention to the person to whom he was talking. "My sister, Gabrielle, is an artist herself, mostly in ceramics. I hear from Lady Helena that you are a superb artist with the needle. Is your work exhibited in the house?"

"Only in the private rooms. Geraint had this house built to display his work. All of its public spaces are devoted to his art and his alone."

The social façade was soon slipping, I thought. I could detect bitterness in Millie's voice. But Fortier's reply merely suggested sincerity. "What a shame, Lady Dorrian-Knowles. In my opinion, you should have your own studio and be known for your own work. It's a great pity that married women put away their interests. My sister would never have countenanced it, and I believe most husbands would come round, given time, if the wife would remain steadfast."

"Geraint's career is our living." Millie's answer was wistful. "And I had a house to run and five children to raise, so I've never put my own needs first. Isn't that the right thing for a wife to do? Especially when her husband is the property of the whole world." Her words could, of course, simply have referred to Sir Geraint's fame, but her glance at me made it clear she was thinking of Odelia.

"And I've taken him away from the family." Seeing an opening, I put my own feelings aside. "You must miss him a great deal. Have any of you been down to Sussex since I saw you there?" I saw Fortier's quick, appreciative glance and felt rather pleased with myself.

Millie shrugged. "Phil and Cass are far too busy to visit their father." She sounded defensive. "Phil has his work, of course. Cass has her house and children—and her husband, I suppose." A trace of humor gleamed at last in her large gray eyes, and I smiled as if she had said something amusing.

"And your other sons? Or perhaps I shouldn't ask." I kept my tone light and amused. "Young men do so resent being required to settle down and stay in the same place."

The housekeeper brought in coffee at that point, and we all took our seats. I thought we had lost control of the conversation until Fortier asked easily, "How many sons do you have, Lady Dorrian-Knowles?"

"Three." Millie handed him an exquisite small cup of Japanese pattern. "Philip, the eldest, is a society portraitist and has his own studio."

"And are the other two artists as well?" Fortier's smile was replete with charm. "Although perhaps they are still at school? I don't believe they can possibly be grown up."

"You flatter me." But Millie did look rather pleased, demonstrating that even the most cynical of women can be vulnerable to a handsome face and a row of even white teeth. "They are young men on the brink of their careers—when they discover them. Edmund says he wants to write, but I'm not sure how dedicated he really is. Galahad will be back from Switzerland soon. He's been improving his French and German with a view to entering the diplomatic corps. Unlike Edmund, he doesn't insist that regular employment is beneath him as a gentleman." The edge had come back into her voice.

"Then I say *bravo* to Galahad," Fortier drawled. "I insisted on studying medicine, and if I weren't detained in London by my father's illness, I'd be putting in a full day's work in Littleberry. I believe work is natural to both men and women, of whatever station in life. Perhaps Edmund has not yet discovered his vocation?"

"Have you forgotten? You told me you enjoyed Edmund's article on the *Nightingale* paintings." I glanced at Fortier for a moment before turning my attention back to Millie. "I suppose the unfortunate events at Lower Broadmere will make it more difficult for Edmund to write more on the subject."

"Of course—I was quite taken by that article." Fortier smiled at Millie again. "Are there any others?"

Millie shrugged. "If there's another article, I wouldn't know. That's the thing with sons—they stop telling you things. One moment they're boys who confide in you and need your approval, and then suddenly they're men who come and go as they please and never tell you what they're doing." Her mouth twisted. "But at least Phil has inherited Geraint's ability to apply himself to work, and Galahad's heart is in the right place."

"Edmund will find his path in time," Fortier said softly. "He must still be very young. To have an article published is a considerable achievement at his age."

Millie's face softened. "You're right, of course. It helps that Cassiope's husband is a publisher, but he wouldn't accept work that didn't show some promise. And Geraint is liberal-handed to a fault with the boys. They're the sons of a baronet, he says, and we can't expect them to live like bank clerks." She looked around the beautiful room, alive with paintings. "We've been fortunate. My husband found success earlier than most artists do."

"He is a great man. A superb talent." And Fortier looked as though he meant it. "I wonder—I have heard that the Hera painting is in this house . . ."

"You'll want to see it." Millie rose to her feet, obliging Fortier to do the same. "And the studio, of course?"

By the time we had seen and admired the paintings in the downstairs reception rooms, Fortier had engaged Millie in a discussion of the work of the Pre-Raphaelites, Sir Geraint's extension of their ideas, and the contrasting values of the Impressionists, about whom he seemed to know a good deal. I began to wonder if his reason for coming to Holland Park with me was more about art than investigation until we had climbed the stairs to Sir Geraint's studio and Fortier ended a long anecdote about Pissarro with an account of how that artist had returned to France, after exiling himself to England during the Franco-Prussian War, to find hundreds of his paintings destroyed.

"I thought of Pissarro when Lady Helena told me about the destruction of the *Nightingale* canvases. Do you not find the destruction of art abhorrent, Lady Dorrian-Knowles?"

I watched Millie's face carefully, but there was nothing in it that suggested the least insincerity as she spoke. "I could cry when I think of all that work ruined. What kind of person attacks a painting? Geraint wrote to me that he thinks it must have been some vagrant taking refuge in the barn. Perhaps someone who was used to sleeping in there and was angry to find it in use. But he has begun again, and they've secured the barn better this time."

"You must wish he were in London." Fortier nodded sympathetically.

"Of course." Millie sighed. "But I won't interfere with the progress of such a work by insisting he return home. I'm the wife of a great artist, Monsieur Fortier. When that artist decides that only a particular location will do, I must bow to that decision. My husband knows what he is doing."

Thereafter, the conversation became more general. I had the distinct impression that Fortier had let go of its reins on purpose. When, after another quarter of an hour, he asked for directions to the washroom, I was quite ready to make the conventional remarks about not overstaying our welcome. Yet as soon as the door closed behind Fortier, Millie turned to me.

"Does your sister go to Littleberry? I saw she had returned to London. Is she visiting Geraint?"

"No." I looked up at the taller woman's face, which had paled a little. "She knows better than to put me in what would be a highly awkward position. One is more *observed* in the country than in Town."

"Thank you." Millie let out her breath in a rush, as if she'd been holding it. "My answer to your friend was that of the dutiful wife, but the woman in me can't help worrying. I fear at times I've driven Geraint away, and I know Odelia's become fonder of him than she used to be. She may fear being left alone. It happens to all of us when our beauty fades." She made a small noise of frustration. "Oh, don't listen to silly Millie. I'm spending too much time alone in this museum of a house, that's all. I'm used to it being full of Geraint's admirers, and now even our oldest friends are starting to talk about Lower Broadmere as if it's the new center of the universe. It's stupid, I know—Geraint's letters are simply full of his work and sketches of Sussex—but all I have is Janie for company, and I'm lonely. Edmund is rarely here. I don't know what he does with himself. I know this commission will take a long time, and I'm . . . I'm frightened."

Her long, strong fingers had encircled my wrist, and now I took them into my hands, looking up at her with a mixture of sadness and anger. How could I have borne it if Justin had treated me thus? I put as much warmth and sincerity into my voice as I could.

"I truly think you have less to worry about Sir Geraint now than you have had for a long time."

It was on the tip of my tongue to tell her that the Dainty Darling had deserted her husband, but she would find that out soon enough. It might be better that she heard it from Sir Geraint himself. "I believe it's simply the desire to make progress with the *Nightingale* that keeps him away from you." I squeezed the hand captured between mine. "You have my promise that if I entertain any suspicions to the contrary, I will let you know."

We could hear Fortier's footsteps on the staircase. Millie, to my surprise, suddenly kissed me on the cheek. "I think you're one of the kindest people I've ever met."

40

THE UNHAPPY VICTIM

Fortier's reappearance brought our visit to a natural close, but he said nothing until the two of us were once more closeted with Guttridge in the seclusion of the moving brougham.

"So did it work, leaving the two of you alone?" Fortier smiled. "I hoped she might have something to say to you in private."

"Why, you devious Frenchman—" I stopped, hearing Guttridge's soft snort of amusement. "Yes, she spoke to me, but as you say, it was private." I thought for a moment. "Though I believe that she genuinely has no idea who destroyed the paintings and no suspicions about any of her children. She confirmed that Edmund spends most of his time out of the house. And I think we can cross Jane off the list. From the sound of it, she's her mother's only companion at the moment, so Millie would notice any absence immediately." I frowned. "Without saying *what* Millie confided in me, I can confirm she's lonely and misses her husband. She seems less angry than before, just unhappy—and who can blame her for that?"

"Who indeed?" Fortier said. "After talking with Lady Dorrian-Knowles, I believe that out of the whole family, Edmund is the most likely suspect. We should look at Philip too. A single man would naturally be at liberty to travel around without anyone noticing, so we should see if we can ascertain his whereabouts at the end of April. Galahad, I suppose, is free of suspicion since he was traveling, but it wouldn't hurt to confirm it. And what about you, Miss Guttridge? Can you add anything to this admittedly slender evidence?"

"I can." Guttridge looked eager. "The servants think Mr. Philip works very hard. Mrs. B's cousin cooks and cleans for him, living out, and says he's the serious sort. Lives quietly, dines out, but never comes home late and never takes too much to drink. He might have a young lady in mind to marry, they think, but he won't pop the question till he's earning a decent living. Or unless his father is generous."

"The very picture of respectability, in other words," I said.

"And Mr. Galahad has been away since the end of March, so that settles *that* question." The satisfaction of imparting information illuminated Guttridge's plain countenance. "They say he's a steady young man too. But money runs through Mr. Edmund's fingers, and he owes everywhere—tailor, vintner, bookmaker, some of it dating from his Oxford days."

I shrugged. "I wouldn't want to point the finger of suspicion at anyone for just spending too freely. No obvious financial motive seems to have emerged so far. Spending beyond one's means isn't uncommon in young men who aren't immediately required to earn a living."

"And who have reasonably wealthy Papas," Fortier added with a smile.

"Mr. Edmund has been known to call on Sir Geraint for a bank draft on occasion," Guttridge confirmed.

"Goodness, do the servants really know all that?" I asked and was rewarded by an enigmatic smile from Guttridge. "Do you think the family's financial position is disastrous, Guttridge?"

"I do not, my lady." Guttridge shook her head. "Mrs. B. hinted that things are much easier now, what with the money Sir Geraint got from you and with him being in Sussex and not out on the town or feeding the five thousand every week. The wine bill used to be eye-watering, she says, but her ladyship and young Jane live so quietly you'd hardly know they were there. Mr. Edmund only dines at home twice a week, and Cook is ever so annoyed about *that* because she's only got those two days when she can make a proper dinner. All the rest of the time she has to make something out of the leftovers for the two ladies, which is a mortification for a good cook. They've had mutton in one form or the other all week." She shook her head sadly.

"Be that as it may, you can't make a case against any particular family member on the basis of thrifty living," Fortier settled his shoulders more firmly into his corner of the carriage.

"And it's not unusual for women to eat simply when the men are away. I was brought up like that," I said. "So let's think about how to proceed. What about Philip?"

"I could easily find a pretext for calling on him at his studio." Fortier put a steadying hand on the carriage wall as the brougham swayed. We were now on Kensington's busy high street, and my coachman was clearly trying to avoid the bustling crowds that were encroaching upon the roadway outside the Metropolitan & District railway station. "I could claim an interest in having a portrait of Gaby and the children, for example. After all—"

But whatever he was about to say was lost as Guttridge, who had been watching the passersby in the street, let out a noise somewhere between "Oy!" and "Ow!" and half rose to bang violently on the front of the carriage with her fist. Naturally, the coachman brought the horses to a standstill somewhat abruptly; since a four-in-hand is a bulky affair, the maneuver brought shouts and swearing from the drivers of other vehicles.

Passersby stopped to see what was happening. I could see them pointing at my brougham and trying to work out which family the coat of arms represented. Guttridge ignored them all, jumping down easily without lowering the step and dashing toward the area where the press of travelers in front of the station was thickest.

She had left the carriage door open. Fortier, who had had to flatten himself into his corner to allow her to pass, kicked down the step and rested one foot on it, leaning out of the door so he could see what was happening. I saw him exchange a puzzled glance with the footman, who was descending from his perch next to the driver. And then in a moment their expressions changed. Fortier climbed back into the brougham, seating himself on my side of the carriage this time, while the footman took up his station next to the open door and stared with the stony malice of a professional flunky at the various pedestrians who had taken it upon themselves to make remarks about our equipage and its passengers, our rudeness in halting where we did, and so on.

"She's buying a newspaper," Fortier explained, and indeed I could see Guttridge hastening back to the brougham with a folded paper tucked under her arm. "I will assume she has a good reason."

"She's not given to such behavior without good cause, as a general rule."

I was amused and entertained by Guttridge's eccentric action, but my levity evaporated as I saw my lady's maid's face. Something was very wrong.

Odelia, was my first, irrational thought. I looked at Fortier and saw my alarm had communicated itself to him so that he started out of his seat, half crouching in the restricted space of the carriage.

Guttridge stepped into the brougham. The footman folded up the step, closed the door, and ascended into his seat at speed, so that we were already moving again as I accepted the newspaper from Guttridge and unfolded it with hands that weren't entirely steady. Fortier was still as upright as the carriage would allow, steadying himself against the frame of the window as he maneuvered himself into the best position for reading.

Our lower limbs were pressed together, and I could feel his warm breath on my face. In other circumstances, I might have found the sheer intimacy of the moment excessive, but in that instance he was an ally, a comforting presence sharing in the shock of the words that took several seconds to register in my mind.

FOUL MURDER IN MAYFAIR, read the thick black print that stained my gloves. DAINTY DARLING FOUND STRANGLED.

41

THE IMPARTING OF
INFORMATION

I pressed a hand to my mouth, feeling sick and cold. The brightness of the afternoon seemed overhung by a thick black sky, even though the rational portion of my mind knew nothing had outwardly changed.

The newspaper article was brief, clearly inserted just before the paper went to press. With just a little journalistic elaboration, it communicated the facts: Miss Elisabetta Aldred, also known as Miss Elsie Aldred, had recently moved to a Mayfair hotel after leaving her position as principal entertainer at the Bulldog Palace of Varieties in the Haymarket. The maid assigned to her by the hotel had arrived to take up her morning duties only to find Miss Aldred, still dressed in the peignoir the maid had put on her the night before, foully murdered by strangulation in a way that suggested she had been accosted by an unexpected caller. The matter was in the hands of the Mayfair police.

"An unexpected caller." I spoke under my breath before looking up at Fortier, who had seated himself again. "I must have been one of the last people to see her alive."

"And she told you things the police might want to know,

my lady." Guttridge, who had been very still beside me, spoke in a small, flat voice. "Things you've told nobody else."

Can I whisper the name to you? "My God, yes." I swallowed hard. "I have to tell them she'd taken a new lover. I might be one of the only people—maybe the only person—who knows his name. She was leaving Sir Geraint for him."

I heard Fortier give a low whistle while Guttridge said, "Ha," under her breath next to me. "Can we know who he is, my lady?" she asked. "It won't hurt the poor woman now, God rest her."

I shook my head unhappily. "I will tell only whom it is absolutely necessary to tell. It's not a question of trust. Of course, I trust both of you implicitly."

Fortier nodded. "It's a question of loyalty," he said softly. "And a deep loyalty, at that. There are times in our lives when such a consideration must override friendship, love—everything. Secrets we must keep, however much it hurts us to do so."

I looked at him, startled to be met by an expression so gentle and sincere that for a moment I was spellbound, aware of nothing but his eyes, the irises a shade between green and amber, and the thick shadowing of his eyelashes. Had he looked into my soul or given me a glimpse of his?

But Fortier had lowered his eyelids to look at the watch he was pulling out of his vest pocket. "It's getting late. I wish to offer you my assistance—in fact, I insist—but I should look in on my father first." He looked up at me again, his expression businesslike this time. "Lady Helena, will you go straight to Scotland Yard? I will try to find you there."

"I can't." My voice was faint. I was finding it hard to catch my breath. "I just want to see that Odelia's all right first. It's silly, I know, but as soon as I saw Guttridge with the newspaper I thought of her. I have a feeling I must look in on her before anything else."

"It's not silly at all." Fortier grasped my hand in his and kissed it gently, heedless of Guttridge's presence, before smartly rapping the carriage roof with his walking stick. "I'll get out here and walk to Kensington Square. Go home. I'll see you at Scotland Yard later. I'll find you."

And he was out of the brougham in an instant, calling for the coachman to set off immediately for Scott House.

"Where is Lady Odelia?" I asked as soon as I stepped over the threshold. Maisie, who had answered the door, looked taken aback.

"Out, m'lady."

"Out where?" The desire to shake the girl seized me, and I saw by the sudden alarm in her eyes that I had not imagined the unaccustomed harshness in my voice. A feeling of dark dread had gripped me, weakening my knees and turning my hands to ice despite the warm May weather.

"I don't know, m'lady." Maisie shook her head. "She went out—probably to visit a friend, I s'pose, since she got a note. She doesn't usually tell us where she goes."

"Can't you even say in which direction she went?" I was almost shouting.

"I'm that sorry, m'lady, but I couldn't tell you." Maisie's pretty face screwed up in consternation, her Cockney accent becoming increasingly apparent in her agitation. "'Er ladyship 'as the key to the side door, and that's 'ow she goes in and out when she's on foot. She don't like us being nosy."

"That's quite all right, Maisie." Guttridge spoke in a reassuring voice, and I felt the gentle—and most unusual—pressure of her hand on my arm. "You're not in any trouble with her ladyship. Would you please tell Cook that we have another appointment and don't know when we'll return?

Have her keep something ready on a tray for when we come back."

"Yes, Miss Guttridge." Maisie almost whispered the words before she darted toward the green baize door that separated the servants' area from the rest of the house.

Guttridge turned to me. "I know you want to leave straightaway, my lady, but it's no use rushing off before I can at least check Lady Odelia hasn't left any clues as to where she went. And I want you to refresh yourself and take a sip of our pick-me-up before we leave. You're looking very pale, and if you faint, you'll just hold us up."

"I won't faint." I looked wildly at Guttridge.

"That's as may be." Guttridge looked down her rather long nose at me. "You need to be at your best for Scotland Yard, my lady, and that's where we must go if I can't find any clue about Lady Odelia. You'll need to tell them what you know about Miss Aldred. And some things that have been private about Lady Odelia might need to be told too." Her dark eyes were fixed on my face. "I'm not a superstitious woman, but I know a premonition when I see one, and you're having one. The quickest way to finding her ladyship is by involving the police."

GUTTRIDGE WAS RIGHT, AS USUAL. UNDER HER PROMPTING, I visited the lavatory, washed my face and hands, and drank a small glass of our herbal cordial with its sharp, bracing sweetness of rosemary, ginger, black pepper, and honey. These small actions restored me. By the time Guttridge reappeared, fresh and neat in her dark dress and smart, plain hat, I was ready to face whatever lay ahead of us.

"You didn't find anything, I take it." I set down my glass. "You'd have told me straightaway if you had."

"No, my lady." Guttridge's expression was sympathetic.

I straightened my back. "Then Scotland Yard it is. Goodness, how strange that sounds. I wonder if Monsieur Fortier will be there before us?"

But there was no sign of Fortier as we walked under the arch of the undistinguished brick building that housed the heart of the London police. The "Dieu Et Mon Droit" of the royal arms reminded me fleetingly of the banner in the church at Littleberry. Here, though, I was anonymous, just another widow with her maid, the brougham left a short distance away to avoid attracting attention.

The announcement, made as quietly as Guttridge could manage it, that I was Lady Helena Whitcombe and had some information regarding the murder of Miss Aldred was enough to make the uniformed man standing behind the wooden desk swivel round and grab the arm of another man, into whose ear he delivered a few terse, inaudible commands. Within some ten minutes, Guttridge and I were sitting in a small room with barred windows, located on the upper floor of another building, to which they had led us in silence.

We emerged two hours later, descending the stairs to find Fortier squeezed into the corner of a bench that ran around the small waiting area. Apologizing, he wriggled himself free of his neighbors—a large police sergeant and a woman in shabby black—tipped his hat to us, and offered me his arm. He didn't speak to us until we were outside, out of earshot of the police building.

"They wouldn't let me in, and I didn't argue. What happened in there? I've been watching various people coming and going. I had a good vantage point for watching the door to the room where you were. Who was that fearfully well-dressed man who arrived soon after I got here?"

"Somebody from the Palace, who must already have been on his way when we arrived." If I hadn't been so worried, I'd have laughed at the almost comical look of enlightenment on the Frenchman's face. "They made poor Guttridge step into an adjoining room while we discussed that part, but I think she now knows why I'm being so uncommunicative. If it weren't for his arrival—and the fact that I am who I am—I don't think they would have believed me. And after that, they kept sending for people. I gather several investigations will now take place."

"And Lady Odelia was at home?"

I shook my head, my dread returning. "They're looking for her as well. She received a note and went out . . ." I swallowed hard. "I had to tell them, Fortier. About Sir Geraint being the lover of both of them." I looked down at my gloved hands. "And do you know what? It didn't seem nearly as bad as I thought it would. I'd countenance any amount of scandal at this point if it meant I could just see Odelia and know she's safe."

"The police won't make a scandal." Fortier looked around the nondescript paved area in front of the equally nondescript building, where two hansom cabs waited, and men, uniformed or in plain clothes, walked purposefully in and out of the various doors. "Is your carriage nearby?"

"I told Dudley to wait in the Strand. I didn't want any journalists recognizing my coat of arms. But where would we go?"

"Back to Scott House, in case Lady Odelia has returned home," Guttridge suggested. "Or perhaps you could accompany her ladyship, sir, and I'll walk back to the house. It's not far."

"Accompany her where?" Fortier shook his head. "Besides, Miss Guttridge, the three of us should stick together until necessity compels us to separate. We can't go haring around London, unable to communicate with one another. We need a plan."

"Scott House first, then," I said. "And then—how about Cynthia Emery's home? As far as I know, she's still in London." I wrinkled my brow. "Of course, the police may go there—I had to tell them about Miss Emery too, although I hated doing it. And they'll probably go to Sir Geraint's home. Poor Millie . . . they'll ask her about Edmund's movements, and she'll remember we were there asking the same thing. She'll feel betrayed, and God knows she's been betrayed enough. The police have wired Sir Edward, at my suggestion, to make discreet inquiries as to whether Sir Geraint is still in Lower Broadmere—and whether he was there yesterday."

"*Bon Dieu.*" Fortier looked faintly disgusted. "But they must pursue that line of inquiry, I suppose. In my experience, it's frequently the man who's supposed to love and protect a woman who does her the most harm. I've seen the result of quite a few beatings. He could have come to see her, heard that she was leaving him, and killed her in a jealous rage." He sighed. "I heard a snatch of conversation while I was waiting, not meant for public ears; my hearing is very sharp. A diamond bracelet was in Miss Aldred's room, which suggests the motive was not theft. I saw one of the detectives make a gesture that suggested to me the strangulation was manual. That means a man—strangulation requires large, muscular hands—and that she allowed her murderer to get near her." He frowned. "If Edmund had been visiting the theater regularly, he would be a familiar face, and she might allow him into her presence. I don't imagine an actress would mind being seen *en déshabillé* as much as a lady would."

I nodded. "The policemen said something similar. We gave them Guttridge's list." I remembered the hard, cool stares of the police detectives as Guttridge had produced the piece of paper. "There's little left for us to do when I think about it. We told all we knew to the police, down to the tiniest detail."

We were heading toward the Strand now, and my mind was racing. What use could I be now that it was all in the hands of the police? I had told them everything . . . everything . . .

I stopped so abruptly that my glove was pulled off, caught on Fortier's arm, through which I had looped my hand. I picked the article up, noting abstractedly that the buttonhole was torn.

"The studio." I looked up at Fortier and Guttridge, who were both now standing close to me. "There's a second studio. I'd completely forgotten when I spoke to the police—it was just a chance remark of Sir Geraint's—he has another studio in his neighbor's stable." I turned around, looking back the way we'd come. "Should we go back?"

Fortier shook his head. "It will take longer to find the right people and explain everything than simply to take your carriage to Holland Park. We're bound to find somebody who can show us where this studio is."

42

THE CHASE

olland Park was bathed in golden late afternoon light as the brougham came to a stately halt outside the Dorrian-Knowles house. Gaining entry wasn't easy; the housekeeper, who answered the door, was adamant that Lady Dorrian-Knowles was at home to nobody. After two minutes of listening to the footman's pleas and Mrs. Bretherton's denials, Fortier jumped down from the brougham and spoke a few words to the housekeeper in a rapid undertone. Whatever he said worked, and five minutes later, we—including Guttridge—stood face-to-face with a red-eyed but stony-featured Millie.

"I don't even know what to say to you." She addressed me directly, her tight, rasping tone evidence of the struggle to control her emotions. "Worming your way into my house and then implicating my son in a murder investigation. They told me it was you." Her voice gained strength. "*Worming*, that's the right word for it. Just as your unspeakable sister *wormed* her way into Geraint's life—all of our lives—all those years ago. If it hadn't been for her, Geraint—well, he wasn't perfect, but he was content. *She* egged him on. She took his ideas and fed them back to him until he believed he was Zeus himself, the giver of life, the giver of freedom. She smiled at his affairs and allowed him to believe he had a right to them, so that he listened to her and not me. Are you listening? Do you have any idea what that kind of fawning nonsense can do to a man?"

"I am listening," I said quietly. "I think you know I don't condone Odelia's behavior."

"Oh, I know I'm supposed to put up with all of it, as a good wife should." Millie wasn't listening to *me*. "And I've tried; truly, I've tried. But I'd take the woman and hang her from the highest tree if I could. My God, I've said that so many times it's like a stain on my skin. And now *you*."

"I'm sorry I had to mention Edmund's name." I took a step closer to Millie, conscious of how her reddened eyes and nose stood out sharply against the whiteness of her face. "Someone strangled Miss Aldred, and I was probably one of the last people she spoke to. I had to speak—to name *all* the people involved, and she had mentioned seeing Edmund several times at the theater. I spared nobody, not even Odelia, whose name is now on the lips of the police as your husband's mistress. If you want revenge, I've probably handed it to you. And you know you wouldn't really hurt her." I could hear a note of pleading creep into my voice. "I just want to find her. You'll help me, won't you, Millie? Please? I'm sure you don't truly wish my sister harm."

Millie stared at me, her hands hanging loosely by her side. Then she gave a great sob and flung herself into a chair, rubbing her eyes and dragging her hand over her face like a child who has reached the uttermost end of weariness.

"Of course I wouldn't really harm her." She closed her eyes. "I slapped her that once, yes, but she had been provoking me for *hours*." She groaned. "I suppose that made me look like a madwoman to you. But if I were the sort of woman who hurts people—*really* hurts them—I would have done harm to Odelia long ago, when I was younger and stronger and less . . . less . . . *exhausted.*" She put both hands over her eyes, as if shielding herself from the golden light that was pouring into the library, flickering as it filtered through the greenery of the garden.

"I believe you." Crossing to where she sat, I knelt on the ground, gently prizing her strong, bare fingers from her face. I had omitted to take off my gloves; the right glove had a sooty smear on it, and its tiny button dangled loosely on a broken thread. "But supposing—just supposing—Odelia is in danger too? That's why I'm here." I took a deep breath, increasing the pressure on Millie's hands the tiniest amount. "Nobody knows where she is, and I simply want to rule out this house and Sir Geraint's other studio. I forgot to tell the police about that one, so they won't go there."

"The stable?" The resistance in Millie's hands eased, and she stared at me, puzzled. "Why should she be there? She's certainly not in this house—the police have been all over it, thanks to you."

"It's a long shot." I didn't tell her that if I didn't find Odelia there, I would invade Philip's studio and Cassiope's home until I found my sister and the sick feeling inside of me went away.

"And time is running on." Fortier looked out of the window. "If you give us directions to this stable . . ."

"I'll take you." Millie sounded weary, but she got to her feet. "It's not far. Geraint had a door put into the garden wall so he could come and go as he pleased. I'll just fetch the key from his desk."

WE FOLLOWED MILLIE INTO THE COOL, TILED HALLWAY AND stood together in silence as she disappeared toward Sir Geraint's study. My companions' faces were grave. Guttridge, who like me had not eaten or rested for hours, had a tired, dragging look to her eyes that was no doubt reflected on my face. Yet her mouth was set in a determined line, her figure upright and stalwart. Fortier seemed full of energy, poised lightly on his feet, as if he were holding himself ready to spring into action. A ray of light from a high window caught his close-cropped black hair, making it gleam with vitality, and spilled onto his trim, muscular figure. Two allies I could trust, I knew. Having them so close to me was an infinite comfort.

Millie was soon back, frowning slightly.

"The key's not there. We may have to go the long way round and disturb my neighbor."

"Is it worth seeing if the garden door's open first?" Fortier asked. "Somebody may have forgotten to close it."

"It's this way." We followed Millie as she led us to the dining room. I spared a glance for the picture of Hera welcoming the dawn, a young Millie holding out her arms to the sun in carefree joy, but the older Millie opened a door, leading us into the loggia with its great empty fireplace. She walked fast; Fortier and Guttridge had a longer stride than I did and had no trouble keeping up with her, but I trotted in the rear and fell ever farther behind as we threaded our way through the garden.

"It *is* open!" Millie's cry as we reached the wall mingled astonishment and annoyance. I saw Fortier dart past her through the unlocked door. By the time I had passed its threshold, he was a good distance from me, running toward a long building some fifty yards away. It was a substantial stable block with a high, pointed roof and double door painted light green. A gravel path led to it, but Fortier was running on the grass. Guttridge was holding up a hand to Millie, speaking in a low voice.

"Do as he's doing, your ladyship—walk on the grass. I think he wants to see what's going on before anyone inside knows we're coming." And indeed, at that moment Fortier halted his steps and, turning, held his finger to his lips in the universal command for silence before swinging round and sprinting toward the building, faster than before.

Hampered by skirts, we all made slower progress on the rough grass, but we obeyed Fortier's injunction to silence. The plot was scythed but resembled a field rather than a garden. In the near distance stood an ancient farmhouse, around which the new brick mansions must have been springing up like mushrooms. I saw Guttridge stumble, but she quickly righted herself. I returned my attention to the grass, which, like any field, was full of dips and holes to turn the ankles of the unwary.

We tiptoed carefully over the last stretch of ground, unkempt gravel well infested with weeds and debris, and came up close behind Fortier's elbow. He had been standing still, listening. Now he was easing up the latch with painful slowness.

It was hard to see much once we were inside because of the serried ranks of canvases. Some loomed far higher than a man, stacked ten deep and at all kinds of angles. Leaning against the huge posts that held up the roof, they formed canyons and fences that turned the interior of the building into a maze. From some unseen window, the light of the sun, now low on the horizon, gilded the upper part of the posts and filled the air with myriad sparkling motes of dust.

I was right behind Fortier now. He turned toward me, motioning to me to remain quiet, and took my hand in his to lead me through the corridors of canvas. Glancing behind me, I could see that Millie and Guttridge had remained close to the door, which Guttridge was pulling shut as quietly as Fortier had opened it.

I grappled with my skirts, pulling them in as much as possible with my free hand, keeping pace with Fortier, conscious of the warmth of his hand through my glove. He was heading toward the light. I thought I could hear faint sounds of activity in that direction, but the enormous canvases seemed to deflect both light and sound, making it hard to distinguish anything.

A squeeze of my hand brought me to a halt. Fortier let go of me and picked up a large, stout-looking piece of wood that lay in front of a stack of small canvases, on which I could discern the half-painted figures of nymphs and dryads. I turned back; Guttridge and Millie were approaching in single file but stopped as I motioned to them.

By the time I faced forward again, Fortier was some six feet from me. His progress forward was cautious, and then my heart almost failed me as he gave a wordless shout at the top of his voice and darted forward with the piece of wood raised above his head. After a moment of paralysis, I too ran forward, wishing I had a weapon but ready to throw caution to the winds.

Light enveloped me, and I saw Fortier swing the piece of wood at someone standing on a heavy ladder of the same kind I had seen Sir Geraint use in his new studio. I saw the man he had hit jump sideways, and a sharp cry informed me he had probably hurt himself landing on the stone-flagged floor. Why was Fortier attacking him? I had seen no weapon of any kind nor any indication of what he had been doing.

Fortier discarded the piece of wood and launched himself forward, landing across the man's body. I grabbed the fallen stick and raised it high above my head as I moved closer to the two men. With a strange feeling of inevitability, I saw the red-blond head of Edmund Dorrian-Knowles, who was struggling vigorously, cursing and wriggling as he tried to free himself from Fortier's weight. The need for silence was clearly over.

"I'll hit you with this piece of wood if you don't lie still," I said as loudly and clearly as I could. "Fortier, why are you—?"

But matters had already proceeded. Edmund had reacted to the sound of my voice with a degree of astonishment that caused him to stop struggling for a second. In that second, Fortier hit him, hard, on the jaw and lowered him, insensible, to the stone-flagged floor.

"What was he—?" But a wail interrupted my second attempt to elicit information from Fortier. It was a sound that made me spin around, forgetting Edmund entirely. It was Guttridge, and I had never heard my imperturbable maid sound so upset.

"Oh, my lady! Oh, my lady!"

She was bending over a large armchair, which was positioned in one of the darker recesses of the studio space next to a small table overflowing with books and papers. I moved toward her, and there was Odelia, slumped on the chair, as silent and still as a broken doll.

43

FROM THE HIGHEST TREE

I flung myself at Odelia, pushing Guttridge out of the way in my eagerness to reach her. I felt a movement of air behind me as Millie rushed to her son's side, calling, "Edmund!" with the same hysterical note as I could hear in my, "Odelia, darling!"

"Don't move her." I felt a restraining touch on my shoulder as Fortier spoke from behind me. "Let me look at her first." Then, over his shoulder: "Miss Guttridge, would you care to bind our friend's hands, fairly tight, in case he wakes up soon and makes a fuss? Tie him to something if you can. There's rope at the foot of the ladder."

"Her face." I clutched foolishly at the front of Fortier's waistcoat. "Is she dead?"

"Good heavens, no." Fortier deposited the lightest of kisses on my forehead before turning his attention back to Odelia. "She's breathing; can't you see? But she's received a bad blow, and I suspect her arm is broken. Let's look at her head first."

He reached out a hand to Odelia, his grimace and sharp intake of breath briefly directing my attention to the rapidly darkening bruises on his knuckles. Touching his fingers lightly to Odelia's wrist for a few moments, he then ran his fingertips over her face, paying particular attention to the dark red bruises that were blossoming near her right temple. He removed hat and hairpins until he could slide both hands under her thick hair, moving slowly and carefully.

After a while, he seemed satisfied and lifted her head slightly, bringing it into a more comfortable-looking position. To my infinite relief, Odelia's eyes fluttered open.

"I don't feel at all well."

"Don't move." Fortier's lips were close to Odelia's face as he continued his examination. "Your arm is probably broken. You're very lucky your hair's so thick. I can't feel any damage to your skull, and your cheekbone's intact, but you'll have to stay very quiet and still for a few days. Do you remember what happened?"

"I fell, I think." Odelia frowned, then winced. "I was struggling—good Lord, it was with Edmund, of all people. I received a note from Geraint to meet him here, only it was Edmund, not Geraint. He said horrible things to me. At least, I can remember that they were horrible. I can't actually remember what he said." She squeezed her eyes shut, moaning as some unpleasant sensation passed through her. "My arm hurts like the devil." Her eyes opened again, widening in alarm. "My arm. My painting arm—"

"I think it's a clean break." Fortier's finely shaped fingers were brushing Odelia's arm with infinite care. "I will set it myself, and it should heal well. Stay still. It's your head that concerns me most at the moment."

"Why are you here?" Odelia's voice strengthened. "Is Helena—?"

"I'm here." I reached for Odelia's uninjured hand. "I won't leave you, darling."

"I've done what you said, sir." Guttridge's voice came

from behind us. "Should I look for a policeman? I can run to Kensington Road, quick as you like. Ah," her voice softened, "her ladyship is awake. You gave me a nasty fright, my lady." She moved so that she was in Odelia's line of vision.

"Guttridge as well?" A little humor returned to Odelia's voice. "Is this a search party?"

"That wasn't the only thing that gave me a nasty turn," I heard Guttridge say to Fortier. "Did you see—?"

"I did." Fortier held up a hand to cut off Guttridge's words. "Finding a policeman is an excellent idea. Helena, could you stay with Lady Odelia and make sure she remains still? I must look at my other patient. I hope I didn't inadvertently do more damage than I meant to. My fear was that he might get the better of me if I didn't act quickly."

"He's moaning a bit," Guttridge remarked heartlessly. "I imagine he'll live." She disappeared into the gloom between the stacked canvases, now quite dark as the sun slid downward. I heard her bump into something and was fairly sure I heard her swear.

In the ensuing silence, I could hear Millie crying, the most heartbroken sound I had ever heard. Was Guttridge wrong and Edmund badly injured? Still holding Odelia's hand, I straightened up to get a better view.

I could see Fortier's back, bent over Edmund, and heard his voice, low and reassuring. Where was Millie? I had expected to see her crouched by her son, staring at him in maternal agony, but all I saw was Fortier. No, Millie was several feet away, huddled between two empty easels, her arms wrapped tightly around her knees, as if trying to make herself as small as possible. She was looking up at a spot a few feet above the wooden stair, and she was whimpering. It took me a few moments to see what she saw—and when I did, it froze the marrow in my bones.

From the great oak beam, almost invisible in the fading light, dangled a hangman's noose.

IT MUST HAVE BEEN TWO—OR WAS IT THREE?—HOURS LATER that I found myself sitting next to Fortier in my carriage. "Found myself" in the sense that my eyes flew open as the brougham rocked before I relaxed as I recognized Fortier. It was strange, I thought sleepily, that I'd known him so easily in the dark.

"Where's Guttridge?" I blinked stupidly into the black void in front of me.

"She returned to Scott House in a hansom half an hour ago to ensure the household is ready for your return and to tell them Lady Odelia's safe. I'm sorry I left you sitting in the carriage. I thought I'd be done sooner."

"I'm quite comfortable. But are you *sure* I shouldn't stay the night with O?" The carriage was moving, smooth on the dry dirt of the road, taking us away from the small cottage hospital to which Fortier had recommended we take Odelia rather than risk the longer journey home.

I felt the fingers of Fortier's left hand gently encircle those of my right, his touch warm and certain. I should perhaps have objected, but I didn't. "She was awake and talking for some time, Helena. She's now sleeping a natural sleep, and someone will be with her all night. I'll be there very early tomorrow." He squeezed my fingers gently.

The action brought another thought to the surface of my half-sleeping mind. "How's your hand?"

"That's why I took so long." There was a note of rueful humor in his voice. "I had them dress it and put it in a sling. Doubtless it helped to use it rather than to let it stiffen up, but it aches like the blazes. I thought I'd broken something at first." His voice deepened. "I'm glad I knocked him out—it was an elegant solution that saved us both further injury—but I had a moment of real fright when I imagined I might not be able to use my hand. I can understand your sister's anxiety. Surgery, like art, requires considerable manual dexterity."

"You didn't look as if you were in pain when you were setting O's arm." I remembered his intent face in the gaslight.

"I was in considerable discomfort, my dear." Now there was laughter in his voice. "But as soon as I knew there was no permanent damage, it just became part of an ordinary day. Like riding myself saddle-sore, or standing up to my—I mean, with my legs in freezing water—in a ditch to help an injured farmer, or falling off Lucifer when something startles him. I never did like the idea of sitting in a warm room in a chair all day."

"You'd make a good sportsman." I smiled lazily into the dark. I was warm, sitting so close to Fortier, and sleepy and weak with relief that Odelia was safe. "The sort who rides to hounds all day and then gets up in the morning to shoot at birds."

"Except that I strongly dislike hunting." Fortier shifted his position, grunting a little. I wondered fleetingly just how much his right hand hurt him. "As a youth, I took lessons in pugilism and still enjoy a fencing match when I get the chance, but blood sports disgust me. I prefer an opponent who has a decent chance." He breathed out a short laugh. "I'll admit the boxing lessons came in handy today."

"Don't sound so smug." It was good to tease Fortier after all the hours of fear and worry. "If you know how to use a rapier, I suppose it's just as well you don't have one of those swords hidden in a walking stick."

"How do you know I don't?" Fortier was laughing properly now, and I joined in. After a few moments, he sobered and continued: "Actually, I left my stick—it's an ordinary one —at the Dorrian-Knowles house, along with my hat and gloves. I'm not sure if I'd be welcome if I went back to retrieve them."

"I've been debating with myself whether I should call on Millie." Her horrified face had frequently come to mind in the darkness of the brougham. "I've concluded I should send a note, although what I can possibly say in the circumstances is beyond me. And where does all this leave me as regards Sir Geraint?"

"I'm surprised you even want to send a note, considering Edmund was going to hang your sister. You really are one of the kindest and most gracious women I've ever met."

There was so much warmth in Fortier's voice that I felt myself blush. Our joined hands, a gesture that had felt innocent and childlike, now seemed to take on a different meaning. But his next words cast a chill over my mood. "You'd be well rid of both Sir Geraint and Lady Dorrian-Knowles. Of the whole family. Where did Edmund get the idea of hanging Lady Odelia after all?"

"He told the police he was only trying to frighten her, didn't he? That's what I thought I heard him say."

"And no doubt that will be his defense." Fortier shuddered. "But I don't like his obsession with a woman's neck. Supposing he *did* kill Miss Aldred? Then it'll be the noose for him."

"Millie admitted she'd said she wanted to hang O from the highest tree . . . . Dear God, Fortier, much as I love my sister, I'm not sure if I'll ever forgive her. I'm inclined to agree with Millie that all this is at least partly her fault. Edmund must have been around seven when his father openly took O as his mistress. Old enough, perhaps, to have understood his mother's anger, to have overheard things." At least, I reflected, Papa's affairs had been hidden from me and

Michael. How could I have listened to him talk about loyalty if I'd known he was making Mama unhappy?

"Will you break your agreement with Sir Geraint because of this?" Fortier asked.

"I don't know. I simply don't know what to do. There's going to be the most awful scandal, isn't there? It isn't going to be possible to keep Odelia's name out of it."

44

SCANDAL

It was later than I'd realized. I stumbled into bed around one in the morning and slept like the dead until nine, woken only by Guttridge bringing me breakfast.

"I didn't think I should let you sleep any longer, my lady." Guttridge gently settled the breakfast tray over my nether limbs. "I know you'll be wanting to visit her ladyship. And, er . . . well, just let me get the post from downstairs. There was too much to put on the tray."

Notwithstanding the vague uneasiness that Guttridge's words had produced, I was ravenous. I fortified myself with toast and coffee before Guttridge reappeared, carrying an alarming number of envelopes.

"You'd better help me with those." I stared at the small harbingers of doom with dismay. "I can't open them and eat at the same time, and I simply *must* eat. Are you well? Fed and rested?"

"I am perfectly well, thank you, my lady." Guttridge's eyes gleamed with pleasure at being included in the revelation of news, good or—most likely—bad.

"Then find a letter opener and start sorting through them

366

while I eat this egg. Do you think there might be a chance of a second breakfast once I've bathed? I'm having visions of chafing dishes full of kedgeree and deviled kidneys and ham. The sort of breakfast I used to lay on for our guests when Sir Justin filled the house for the pheasant shooting." I grinned. "But I'll settle for a kipper."

"I'll arrange that once I've readied your bath, my lady." Guttridge, having found a small ivory letter opener, brought a chair to my bedside and got to work. By the time I'd devoured every scrap of my breakfast, she had sorted the letters into piles.

"These are the important ones." Guttridge removed the depleted tray and handed me some sheets of paper. "These should be answered later—they're from concerned acquaintances—and *these*," she indicated the largest pile, "are impertinent letters from journalists and ill-wishers and should probably just be burned without reading."

"Right." I flicked through the letters in silence, knowing that Guttridge had probably already registered their contents with a glance. One from the hospital to say Odelia passed a comfortable night and was in tolerable spirits—excellent. One from Fortier, the handwriting cramped and painful-looking, saying much the same. I put it aside on my nightstand, feeling a little ashamed of sleeping late.

"Oh dear." I wrinkled my nose at the third letter, which had a nastily official look. "The police want to see me again. Well, there's no help for it." I turned back the bedcovers. "Forget the kipper. I'd better bathe straightaway."

"Yes, my lady."

"The worst thing is," I remarked as my feet touched the faded but soft rug, "by the end of the day, the London papers will have reached Littleberry. Even before that, I imagine people will send telegrams to Sir Edward or Lord Broadmere." And what Ned and Michael would make of *those* sent my imagination into a fever. "I'll have the whole family sending me letters."

WE FOUND ODELIA SITTING UP IN BED, VERY PALE AND MUCH bruised on the right side of her head. Her arm was swathed in bandages and supported by a large sling.

"We've brought you some things," I said after kissing the unbruised side of her face and enfolding her in a long, gentle hug. "Your nightdress, hairbrush, and other indispensables. Guttridge has a bag of things to help make you what she calls 'presentable.' Naturally, she insists that nobody but she should have the grooming of you."

"They say I should stay till I can walk around steadily." Odelia's voice was a little faint. "I get dizzy. What a fool I was to have fallen over like that."

I looked at Guttridge. Seeing her faint frown, I tried to wipe the look of worry off my face. "What on earth happened?" I asked my sister since the best course seemed to find out what she thought had transpired.

O started to shake her head but winced. "I'm not entirely sure. I had a note from Geraint to meet him at the studio. It made me so happy to think he was back in London, and I was so eager to see him." Her mouth turned down. "But he wasn't there. Just Edmund, with some story about his father being delayed, I think. I don't really remember. He was talking to me in that supercilious way he has. I can hear his voice in my memory, but the words escape me. Then he was angry. And then all I remember is you all being there, making a fuss over me. Were you looking for me, darling? I'm sorry I didn't leave word about where I'd gone, but it was silly of you to worry. You can't possibly chase me all over London."

"Yes, I can." I put my arms around Odelia again, breathing

the scent of her hair and warm body. I was going to have to tell her what had really happened before somebody else did, but I needed some time simply to feel grateful she had survived.

"How's your arm, my lady?" Guttridge asked.

Odelia waggled the fingertips peeping from under the heavy bandage. "Dr. Fortier says it's doing very well. It doesn't hurt much because when it starts hurting, they give me something and the pain just sort of washes away." She smiled lazily at me. "He's rather nice, your physician. He managed to hurt his own hand. Isn't that a coincidence? He says it'll be quite some time till my arm is healed but that I'll be able to use it just as before. I'm going to be dreadfully bored if I can't paint or draw, but there's nothing to be done about it."

She smiled again. "I think whatever they're giving me must be quite strong. I feel as if everything should matter a lot more than it does. Will you look after me when I come home, Helena? You're quite the nicest person to have around when one is under the weather. You can stay in London for a few more weeks, can't you?"

I thought of the pile of "impertinent" letters that I had locked into my writing desk. I thought of the cynical-eyed men waiting outside the gate of Scott House as my carriage picked up speed, Dudley waving his whip at one or two of the bolder ones who'd tried to impede our progress. My eyes met Guttridge's, and she spoke.

"Sometimes it's best to get the medicine over with, my lady. Especially since her ladyship's so cheerful."

"Could you leave us?" I asked her. I knew I would cry, and although Guttridge was quite accustomed to seeing me in tears, it embarrassed me. Mama had always made me feel that crying was below the dignity of the Scott-De Quincys.

Guttridge's answer was to rise to her feet and leave the room with a sympathetic glance at the two of us.

"O." My voice sounded small. "I need to tell you something."

SOME FORTY MINUTES LATER, A SOFT KNOCK SOUNDED ON THE door. I swallowed back my tears—they had not been too abundant, to my relief—and wiped my eyes before calling, "Come in."

It was Fortier. His right arm was also in a sling but a much lighter one than Odelia's, the bruises livid on his unbandaged hand. He exuded what I could only call a professionally reassuring air, as if his surroundings dictated that he must show confidence in the presence of a patient.

"I've been telling Odelia what happened yesterday," I informed him as our fingers touched in greeting, bringing back a memory of his hand on mine in the dark. "I thought it best."

Fortier slipped his injured hand out of the loop of cloth that supported it and grasped Odelia's wrist lightly. "Ordinarily, I would advise against administering a shock to someone who's so recently suffered an injury to the head." His gaze took in Odelia's white face. "But the pulse is steady. Lady Odelia, you are made of tough fiber. Of course, morphine has a reputation for inducing detachment, but I've been giving you very small doses. Are you feeling any pain?"

"My arm throbs horribly, and there's an itch somewhere under the bandages." Odelia tried to smile. Her eyes, unlike mine, were dry but infinitely weary. "I think the morphine is wearing off, but I'd rather not have any more for the moment. I need to feel the reality of what I'm inflicting on my family." She put her good hand on mine. "That's a pain I must endure. There's no medicine for it."

"I wasn't trying to hurt you." I took her hand in both of mine. "The family will survive, and it'll all be yesterday's news soon enough. Still, I don't think you should return to Scott House for the moment. Come to Whitcombe, where I can make sure they leave you alone."

"I don't deserve you." For a moment, I thought the tears would come, but Odelia mastered herself and gave me and Fortier a tremulous smile. "I don't care about scandal attaching to *me*—I've run that risk for years—but I find the thought of my family being smeared with the kind of dirt one sees in the gossip columns is producing an unusual effect. I believe it's called shame." She bit her lip. "I suppose it'll get out that I'm not Geraint's only mistress. They're bound to connect me with the Aldred woman. I can just imagine what all the old biddies in Littleberry will say. Strictly speaking, Helena, darling, you shouldn't receive me at Whitcombe."

"Hang all of that." I kissed the hand that lay in mine. "I wouldn't turn you away if you'd had a hundred lovers. If Blanche objects to your presence, she can stay at Hyrst or with her hidebound friends in Broadmere. I'm not Baby any more, O. I've grown up. I know what my values are. Ultimately, I care more about my sister than about other people's morality." I turned to Fortier. "Do you think Odelia will be well enough to travel straight down to Whitcombe with me? Just until things die down a bit. I suppose Edmund will be put on trial, so there'll be more fuss to come."

"The correct procedure would be for me to go back to Italy." Odelia grimaced. "I can just see Gerry insisting on it."

"I will write Lady Freestone a letter explaining that such a voyage would be injurious to your health," Fortier said gravely. "To answer your question, Lady Helena, she should be able to travel after another two or three days' rest. While she is here, we will not allow her to be importuned."

"There." I smiled at Odelia. "You'll be perfectly safe at Whitcombe. We can hide there until every last shred of scandal has died down. After all, that's what country houses are for."

I felt a surge of joy at the notion of returning to Whitcombe House. It would mean deserting Fortier, of course, and I knew I would regret that. Yet a sensible corner of my mind told me that it might be better to see less of each other for a while after the highly interesting—one might even say romantic—events of the previous day. He was not free, and I was still in mourning for Justin. At Whitcombe, I could think, without the noise and rattle of London, and the blossom would still be on the trees, and—

I realized that Fortier's face had taken on a very grave aspect. Did he reproach me for wanting to return to Littleberry, whence he could not go? But his words told me he'd been thinking of something entirely removed from matters of the heart.

"You realize, don't you—?" He hesitated, then plunged on. "You do realize you'll both be expected back in London for the trial?"

45

NO AMOUNT OF INFLUENCE

The return to Littleberry was, unsurprisingly, a little trying.

"The fact is," said my brother-in-law Ned ten days later, "no amount of influence can prevent the two of you being called to give evidence against a man charged with feloniously injuring O with intent to murder. And Helena is a material witness in the Aldred case. Those among us who have suggested an attempt to influence the course of justice might be made should have more regard for my position." He cast a severe eye upon his wife. "Besides, my influence doesn't extend to London. So there's the question of practicality as well."

I watched Gerry assume her haughtiest expression, eyebrows delicately arched as if she hadn't just been arguing that Ned "should really *do* something about this." Odelia and I had been back at Whitcombe for less than a week, but Odelia was well enough that I'd invited the family to tea, to get it all over with in one afternoon. The glaring absence was Blanche; oddly enough, she had only sent one letter, and since that was to Gerry, I wasn't privy to its contents. Apparently, Dederick was staying with her in Tunbridge Wells and she was far too busy with her son to even bother with the scandal that had broken over our heads.

"We've been bound over to appear, Gerry," I said softly.

"Bound over—what a dreadful phrase." Gerry sniffed. "For once I'm grateful Mama cannot know what's happening. To think of her daughters—ladies, Scott-De Quincys—appearing at the Old Bailey. And in a murder trial too. Why did the two of you have to get mixed up with such ill-bred, unregulated people? Even if he *is* a baronet. And you, Helena, poking your nose into Odelia's business—"

A chorus of objections silenced my eldest sister. Odelia, still heavily bandaged but now swathed in an elegant silk shawl in place of her utilitarian sling, sat up straighter in her chaise longue.

"If Helena hadn't poked her nose into my business, I'd be dead. It's all my fault, not hers, and I won't hear a word against her." She smiled fondly at me. "It's like having the old Helena back, doing the most unexpected things because you'd found a reason to. And such good reasons too. You'd just look at us with those big serious eyes, and we'd know you were only trying to help."

An amused grunt and a vigorous nod from Ned greeted her reminiscences, and even Gerry's expression became a shade less frosty. Alice and Annette, sitting so close together they were touching, favored me with identical smiles. Thomas, by dint of his residence at Whitcombe the only representative of the younger generation in attendance, smothered a wide grin behind his good hand. Julia raised her eyebrows at me in mock horror.

Only Michael didn't react, continuing to fidget impatiently with the ornaments on the green drawing room's mantelpiece. He had already told me that he refused to have an opinion about the various threads of scandal woven around the two of us. His ostensible reason was that as the earl, he had to remain neutral, but I suspected he didn't want anyone to find out he had already known about Odelia's affair with Sir Geraint.

Gerry had already forgotten about me in her hunt for bigger prey. This meeting was her first proper opportunity to speak her mind since our return, as I had deliberately surrounded Odelia with nurses and servants to keep the family from persecuting her. She addressed our brother in her most imperious tone. "Michael, do stop fidgeting and listen to me. I *insist* you no longer allow O to live at Scott House. Mama and Papa should never have permitted it. I said at the time she'd get herself into trouble. You'll have to have her at Hyrst. She'll never marry now."

"Oh, surely not at Hyrst, Gerry." It was Alice, speaking at last. Her twin chimed in with, "But what would she *do*?" at the same time, before the two of them launched into one of their strange flurries of speech where one could barely distinguish which one of them was speaking, as if they were two halves of the same person.

"She would get under our feet—"

"She'd expect us to do everything for her—"

"Poor Michael, as if he doesn't have enough—"

"Responsibilities—"

"And what would the county think?" they concluded in unison.

"I will certainly *not* live at Hyrst." Odelia's color was high. "Besides, Michael's known for years and never bothered me about it." She ignored Michael's furious glare and the ripple of shocked gasps and continued in a louder voice, while I tried not to see Julia collapsing into a fit of the giggles so severe she had to hide behind a cushion. "I admit it might be a good idea to leave London for a while. Once my arm is healed, I will return to Rome. One can live cheaply there, and I've made a few friends. I'm sure I can sell a painting or two—"

"Michael ought to cut off your allowance." Gerry was clearly not about to give in. "And you may not find it easy to get commissions. I know for certain Lady Woollven-Lowrie has withdrawn her patronage because she wrote to tell me so." Her mouth set in a firm expression that betrayed the tiny lines of age beginning to appear around her lips. "*You* do not seem to care about your reputation, Odelia, but other people do. It makes every kind of difference to a woman what people think."

"You lost the commission for the Lynette painting?" I asked my sister. "You didn't tell me."

"The old hag only wrote to me yesterday." Odelia's expression was decidedly sulky, but then she brightened. "And do you know something? I've had a much better idea for that painting. I shall repaint Lynette's face and put in a few symbolic touches so that everyone knows the high and mighty Lynette is hiding a secret past. That she's a hypocrite. Because most people who look too good to be true are." She glared at Gerry. "And once it's finished, I'll find someone to sell it to, you see if I don't."

"Nevertheless, you lost the commission." Gerry was flushed by now, speaking even louder than Odelia. "And you may not get any work for a while. And Michael—"

"I will not cut off her allowance, Geraldine." Michael had been listening to the exchange with one hand on his hip, forgetting to fidget in his impatience to assert his authority as head of the family. Close to him, Julia raised a rosy face from her cushion and gazed at him with undisguised adoration.

"Papa set Odelia's allowance up for her lifetime or until her marriage, at which point it will be converted to a dowry," Michael continued. "It is a burden on the estate, but I never shirk my responsibilities. As for you living at Hyrst, Odelia, I'd far rather you went abroad than stayed with us. It would be inconvenient to have you at Hyrst. And when people stop gossiping, you should move back to Scott House. I haven't made up my mind to sell it yet, and Brandrick says it's a bad idea to leave a property uninhabited. I can't afford to improve it, and you're the only person willing to live there in its present state. And when you're there, Helena stays with you and spends money on the house, which is much to my advantage."

"Devastating honesty," Odelia murmured before turning to Gerry. "I'm sorry—truly, I am—that you and the others will lose face in the county because of me. It's a bad show after all the years I've spent being discreet for your sakes. But why don't you take a leaf out of Michael's book and be honest for once? Admit it, you're only cross because I've been caught out. We all know how the game is played. That's what Mama never seemed to understand, and look what it did to *her*. She knew I had a lover, by the way, although I never told her who it was."

"*Odelia!*" Gerry spat out the name, her face now quite red. "May I remind you that my son is present and that there are things we *do not* discuss in this family—"

"Well, *maybe* we should. *You*—"

"Gerry." Ned's growl, deeper and stronger than usual, had the effect of silencing both Gerry and Odelia, but it was to his wife he spoke, placing a large hand firmly over hers. "You're making things worse. This family is going to have to put up with a fair amount of unpleasantness for a while, and it needs to stick together."

"Whew." Thomas returned from seeing his parents into their carriage and lowered himself down into an armchair with the support of his good arm. "Are you all right, Auntie O? I h-have to say that m-my eyes have been opened—and I s-suspect that without my father's intervention, there m-might have been even m-more revelations." He looked at Odelia with a small, puzzled frown, and I went back in my mind over the argument between Gerry and Odelia. Had O been about to say something about our eldest sister?

"I hope you're not shocked." Odelia had recovered her usual sardonic poise.

Thomas shook his head. "A clergyman must be familiar with every t-type of sin." He leaned his head on his hand. "Although I had rather expected to g-get acquainted with it in the slums, not the c-country houses."

"I think you'll find the country houses have a great deal to offer in terms of immoral education." Odelia's smile was mischievous. "You can pray over me if you really want to, Thomas. If you were ordained already, you might feel obliged to do it."

"I'll pray *for* you and spare our b-blushes."

"Pray for Millicent Dorrian-Knowles," I said sharply, with a sudden stab of irritation. "Why do you have to be so cyni-cal?" I took a deep breath and moderated my tone. "I love you, O—and I know it took two of you to have this affair, and that you were very young when it began, and that Sir Geraint should have known better—but you didn't see Millie's face when she saw the noose Edmund was going to use to hang you. And perhaps you don't know that she told me she'd often said she wanted to hang you from the highest tree."

"Ugh." Odelia made a face. "Trust you to tell me *that*. Now

I'll have nightmares. Do you think she said the same about the actress? Because it's for her that Edmund will hang." She looked down at the slender, beringed fingers of her uninjured hand. "I've been reading the newspapers—I know I shouldn't, but I can't seem to stop—and it looks fairly certain that the evidence against him is conclusive. Including *your* evidence."

I bit my lip, remembering the ordeal of sitting across a scuffed desk from a stony-faced officer of the detective force, explaining—in more detail than before—everything I had known and done and thought in connection with Odelia and Sir Geraint and Millie and all the rest of them. I would no doubt have to explain it all again in the court—in public— and the very thought made me feel sick.

"Don't look so tragic." Odelia's tone was dry. "At least you have the advantage of virtue. None of this is *your* fault."

"The police didn't seem so sure. 'Meddling' was the way they put it." My voice was unsteady.

Odelia shook her head. "You'll get a relatively smooth ride, unlike your abject sister." She essayed a smile, but it didn't seem to work. "I will have the entire world against me. You won't be able to fend the busybodies off forever. In addition, I have to be grateful to you for shutting Whitcombe's doors to the world while my head healed. And furthermore —oh, what's the use. I'm tired."

She rose to her feet in a graceful movement, seemingly unhampered by not having the use of one arm, and left the room without any kind of farewell nor any gesture of affection to Thomas or me. A dull dismay flooded my heart as the door closed behind her.

"Should I go to her?" I asked my nephew. "I don't like her being alone in this black mood."

But Thomas was shaking his head as he came to sit beside me. "It's self-p-pity, Auntie Helena, and it's unfair to you." He reached out his good arm toward me. "Very unfair. Auntie O's self-centered—selfish—she's never really cared what other people f-feel or think, even y-you. D-don't let her m-m-make you feel you're in the wrong wh-when all you've done is try to h-help."

"She didn't like me criticizing her about Millie." I accepted the comfort of Thomas's encircling arm, leaning into my nephew's shoulder and closing my eyes to ward off the headache that had been forming. "It's not my role in this family to criticize, is it? Everyone else can do it, but not I."

"Don't let h-her make you sad." Thomas rested his chin on the top of my head. "P-poor Auntie Helena, having to contend with such a family."

"I've never stood a chance against them." But I smiled into the rough tweed of Thomas's jacket, remembering Julia's warm hug and the way Michael had stood a little closer to me than he would normally tolerate. I *did* have allies, and Thomas was one of the best of them.

"It's just that O and I have never really been at odds before," I said. "It's all so difficult. I almost wish the trial *had* been set for yesterday's sessions instead of being put off till the twenty-fifth of June. We have so much to go through, she and I, and I don't want to have to go back to London. I just want to hide away in my home and be comfortable again."

"Except that you d-don't have a drawing room." Thomas hugged me closer. "The heart of your house lies b-bleeding. What are you going to do?"

"I have no idea." I groaned. "I could call someone in to take down the work done on the frames and just decorate the room as it was, I suppose. But will I ever be happy with it after the wonderful vision Sir Geraint and O between them put into my head?"

"Have you written to Sir Geraint? I suppose you must."

"I know I must, but I keep putting it off. How can I

intrude at a time like this? How can I even discuss *my* needs? Sir Geraint is in London with Millie, and I shouldn't think she'd even want to hear the name of anyone connected with the Scott-De Quincy family. My acquaintance with Sir Geraint is doubtless sundered forever."

46

THE FRAGILE BOND

I was wrong—more wrong than I could ever have anticipated. The first indication came when Ned paid me a visit the following Thursday morning.

"Bearing up?" he inquired kindly as we settled down to drink coffee together.

"Just about."

"It'll all be over by the end of the month." Ned smiled reassuringly at me as he took a sip of coffee. He made a small noise of appreciation at the beverage and swiped at his mustache with a finger in a gesture that would certainly have annoyed Gerry. "I've brought you some news. It may not be entirely welcome, but I thought I'd better tell you before it reaches you some other way." Another sip and then Ned put down the coffee cup and regarded me gravely. "I heard from a man I know that Sir Geraint Dorrian-Knowles has bought the Bennett farmhouse."

"What?" I put down my own cup and stared at my brother-in-law. "When did this happen?"

"Yesterday, so I'm told. He made an offer a week ago and sent an agent down to negotiate the details. Bought it for a song. If you ask me, Bennett's made a foolish bargain, but he seems pleased enough with the cash. He's been bragging about having rid himself of the place at last."

After Ned's departure, I spent some thirty minutes staring blankly out of the morning-room window before resolving that there was nothing for it but to write to Sir Geraint straightaway. I was at leisure to do so since Odelia breakfasted in her room and I was unlikely to see her for an hour or two. I fervently hoped that the coolness I had felt between us the day before would be dissipated by a good night's sleep. Perhaps regularizing matters between Sir Geraint and myself would help.

I was working on my rough copy—feeling my way carefully through a mild inquiry into the state of things in Holland Park and an even milder suggestion that Sir Geraint and I needed to discuss our business relationship—when a footman interrupted me. Was I at home to Sir Geraint Dorrian-Knowles?

I put down my pen so hastily that a fat drop of ink instantly bloomed on the paper. Given that Sir Geraint had more or less had the freedom of Whitcombe House while engaged on the *Nightingale* pictures, this cautious approach seemed significant. I dispatched the footman to fetch Sir Geraint and spent the intervening moments steadying my breath, trying to slow the sudden, rapid beating of my heart.

"Lady Helena." The man who took my hand, smiling at me with the familiar, intense look in his eyes, was perhaps a little thinner than before but still imbued with the same vitality. Should I have expected much of a change in the five weeks or so since I had last seen him? His skin was even a little tanned, as if he had been spending much time outdoors.

I stepped back so that I could see him better and motioned him to a nearby chair.

"I was writing to you." I glanced back at my writing desk, where the letter lay. "I should have done it before, and I'm sorry. I thought you were in London."

"I have traveled down to sign the papers to buy Eden-holme. Have you heard about that?" At my nod, a grin appeared on his face. "Yes, I've learned how fast gossip flies around Littleberry. I'm going back to Holland Park this afternoon."

"How is . . . everything?" I hardly knew how to ask. "How is Millie?"

The levity vanished, but the rich voice was steady. "My son is being held at Newgate Prison awaiting trial, as you might have seen in the papers. Millie is . . . suffering." His thick, dark eyebrows drew together, deepening the line between them. "But I suppose you must know all about the trial. You and O are both witnesses, aren't you?"

Had that thought not been uppermost in his mind? "I'm so sorry about all of this." I half whispered the words as his frown deepened further, but when he spoke, I realized it was perplexity, not anger, that had caused his countenance to darken.

"I'm wondering whether I should even be visiting you—in the circumstances." He took a deep breath and shrugged. "But here I am, and let the lawyers make what they wish of it. Don't be sorry, Lady Helena. We needed to speak. Isn't a visit preferable to a letter?"

I nodded dumbly. Sir Geraint cleared his throat and went on. "My other sons are in good health, as are Cassiope and her family. Janie is in Wales, staying with my cousin, since I thought it best to remove her from London for a while. She'll have to come back for the trial." Now the bunching of his brow was unmistakably anger, and his voice hardened. "Did you know Ed had her deliver some of the letters? She'll have to go through the ordeal of testifying. I find that . . . *unforgivable*." He delivered that last word with a kind of controlled rage that chilled me. "Millie is in a small private asylum near Hampstead Heath, having suffered a complete breakdown. They think she'll recover, but it will take a long time."

"Dear heaven." I wanted to reach out to him, and yet at the same time I felt that I could not have touched him under any circumstances. We were like two warriors on a battle-field, with scorched earth and victims around us, and the horror of what had passed in our eyes.

"I apologize for not having written to you before," Sir Geraint continued, his face clearing as if the worst moment had passed. "I've had a lot of thinking to do. The upshot of it all is that I'm taking Millie and Janie out of London for good, whatever happens. If Edmund survives, it is likely to be on the basis of insanity, I'm told, and if he does, they will commit him to an insane asylum. If not, they will bury him in the precincts of Newgate. Our family is broken. The older children can continue to forge their own paths, and my responsibility is to Millie and Jane."

"And Galahad? I suppose Cassiope has her home and Philip his studio."

"Galahad is returning to Switzerland next week at my insistence." Sir Geraint's voice strengthened. "None of the older ones are needed at the trial because they knew nothing. Cass has been an absolute tower of strength, organizing me and visiting Millie. Phil is sensibly trying to distance himself from us for the sake of his career. Galahad won't have the diplomatic corps just yet, thanks to the scandal I've caused, but he can find tutoring work in Switzerland and improve his languages some more. In a year or two, I hope, Phil will have the right friends to help him, and many of mine have stuck by me."

"I'm glad," I said. "I'm deeply sorry for all of you. Millie in particular."

"I would have deserved it if you'd spat at me." Sir Geraint seemed to relax a little. "How is O?"

I realized this was the first time he'd mentioned my sister. "She's making a good recovery." I hesitated as a thought struck me. "You're not hoping to see her, are you? Allowing that would put me in a hard position with my family."

"I wouldn't dream of embarrassing you." He leaned forward suddenly, grasping my hand. His touch was so warm and normal that my earlier qualms vanished. "Believe me, Lady Helena, I have no intention of seeing Odelia, now or in the foreseeable future. Millie must be my priority henceforth. By the time she's well enough to come home, we will all be living at Edenholme. There will be nothing there to remind her of our life in London. I plan to convert one of the outbuildings into a studio of her own, and I am designing a garden in the courtyard where we can work together on fine days. We will have silence and sunshine and the sea air, and I will put my former life behind me. I've let the London house to a fellow artist who's coveted it for years, at a stupendous rent. I sold him *In the Halls of the Snow Queen* into the bargain and will probably dispose of some of the other paintings in the house. That will cover a good many debts."

"But why *here?*" I sounded as astonished as I felt. "I would have thought this would be the last place Millie would want to be."

"Because of the *Nightingale,* of course." Sir Geraint let go of my hand and leaned back. "I can't possibly leave Millie with anyone else. I've vowed that she will be by my side and I by hers. Janie will be responsible for running the household, but the adjustment in my expenses will allow for more servants so that she has little more to do than supervise." He smiled expansively. "I will devote myself to *The Nightingale* almost exclusively, except for one or two small commissions I must bring with me, and we three—plus Hay and Scoff, of course—will live in the quietest way possible. *The Nightingale* will be my greatest work. I feel it here." He laid a long-fingered hand on his heart. "So marvelous that nobody will remember the story behind it. Or if they do, it will merely add piquancy to the masterpiece."

I stared at Sir Geraint, momentarily dumbfounded. "That's pure fantasy," I said eventually. "Do you really think Millie will be happy living so close to the family of the greatest rival for your affection?"

"Millie has no rival. I have come to my senses."

He said it with the calm assurance of the religious convert and continued in the same even, confident tone. "Even in her broken state, Millie too believes this commission must proceed. She's said to me often enough that my best work is done when I'm devoted to a single object, and I've finally conceded that I am wrong to divide my affections in art as in life. The story of *The Nightingale* is that of a man who forsakes truth for everything that glitters, but who, at the utmost end, sees his error and is saved. Can you not see the significance?"

It was, I realized, what I had wanted from the beginning. Yet I was still a sister, and so I spoke. "But Odelia—"

"O has always known I will put my family first, above all my wife. We have had a wonderful friendship, but it is broken now, like the false nightingale. It must come to an end."

I gaped at Sir Geraint in astonishment and confusion, trying to find a response that sounded neither like narrow moralizing nor an encouragement of sin. I didn't know what I thought about the commission. Its continuation seemed impossible, and yet there was a kind of relief in knowing that all the work and disruption of the last six months might not be wasted. Still, I couldn't find the words to agree with the artist. I did not, in fact, know my own mind.

Sir Geraint was sitting with his back to the half-open door of the morning room. I sat opposite him so that it was I who saw Odelia enter slowly, her head high and confident. When she spoke, her voice was steady, holding a hint of amusement.

"Dear Geraint." O smiled as her lover gave a start at the sound of her voice. "Are you really breaking with me and informing Helena first? That's putting business to the forefront with a vengeance."

SIR GERAINT RECOVERED QUICKLY. HE ROSE POLITELY TO HIS feet and waited for Odelia to take her seat. She lowered herself into a chair with perfect poise despite the sling and the heavy bandage around her arm. Nearly two weeks after being knocked senseless—which she still attributed to falling despite the police detectives' conviction that Edmund had hit her—the bruises on her face had faded to a mottled green and yellow, a streak of purple flaring above one eyebrow.

Not that her injuries detracted from her beauty. With Guttridge attending her, she was even better turned out than usual, her thick blond hair arranged in a deceptively simple style crowned with a single braid. She was wearing one of her best day dresses, a claret-colored gown. Guttridge had cleverly removed one sleeve and replaced it with another silk scarf, ingeniously arranged so it appeared to be a deliberate part of her ensemble. Had she heard of Sir Geraint's arrival and dressed for the occasion? How long had she been outside the door?

"Of course you must put your family first." Odelia's voice was silk, her eyes unfathomable. "Or is it your art you're putting first? How terribly convenient that Millie's opinions and best interests happen to coincide with the most favorable arrangement for your ambitions and, dare I say it, your finances."

"You know it's not like that." Sir Geraint's voice was equally unemotional. "This is an important work of art. Haven't you said so often enough? You can't expect me to just abandon this commission without a backward glance."

"And I'm not so sure about the artistic merit of isolating yourself," Odelia continued as if he hadn't spoken. "After all, you've criticized painters who turn their backs on the community—on London. Their work turns in on itself, becomes insular and irrelevant."

"Not if it's driven on by a greater truth." Sir Geraint raised a thick black eyebrow. "Did you think I was incapable of recognizing it when it revealed itself to me? As for my finances, I have a family to support. That's a feat I have to renew every day by expending my skill and intelligence. Don't sneer at my concern for money. It's not for myself that I must think of it."

"You've a smooth tongue." There was no malice in Odelia's smile. "That bit about our . . . friendship . . . being like the false nightingale was brilliant." She shifted in her seat, stifling a small yawn behind her hand as if she were at a social event that was becoming tiresome. "Ah, well. I don't suppose I can change your mind. The events of recent weeks have certainly placed us in a false and awkward position, and I don't blame you for wanting to distance yourself from it— from me. To be frank, I'm as anxious as you are to avoid making ourselves and our families the object of any more interest."

"Then you agree we must part?" Sir Geraint looked relieved.

Odelia shrugged. "We have already parted. The bond

between us wasn't strong enough to survive Edmund, was it? In a few days, I will give evidence against your son while my name is dragged in the dirt." She looked down at her broken arm. "What we had together was surprisingly fragile."

There seemed absolutely nothing any of us could say after such a pronouncement, but as the silence stretched, I knew I had to speak. "I'm still not sure if this makes any difference. Won't the world see the continuation of the commission as . . . well, as my support of an irregular state of affairs?"

"Do you really care about the sort of people who would think and say such things?" Odelia made a face.

I thought for a moment. "I don't suppose I do." And with that realization, a weight lifted off my shoulders.

"Then to Hades with them." Odelia waved her uninjured hand, the morning sunlight making colored sparks of her rings. "In any case, by the time—well, once Edmund's case is settled, I'm off to the Continent, as I've already told the family." She tilted her head toward her former lover. "You see, my dear, I was leaving you in any event. I have new worlds to conquer."

"No hard feelings, then?" Sir Geraint's poise deserted him for a second, his shoulders slumping like a man who had laid down a burden. Odelia smiled brilliantly.

"Best of friends, as always."

Sir Geraint stayed on for a while after Odelia returned upstairs, and we talked in a somewhat disjointed manner of the commission and of Edenholme. By tacit consent, neither of us mentioned Odelia or Edmund, but their shadows hung over us. I was not sorry when Sir Geraint left.

Within a few minutes of our guest's departure, I was at Odelia's bedroom door, knocking gently.

"I'd rather you left me alone." Odelia knew it was me, of course. A servant would not have knocked.

"I know you're upset. Don't try to hide it from me." I pushed the door open a crack. "Do let me come in, dear."

Receiving no answer, I pushed a little harder. Odelia was standing by the window, staring out at the distant sea. She was blotting her eyes with an inadequately sized lady's handkerchief.

"Mine's clean." I held out the square of linen I had fished from a pocket. O dropped her own sodden handkerchief and applied mine to her reddened eyes.

"You were very brave." I put an arm around my sister's waist. "Exactly the right tone. Do you really think I should go on with the commission? I can write to him and give him his marching orders if you wish."

"Commission or no commission, he's clearly decided to live at the farmhouse." O sniffed. "*Edenholme*. What a vulgar name. Suggestive, I suppose, of an earthly paradise." She took a deep breath. "I hope his chimney smokes, his walls creep with black beetles, and his foundations develop both dry and damp rot. I hope we have a storm like the one that washed Old Broadmere under the waves and that the sea wall falls down, and—well, damn him all round." The tremor in her voice was subsiding. "Now all I have to do is to stop feeling sorry for him over Edmund and I'll be quite myself again. I suppose it had to happen eventually."

"What about Cynthia Emery?" I couldn't help wondering. To my relief, Odelia gave a shout of genuine laughter.

"You can't break something that has no substance. You should *see* Cynthia making eyes at the Italian men. I suppose she'll be mentioned at the trial even if she doesn't have to give evidence, but she's welcome to stay with me in Rome if she feels the need to lie low for a while."

"You like her—so do I." I grinned, but then my smile faded. "I liked Miss Aldred too, actually."

"I didn't." O dropped my handkerchief on the floor but then smiled ruefully and picked up both damp articles, shoving them into a pocket. "Sorry—disgusting bohemian habits. But I regret her death, of course. No woman should have to suffer at the hands of a man."

"No woman should." I reached up to caress the bruises on Odelia's temple. "You need some more salve. I'll fetch it."

"I'm almost healed." Odelia put her uninjured arm around my shoulder for what seemed like the first time in months. "Thanks to you. You were a clever little thing to realize I was positively *screaming* inside when I was talking to Geraint. I hope I played my part well enough."

"You were magnificent." I tightened my arm around Odelia's waist. "Just as well. I don't suppose we'll ever escape Sir Geraint now I've been foolish enough to let the commission go on."

"I'm certainly not going to run away from him." Odelia's upper lip lifted in the faintest of sneers. "Besides, we'll see him at the trial. No point in cowardice. Have you ever known me to ride around a fence or a ditch?"

47

TRIALS

*T*he trial of Edmund Dorrian-Knowles began less than two weeks later. Michael and Ned accompanied us to the Old Bailey, where we were due to report to the witnesses' waiting room.

"Do you think our brother considers us too weak and feeble to attend a courtroom by ourselves?" Odelia watched Michael, easily distinguished in the crowd by his height, corn-blond hair, and awkward gait, depart in the direction of the public gallery. He had left us—"us" included Guttridge—in the care of some sort of usher who guarded the room reserved for witnesses.

"I think he believes he's protecting us." I ignored Odelia's snort of derision. "Ned too. Although in his case, I'm not entirely sure he's uninfluenced by vulgar curiosity, as Gerry claims." I smiled at my sister, trying to remain cheerful despite the butterflies in my stomach. "At least one could never accuse Michael of curiosity. He's quite incapable of such a human weakness."

"Where's Guttridge?" O turned to look behind us. Despite her protestations to the contrary, I knew she was nervous

393

too, as jumpy as a thoroughbred before a race. "Ah, Guttridge, is my hat quite right? I swear I felt it being knocked sideways when we were being herded through that doorway. What a ridiculous crowd. Can they possibly all be witnesses at this trial?"

"I'll just adjust the hat a little, my lady." Guttridge, severe and respectable in her best black silk, deftly removed the hatpin from Odelia's thick hair. She altered the angle of the hat the smallest degree and re-pinned it before surveying me carefully from head to toe.

"The new dress is excellent, my lady." She nodded approvingly at my dark gray ensemble.

"Far too dull." Odelia sighed. "Like a *grisaille* figure in a painting. We're all much too *oscura* for my liking, but I suppose you're right about looking as little like the scarlet woman as possible." Her own elegant outfit was a rich chocolate brown. Guttridge had persuaded her to exchange the deep crimson feather on her hat for a black one that belonged to me.

"That's not what I said, my lady." Guttridge gave Odelia a reproving look.

"But you thought it. Ah, we're finally going somewhere. How tedious it all is."

At least Odelia had recovered her spirits, I thought as I followed the two taller women through the press of the slowly moving throng. The days following her separation from Sir Geraint had been marked by a certain degree of dull misery, which she failed to hide from us, and I had been hard put to it keeping her entertained.

We were shown into a large room fitted out with pews a bit like a church. Sir Geraint and Jane, seated near the back of the room, did not look at us as we passed. I was astonished at the sheer relief I felt when I spotted the back of Fortier's dark head, bare of any hat, in the front rows. As if warned of our presence by some instinct, he turned and nodded a greeting to us.

"Ah, your doctor is here." O leaned over to murmur into my ear as I took my seat. "You know, I like that man more every time I see him. Is he going to remain in London, do you think?"

"I wouldn't be so impertinent as to ask." I jerked my head away from Odelia.

"I'm not interested in him for *me*, you ridiculous Baby." My sister pinched my side with her uninjured hand. "I was simply thinking I'd be prepared to love him as a brother despite his social unsuitability. Although that house of his father's is rather splendid. Did you ever find out whether he's a gentleman?"

"How can you even think of such matters in . . . in *this*?" I gestured at the sides of the room, where two policemen and a hollow-eyed clerk stood, no doubt to watch us in case we conspired together or ran riot or got into a fight. Did such things happen? I sighed, wishing heartily that I had never heard of the Dorrian-Knowles family, and fixed my eyes on Fortier's back. My nerves were strained, my stomach uneasy, but he—Fortier—somehow represented the calm and safety of a world away from London and its manifold dangers.

"I need something to distract me, that's all." Odelia looked sideways at me. "I'm nervous too. Now then, Helena, chin up. We are Scott-De Quincys and we will come through this with our heads high and our colors flying."

MY APPREHENSION WAS NOT HELPED BY THE PALLOR OF Odelia's face as she returned from giving her own evidence. I was the next witness and had already been called. When I stood, my legs no longer felt as if they were made of bone and sinew, and I was barely aware of Guttridge's reassuring nod.

I tried not to look directly at Fortier, but I knew he was there, and that knowledge enabled me to walk up an aisle that had somehow become much longer than it should be. As I passed Odelia, she met my eyes, and I answered her attempt at a smile with an effort of my own.

And then I was through the dusty curtain leading to the witness box, and the courtroom felt both impossibly cramped and uncomfortably vast and open. I felt a change in the air as heads turned to see me. Then I heard myself answering that I was indeed Lady Helena Whitcombe of Whitcombe House near Littleberry in the county of Sussex. Yes, I would tell the truth, the whole truth, and nothing but the truth. I wondered at the steadiness of my voice.

I became aware of the scents of hair oil and men's sweat from the packed benches far below me and the fragrance of old leather from the rows of books that lined a sort of book-case built into the front of a box containing several men. Nothing but men, and all in boxes. To the side of me was a dyspeptic-looking man in a bright robe and great wig, undoubtedly the judge, contained in a box of his very own. Bewigged and berobed lawyers were easy to identify. Two of them were conferring together, ignoring me for a moment.

A flash of color drew my attention to a large box, high up. There were two women present after all. And there were Michael's blond head and Ned's bushy beard, so that must be the public gallery. Where was Edmund?

With a shock, I realized he was right in front of me, sepa-rated by the gulf below me where men swarmed, seated at benches or standing, in various attitudes of alertness or boredom. Edmund's thinness was accentuated by the large box in which he stood like a solitary sapling in a forest clear-ing. To one side of him sat a uniformed man, his eyes on the prisoner. Above our heads, a huge mirror was suspended at an angle. Below it were two gas lamps, lit to counter the leaden dullness of the sky outside. After a few days of dry weather and bright sunshine, we had rain at last, and the open windows admitted the odd metallic odor of rain falling on dry dust and soot. Edmund looked ahead, indifferent. Although he was looking in my direction, I didn't think he was looking at me, and I made no attempt to catch his eye.

A man was talking to me, important in his gown and wig. The first questions were straightforward. Yes, I had come to London at the end of September last to stay with my sister Lady Odelia Scott-De Quincy at our family home, Scott House. Yes, I had met Sir Geraint Dorrian-Knowles. These were familiar, easy questions that I knew well from the endless hours spent talking to police detectives. I knew they would get harder.

It was about a quarter of an hour later that the barrister cleared his throat and regarded me sternly. "I would like to go over a few points for clarity's sake. When you became aware of the letter and so forth aimed, apparently, at Lady Odelia, you decided to undertake some *investigations* of your own, didn't you? Why did you not have recourse to the police? Surely, they are far more qualified to *investigate* serious matters than a widow who lives in relative retirement in the country?"

I flinched, struck dumb for a second. And then somebody sniggered below me and my nervousness evaporated, everything around me snapping into sharp outlines as if I were looking through a piece of glass from which the grime had just been washed.

"I didn't consider myself to be investigating anything." I straightened my back, trying to make myself look as tall as possible. "My aim was simply to make a few inquiries to help my sister. I didn't consider the matter worth going to the police about. After all, people do send unpleasant letters, especially when one has a certain standing in society. Should we run to the police for help at every criticism? The nobility would be hammering on the doors of Scotland Yard day and night."

My voice was clear and loud, easily projecting over the whispering and fidgeting of the men in the room. I heard a rumble to my right that was almost certainly Ned, voicing his approval under his breath.

"But then there were more unpleasant occurrences than a mere letter, were there not?" The man sounded genuinely disapproving. "A word—that I will not repeat with ladies present, but that began with a *B* and ended with an *H*—painted in letters as high as a man on the gate of your family's house."

I acknowledged the truth of this occurrence, pointing out that we had drawn it to the attention of the police. The barrister smiled thinly and went on. "And then there was a most unpleasant parcel—the rotting carcass of a cat mixed with some offal."

The ladies in the public gallery gave small squeals of disgust, and the lawyer nodded gravely at them. "It was the sort of revolting object that would sicken most ladies. Indeed, it produced a physical reaction in Lady Odelia."

There was a faint ripple of laughter, and the barrister smirked. I again acknowledged the truth of his words.

"It sent the maid into hysterics, as might be expected of that class of person." The Queen's Counsel smoothed the front of his robe. "But you, Lady Helena, coolly ordered the disgusting mess to be kept overnight and then *investigated* it for clues, did you not? Along with Monsieur Fortier de Maival." He pronounced the name with an excellent accent, lingering lovingly over the syllables, as if proud of his good

French. "Surely, you might by *then* have thought of speaking to the police. These were serious matters, were they not?"

Laughter again from somewhere. I narrowed my eyes, pitching my voice to the tone Mama used when dealing with impertinence. "I didn't consider it necessary. These were pranks as far as I was concerned. Naturally, I was interested in finding out who the sender might be so that I could attempt to prevent further upsets to my sister."

"Very loyal of you. And your loyalty extended to identifying and interviewing Miss Cynthia Emery, did it not? And ultimately Miss Elsie Aldred, the victim of the foul murder with which we are today concerned?" He turned his head to look at Edmund before returning his attention to me. "The late Miss Aldred, also known as Elisabetta Aldred or the Dainty Darling?"

"Yes, I spoke to both Miss Emery and Miss Aldred." It surprised me how unconcerned I sounded.

"It all sounds remarkably like an *investigation* to me." The lawyer waved a dismissive hand. "But we will no longer dwell on the eccentricity of your actions, Lady Helena. We may, perhaps, put them down to the aristocracy's instinct to take charge, may we not? We have much ground to cover, so let us turn the page and examine your last meeting with Miss Aldred. What, as a preliminary thought, is your opinion of that young woman?"

I saw her then, pictured clearly in my mind. Her impish smile, her hard and yet vulnerable eyes. What *was* my opinion of her? That she had pursued ambition far beyond her origins. That she had turned Sir Geraint's pursuit of her into an arrangement that served as a stepping stone to something greater. That I had seen, perhaps, the final efforts of a long, hard climb. I took a deep breath.

"My opinion," I said, "is that she didn't deserve to die."

48

THE LADY DETECTIVE

"*H*ow are you all bearing up?" Ned asked solicitously when we all finally met up again amid the jostling crowd in the shabby corridors that led to the outside world. "A terrible business, this, very bad indeed." He tugged at his bushy beard. "You ladies couldn't hear the details of Miss Aldred's demise, could you? No? Good. You were quite right, Helena, my dear, she didn't deserve to die. If she died at the hands of young Mr. Dorrian-Knowles, he is a villainous man indeed. But that's for the jury to decide." He shrugged. "No doubt the press will also have its opinions."

"Opinions are of no use whatsoever." Michael pulled out his pocket watch and glared at the dial. He could read the time by the position of the hands, but it took him far longer than most people needed. "I suppose tomorrow will be just as bad."

"Worse, no doubt." Odelia looked glum. "I feel as if I should go down on my knees and apologize to all of you all over again."

"Nonsense." Michael snapped his watch shut and pushed it back into his waistcoat pocket. "There's no point in endlessly going over the past. And it's all wrong anyhow. I counted five mistakes in what the lawyers said. It's like sitting through a debate in the Lords, but I'm not allowed to correct anyone. Let's go home now."

"I'd like a word with Fortier first." Ned looked around, surveying the crowd. "Do you think he's already left? My word, that was a surprise—Fortier *de Maival* indeed. Although there's nothing in his bearing or manner that argues against him being of noble birth."

Odelia, to whom this detail would have been news, turned to stare hard at me. "Helena already knew, if I'm any judge. She doesn't look the least bit surprised." She laid her uninjured hand on Ned's arm. "What did he give as his profession?"

"Gentleman." Ned's teeth showed white amid his abundant whiskers. "Although he readily admitted he works as a physician and surgeon. I say, that story about him socking Dorrian-Knowles on the jaw was quite something, wasn't it? The ladies have been holding out on us, Michael. An interesting fellow, that—ah, there he is."

Ned reached out to clap Fortier on the shoulder in a friendly manner. "I was just saying you're a bit of a dark horse, Fortier. Or should I call you de Maival?"

"Fortier is the name I prefer." Fortier spoke lightly, but his face was grave. "A title is an empty thing when it's backed by neither land nor position. My father does not use his *particule de noblesse*, and neither do I—but it is my legal name, and I couldn't avoid giving it in court."

"Titles are a blasted nuisance," Michael said with as much feeling as I was accustomed to hearing from him. "One has to live up to them, do one's duty to one's country and all that."

"Exactly." Fortier smiled at my brother. "Far better to be a private gentleman. Far better still to pursue a worthy calling."

Michael's brow wrinkled. "Dashed if I know what my

calling would be if I weren't an earl. Nobody ever gave me the chance to find out. What in blazes were all those names you rattled off?"

"Armand Benoît Paul Antoine Fortier de Maival," Fortier said in measured tones.

"Hmph. I have it now." Michael's expression assumed the inward look that meant he was committing a fact to memory permanently. "Always have trouble with foreign names. I could never learn French, you know. Even Mama gave up. It made me angry when people spoke French at me, and I was rather prone to biting people when I got angry. I don't do it now, of course." He looked directly at Fortier for a second. "Well, let's send someone for our carriages and go back to Scott House. I want my tea. I suppose we'll be in this vile place for all of tomorrow. Fortier, you'll join us, won't you?"

He turned on his heel and strode rapidly away from us, presumably to bully anyone who looked official into finding our carriages. Ned, who was closest to Odelia, offered her his arm. She took it, but not before pantomiming a highly amused, wide-eyed glance at me and Fortier. Guttridge hurried forward, possibly to limit any offense Michael might inadvertently give, and I was left alone with the future Duc de Maival.

"Michael *likes* you." I slid my hand under Fortier's proffered arm. "That was closer to friendly speech than I've ever seen him get with a man, except for that odious steward of his. And Ned, I suppose."

"I'm honored." Fortier's eyes were dancing with amusement. "Did Lord Broadmere really bite people?"

"I don't remember that. I remember him screaming blue murder every time the French nursemaid came into the room. The poor woman, it was her *job* to speak French to us. Mama's French wasn't good, you see, and she always felt she had been disadvantaged, so she insisted on us having the language drilled into us from an early age. Mind you, Michael still hates it when people speak any foreign language in his presence."

"I quite understand." Fortier drew himself up to his full height, trying to see across the throng of people into which all the others had disappeared. I, of course, could see absolutely nothing. "It's bad manners to converse in another language if you're not sure all the company knows it." He directed a severe look at a nearby group of people and raised his voice. "It's also bad manners to stare at people as if they're exhibits in the zoological gardens."

Various people looked away. Fortier spied a gap in the crowd and steered me toward it.

"I suppose we'll all have to put up with a certain notoriety," I said. "You may decide it's better not to know us."

"Nonsense." Fortier gave me a sideways smile. "What people think of you doesn't change who you are. There's Lord Broadmere—let's hope our carriages are coming. I saw Sir Geraint and his daughter leave some time ago."

"Wait—O's not crying, is she?" I let go of Fortier's arm and darted forward. "Odelia, darling, what's wrong?"

O had her hand over her face. Her shoulders were shaking. I imagined all the terrible insults that might have broken through her shield of insouciance and prepared to do battle with the perpetrators.

"Odelia, please don't." I was only about four feet from my sister by now. She had seen me, I thought, but she turned toward Ned and buried her face in his broad shoulder. Dismay filled me.

And then I saw Ned's face. He was waging a valiant—and losing—struggle against the desire to laugh. Confused, I looked at Odelia again and realized that what I had taken for distress was, in fact, convulsions of mirth. What on earth could have happened?

I was in the street now, with the great hulk of Newgate Prison nearby. Above the din of the crowd, I could hear the Great Tom bell of St. Paul's chiming four o'clock. I looked around, puzzled, for the source of Odelia's hilarity; and then it became nastily clear.

I had almost missed it, so commonplace was the sight of the newspaper sellers who haunted the City of London. They either huddled in a corner if they were the dejected kind or, if a little bolder, strode among the passersby or ventured into the road with a poster clutched in one hand and a sheaf of folded newspapers under the other arm. These posters were invariably emblazoned with words designed to catch the eye. Today Egypt, Ireland, and the dreadful deaths of children in a Sunderland theater all figured prominently. But it was the last item that arrested my attention.

At the very bottom of more than one poster was the legend DAINTY DARLING MURDER TRIAL—and below it, in large solid letters, words that aroused feelings of cold horror in my heart:

LADY HELENA INVESTIGATES.

49

A CLOUD OVER THE SUN

he trial dragged on to its ineluctable end. I saw little of it, being sequestered in the witness room or at Scott House with Odelia when our presence was not required in the court. I learned enough of the proceedings from Ned to feel no surprise or shock—nothing more than a dull ache in my heart—when the jury found Edmund Dorrian-Knowles guilty of murder and the judge sentenced him to hang by the neck until he was dead.

What astonished me the most was the way life simply continued, flowing around the verdict the way a stream flows around rocks. I had seen a hanged man before, and sometimes, during some ordinary activity, the reality of what lay in store for Edmund would appear in my mind's eye in nastily vivid detail. Yet all I could do was concentrate on the business of leaving London. I hoped to do that before Edmund took his last walk through Newgate Prison to the gallows.

Our departure for the country was also, admittedly, a flight from scandal. I had never been so grateful for Scott House's high walls and heavy gate, and for once I was glad that Odelia left the management of the house to me, as it meant I had something to do. I dismissed the footman, George, for accepting payment from the gentlemen of the press in return for information, but kept a grateful Mrs. Coles and Maisie on at half pay for the indefinite period during which Scott House would be closed up. A week of gently chivvying a subdued Odelia through sorting her canvases and effects, sending some to Italy and others to be stored, and packing her trunks was all that was needed to make us ready for departure.

Given the circumstances, social calls were currently out of the question, but there was one visit I needed to make.

"It's so kind of you to call on us." Gabrielle Dermody reached out to take my hands in hers as I stepped into the hushed elegance of the house in Kensington Square. "Armand will be down soon, I'm sure."

"How is your father today?" I asked.

Gabrielle glanced upward to where the staircase disappeared into the house's upper regions. "Not so good." It was the answer I had expected. Gabrielle had written to tell me she had arrived in Town at Fortier's request to wait out their father's last days.

"I feel guilty whenever I think of all the time your brother has devoted to my concerns instead of remaining by your father's side." I let Gabrielle draw me into the library, where the open windows let in the pleasant July sounds of birdsong and the rustling of the trees in the square's central garden. "His absence hasn't made things worse, I trust?"

"Worse than dying?" Gabrielle's smile was gentle. "Armand has always been here when it counted. He's delighted he could be of service to you and your family. I think you know why."

I knew I was blushing. "Odelia should have come, really." I said, to cover my confusion. "She owes your brother a great deal. But stepping outside Scott House is an ordeal at present."

"Notoriety doesn't last." Gabrielle smiled. "Even in Littleberry. Before I left, I heard that Lady Geraldine and the countess have let everyone know they will continue to receive Lady Odelia at Four Square and Hyrst. And you will make your loyalty clear by keeping her close to you at Whitcombe. Where you all lead, everyone else will follow, isn't that the truth? It goes without saying that I would welcome your sister into my home should she care to call on me. How is her arm?"

"Healing well. She's been trying to draw, although she doesn't feel up to painting yet. We're both a little melancholy." I sighed. "If only I could do more for Lady Dorrian-Knowles, the poor woman. I feel terrible about suspecting her, even for a short time. I'm no use as a lady detective, whatever the papers call me."

"That too will pass."

"Hmph. I can't tell you the number of people who've written to me about that ridiculous sobriquet. Oh, Gabrielle." I closed my eyes. "I'm longing to get back to my home and my herbs and some measure of peace."

"I hope you find it."

The voice was Fortier's. My eyes flew open to discover him standing in the doorway. He was smiling, but the shadows under his eyes bespoke long nighttime vigils and much worry.

"Shame on you, creeping up on us like that and listening to our conversation." Gabrielle held out a hand to her brother, her tone deliberately light. "We might have been talking about you."

"Then I would have all the more reason to listen." Fortier gave his sister's hand a light squeeze before dropping, rather heavily, into a chair. "I'm glad you're here," he said to me.

"I've been hoping to call on you before you left, but Father has needed me so much over the last few days."

"Is this a permanent change for the worse, do you think?" I asked.

"Yes." Fortier pulled a large handkerchief from a pocket and used it to wipe his brow. "Afternoons always seem to be difficult, especially now the weather's so warm."

"I could read to him." Gabrielle rose rapidly to her feet. Fortier stood perforce, a wry smile on his face at having to make the effort, and I wondered just how much he needed rest. I stood as well.

"Perhaps I should go . . ." I began.

"Please stay." Fortier looked alarmed. "It could be months until I see you." He frowned at Gabrielle. "You haven't even offered our guest any refreshment, and now you're driving her away."

"I'm happy to stay—" I began, but Gabrielle spoke across me, addressing her brother.

"I thought you might prefer a moment alone—"

We both stopped talking, and the three of us looked at each other, all equally flustered. Gabrielle was the first to break the silence.

"Perhaps we should all sit down and start again."

Her tone and expression were so droll that I could not repress a smile, and the awkwardness of the moment seemed to dissipate immediately. Fortier grasped his sister's elbow and turned her firmly toward the door.

"Now that you mention it, my dear Gaby, Father may settle better if you read him some more Balzac. *Eugénie Grandet*, isn't it? A wonderful tale of romance spoiled by family meddling."

FORTIER SHUT THE LIBRARY DOOR FIRMLY, AND THE SOUND OF Gabrielle's footsteps was immediately hushed. All I could hear was the rapid thrumming of my heartbeat.

Yet Fortier's expression was not that of a hopeful lover as he turned back to me. He let the silence build between us for a few seconds before once again dropping into his seat without even waiting for me to sit down. Disconcerted, I made my way to an Empire sofa and perched warily on its striped satin brocade.

"I hope I didn't give the impression that I was about to make a nuisance of myself." One side of Fortier's mouth lifted, but his eyes were serious. "Gaby has a more optimistic view of my situation than I do myself, I believe." He leaned back into his armchair, stretching out his legs and sliding down a little so that he was staring at the ceiling, his arms folded. "I don't mind admitting that, romantically speaking, I'm in a state of utter despair."

"You said once that matters in France are damnable. Is that it?"

"I can always trust you to understand." His gaze was still on the ceiling. "Louise—she's my cousin, did I tell you?—has been begging me to bring her to England. I'll have to do it once . . . once Father is gone. I've promised to leave by the first boat train I can catch."

A cloud seemed to pass over the sun. "Will she live here? Will this be your house?"

"It will be mine, but it wouldn't be wise to settle her in London. Besides, the country would be much better for—" He took a deep breath and held it for a moment before releasing a torrent of words. "For the boy. His name is Jacques. Jacques Fortier. It's Louise's name too, you see. He's known me as his father all his life, but he's not mine. That would be impossible."

"Ah." I could see it plainly—a woman with an illegitimate child, turning to her cousin to save her from disgrace.

"It was idiotic of us to use our family name. But we were so young." He turned his head so he was looking straight at me at last. "I was barely eighteen, Louise only a little older. It was a game to us then—an exciting adventure. A little alarming to have a tiny baby to care for, but I've always liked children. We had to find a wet nurse, you see, and somewhere to stay, and that meant inventing a story. It was far too much responsibility for the pair of infants we were, and I suppose it never occurred to us that we would have to look after the child for more than a month or two."

I frowned, the picture of Louise as a fallen woman evaporating as I mentally worked through the implications of Fortier's words. "Do you mean he's not Louise's child either?"

"He is not."

"So whose—?"

A soft knock on the door interrupted my question. "Armand?" It was Gabrielle. Fortier immediately extricated himself from the armchair, crossing the room rapidly to open the door.

"It's all right, *p'tite mère*. We're just talking. What's wrong?"

"More blood." Gabrielle glanced at me, her face strained. "You told me to tell you . . . I'm sorry—how can he bear it?"

"Go to him." Fortier kissed his sister on the forehead. "I'll be up in a moment."

She turned, and I heard her footsteps hurrying upward. I rose to my feet.

"Now I should really go."

"Yes. I don't suppose I will get a moment more with you today." He closed his eyes, looking both exhausted and exasperated. "You don't know how much I'd like you by my side right now, but you have enough to worry about, don't you? I'll ring for somebody to see you out."

He moved so that he was close to me, taking my hand in his. "Are you beginning to understand why I don't wish to embroil you in this mess? Perhaps once I've fetched Louise and Jacques from France, we'll have thought of a way through. For various reasons, I can't write to you about any of this, so—"

"So I'll have to be patient."

Fortier's only answer was to touch his lips to mine in a gentle kiss. And then he was moving around me, tugging on the bellpull near the door as he pushed it open with the other hand, and with only the briefest glance behind him, he left me alone, listening to the sound of his rapid footfalls on the stairs.

50

ALL THEM THAT TRULY REPENT

The church of St. Michael and All Angels seemed very full the Sunday after Edmund Dorrian-Knowles's appointment with the hangman. Possibly, the county was attending to stare at us Scott-De Quincys, to see how we fared amid the renewed publicity of Edmund's doom. Or perhaps they had another object of curiosity in mind.

"He *is* here." Gerry's voice was hard with disapproval as she looked out of the carriage window. She had visited Mama at my house before the service and had consequently ridden to church with me and Thomas. Odelia was not present, having flatly refused to attend because of the rumor —evidently accurate—that Sir Geraint and Jane would be present.

"There are *some* fences it's idiotic to jump, Gerry." Odelia, her arm now free of sling and bindings, had flung herself back onto her bed and frowned rebelliously at our eldest sibling. "I'll never manage the service without breaking down." She had smiled, but it was a tremulous attempt. "Not because of Geraint, of course. I knew Edmund as a small boy, remember? I'll make a fool of myself and the family if I blub."

Having experienced O's self-control, I was not convinced she would really have given way to tears. All I knew was that I was near to weeping myself when I saw Jane, dressed in black, on the arm of her father. It was only the annoyance radiating from Gerry that held me in equilibrium as the carriage jolted to a halt.

"Couldn't he have gone elsewhere?" she muttered between clenched teeth as I stepped onto the cobblestones behind her.

"Obviously not. After all, he attended this church when he stayed with me." It surprised me how calm I sounded. "Well, it saves me from paying them a condolence visit. I see Ned's going to get there before us."

And before I could give myself time to hesitate, I swept past Gerry and approached the two mourners. I could hear the deep bass of Ned's voice, kind and comforting, and after his steady example it was not difficult to say a few simple words of sympathy. Gerry had no choice but to follow suit. Michael and Julia, who had been waiting for us outside the church, were not far behind. Thomas was last, having descended more slowly from the carriage.

None of Ned and Gerry's other children were there, and we hadn't seen Blanche for months. Alice and Annette were attending the church in Broadmere, so we were a small, subdued group with plenty of room to spread out in the family pews. Sir Geraint and Jane took a distressingly prominent position in the front pew of the north side of the church. I heard a muttered, "*Right* under our noses," from Gerry behind me and caught a sympathetic glance from Julia, who sat on my right.

"I really don't care, Gerry," Odelia had said earlier when our sister had continued to insist that the family dignity would be better served if Odelia were present at the service. "Call me a coward if you wish. I intend to go to Paris this week and on to Rome as soon as the weather cools a little, and I've put up with people staring at me in church for two Sundays. Why shouldn't I be indisposed for once? You and this whole nasty, gossiping little town can go to blazes, and so can Geraint. My entire life here has gone sour."

Not nearly as sour as theirs. Sir Geraint wore a crape hatband, his gloves and cravat the deep midnight hue of mourning. Jane was in unrelieved black, her eyes red and swollen. Couldn't her father have insisted she wear a veil? But I remembered too well the feel of my own heavy veil and how much I had hated it. Perhaps Jane felt the same way.

Despite the disgrace that Odelia—and to some extent, I—had brought to our family, Littleberry was a small town, and we were still the most important people in it. I caught a few friendly glances and small, sympathetic nods from acquaintances as we stood for the ecclesiastical procession to pass, and I knew that eventually all would be well.

And, scandal or no scandal, Sir Geraint was a famous artist and a baronet. Thanks to me, he had made the acquaintance of most of the county gentry present. He might fare better than us. Most people, I found, had some measure of sympathy for grief, and they certainly had a generous portion of curiosity.

The long file of choirboys had finally settled into the choir stalls, and the first hymn had begun. It was one of those comfortingly intricate tunes from the last century, difficult to learn but most satisfying when mastered. It lent itself well to the high voices of the youngest boys, rising pure as silver into the church's lofty rafters, and in concentrating on getting the tune right while ignoring Michael's eccentric version, I forgot my troubles for a few moments.

Sir Geraint was singing lustily in his remarkably fine

voice, no sign of grief discernible in his demeanor. Jane was inaudible. In front of me, the great pendulum swung, maddeningly out of rhythm with the measure of the hymn, its whisper of Loyalty and Eternity equally out of rhythm with my intrusive thoughts.

Would I approach Quinn Dermody after the service to ask after Gabrielle and her family in London? Yes, I would, as I had done the past two Sundays. He had promised to inform me of his father-in-law's demise as soon as it happened, so I knew that the long ordeal of the sickroom was not yet over. My heart went out to the dying man and his watching children, and for the thousandth time I felt the touch of Fortier's lips on mine.

The hymn had finished. A tiny squeak of annoyance from Gerry made me sit down hurriedly, realizing I was still standing when everyone else had seated themselves. I unclasped my prayer book—*To his beloved wife, Helena, on the occasion of their wedding*—and found my place among the petal-thin pages with their bright gilded edges.

I felt more alone than I had after Justin's death, and yet not lonely. I had, in some senses, lost Odelia. Although we were as affectionate toward one another as ever, and I still loved her, it was no longer with the uncritical adoration of a much younger sibling.

What had I gained in return? Knowledge, I decided. I had seen Odelia at her worst and occasionally at her bravest, and she had become a far more complicated and interesting person to me than the elegant façade I had accepted for so long. The ten years that separated us had been a barrier of sorts, but it was gone.

It was up to me to maintain this new sense of closeness, to fight against the secretive side that I suspected Odelia might have inherited from our father. I suddenly wished I could go straight home to her, to sit and talk without criticizing, as our older sisters invariably did, making the most of the precious few days left before she exiled herself to the Continent.

And what of me? I didn't have an easy time ahead. It would have been unjust to deny that my feelings for Fortier had deepened and strengthened over the last year. As frustrating as I found his reluctance to entrust me with his secrets, I was confident that I would eventually know them as he knew mine, and then we could decide what we wanted to be to one another. I had more than yielded to his kiss—I had been unable to stop my own lips parting and returning the pressure of his for those brief seconds—and I knew he would understand my response as a promise not to judge until I was in full possession of the facts. Yet a wife who was not his wife and a child who was not his child were thorny problems indeed . . .

The air around me moved, and I automatically knelt with the rest of the congregation, realizing with a guilty start how inattentive I had been. Behind me, I could hear Ned's growling bass and Gerry's clear, soft voice: *"We have followed too much the devices and desires of our own hearts . . ."*

A sob sounded from across the aisle, and I knew it was Jane. My throat constricted with sorrow for the girl, whose troubles were surely so much greater than mine. The evidence she had given against her brother had apparently been damning, however hard she tried to excuse him, and now Edmund was beyond the reach of any redemption or reconciliation. I squeezed my eyes tight shut to stop the tears coming and tried to concentrate fully on the Absolution. *He pardoneth and absolveth all them that truly repent.* Had Edmund repented at the last?

We rose to our feet, and I could open my eyes, relieved to see that Jane had conquered her tears. She and Sir Geraint would continue to be a part of my life for some considerable time, and when Millie was well enough, I would visit her whether or not my family approved. Odelia's secrets were hers alone no longer, and as my eyes automatically sought the ponderous swing of the great pendulum, I was suddenly afraid of the inexorable march of time it represented. Time, it seemed, had a nasty tendency to reveal all things. What else did I not know about my family?

The House of Closed Doors series

The House of Closed Doors
Eternal Deception
The Shadow Palace
The Jewel Cage

My stepfather was not particularly fond of me to begin with, and now that he'd found out about the baby, he was foaming at the mouth.

Nell Lillington is a heedless, cosseted seventeen-year-old when she chooses not to reveal the name of her baby's father. In 1870s Illinois, such a decision has far-reaching consequences, and Nell finds her path to happiness strewn with murder. Join Nell as she struggles to reconcile love, independence, and respectability in these engrossing Victorian mysteries—great clean reads that will keep you entertained for hours.

"This entire series has kept me spellbound…couldn't wait for the next page or book. Loved the story line, and the characters. Enjoyed the history background. Highly recommend the complete series."—*Carolyn G., Amazon reader*

FROM THE AUTHOR

Dear Reader,

I hope you enjoyed reading *Lady Odelia's Secret* as much as I enjoyed writing it. I'm an indie author paying bills by doing what I love the most—creating entertainment for other people. So my most important assets are YOU, the readers, without whom I'd just be talking to myself. Again.

My promise to you is that I'll do my best. I'll research to make the historical background to my stories as accurate as I can. I'll edit and polish until the book's up to my (high) standards. I'll give you a great-looking cover to look at, and I'll make sure my books are available in as many formats and in as many places as possible. I'll keep my prices as low as is compatible with keeping my publishing business going.

What can you do for me? If you've loved this book, there are several ways you can help me out.

Let me know what you think. If you go to www.janes teen.com, you'll see a little envelope icon near the bottom of the page. That's how you contact me by email. I'd love to hear what you thought of the book. Or find me on Facebook, Twitter, or Goodreads.

Leave a review. An honest review—even if you just want to say you didn't like the book—is a huge help. Leave it on the site where you bought the book, or on a reader site like Goodreads.

Tell a friend. I love it when sales come through word of mouth. Better still, mention my book on social media and amplify your power to help my career.

Sign up for my newsletter at www.janesteen.com/insider. That's a win-win: my newsletter is where I offer free copies, unpublished extras, insider info, and let you know when a new book's coming out.

And thanks again for reading.

Jane xx

AUTHOR'S NOTE

One of the joys of writing fiction is that you can give your characters as much money and house room as you want. I endowed Lady Helena Whitcombe with a perfectly located, 24-bedroom, grand Georgian stately home—and why not?— but I didn't become fully aware of the potential of such a space until early 2019. We were in London to watch a friend's show and had a couple of hours to spare, and I happened to notice that there was an exhibition of Edward Burne-Jones's work at Tate Britain.

As a fan of the late Victorian period, I naturally have an interest in the pre-Raphaelite painters and was familiar with Burne-Jones's work, but I had never seen the Briar Rose paintings. These four large canvases, entitled *The Legend of Briar Rose* and based, as so many Victorian artworks were, on the familiar *Sleeping Beauty* fairy tale, were completed between 1885 and 1890. For the Tate Britain exhibition a custom-built space housed the paintings, with inscriptions below them of specially written verses by William Morris, and the overall effect was immersive and strangely tranquil.

The paintings show just one moment in the Sleeping Beauty story, when the prince arrives at the castle to find it surrounded by a thick growth of thorny briars and everyone inside it asleep, including the princess whom he must awaken with a kiss. With the side panels included, over forty feet of thorns separate the arriving prince and the sleeping beauty, who is based on Burne-Jones's daughter Margaret.

I later found out that the paintings were purchased for a splendid neoclassical country house in Oxfordshire called Buscot Park, where they are housed in a grand "saloon" or drawing room, nestled in custom-built frames on which Morris's verses are carved. The whole installation is a true Arts & Crafts melding of words, visual art, and decoration, and enhances the grand drawing room in a most inspiring way. The house belongs to the National Trust and can be visited in the summer.

Because of the exhibition, I also read Fiona MacCarthy's biography of Burne-Jones (*The Last Pre-Raphaelite*) and discovered that despite his long attachment to his wife Georgiana (Georgie), he had loved other women—notably Maria (or Mary) Zambaco and, later, the socialite May Gaskell, to whom he wrote startlingly passionate letters only rediscovered a century later by her descendent, the author Josceline Dimbleby (there are excerpts in her book *A Profound Secret*). After Burne-Jones's death, Georgie wrote a very readable biography of her late husband. Like a good Victorian wife she left out any allusions to his affairs, but there's a subtle change of tone from the happier reminiscences of their early days together.

And that, dear Reader, is how plots begin in a writer's mind. I had a heroine with a grand house just crying out to be used more in a novel. I had an artist sister. I had a great Victorian painter with a penchant for romantic attachments to women who were not his wife. I had a series of huge paintings based on a fairy tale.

I also had a book of Hans Christian Andersen's fairy tales from my childhood, rescued on a whim from the boxes in my parents' garage some twenty-five years after I left home. It is lavishly illustrated by one Ralph Gore Antony Groves-Raines (1913 or 1928-1993), and it was undoubtedly his drawings that made me love the book. They are lively, colorful, and clever, showing a remarkable depth of artistic knowledge and imagination. To the art-starved child that I was, they were inspirational, and I knew that my famous fictional artist should turn them into high art for the purposes of a novel that would explore Odelia's world.

Sir Geraint Dorrian-Knowles was never intended as a direct fictionalization of Sir Edward Coley Burne-Jones, but I have dropped in quite a few Burne-Jones references for my own amusement, including the later hyphenation of his names (Burne-Jones started out as plain Ned (or, earlier, Ted) Jones) and the fact that he has a son called Philip who becomes a portraitist. Chapters 6 and 7 contain extremely brief, non-speaking appearances by Burne-Jones, his assistant Thomas Rooke, and his great friend William Morris, whose designs are still popular.

The Dorrian-Knowles house in Holland Park is based on the Leighton House Museum, once a private residence built by Sir Frederic Leighton. For the purposes of the story I had to add a family wing since Leighton, a lifelong bachelor, only included one bedroom in his huge studio house. The Leighton House was just one of several beautiful studio houses built by well-to-do artists, who became known as the Holland Park Circle after the (then) new district in which they lived. Several of the houses still exist, and as well as visiting the Leighton House it is possible to see them via walking tours.

Fans of Littleberry, fear not—Lady Helena will spend a great deal more time in the countryside in future. My original draft included far more scenes in Littleberry, but these strayed from Odelia's story and so I cut them—with plans to rewrite them as stories in their own right. Like Helena, I love my quirky little town.

ACKNOWLEDGMENTS

This novel was written over a long period of time, interleaved with work on the fourth novel in the House of Closed Doors series, *The Jewel Cage*, and with an extended period of planning for the whole Scott-de Quincy series. It began to get up a head of steam in the middle of 2021, from which point onward I left the solitary writer-cave and relied on a host of helpers. Imagination can only take you so far—at some point you have to tackle the hard work of turning the pictures and words in your head into a book that can be read by others, and I don't think any author can really do that alone.

I am grateful to the readers who tackled my messy first draft and gave me their trenchant opinions: they are Brandi Coffey, Deena Nataf, Hilarie Berzins, Jacomien Zwemstra, Jenna Matheson, Leslie McKinnon, Rebekah Giese Witherspoon, and Shirley Stephens. Most of them came back for the beta read, with the worthy addition of Alisha Moore Cole, Candace Webster, Kristen Tate, Regina Newman, Sharon Beechy, Sheila Matthews, and Sheri Mahalick. My beta readers deserve special praise for submitting to my grueling process, and although I'm exhausted at the end of it, I'm always sorry to say goodbye till next time.

I am eternally grateful to the professionals who, year in year out, have provided me with such excellent services. Rachel Lawston (www.lawstondesign.com) is an incredibly talented designer and now a fellow author! Jenny Quinlan (historicaleditorial.blogspot.com) makes me actually look forward to that all-important final edit. Elizabeth Klett (eliza bethklettaudio.com) is a joy to work with and to listen to, and I'm proud of my audiobooks. Susan Kings and Helen Turner of Kings Accounting take the huge burden of getting the numbers right off my shoulders and present me with beautifully neat pages instead, saving me about a hundred tons of stress.

And then, closest to me of all, there's my Aspidistra Press team: Kate Burgess, Leander Couldridge, and Ellen Hills. Many thanks to all three of you for your sense of organization and discipline, traits that I wish I had! And for all the hard work, and putting up with my random thoughts and assumptions that you can read my mind.

ABOUT THE AUTHOR

The most important fact you need to know about me is that I was (according to my mother, at least) named after Jane Eyre, which to this day remains one of my favorite books. I was clearly doomed to love all things Victorian, and ended up studying both English and French nineteenth-century writers in depth.

This was a pretty good grounding for launching myself into writing novels set in the nineteenth century. I was living in the small town of Libertyville, Illinois—part of the greater Chicago area—when I began writing the *House of Closed Doors* series, inspired by a photograph of the long-vanished County Poor Farm on Libertyville's main street.

Now back in my native England, I have the good fortune to live in an idyllic ancient town close to the sea. This location has sparked a new series about an aristocratic family with more secrets than most: *The Scott-De Quincy Mysteries*.

I write for readers who want a series you can't put down. I love to blend saga, mystery, adventure, and a touch of romance, set against the background of the real-life issues facing women in the late nineteenth century.

I am a member of the Alliance of Independent Authors, the Historical Novel Society, Novelists, Inc., and the Society of Authors.

To find out more about my books, join my insider list at www.janesteen.com/insider

facebook.com/janesteenwriter
twitter.com/JaneSteen
bookbub.com/authors/jane-steen
goodreads.com/janesteen
pinterest.com/janesteen

www.ingramcontent.com/pod-product-compliance
Lightning Source LLC
Chambersburg PA
CBHW010546170726
48285CB00011B/2774